Praise for Fern Michaels's first novel in the bestselling Texas series, *Texas Rich*

"A steaming, sprawling saga . . . As always, Fern Michaels writes a full story with bigger-than-life characters we would look forward to meeting. . . . A rags-to-riches saga that would make a colorful movie."

—*Romantic Times*

"Talk about action! There is more in this epic than in five novels. And it's fascinating, interesting, and exciting. One of those rare books, the kind the reader doesn't want to end. A real winner!"

—*Green Bay Press Gazette*

"Fine fare for Fern Michaels's fans!"

—*The Philadelphia Inquirer*

TEXAS
SUNRISE

Fern Michaels

BALLANTINE BOOKS • NEW YORK

A Ballantine Book
Published by The Random House Publishing Group

Published in the United States by Ballantine Books, an imprint of The Random House Publishing Group, a division of Random House, Inc., New York, and simultaneously in Canada by Random House of Canada Limited, Toronto.

www.ballantinebooks.com

ISBN 0-345-36593-3

Manufactured in the United States of America

First Hardcover Edition: February 1993
First Mass Market Edition: March 1994

OPM 39 38 37 36 35 34

*I would like to dedicate this book to two very special peo-
ple, Doris and Buzz Parmett. You're always there for me
and besides, you love Fred and Gus as much as I do.*

—F.M.

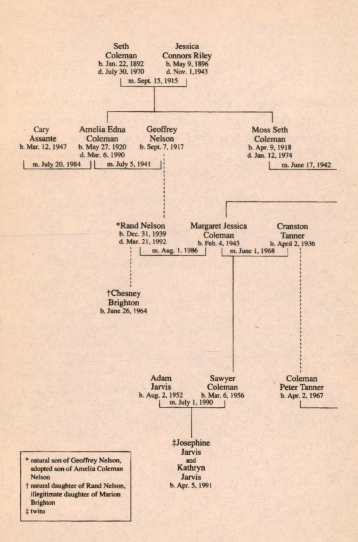

Seth
Coleman
b. Jan. 22, 1892
d. July 30, 1970

Jessica
Connors Riley
b. May 9, 1896
d. Nov. 1,1943

m. Sept. 15, 1915

Cary
Assante
b. Mar. 12, 1947

m. July 20, 1984

Amelia Edna
Coleman
b. May 27, 1920
d. Mar. 6, 1990

Geoffrey
Nelson
b. Sept. 7, 1917

m. July 5, 1941

Moss Seth
Coleman
b. Apr. 9, 1918
d. Jan. 12, 1974

m. June 17, 1942

*Rand Nelson
b. Dec. 31, 1939
d. Mar. 21, 1992

m. Aug. 1, 1986

Margaret Jessica
Coleman
b. Feb. 4, 1943

m. June 1, 1968

Cranston
Tanner
b. April 2, 1936

†Chesney
Brighton
b. June 26, 1964

Adam
Jarvis
b. Aug. 2, 1952

Sawyer
Coleman
b. Mar. 6, 1956

m. July 1, 1990

Coleman
Peter Tanner
b. Apr. 2, 1967

‡Josephine
Jarvis
and
Kathryn
Jarvis
b. Apr. 5, 1991

* natural son of Geoffrey Nelson,
  adopted son of Amelia Coleman
  Nelson
† natural daughter of Rand Nelson,
  illegitimate daughter of Marion
  Brighton
‡ twins

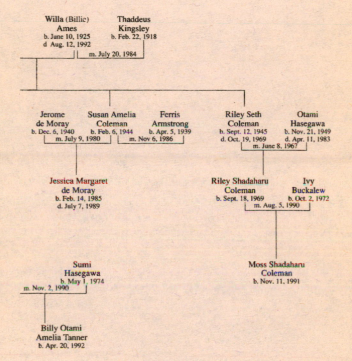

Willa (Billie)
Ames
b. June 10, 1925
d Aug. 12, 1992

Thaddeus
Kingsley
b. Feb. 22, 1918

m. July 20, 1984

Jerome
de Moray
b. Dec. 6, 1940
m. July 9, 1980

Susan Amelia
Coleman
b. Feb. 6, 1944

Ferris
Armstrong
b. Apr. 5, 1939
m. Nov 6, 1986

Riley Seth
Coleman
b. Sept. 12, 1945
d. Oct. 19, 1969

Otami
Hasegawa
b. Nov. 21, 1949
d. Apr. 11, 1983
m. June 8, 1967

Jessica Margaret
de Moray
b. Feb. 14, 1985
d. July 7, 1989

Riley Shadaharu
Coleman
b. Sept. 18, 1969
m. Aug. 5, 1990

Ivy
Buckalew
b. Oct. 2, 1972

Moss Shadaharu
Coleman
b. Nov. 11, 1991

Sumi
Hasegawa
b. May 1, 1974
m. Nov. 2, 1990

Billy Otami
Amelia Tanner
b. Apr. 20, 1992

{{{{{{{{ PROLOGUE }}}}}}}}

Billie Kingsley blinked. It was the only outward sign that she'd heard what the specialist had said. But inwardly, time stood still for her. What would happen to her family, to her children, her grandchildren? To Thad, her husband? They were her reasons for living. Now this man in his wrinkled white coat was telling her it was all coming to an end. He looked miserable, as if he were going to cry. She had to make the look go away. Her thin hand stretched across the desk. "It's not your fault, Aaron. I've always believed our death is ordained the day we're born."

Aaron Kopelman had known all the Colemans, had been invited to their Texas barbecues, had gone to school with Moss Coleman, Billie's first husband. He remembered being introduced to Billie for the first time and wondering if she would be a match for the robust Colemans. How would this shy, pretty, inexperienced girl from Philadelphia fare among them over the years? It didn't take him long to find out and since then he'd loved her like his own sister. Billie Coleman Kingsley was unique, and God simply didn't make them any better. Or if He did, He kept them for Himself. "How will you tell Thad?" was all he could think to say.

"I don't know, Aaron. I told Thad I was coming to a fabric show, that I was thinking of doing some new de-

{1}

signs. I'm not sure if he believed me or not. I've never lied to him, not once in all the years we've been married, but I just couldn't bear to give him even a moment's worry. I think maybe I'll go back to the hotel and do some thinking."

"No you won't," Aaron said spiritedly. "You're coming home with me. We have to talk about ... treatment." She was so beautiful, Aaron thought, and never more so than at this moment. How was that possible? Was it her essential goodness, her kindness and selflessness showing through? Even now she wasn't thinking about herself, but about her family, her husband, and how her illness was going to affect them. He felt a fierce protectiveness he'd never experienced before, and wondered if it showed on his face.

"No, Aaron," Billie said gently, "I need to be alone. I need to absorb all of what you've told me, and I can only do that if I'm by myself. But I appreciate your invitation. You're a dear, wonderful friend, Aaron. Now," she said briskly, with barely a break in her voice, "let's talk about my ... limited options."

It was mid-afternoon when Aaron Kopelman walked Billie to the lobby. Promises had been made, commitments would be honored. "I'll be back a week from today, Aaron. Give Phyllis my love. I'll give Thad yours."

Aaron felt hot tears prick his eyelids. He knew they were going to roll down his cheeks, but he didn't give a damn. Why Billie? Why not the killers, the drug dealers, the rapists? "If it were possible," he said, "I'd change places with you. I swear to God I would."

Billie laid a gentle finger against his lips. How dear this homely man was, how sincere, how loving. "Shhh. You're needed here. God knows that. And, if it were possible to change places, I wouldn't do it, you're much too important to leave this earth ahead of schedule. I, on the other hand, am not eager to go, but if it's my time, then I must accept it. I just hope I can meet my Maker with all the dignity Amelia had. I only want to be strong. Do you think, Aaron, that God will allow me that one request? You know, I never bargained with God for anything. I mean I've prayed, but never for myself. Maybe He doesn't know I'm here. Do you pray, Aaron?" she asked fretfully.

"Every single day of my life." His voice sounded just as fretful as hers. "But like you, it's always for someone else."

They said their good-byes, and as he watched her walk away, he said today's prayer there in the open doorway. He asked that God not let her suffer, but instead give her the strength and the dignity she needed.

It was six o'clock when Billie entered her hotel. She was glad she'd rented a suite instead of a room. She liked to walk around, and in its mini-kitchen area she could make a cup of coffee or have a drink without having to call room service. It rather felt like home. She also liked having a telephone in the bathroom, although Thad always said that it was obscene. A small smile tugged at the corners of her mouth.

Billie popped a can of 7UP and kicked off her shoes before she sat down on a dark, chocolate-colored love seat. She stretched out her legs, frowning at their thinness. After pressing the remote to turn on the television, she adjusted the volume to the lowest setting.

She was alone now. Now she could react in private. Howl, yowl, curse, scream, cry, rant and rave. Instead, she thought of all those who'd gone before her and those whom she was about to leave behind. She sipped at her cold drink. She had to call Thad. She had to call everyone. She needed to hear their voices. All those she loved would give her the courage to do what had to be done.

Her husband picked up on the second ring.

"Darling, how are things at home?" Billie asked lightly.

"When are you coming back?" Thad grumbled.

"Tomorrow morning. I want you to meet me with a large bouquet of spring flowers. Artificial will do if you can't find any in bloom." Billie giggled.

"For you, my darling, anything. A slice of the moon, a sunbeam, a sparkling star. Me. What time?"

"Eleven o'clock."

"Wonderful. We can go to O'Malley's for lunch. I haven't had anything decent to eat since you left. I hate eating peanut butter and jelly for breakfast. Actually, it isn't the peanut butter and jelly, it's eating alone. God, I miss you, Billie. Did you find the fabric you were looking for?"

"No. They're going to send me some samples next week. New ones."

"So what's new in the Big Apple?"

"Not much. But I've missed you too, Thad. This city frightens me to death. I can't wait to get back to the farm."

"I volunteered to go with you, but you said no." Thad chuckled. "Serves you right, old girl."

Billie forced a smile into her voice. "A mistake I won't make again. I'll see you tomorrow. I'll be the girl in the red dress."

"Sweetheart, you could be dressed in burlap and I'd pick you out of a crowd of thousands. I love you, Billie."

"Tomorrow you can prove how much. Have a nice evening, darling. I'm going to curl up with a book. Maybe I'll call the children or maybe I'll turn in early. 'Night, Thad."

" 'Night, honey. Dream about me."

"Count on it," Billie said cheerfully.

Exhausted with the effort she'd put into the phone call, Billie leaned back into the depths of the love seat. She realized that Thad was going to fall apart at the news, and the thought made her straighten her shoulders. *She* would have to remain strong for all of them. Lord, how was she to do it? The family she so loved paraded behind her closed eyelids. A lone tear escaped and rolled down her cheek. She wiped it with a trembling finger.

The long, lonely night stretched ahead of her. What to do with it? Eating would take up some time. Tea, lots of tea. Tea always made things better. It didn't make sense; tea had caffeine. Maybe some plum wine. Both she and Thad adored plum wine. No, she needed a clear head so she could think about the situation. She picked up the phone and dialed room service. Her order rolled off her tongue: two glasses of plum wine, two pots of tea, a side of raw vegetables, and a ham and cheese sandwich.

She had thirty minutes until her food arrived. Do something, her mind ordered. Remove your makeup, take off your clothes, put on that snuggly, yellow flannel robe Thad likes so much. Brush your hair, the gray hair Thad asked you not to color. Remove the pearl earrings Thad gave you for your birthday. She found herself staring at her wedding ring, a wide, plain, gold wedding band. Would they leave it on her finger when it was ... when it was time to go? Of course they would. She would need it when it was time to meet Thad in Eternity. *Write it down. Write everything down so there's no problem later.* The words ricocheted around her mind.

She finished writing just as the room-service waiter knocked on her door. With greedy hands, she reached for the wine and drank it in two fiery swallows. Her insides rebelled instantly, and she ran, blinded by watery eyes, to the bathroom.

When she was back in the sitting room, Billie nibbled on the sandwich, which wasn't like any sandwich she'd ever seen. Even Thad, who was a big eater, wouldn't be able to finish it. It was a creation, she thought as she picked at the ham and thinly sliced cheese. It looked pressed, like someone had used a hot iron to flatten it so that more meat and cheese could be added. She had to remember to tell Thad about this sandwich.

Enough already, her mind ordered. A moment later the phone was in her hands.

"Mam, what's wrong?" Maggie whispered fearfully.

"I'm so sorry, darling. I've had this feeling all day that I should call you. Is everything all right with you and Rand?"

"Mam, hold on, I'm going out to the lanai. Don't hang up now." While Billie waited for one phone to be picked up and the other to be hung up, she allowed herself to imagine the lanai, that wonderful, glorious patio, half indoor room and half outdoor room, which was full of colorful, vibrant flowers and greenery. Maggie had said, just a short time ago, that she had reupholstered all the lanai furniture in a wild fuchsia and purple pattern.

"Mam, I'm delighted with this call," Maggie said when she came back on the line. "How are things in Vermont? What's going on? We just talked a while ago.

I know you want to know what I'm going to do about Billie Limited, right?" Billie Ltd. was her mother's design firm. Billie had decided to give up managing it and had asked Maggie to take over.

"Well, I do think you should be doing something besides swimming and sunning yourself. Sun isn't good for you, Maggie. What do you *do* all day, darling?"

"Hang out with Rand, read, walk, swim, cook a little, hang out with Rand, swim some more and hang out more with Rand."

"It almost sounds," Billie said lightly, "as though you can't let him out of your sight." She wondered if Maggie had finally become aware of her husband's wandering eye.

Maggie's voice changed slightly. "It does, doesn't it? I think we're both caught up in this place. We call it our personal paradise. Rand goes to Hilo a few times a week to oversee the sugar refinery. I have to admit that he does more than I do. I've been thinking more and more about your offer. I guess I put it off because . . . well, because, you know me, I jump in with both feet and have no time for anything but whatever it is I'm doing. Rand would be . . . I think he would be lost. Are you calling for a definite answer or . . . ?" Maggie let the rest hang in the air.

Something was wrong. Billie could feel it sing over the wires. Motherly intuition. "Darling, if you could just give me some indication if you feel positive or negative about taking over, I would appreciate it. Otherwise, I've had an offer to sell, although I cannot believe the amount. Can you imagine, the little design business I started when you were born is now worth over a hundred million dollars? I'm sure the Colemans' coffers could use the money if you aren't interested." What she didn't say was that, in her own limited way, she would be ensuring her family's security. Billie Ltd. had always been separate from Coleman Enterprises.

"My God, Mam, you can't sell Billie Limited. Who offered you that much money? The Japanese, right? They're the only ones that have it. What kind of terms?"

"Cash," Billie lied.

"My God!"

"I was stunned, Maggie, considering I haven't really done anything with the company for the past year and a half. It's more or less been running itself, and, I have to admit, going down in revenues. I need to spend time with Thad."

"Let me talk to Rand, and I'll get back to you in a few days. Will that be all right?"

"Of course. Now let's talk about something *really* interesting. Have you spoken to Cole lately, or Sawyer? And how is the weather?"

"My children are fine, Mam. The weather is balmy, I'm here on the lanai, and the breeze is just heavenly. It is paradise, Mam. Did I tell you, I covered the cushions? Bright fuchsia and purple. They keep me awake during the day, the colors are blinding."

Billie chuckled. "And Susan?" she said cautiously.

"Suse is Suse, Mam, you know that. One minute she's the world's biggest bitch, the next she's sweet as sugar. I think she needs to join 'the world' and grow up a little. That whining and helpless act she uses is getting a little dated, if you want my opinion. Listen, Mam, I know you take all this to heart and you blame yourself for Susan's . . . life, but don't do that to yourself. Susan is . . . what, forty-eight? She's certainly old enough to take charge of her life. Aunt Amelia was . . . look, Susan wanted to go to England to study music. She wanted to live with Aunt Amelia. So now she's a renowned concert pianist. Not too shabby."

"No, it isn't, but I never should have sent her. I feel that sending her off like that was the biggest mistake of my life. She was too young, too vulnerable. She needed me, but I gave in to your father and Amelia. What I did, Maggie, was to give my daughter away to Amelia. In my heart I believe she hates me for it."

"Mam, no! You are the dearest person in the world to Suse. That simply isn't true."

"But it is, darling. Susan wanted it all: England, the career, Amelia's twenty-four-hour doting, and all of us. As you say, Susan has to grow up a little. Listen, darling, I've kept you long enough."

"I'm glad you called. Give Thad my love, and I'll call you in a few days with my answer."

"Good night, darling. We'll talk again in a few days. Give my regards to Rand."

"I love you, Mam."

"I love you too. Bye, darling."

Billie wiped at the tears on her cheeks. Her head dropped to her hands. She wished, as she wished every day of her life, that her only son hadn't died during the war. Maggie and Susan both needed a brother, now more than ever. How was she to secure their lives? Should she even try? She needed to know that her family was safe and secure before she ... She would do whatever she had to. All she needed was strength and a little more time. But time was her enemy now. It wouldn't be enough to simply persevere. She would have to prevail.

{{{{{{{{ CHAPTER ONE }}}}}}}}

"So, Coleman-san, you have failed."
Cole Tanner looked around, his eyes widening in stunned surprise, certain what he thought he was hearing was real; his father-in-law, Shadaharu Hasegawa's voice crying on the gentle April breeze. A second later he realized it was his own thought he'd actually voiced aloud. "That about sums it up," he said bitterly, his eyes raised to the umbrella of shell-pink blossoms overhead. He remembered the time he carried the frail old Japanese down the hill, the fragile blossoms covering his wasted body. He'd come many times to this peaceful, tranquil spot in the past three years. He held out his hands, palms upward, and watched as the pale, pink blossoms filled his hands. They were beautiful this year, the petals almost translucent. He wondered if it meant something special or if this was just an exceptional year for the cherry blossoms.

He talked because it was the only thing he could think of to do. "I did nothing different. I studied and followed your methods, and it wasn't enough. I worked hard, stretched myself thin to do all that was required. I never slacked off, not once, and yet I failed to move Rising Sun forward. I don't know what I'm doing wrong. Most of the others, those closest to you, are certain you . . . made the wrong choice. I can see it in their

{11}

eyes, and right now I feel the same way. I don't know where to turn. I came here to meditate as you used to do. I have to believe your trust in me was misguided, that Riley is the one who should be in control of Rising Sun, not me. I'm not worthy." Cole bowed his head in shame, his eyes burning.

Cole meditated silently, and eventually slept, his weary mind succumbing to the tranquility of the cherry blossom hill. Tortured dreams took him to a faraway place he neither knew nor understood. When he awoke, it was with the name Shigata Mitsu on his lips, though he had never heard it before. Sumi was on her knees next to him.

"I came to tell you that Sawyer called. She will call back in an hour. She says it is important to talk with you." She was panting with her walk up the hill.

Cole felt instantly contrite. "Why didn't you just call me instead of walking all this way?" he admonished gently.

"Because I wanted to come here with you. The exercise was good for me, but I think you can carry me down."

"All ninety-seven pounds of you?" Cole teased.

"Actually, it is ninety-eight and a half as of this morning."

"That's because you ate a bowl of ice cream and a slice of cake for breakfast," Cole continued to tease. "You're worrying too much about me. I don't want you worrying. Things are going to turn around."

Sumi laid her head on Cole's knee. "I know they will. My father chose you, and he never made mistakes in his judgment of people."

He wanted to tell Sumi there was a first time for everything, but instead he asked, "Who is Shigata Mitsu?"

Sumi shrugged her shoulders. "I do not know. Both names are common in Japan, much like the names Michael and Jones in your country. Why do you ask, Cole?"

As Cole stroked his wife's black hair, his voice grew thoughtful, more thoughtful than Sumi had ever heard it. "I was meditating and I guess I dozed off. When I woke, I saw you, and the name was on the tip of my tongue. I don't know if I dreamed it or if it means something. I asked your father's spirit for guidance. Is it possible the name came from him?"

Sumi thought the spirit business silly; she was, after all, a modern Japanese in all ways. She had no time for spirits and legends and the like. She only wanted to deal in the here and now. In her opinion, it was highly unlikely that her father would venture from that nether world where he rested to somehow place a meaningless name on her husband's lips. No. Her father, if he did indeed leave the spirit world, would have asked for a glass of sake and a cigar.

"I do not know, Cole," Sumi said honestly. "The name has a certain ring to it, a cadence, if you will. I personally never heard of it. We can ask my sisters and their husbands. Perhaps someone down at the paper or in one of the offices has heard it. The library!" she said with a sudden burst of insight. "Librarians know everything."

"I knew I married you for a reason," Cole teased. "I'll do that, first thing tomorrow. How are you feeling, Sumi?"

"Wonderful, now that you are paying attention to me." Sumi sighed, loving this warm contact with her husband. These times now were few and far between, much to her chagrin. Her husband was always preoccu-

pied, worried, and lately he was becoming so with-
drawn that she was starting to become alarmed. So
much so that she was thinking of writing Sawyer a long
letter in the hope Cole's half sister would have some insight and perhaps offer some advice.

"Have I been that neglectful, Sumi?"

"Yes, Cole, you have. I understand how you feel, but
my father did not make a mistake when he chose you to
run Rising Sun. You must believe this."

"Then why am I feeling this way?" He caught a lacy
pink petal and placed it gently on his wife's lips. "It's
almost as beautiful as you are," he said, tracing the line
of her lips and the petal at the same time.

"I don't ever remember the blossoms being this beautiful. I am sad that my father isn't here to see them.
This was always such a special place for him. When I
was very little, I would follow him up here and hide behind a bush and watch him. He prayed for us and . . .
and . . ."

"And what?" Cole asked, curious, as he caught another petal. "You know, my grandmother made a dress
for Sawyer once that was this color. She took some of
the blossoms home with her after a trip over here. Sawyer looked beautiful in her Billie original. See? I know
a thing or two about fashion," he said lightly.

"My father was offering up prayers of thanks. As a
child I seem to remember . . . he was talking to someone, but no one was on the hill. I ran down and told my
mother, and she said . . . she said he was probably talking to his . . . friend. Even back then, at the age of
seven, I was a skeptic. I demanded to know what friend
and if he was invisible like my imaginary playmates.
My mother said . . . my mother said . . . what she said
was . . . oh, dear, I can't remember. It was so long ago.

Come, we must get back, because Sawyer is going to call you. She said it was important."

Cole was careful to keep his arm around her slim shoulders for support as he helped her to her feet. She was so tiny that she came only to the middle of his chest. If she'd been taller, he would have noticed the wild look in her eyes. As it was, he felt her body tremble and thought it was from exertion. He scooped her into his arms and started down the hill, the gentle breeze sending a wave of fragile, pink petals ahead of them.

"I think, Cole, that it is time for you to go back to Texas for a visit," Sumi said.

"Later, after the baby is born. We'll all go. Don't you want to show off our firstborn?"

"Of course I do, but this time I think you need to go alone. I think you need to talk to your family. You may go as long as you swear in blood you will return."

"In blood? Never!" Cole said in mock horror.

"Ha!" was all Sumi had to say.

When they reached the garden, he set her down and she said, "Sit, Cole, and I will bring you some Sapporo. It is time for me to take my vitamins and drink that awful tea the doctor prescribed. I'll bring the phone to you when Sawyer calls. Now relax."

"You are the bossiest female I ever met," Cole said, whacking her gently on the rump. "Fetch the Sapporo and I'll go for a walk in the garden. Go, go, go!"

Next to the cherry blossom hill, this garden was probably the most tranquil spot in the entire world. It had been planted and sculpted by a Zen master. When Shadaharu was alive, this garden had been his favorite spot. He'd said he wanted to die here, if only it wouldn't leave unhappy memories for his family.

Cole skirted a waterfall and crossed a rustic bridge before he sat down on a nearby bench. When it was time for *him* to die, would he want to die here on foreign soil, or would he want to go back to Texas? He shook his head to clear away these morbid thoughts. Where did they come from? Death was a long way off. He stared off into the distance and barely noticed Sumi when she set down a bottle of beer and the portable phone. She waited a moment, hoping he would ask her to join him. When he continued to stare at a banzai tree, she quietly withdrew, her eyes filled with tears. They were growing so far apart.

Whoever and whatever you are, Shigata Mitsu, you have been here in this garden. I feel it. He thought of words like karma, spirits, and guardian angels, and Shadaharu Hasegawa. There was always something bordering on the ethereal about the old Japanese. He'd mentioned it to Riley's grandfather the first time he set foot in the garden, and the old man had just smiled. He remembered that smile now because it had made him feel so alive and wanted. He also remembered the awe he felt when in the old man's presence. What's more, he had said so, to the old man's delight.

Many times here in this garden, sitting in this very spot, he'd felt Shadaharu's spirit. He felt the old man's hand on his shoulder when he allowed it to slump here in the privacy of this garden. He didn't see ghostly apparitions or trailing bits of fog or even hear singsong words. It was nothing like that at all. He just always knew the old man was there, which somehow made him more aware of the gentle breeze and the sound of his own footsteps. Once, not long ago, when he was feeling very vulnerable, he'd childishly set what he thought was a ghost trap. He'd brought out a small glass of sake, lighted a cigar and laid it carefully in an ashtray on a small table. He himself didn't like sake and never smoked cigars. He sat down to wait, his eyes on the little table. Then one of the children had called him to the phone. When he returned a long time later, the sake was gone and the cigar was nothing but a stub. One of the children, he told himself, or more likely, the cigar had simply burned out. Until he walked the same path the old Japanese had so many times, the same walk he'd taken with him. There, right in front of his eyes, were little piles of ash. He'd gotten goose bumps that day and never mentioned it to anyone. It was a secret he kept to himself. There was no doubt in his mind that Shadaharu's spirit was trying to help him. If what he was experiencing wasn't real, then he was losing his mind. The question was, what was the old Japanese trying to tell him? Was he trying to warn him of something? Cole was tense, impatient, traits the Japanese frowned upon. He had to relax, meditate. What or who was Shigata Mitsu?

He realized he was waiting, but he wasn't sure what he was waiting for. A sign of some kind. He drank his beer, his eyes on the portable phone. *Shigata Mitsu.* He whispered the name, his voice soft and full of sadness. When nothing happened, Cole said, "I understand, old friend, one clue at a time." He didn't know if he felt stupid or not, and he didn't have time to think about it then, for the phone rang. It was Sawyer, his port in a storm. She was always there for him, whenever he needed her. He loved his half sister, but not because she was always lovable; more often than not she was a royal pain in the ass.

"For Christ's sake, Sawyer, do you always have to come on the phone like a tornado? I can hear you just fine. What's up? How are the kiddies, my godchild in particular? How's the weather in New York? Have you ever heard of Shigata Mitsu?" Cole asked, his voice dropping to a low mutter.

"Everything is fine. Kids are fine, Adam's fine. It's raining. My au pair is working out just great. I have time to myself once in a while. That's kind of the reason I'm calling you, Cole. I need some money from that dynasty you control," Sawyer trilled. "What was that name again?"

Cole's stomach flip-flopped. "How much?" he asked gruffly. "Shigata Mitsu," he almost snapped.

"A bunch. Listen, I need to talk with you. I've designed this . . . Cole, it will bend . . . it's a plane that will bend the laws of aerodynamics. I did it in between changing diapers and wrestling with Adam. Coleman Aviation hasn't got the financing I'm going to need. I need big bucks, little brother." Her voice was so airy, so confident-sounding, Cole cringed. "Millions. Maybe a hundred million." His stomach lurched a second time. "Don't you want to know about this splendid plane? Adam is impressed. Riley said, and this is a direct quote, 'It will put us back in the running when Cole comes through.' End of quote. I guess I overwhelmed you. Listen, I see this as tomorrow's *Top Gun*. I'm talking about super-maneuverability, within seconds. A decisive advantage in air-to-air combat. Vectored thrust engine. Canard wings. You interested, Cole?"

"What do I get out of this?" Cole asked coolly.

"The chance to be my financial backer. It'll fly, Cole. Trust me. It's like we're coming full circle. Just like Grandpa Moss did the first time around. It's our chance to get out from under. Megabucks. Are you in, Cole?"

Her voice was fretful-sounding now, Cole thought. She probably hadn't expected any questions, any opposition.

Cole thought about profit margins, his past three years, and his miserable time at the helm of Rising Sun. "Seventy-five percent and twelve percent interest. I could charge fifteen, but since you're family, I'll go with twelve." This must be what he'd subconsciously been waiting for, a sign from the *other side*, from Shadaharu. Jesus, it was his first goddamn clue. What else could it be? His thoughts grew frenzied. Seventy-five percent and twelve percent interest would put him where he wanted to be, in control, showing a profit. For sure he was a believer now. A niggling voice intruded in his thoughts. *At Sawyer's and the family's expense.* His mind continued to race. Was it too high, too much? Guts, he needed a bushelful now. The numbers were high, but given the vagaries of government contracts, it could also alienate the family, plus . . . plus he could be betting the ranch on a *ghost*. Was he losing his mind? Ah shit! He wished now he hadn't rattled off the numbers at the speed of light. He was about to speak when Sawyer's shrill voice pierced his eardrum.

"Did I hear you right, Cole?" she said coldly. "Seventy-five percent and twelve percent interest?"

In his life he'd never heard such a voice from her. He wanted to say no, take the words back. He thought about Rising Sun's profit margin. He thought about his father-in-law, who just happened to be a ghost, a spirit. Well, either he believed or he didn't. He decided he believed.

"I'm open to negotiating this matter," he said. "Nothing is ever carved in stone. Isn't it about time for you to come over here? Let's sit down and hammer out a deal we can all live with."

"In your dreams, Cole," Sawyer snarled. "I guess I did hear you right. You give some people power and money, and it's all over."

Cole didn't think her voice could get any angrier or any colder, but it did.

"Good-bye, Cole."

"Son-of-a-fucking-*bitch*," Cole hissed.

Hovering discreetly at the entrance to the Zen garden, Sumi trundled her way down the winding path to where Cole was sitting. "What is it?" she asked fearfully. "Did Sawyer . . . is it bad news?"

"Depends on your point of view. She wants . . . she expects me to finance a plane she's designed for Coleman Aviation."

"Oh, is that all? I thought it was something terrible, from the way you looked. You told her you would, didn't you? How I admire her ability. To think that both of you, brother and sister, became aeronautical engineers . . . well, it's just wonderful. My father had such respect for Sawyer. It was hard for him to believe a woman could do the things she did. He loved your family very much."

Shame coursed through Cole. "I made her an offer, which she rejected. Obviously, the thought never occurred to her that I might . . . that it is after all a business deal and I'd want to see a profit." When he saw the look in her eyes, however, he grasped her arm, knowing he had to say more. "I know you don't understand, and I really can't explain this, but I did what I did for a reason. I truly believe your father . . ." How was he to say it? "Honey, I believe your father's spirit is trying to help me out of the quandary I'm in. I am doing what is supernaturally expected of me at this point in time." He sounded like a lunatic.

"What *exactly* did you say to Sawyer?" Sumi asked quietly.

"I said twelve percent interest with a seventy-five percent share of the profits."

"I see."

"I've shamed you. That's what that look on your face means, doesn't it?"

"Yes," Sumi said sadly. She pulled her arm free of her husband's grasp. She turned once and almost stumbled on the path. "I wonder what would have happened to your family the first time if my father had acted with your attitude." With one hand on the door, she called out, "My father charged no interest. There was no time limit on the payback and the check was blank. I heard that story so many times I know it by heart."

Cole's eyes were glued to the doors as they closed. He felt like the scum of the earth. Worse. Until this moment, he could do no wrong in his wife's eyes. Now her beautiful, gentle face was full of shame—for him.

Did he have the nerve to say the same thing he'd just said to Sawyer to his whole family? Was there one among them who would understand, even if he could explain the way he felt? He'd boasted when he took over the Japanese empire that he had ninety billion dollars at his disposal. His *personal* disposal. Three years later he still had ninety billion dollars. He knew what all their faces would look like when Sawyer told them, and she *would* tell them, of their conversation. They'd say, among themselves, that ninety billion dollars had turned his head. They would call him a disgusting, greedy bastard. His heart felt bruised and sore.

Cole reached for the Sapporo, but the bottle was empty. He'd taken no more than a few swigs, and hadn't poured any of the beer into the glass on the black lacquer tray. When he picked up the glass, he wasn't at all surprised to discover beer suds in the bottom. The old Japanese had always liked beer with his dinner, no matter what he was eating. Cole looked at his watch. Fifteen minutes past six. He looked around wildly. The late afternoon sun dimmed. Another sign. He was sure of it. Shadaharu's spirit was here, listening. If he truly believed that, then he had to believe he'd done the right thing with Sawyer. Numbers could always be adjusted. Still, his sister was a tight-ass and would view this as a betrayal. Well, he'd just have to convince her she was wrong. Right now he had to concentrate on his loyalty to his father-in-law. The old Japanese came first.

Overhead he could heard the rustle of birds as they readied themselves for flight. He thought it an angry sound. Each rustle, each flap of the wings, seemed to say, Shigata Mitsu, Shigata Mitsu.

Sawyer Coleman Jarvis stared at the pinging receiver in her hand, her eyes full of stunned disbelief. She felt like crying, but she fought back her tears. Behind her, the twins, Katy and Josie, tussled and squealed as they both tugged at a flop-eared rabbit. Both girls were as stubborn as she was. Each of them would end up with one of the rabbit's ears, and then she'd have to sew them back on when they napped. It didn't matter that each had her own rabbit. So far she'd sewn the ears back on both rabbits a dozen times. The terrible twos. She loved and treasured each minute she spent with the twins, who, she said, looked just like Adam, although they had her blond hair and blue eyes.

"Damn," she muttered as she picked her way past an oversize playpen, then tripped over a Raggedy Andy doll, which she kicked out of her way. The twins stopped tugging on the battered rabbit and stared at the colorful doll flying through the air.

"Adammmm!" Sawyer bellowed.

"Are you trying to wake the dead?" Adam bellowed in return. "It's a damn good thing no one else lives here but us, with the crazy hours we keep. What's wrong?"

Sawyer sat down on the high stool at her drafting table, which was alongside Adam's. His and hers drafting tables. Most times she thought it amusing that they could work side by side, Adam drawing the political cartoons that provided their living and she doing her designs. Right now she didn't see anything amusing in it.

She told him about her conversation with Cole. "Do you believe that! He actually said that to me!" Sawyer snorted angrily.

Always the peacemaker, Adam said, "Maybe you caught him at a bad time. Sumi is pregnant, and he's probably worried about her. He's got a hell of a load to carry around. He's responsible for the whole shooting match over there. Cut him a little slack, call him back."

"No way," Sawyer seethed.

Adam's brow furrowed. "Maybe his business practices changed." He was remembering Cole and Riley when they were young, when he acted as mediator, as if he were their big brother. "Do you want *me* to call him? You're a hothead, Sawyer, and Cole's no slouch in that department either. I'm sure this is . . . Jesus, you're asking for a couple of hundred million dollars. I don't know how quick I'd be to say yes. I'm sure he needs time to think about it, to speak with his advisers."

"No, no, no," Sawyer snapped. "He was real quick to say he wanted seventy-five percent and twelve percent interest. Does that sound like he has to confer with his advisers? Cole is the adviser. He's everything. Whatever he says goes. Another thing, Adam. When my family needed money last year to pay off legal suits, you were the first one in line to offer money. Grandmam Billie didn't even have to ask you, so don't go telling me you'd have to think about all this."

Adam scratched his stand-up red hair, the tight curls giving the appearance of corkscrews. He hated arguing with Sawyer, because he never won. She wore him down by sheer persistence. Still, he tried. "I realize this sounds like I'm playing devil's advocate, but has it ever occurred to any of you Colemans that Cole is not your personal banker? Where is it written that he has to come through every time you guys get in a bind?"

Sawyer started to sputter. They'd had this argument once before, and she'd come out on the short end simply because, logically, Adam was right.

"Look," she said hotly, "the point is, I never dreamed he would take the position he just took. He's a little shit, Adam. The money and power have gone to his head."

"But you're willing to tap into that power and money without a second thought." Adam smirked. He was getting to her. Finally.

"If you put it like that," Sawyer snapped, "I guess you're right. But he could have been a little more fair. We'd all make money. You weren't around the first time, when we were scrambling to raise the money for Grandpap Moss's first plane. I remember what *that* was like. It was a nightmare, Adam. It was Mr. Hasegawa who bailed us out."

Adam threw his hands in the air. "I rest my case."

"We didn't ask," Sawyer said tightly, "he offered."

"Has anyone ever questioned how that old Japanese became so successful? What did he do that your family didn't do? I think it was Thad who said at one time Mr. Hasegawa wasn't born with a silver spoon in his mouth and that he came from humble beginnings. At his death he was one of the three richest men in the world."

"What does that have to do with anything? Come here, Josie, Mommy will fix it," Sawyer said, reaching for the Raggedy Andy doll. She looked at the battered face, at the yarn hair, and sighed. "Isn't it your turn to sew this?"

"No, it's not my turn. And it has everything to do with what we're talking about," Adam said. Sawyer reached for the sewing box that was always near her drafting table. Somehow that warmed his heart. His tone softened. "Oh, okay, I'll sew it this time."

"You might be right. Maybe I did come on too strong," Sawyer said, biting off the end of the thread. "So I'll call him back and apologize. In true Sawyer fashion. What do *you* think is a fair percentage?"

"Oh, no, you don't. Don't get me involved. You work this out with Cole and the family." He risked a glance at Sawyer's blueprint. It was Greek to him. Half the time he didn't understand a thing she was talking about. She liked to mutter while she worked. About the only thing he really understood was the term dogfight, and the only reason he knew that was because Sawyer made him sit through *Top Gun* five times. He'd really been out of his depth when his wife, pregnant with twins, had said she wanted to go to England to the Farnsworth air show. She'd been impossible to live with when she got back, with her constant chatter about the MiG-29 that so impressed her by climbing almost straight up, slowing to a stop at about four thousand feet, then sliding back tail first. His wife, the aerodynamicist. Jesus, he even had trouble pronouncing the word.

"There you go, sweetie. Show it to Ellen. In the kitchen, Josie."

"Where's Katy?" Adam said, a frown on his face. "She gave up on the doll too easily."

"In the kitchen getting a cookie," Sawyer smiled. "I have to get back to work. Can you handle things? I mean really handle them?"

"Hey," Adam scoffed, "I know how to hand out all-day suckers and cookies as well as you do. I can also sew and open cans. Ellen's here."

"You're the boss," Sawyer said happily, one hand on the phone, her eyes on a set of blueprints.

Adam snorted. "Get to work."

He could have saved his breath. Sawyer was already lost in the maze of blueprints. He swung back to his own drafting table and the political cartoon he was drawing of President Bush. Political tomfoolery he understood.

{{{{{{{{ CHAPTER TWO }}}}}}}}

It was a beautiful house, perhaps the most beautiful house on the island of Hawaii. Lush hibiscus and fragrant plumeria surrounded the estate. A monstrous banyan tree that resembled a giant umbrella shrouded the timeworn iron gates at the entrance to Maggie and Rand Nelson's estate. The snakelike drive, which eventually widened and became circular, was edged on both sides by regal palms. The house itself was long, low, and sprawling, with the sparkling Pacific as a backdrop.

The house was spacious, yet not overlarge, and it gave off a cozy feeling of coolness and light, so different from Sunbridge, with its heavy leather furniture and somber colors. Every room opened to the outside. The French doors leading to the patio were sheltered from sun and rain by a sloping overhang of the tiled roof. Beautiful gardens were part of the view and seemed to come indoors to blend with the light bamboo furniture and vivid greens and whites of the walls. Graceful paddle fans, centered on every ceiling, created a pleasant breeze, and the tang of the sea far below seemed to fill each room.

Every room in the house had sheer curtains that billowed in the scented sea breeze. The carpets were eggshell-white, bringing into relief the dark tones of the native mahogany furnishings of the bedrooms, while in other rooms it complemented the light bamboo furniture.

Billie, who had been the estate's first owner, had called it her own personal paradise. Maggie and Rand referred to it simply as home.

Maggie Coleman Tanner Nelson, wearing a bikini, settled herself on the lanai. The breeze was gentle today, causing the ferns hanging overhead to dance.

She looked around uneasily. Always when things were perfect, something went awry. She felt a tug at her heart and knew instantly that something was wrong, either with her mother, her son Cole, or her daughter Sawyer. It was a seventh sense the Coleman women had, her mother always said. So far, Maggie thought uneasily, that seventh sense had never been wrong. The feeling had been with her for several days now, and last night's call from her sister Susan accentuated it.

Maggie draped the vibrant beach towel, a Billie original, around her shivering shoulders. It was eighty degrees, so why was she shaking and shivering? Was it Susan's imminent arrival? This visit was unexpected, a total surprise. Susan never, ever, acted spontaneously. That in itself was cause for worry. She'd said her husband, Ferris, was out conquering the medical world, and she'd laughed when she had said it; a bitter sound as Maggie recalled. She'd even mentioned it to Rand, who had pooh-poohed the whole thing away, saying Susan probably just needed to be with her family for a few days.

Maggie walked to the edge of the lanai. How beautiful it was here, she thought, how calm and peaceful. She closed her eyes, forcing her mind to blankness. "Please," she whispered, "don't let anything intrude, don't let anything spoil my happiness."

The towel dropped and she ran straight down the white sandy beach and into the sparkling blue water. Her strokes were strong and sure, testament to the daily workout she gave her muscles. When the tension in her shoulders eased, she flopped over and floated on her back to let the sun caress her body.

Life hadn't always been this idyllic. She'd wasted years both hating and loving her father, Moss. There had been times when she'd hated her mother as well. And she'd caused the family so much grief and sadness when, at the age of fourteen, she'd given birth to Sawyer. A child herself, she knew nothing about babies, but she'd known enough to get herself pregnant. She'd wanted to give the baby away, but her mother and father refused even to consider it. Her mother had taken Sawyer and raised her as her own daughter, while Maggie had been sent to a private school that dealt with incorrigible children. When she came of age, she'd struck out on her own, ignoring her daughter and her family. Eventually she'd married Cole's father and, at the age of twenty-six, became a mother for the second time. Then she'd divorced Cranston Tanner and fought for custody of Cole. The day she had finally settled her son in military school, she attacked the bottle with a vengeance. For a long time her days were spent sleeping off hangovers. The realization that she was an alcoholic came to her the day she received the deed to Sunbridge, her father's legacy. It was then that she had managed to turn herself around. Coleman guts, she told herself every day of her life.

Maggie rolled over in the water and struck out for shore. She hated her thoughts when they carried her back to that part of her life. She always cried when she thought of Sawyer and all she had missed with her.

When Sawyer had been diagnosed with a brain tumor she had turned on Maggie, rebelling as Maggie had with her family. Sawyer had refused an operation. Maggie had tried to talk her out of her decision, to be a mother to her daughter, but Sawyer had told her to go to hell, to get out of her life. Too little too late, she'd said, but Maggie had refused to listen. Instead, Maggie had trenched in and fought Sawyer every step of the way. Her brother Cole and his cousin Riley, sixteen at the time, had joined forces with her, and in the end, tired, weary, and beaten, Sawyer agreed to the operation. Maggie would never forget the day she saw Sawyer's cocky thumbs-up salute as they stood outside the plate-glass window in the intensive care unit. She'd heard the angels sing that day. God, in his infinite wisdom, had given both her and Sawyer a second chance at life.

She was at the shoreline now and could see her husband on the lanai. Leaving the surf behind, she waved as she ran.

Rand's heart hammered with excitement when Maggie reached up to kiss him full on the mouth, but he sensed her inward trembling, saw the concern in her eyes. Something was wrong. Maggie was like Billie, a rock when it came to emotions. It was one of the reasons he loved her. He, on the other hand, only knew one way to deal with emotions.

"C'mere," he said, crooking a finger at his wife.

Maggie laughed. "Oh no, Lord Nelson, I know that leer of yours. Uh-uh, not now. Lela is due to come in here any second to clean, and . . ."

"And . . ."

"And you think I'm easy. . . ." And why now? she wondered.

"Sort of . . . we are married, you're supposed to be easy." Rand laughed, his eyes sly.

Maggie's heart fluttered, but her eyes took on a wary look. She supposed she *was* always willing, even when she wasn't in the mood. Yet they hadn't had sex in over three weeks, if you were counting the days. She was counting.

During those weeks she'd done a lot of thinking. Was she becoming unattractive, uninteresting in Rand's eyes? What, after all, did she contribute? All she ever had to talk about was the cleaning lady, her trips to the grocery store, and the latest book she'd read. On a really interesting day when she found a unique shell on the beach or the water changed color, she had to struggle less for conversation.

Lately, all the slick magazines said that the woman in a marriage had to initiate sex at times. What the magazine didn't say was what a forty-nine-year-old woman approaching fifty was supposed to do when she was rebuffed, even if the rebuffing was done nicely.

She was damn tired of pretending it didn't matter, damn tired of being perky all the time, damn tired of struggling after witty, charming conversation. And she was damn, fucking tired of Rand's trips to Hilo and Maui and being left alone for days at a time.

She felt like crying suddenly, but Rand hated what he called her sniveling. To cover the bad moment, she allowed her eyebrows to shoot upward. "How about a swim? In the buff!"

"You're on!" Rand said, stripping off his madras shorts. Maggie squealed the way she always did and ran out across the lanai, her nude husband in hot pursuit.

She hit the deep, blue water of the ocean a moment after her skimpy bikini fell to the sand. She struck out, her powerful arms slicing through the water. Within seconds she slacked off purposely so her husband could catch up with her. When he was almost abreast of her, she jackknifed and her bare bottom upended. Rand whooped and followed her down into the silent, sapphire water. They swam alongside one another as if their movements were choreographed, then together they surfaced, their heads breaking water at the same moment.

"I love you," Maggie whispered.

"How much?" Rand said, locking his body against hers.

"More than yesterday and half as much as tomorrow," she said. "How much do you love me?"

"A lot, you brazen hussy," Rand said hoarsely. He entwined one of his legs with hers to bring her closer. "Want to make love in the water?"

"Yeah," Maggie drawled.

"It might be a little tricky out here."

"Is that your fifty-three years talking, or am I too much woman for you?"

Rand grinned. "More likely the other way around."

"Show me," she whispered. Maybe this time things would be the way they used to be. Maybe this time Rand's lovemaking wouldn't be so . . . mechanical.

He brought his mouth close to her ear and whispered.

"Really!" Maggie laughed.

"Really. And then some." Rand grinned, striking out for the shore line.

A devilish light in her eyes, Maggie jackknifed into the water. She surfaced, her powerful strokes enabling her to overtake him easily. They hit the beach within seconds and rolled on the sand together.

Maggie tensed for what she knew was about to come. Rand's arms tightened despite her pretended struggles. Then he forced her closer, crushing her, his body hard and muscular. She felt herself caught in the intensity of his gaze, aware of the power he had over her. Her pretended outrage was gone, replaced now with passion as he drew her into the depths of his dark eyes.

She lowered her head imperceptibly, digging her body into the soft white sand, bracing herself for his kiss, preparing her mouth for his expected onslaught. Instead, she felt his gentle lips against her brow, slipping into her hairline and descending in a path to the sensitive skin at her ear. She was aware of the faint spicy scent of his cologne, of the close stubble of beard on his chin, of the softness of his lips as they traced patterns across her cheeks.

Maggie felt her body relaxing, yielding, as his hand cupped her face, raising her lips to his own. When she thought she couldn't bear the sweetness another moment, his kiss deepened. The moist tip of his tongue smoothed the satiny underside of her lips and penetrated ever so softly, ever so slowly, into the recesses of her mouth.

Feeling her moist, anxious lips soften and part, offering themselves to him, Rand groaned and moved his mouth hungrily over hers, tasting the sweetness within.

When he released her, his eyes searched hers for an instant, then her long, thick lashes closed, and she heard her breath coming in ragged little gasps of surprise and wonder. How could this man, whom she loved with all her being, still evoke in her these wild animal feelings? She kissed him deeply, and everything was blotted out—the glorious sun, the soft lapping water at their feet, even Susan and the household staff, who had a clear view of the beach. Nothing mattered but this man and the feeling he evoked in her.

It seemed to Maggie that his mouth became part of her own, his white teeth large and square, his lips full, sensuous. It was a clean mouth, tasting of the wine he'd had with lunch. She clung to him, unwilling to allow even the narrowest space between them. His kisses intoxicated her, making her lightheaded, heightening her craving. They strained toward one another, captured by the designs of sensuality, caught in a yearning that penetrated the barriers of the flesh and drove them to join breath and body, spirit and soul.

When at last they could bear to part, he again looked deeply into her eyes. No man could ever take his place in her life. It was fated that his eyes should be looking at her as they were now, filled with desire, brimming with expectation; it was fated that his voice should be so soft, so gentle, yet vibrate through her like the deep, rumbling note of a violin plucking at her senses, casting a spell over her.

Beneath the sun's golden, warming rays he nuzzled her neck and inhaled her fragrance. His tongue blazed a trail from her throat to her bare breasts, and she trembled with exquisite anticipation. All things moved to the distance, nothing and no one existed beyond this moment and place. The only reality was the way her body reacted to her husband. Pleasure radiated upward from some hidden well within her, and she allowed herself to be carried by it, unable to hinder the momentum of her own desire.

Maggie's sensations heightened wherever he touched her; her emotions hurled and spun, wreaking havoc upon her. Her hands were eager, her fingers greedy as she held him to her as closely as a secret.

She watched him now with half-closed eyes, aware of his sun-bronzed chest, of the curling patterns of chest hair that narrowed to a thin, fine fur over the flatness of his belly. His erection pulsated with anticipation. The paleness of his lean haunches delineated the dark patch of hair surrounding his manhood, and his tapered hips flared into thighs thick and strong with muscle.

As her hands moved over him, Rand was filled with a sense of his own power and exulted in her undisguised passion for him. She was so beautiful, this wife of his, with her lips red from his kisses, seductive now, and her languid, heavy-lidded gaze, which hinted at a depth of passion that excited him unbearably. He was so hungry for her, he wanted to spread her beneath him and plunge into her fiery depths, to feel himself become a part of her. Each curve of her body was eloquent: the roundness of her breasts, with their pink crests; the slender arc of her hips, which narrowed into long, lean legs; the golden hue of her skin, gleaming softly with the sheen of her desire. But he would take her slowly, savoring every inch of her, delighting in the pleasure they would share.

When he moved to cover her with his body, it was her turn to protest. As she rolled over on her side next to him, her cloud of dark hair tumbled around her face, grazing his shoulder and tickling his chest. She smoothed his chest with her fingertips, trailing through the patch of dark curls, exploring the regions that were smooth and hairless, then moving to the flat hardness of his belly. He heard himself gasp as her hand wandered close to his groin and then flew upward again. He wanted to applaud her daring, yet he almost laughed at the innocent look in her eyes. "Touch me," he demanded, taking her hand in his, moving it downward again. It was their first time again, something only Maggie was capable of making him feel. "Do you like it when I touch you? Here?" He caressed her breast, feeling its weight in the palm of his hand, relishing the softness of it and the hard little crest that jutted into his palm. "And here?" he asked, sliding downward to the softness of her belly. "Here?" His fingers grazed the satiny flesh of her inner thighs, whispering past the fleecy curls between her legs.

Her hand followed his, combing past the thicket that surrounded his eager shaft. Hesitantly, her fingers explored him, moving upward to touch the velvet-smooth tip, upon which poised a drop of moisture, like a glistening pearl. As she turned her head to watch the progress of her fingers, her hair hung like a curtain, shielding her face from his view. It pleased her to hear his sharp intake of breath as her fingers traveled the length of his manhood downward to the surprising vulnerability between his thighs. She felt desire ripple through him and realized with a curious, proud excitement that she was in command of his passions.

When she lifted her head to look back at him, her eyes were heavy with desire; he was reminded of a sleek cat who has just discovered the cream bowl. The little smile she bestowed upon him was dripping feline self-satisfaction.

She reached out to touch him again, this time watching him, aware of his every reaction, relishing the masculine hardness of him and feeling it pulsate in anticipation of her touch. When she closed her hand over him, a deep throbbing sounded in his chest and rumbled from his lips. Unable to resist her a moment longer, he reached up, pulled her beside him and took the superior position. Only having her, losing himself within her, would satisfy.

A golden warmth flooded through Maggie as he brought his mouth to hers once again. His movements were smoothly executed as he drew a path from one breast to the other, covering each first with his hands and then with his lips. She clung to the strength of his arms, holding fast as though she were fearful of falling in on herself, never to be found again.

His hands, at her waist and buttocks, lifted her slightly. The tortuous, teasing exploration of his tongue made her shudder and heightened her passion. Her fingers clutched and pulled at his dark, ruffled hair as though begging him to stop while her body arched into his, feverishly exposing herself to his maddening mouth. He searched for and found the secret places that pushed her to the brink of release, only to have his kiss follow another path before returning to the first.

A yawning ache spread through Maggie, demanding satisfaction, settling at her core and forcing her to seek relief by writhing and thrashing about restlessly. Rand held her there, forcing her to him, adoring her with his hands and lips until she could deny herself no longer. Her body flamed, her back arched, and her world divided into two parts—her need and his lips. And when the tremors ceased and his mouth covered hers once again, she tasted herself there. She was satisfied, yet discontented. She had feasted, but she was famished. She wanted more, much more. She wanted to share with him the release of his own passion.

She urged him onward. Grasping her hips, he lifted her, and she wound her parted thighs around him. She guided him into her, pulling him forward, driving downward, now with a different desire, cooler than before. As she moved with him, became part of him, Maggie fueled his passion and renewed her own. Together they were flung upward; together they found the sun.

For what seemed an eternity they lay together, whispering and touching. They loved.

"Not bad for an old broad, eh?" Maggie gurgled with laughter.

"Not bad at all," Rand said smoothly.

Stark naked, Maggie and Rand walked up to the lanai arm in arm, their suits draped over their shoulders. They showered together on the concrete pad, and they wrapped themselves in colorful towels.

"Are you still going over to Maui?" Maggie asked as she popped open a can of iced tea.

"Are you kidding? This old man is heading for the bedroom for a nap."

Maggie hooted. "I knew it, I knew it. Let's do it again!"

"You looking for early widowhood?"

Maggie's face became serious. "Don't ever say that again to me. I hate that word. I don't know what I'd do without you, Rand," she said harshly.

He was supposed to say, And I wouldn't want to live without you, Maggie darling. But he didn't. Instead, he said, "I am going to Maui, and yes, I will pick Susan up from the airport on my way back."

"Sounds good to me," Maggie said quietly.

When Maggie heard the sound of Rand's car spewing gravel in the driveway, she walked down to the beach to sit in the sun. Why did she feel so cold, so alone? She ran the past hour over and over in her mind. The lovemaking was wonderful, but it had been *her* idea, not Rand's. She thought of all the excuses he had made over the past three weeks. He had headaches, his back hurt, he had paperwork to do, he fell asleep before she finished in the bathroom. If she had to come up with a word to describe her husband, she would say he was bored. With her. Oh, he still said he loved her, wanted her, needed her, but she wasn't sure if she believed him any longer. Maybe Rand was going through the male mid-life crisis. Maybe, maybe, maybe.

Maggie inhaled deeply, loving the scent of the salty ocean. A spray of frothy blue water rushed about her feet, leaving behind little droplets that looked like tiny jewels on her sunbronzed ankles. It was such a perfect day, the way most were. Not a cloud in the sky, and where it met the horizon, it was impossible to tell where sky ended and ocean began. Breathtaking, utterly breathtaking.

Lord in heaven, she was blessed in so many ways. Why couldn't she just accept that? "Because, damnit, something is wrong," she said aloud. Was it Rand? Her mother, her sister's visit? Or was it her?

A sudden gust of plumeria-scented air swept past. It was so heady, she closed her eyes to savor the fragrant breeze. Next to the tantalizing aroma of fried onions and peppers, plumeria was her favorite smell in the world. Another wave washed against her legs. She looked down and imagined a string of diamonds circling her ankles. A strange sound slid past her lips. Water drops that were like strings of diamonds, flowers that reminded her of frying onions and peppers, mechanical lovemaking. Her do-nothing life. Maybe that was what was bothering her. She wasn't contributing. Instead, she was monitoring her husband, spending as much time with him as possible so he wouldn't spend time with anyone else.

If she took over Billie Ltd., Rand would be left to his own devices. She would have to do a fair amount of traveling, work the same long, arduous hours her mother had put in when the company was at its peak. What it was coming down to, she thought, was Billie Ltd. or Rand. I must not be much of a woman if I can't hold my husband just because I'm nearing fifty, she thought. Fifty. The magic halfway mark in a woman's life. Was it true that women grew older and men grew distinguished? It wasn't fair. She needed a Billie pep talk. Or maybe she just needed to unload on family. A sister could be as good as a mother. Susan might be a good sounding board. Sawyer would be good too, but she had her hands full with the twins. No sense unnerving her.

Maggie dug her toes into the bare sand as deep as they would go. "Nobody ever gets it all," she muttered. "You get close, and then, because you don't deserve it, it's snatched away." Now, where did that thought come from? There were no answers here on this white beach. Her mother said that the answers always lay within one's self, and Billie was never wrong. Never.

A walk on the beach and then a brief snooze under the monkeypod tree might give her some perspective. "All I have are brief moments of happiness," Maggie muttered as she trudged along the water's edge.

As the sun was beginning to set, Maggie woke to voices from the lanai. Her heart fluttered in her chest when she heard her husband say, "Maggie usually takes a nap late in the afternoon. Five will get you ten she's under the monkeypod tree. Maggie doesn't . . . Maggie doesn't do much these days but hover."

Hover. Dear God. She sprang from the hammock,

rubbing the sleep from her eyes. A moment later she was speaking to Rand, forcing a lilt into her voice. "I was reading this awesome book Mam sent a few weeks ago. I'm going to call her later, and I wanted to be able to discuss it with her."

"Are we having dinner this evening?" Rand said. "The kitchen is cool, dim, and there are no fragrant odors," Rand teased lightly.

Maggie refused to look directly at her husband, refused to acknowledge she'd heard his words. *Hover.* God in heaven. Instead, she focused on her sister. "Let me look at you, Suse," she ordered. "Too thin," she said, clucking her tongue. "I don't see a sparkle in your eyes either. Well, we can fix that up in a hurry. The lei becomes you. I made it myself this morning. Doesn't the scent just drive you crazy? I guess Ferris was too busy to come with you. Oh, I get it, this is one of those getaway vacations. Well, this is the right place for a quick getaway. Juice? Some fruit? Come on, I'll show you your room. You can change into a suit and we'll hit the water." She knew she was babbling, but her eyes pleaded with Rand not to question her as she ushered Susan into the house.

"So, this is the magical paradise where everyone has found happiness," Susan said with a bitter edge in her voice. "I'm the only one who's never been here, and yet I'm the one who was conceived here. Can you imagine that?"

"If I remember correctly, you never *wanted* to come here," Maggie said, matching her sister's tone. "I invited you and Ferris dozens of times, but you always had a reason why you couldn't visit."

"Mam *gave* you this place, didn't she?" Susan said tightly.

"Only for a year. Then Rand and I bought it from her. She wanted us to see if we'd like living here on a full-time basis. Where did you ever get the idea it was a gift? Mam is generous, but not that generous. Besides, Rand would never have accepted it. Isn't that right, Rand?" Maggie said, looking directly at her husband for the first time.

"True. But it looks like you two have some squabbling to get out of your system. Why don't you do it while I go to Mickey Dee's and bring home some food?"

He was gone a second later.

"Why are you here now, Susan? What's wrong?"

"Maggie, I'm dead on my feet. I have jet-lag and I haven't been sleeping well lately. Would you mind terribly if I took a nap? Just an hour or so. I ate on the plane so don't worry about me. And don't let me sleep any longer."

"Oh, Suse, I'm sorry," Maggie said, hugging her sister. "Of course you must be tired. We can talk later, stay up all night if necessary. Remember how we used to do that until we got all caught up?"

"I remember," Susan said sadly, her eyes misting.

Maggie pretended not to see her sister's tears. "The bathroom is over there, and in the top drawer are some night things Sawyer keeps here. I'll turn down the bed and all you have to do is hop in. A word of warning, though. Don't sleep on the eyelet ruffle or you'll have creases in your face when you wake. Or," she added thoughtfully, "does that just happen to women my age? I'm forty-nine, you know. What are you, forty-eight? My God! It's awesome, isn't it?" She was babbling again and still didn't know why. "Sleep tight, Suse."

In a flash Maggie was down the hall and into her

husband's small office. As always when she was around her sister, Maggie left her feelings aside; now she spoke boldly to Rand. "Something's wrong. I can feel it. Did she say anything on the ride from the airport?"

Rand stared at his wife. "She said Hawaii is beautiful and she loved the ride up here to the North Shore. We talked about the lei, and I told her you made it just for her. She said they had a hard winter this year. She did say she was homesick, but didn't know where home was. I felt sorry for her. Mother Maggie's magic is what she needs, I think. Maybe she and Ferris had a tiff. She misses Jessie terribly. She hasn't gotten over her death, that's for sure. Don't look so troubled, darling. Susan is a grown woman. She can handle it. Time is all she needs."

"*If* there is a problem, why didn't she go to Mam's? I always want to run to Mam when something goes wrong. It's not just Suse either. I've had this ominous feeling for a few days now that things aren't what they seem with Mam. You know me and my feelings."

"I think you're just overexcited. Let's you and I skip out to Mickey Dee's and grab ourselves some succulent, greasy, deep-fried mahi-mahi, and greasier french fries."

"I'm not hungry. Why don't you go and get whatever you want, or I can make a salad. There's some very good crabmeat in the refrigerator. It's up to you. I want to make some phone calls before it gets too late. You don't mind, do you?" Her tone of voice let him know she didn't much care one way or the other.

"Guess I'll see you in a bit then. I can taste the grease already. Give my regards to everyone."

The soft knock on the door caused both Maggie and Rand to turn around. "Oh, Lela, are you finished?" Maggie said. "Yes, I guess you are. That was a silly question now, wasn't it? I think my checkbook is here somewhere." Feeling uncomfortable about Lela's presence, she rummaged in Rand's desk drawer for the household checkbook.

Lela, the nineteen-year-old daughter of Maggie's housekeeper Addie, filled in when one of Addie's numerous children needed her. Lela was so beautiful, it almost hurt to look at her. Her hair was long and blacker than a raven's wing, her heavily fringed lashes sweeping upward to reveal jet-dark eyes that always seemed to Maggie to be speculating or calculating. She was model-thin, but rounded in all the right places. She was the color of rich honey, perfection dressed in island attire. At the moment, she was engaged in bantering conversation with Rand. Nineteen going on thirty, Maggie thought. Addie should put a leash on her.

Maggie ripped the check from the book and straightened up in time to see Rand tap the girl's derriere. As Lela reached for the check, her eyes playfully challenged Maggie.

"Close the door on your way out, Lela. Tell Addie I won't need you the rest of the week." When the girl had gone, Maggie turned to her husband. "Would you mind telling me what *that* was all about?" she bristled.

"What?" Rand said.

"That little pat on Lela's tush. I don't like it when you do things like that, and I don't like the way that girl looks at me."

"Is that why you told her you didn't need her the rest of the week? That means, darling Maggie, *you* will have to cook and make the beds," Rand said quietly. "Won't that eat into your routine? Anyway, it didn't mean anything."

"If it didn't mean anything, then why did you do it?"

"I don't know. I just did it. Jesus, I'm sorry. It won't happen again."

"See that it doesn't," Maggie said quietly.

"I guess I'll be going," Rand said stiffly. "Say hello to everyone when you make your calls."

"I will," Maggie called over her shoulder as she headed down the hall to their bedroom.

Maggie pulled a mint-green muumuu over her head and slipped into thong sandals, her island attire. She walked down to the beach with the portable phone in her hand. She had decided to call Sawyer. There was a smile on her face when she thought about her daughter's two children, Josie and Katy.

The connection was clear, Sawyer's voice crackling with something that sent chills down Maggie's arms. "I was just going to call you," Sawyer said.

"Is everything okay? Adam? The twins?"

"The girls are eating cookies, Adam is trying to glue a toy together, and I'm . . . I'm pissed to the teeth. Have you heard from Cole?"

"Last week," Maggie said with a catch in her voice. "Why?"

Maggie listened to Sawyer's story until she heard Adam order his wife to lower her voice.

"Well, what do you think, Maggie?" Sawyer asked. She had been calling her mother by her first name since childhood.

"I don't know what to think. That doesn't sound like Cole. Do you want me to call him?" Without waiting for a reply, she rushed on, "For the past few days I've had this awful feeling that something is wrong somewhere. Your aunt Susan arrived today. At first I thought my uneasiness had something to do with her, but nothing she's told me explains the feeling I have. I planned on calling Cole anyway. What should I say?"

"I don't know," Sawyer muttered. "Adam says I should call back and apologize for my attitude. He says it sucks. Maybe he's right. I had no right to assume Cole would be willing to go on the line for us. When you talked to him last, did he act as if anything was wrong? I mean, Sumi is okay. I talked to her a few days ago. It's Cole, Maggie. If you call him, I'd appreciate it if you'd get back to me. I'm going to start beating the bushes for some financing if he doesn't come through. And you can reiterate to him for me that I'm not paying loan-shark rates."

"All right, Sawyer, I'll pass the word along. Now tell me about the girls. Are they talking yet?"

"They're like magpies. All they do is chatter. They seem to understand each other. Adam says they're speaking Greek at an early age. He said to give you his love. Oh, God, Adammmm!"

"What's wrong?" Maggie demanded when she heard a crash and loud wailing.

"They just got into the jelly bean jar and broke it. They climbed up on the table. Ellen, the sitter, is in the bathroom. You can't take your eyes off them for a minute. The terrible twos. And Adam wants to get them a puppy!"

"I guess I better let you go. Give them a kiss for me. Adam too."

"I'll send some pictures. Give Rand and Chesney our love, Aunt Susan too, okay? And call me if you find out anything from Cole."

"I will, Sawyer. Remember now, patience is the name of the game with the girls."

"I always do. Oh God, they threw a pillow into the fish tank. 'Bye, Maggie."

There was a smile on Maggie's face when she dialed Cole's number. She didn't care what time it was in Japan. She loved talking to her son, and especially now that he and Sumi were expecting.

It was hard to believe that Cole was going to be a father, and harder still to believe she, Maggie, was going to be a grandmother for a second time. Grandmother Maggie. She liked the sound of that.

"Cole, how are you?" she asked cheerfully when she heard her son's deep voice.

"Fine, Mother, and no, Sumi isn't ready yet," he said with a chuckle. "She's waddling like a duck and has constant heartburn. She says that means the baby has a lot of hair. Is that true?"

Maggie laughed. "I've heard that. Not to change the subject, but guess who came to visit?" Without waiting for her son to reply, she said, "Susan. She's sleeping right now, so we haven't had a chance to visit, I mean really visit. I'm so excited. I just love it when family comes. By the way, Ivy sent me a picture of little Moss. I can't tell you how much he looks like your grandfather. Even Mam says so. Same name, same face. It's uncanny."

"We got a picture too. Sumi says he has her father's ears."

How flat his voice was, Maggie suddenly noticed, how dead-sounding. She felt her heart thump in her chest. "Have you decided what you're going to call the baby?" Any minute she was going to do what she did best—babble.

"If it was up to Sumi, it would have seven names.

She can't seem to make up her mind. But I get to name it if it's a boy."

"Sounds fair to me. What's your choice?"

"I haven't decided." There was an uncomfortable moment of silence, as if he couldn't think of anything to say. "How's Chesney?" he finally managed.

"She's in Hong Kong. She left this morning on a flight and won't be back till the end of the week. She calls Rand 'Dad' now. He's going through a bit of anxiety, because she's getting engaged to that Navy flier. What's his name? Brian, that's it. He has six more months to go in the Navy and then he's out. He said he's willing to test-fly Sawyer's plane if she gets it off the ground. *That* was what convinced Rand he's an okay guy. Rand flew the test flight for your grandfather's plane, you know. He says history is repeating itself, that we're coming full circle, and I think it's true."

"So you've talked to Sawyer." There was a faint sound of accusation in his voice.

"A little while ago, as a matter of fact. I try to call twice a week. She was . . . upset. Mostly with herself, but she did say she was disappointed in your response. Cole, she loves you so much."

"Sawyer came on real strong. I gave her some numbers off the top of my head. I'm the first to admit they were high. As a matter of fact, I was reworking the numbers when you called. I was going to call her back in the middle of the night and give her a dose of her own medicine."

Maggie strained to hear the chuckle that was usually in her son's voice when he spoke of Sawyer. Not only were they sister and brother, they were friends as well. There was no chuckle. "Cole, is something wrong? I mean really wrong? You've always said that what was yours was ours. I remember thinking that was the most wonderful thing I'd ever heard," she said, then added more firmly, "If you didn't mean it, you shouldn't have said it. You know your sister better than anyone."

"I know that she's damn pigheaded. If you don't do things her way, she takes her marbles and goes home."

Maggie took a deep breath. *God, what was happening to her family?*

Cole snorted. "Look, Mother, don't worry, okay? I'll call Sawyer tomorrow and work it out with her. Give everyone my love, and I'll call in a few days."

"All right, Cole. Give my love to Sumi."

Maggie clicked off the portable phone. She felt like crying and didn't know why. The sun was down now, and the moon was rising. From her position on the beach she could see the ocean's silvery ripples extending to the horizon. Golden by day, silver by night.

"You feel it too, don't you?" Susan said, coming up behind her. She squatted on the sand alongside Maggie and reached for her hand. "I feel," she said, choosing her words carefully, "as if some unseen force is chipping away at the internal workings of this family. You must feel it even more than I do. We all dump on you. That's why I'm here now. I need to do a little dumping. I'm not going to cry, I'm too numb for that. Besides, I've done nothing but cry for months. Just listen, okay?"

"Oh, Suse, I'm sorry. It's Jessie, isn't it?"

"No. A parent isn't supposed to bury a child, and I'll grieve every day of my life for Jessie, but life goes on. Mam made me see that. No, it's that Ferris wants a divorce. He's found a young woman, one who likes to bake cookies and pies and give back rubs. She's a nurse at the hospital. She's drop-dead gorgeous, Maggie. She goes to church and sings in the choir. She has the most beautiful smile, and she's . . . God, she's twenty-two. I went to see her. I didn't want to believe the man I loved would do that to me. But he's been doing it for two years. I never knew. My God, Maggie, I never knew. What does that say about me? He said . . . he said I was boring, that I play boring music. He wants excitement in his life. Martina, that's her name, makes him feel young and alive. I guess that means she's good in the sack. You know, he's always encouraged me to go on tour twice a year. Now I know why." Her voice hardened. "He said I could have the house. Do you believe that? He's keeping the house in the Virgin Islands. I get the Jeep and he gets the SEL. Is that fair or what? He said there's no money to divide. No money, Maggie. He cleaned out the accounts months ago."

"Nothing!" Maggie gasped.

"Zip," Susan said bitterly.

"What happened to the money Aunt Amelia left you, and the money Mam settled on you?" Maggie's voice betrayed her shock.

"Gone. If I'm lucky, I might get seventy thousand for the house. The Jeep is four years old. I have six hundred dollars in my personal checking account and eighty dollars in my purse. I was going to ask you for a loan to tide me over. My God, I don't even have enough to pay the lawyer." She began sobbing. "I guess I'm the world's biggest fool. Jerome did the same thing to me. Can I pick 'em or what?"

"Hey," Maggie said soothingly, "I walked down that road myself. The money is no problem, so don't worry about that. We'll talk to Rand and see what he says. You need a good lawyer, one of those barracudas. We'll

work it out, Suse. That's what family is for. Go ahead
and cry." Maggie cradled her sister against her breast,
patting her shiny blond hair.

"He moved out of the house last week," Susan said
vehemently. "He took everything that belonged to him
and a lot of the treasures I brought back from my tours.
All the jade is gone. The bastard even took the pearls
Aunt Amelia gave me for my sixteenth birthday. What
did I do wrong, Maggie? Is it because I'm almost fifty
years old? Do you think I should get a face-lift, a
tummy tuck?"

"I don't think any such thing. You're beautiful just
the way you are. Fifty is prime, Suse."

Susan choked and sputtered, then blew her nose.
"Get off it, Maggie, fifty is over the hill. Ferris said it.
I can see the wrinkles, the beginning of jowls. My ass
looks like cottage cheese. My knees are wrinkled, my
hair is thinning. Don't tell me I'm beautiful. I've never
even been close to pretty. I've always been plain, and
you know it."

"You're hurting, Suse, so don't be so hard on yourself. I don't see one thing wrong with getting a face-lift
if you do it for the right reasons. And if you want to get
your gut sucked out, go to it. But you can't run to a
plastic surgeon for every little wrinkle and ounce of fat.
I know it sounds corny, but beauty really *is* in the eye
of the beholder, and you're a beautiful person inside,
Suse."

"Thanks, Maggie." Susan sighed. "I just get to feeling so desperate, and I try to come up with things that
will make me feel better. God, Maggie, what *am* I going
to do?"

"You're going to stay right here with me. I might
even have a temporary solution to your problems. Lis-

ten to this. Mam turned over Billie Limited to me as of
the first of the year. I don't mean she gave the business
to me, but she asked me to run it for her. Rand thinks
it's a wonderful idea, so I thought I would take a crack
at it and head for the Orient next month on a buying
trip. We could go together. We both have an eye for
color. I've been working on the colors in my head for
the past few weeks. I want to elaborate on Mam's
popsicle-colored silks. I came up with a firecracker-red
that will blow your socks off. Are you interested?" My
God, Maggie thought, I've just made a verbal decision,
a commitment. She felt lightheaded.

"Yes, I'll do anything! Oh, Maggie, thank you. Just
tell me what to do."

"Tomorrow morning we can draft up letters to all of
Mam's clients telling them we're back in business full-
time. You can stay here with us. We have so much
room, and Chesney is never here for more than a day
and a half at any one time. You're going to love her,
Suse," Maggie gurgled. "Oh, it's going to be wonderful!
See, in some miraculous way, Mam has taken care of
you. It's uncanny the way she's always been able to . . .
what's the word here . . . you know, step in when the
going is tough, when we're at our lowest ebb. She never
gives us the answers, but somehow she sends us off in
the right direction and we think we did it ourselves. I've
never quite figured out how she does it. Let's call her
later and give her the good news, okay?"

Susan groaned. "Oh, Maggie, I don't want to upset
her."

"Trust me, she won't be upset as long as she knows
you're all right. In fact, she'll be thrilled. She's always
wanted us to work together."

Susan sniffed and wiped at her eyes. "I don't want to go back there," she muttered.

"Then don't. We'll get a lawyer on the mainland. Hey, let's get in touch with Valentine Mitchell and let her handle the whole thing: the foundation, the sale of your house, the whole ball of wax. You said Ferris took everything of value, so what's the point in going back?"

"My piano," Susan said weakly.

"There's a piano in the music room. Rand has had it tuned every month on the off chance you showed up for a visit." Maggie's eyes filled with tears. "Wasn't that wonderful of him?"

Susan's eyes also misted. "Rand has always been so good to me. He's more brother than anything. You're so lucky, Maggie, so very lucky."

"Am I?" Maggie said quietly. "We do have a good life, I suppose. And now that he's found his daughter after so many years, he's . . . I don't know. It must seem like we have it all, if there is such a thing."

Susan wiped away her tears. "You're worried about something. I see it in your eyes. Let's take a walk on the beach and you can tell me what's going on."

"I guess I'm not very good at hiding it. I wish I were more like Mam. If I could just have her inner serenity, I'd damn well bottle and sell it. She is the most serene, peaceful, loving person I've ever met, and it's just there, she doesn't have to work at it the way we do. We're damn lucky, Suse."

It was after nine when the lights in the lanai beckoned the sisters. They ran back like young girls, the sand spewing up behind their pounding heels.

Over crabmeat and pineapple salad Susan told Rand the reason for her visit. "Maggie said I can stay here until I get myself together. I'd like to take her up on her offer, if it's okay with you."

Rand reached across the table in the lanai to take Susan's hand. "Stay as long as you like. Our home is your home. Forever, if you like. Everyone who comes here says it's a magical place. Maybe its magic will rub off on you. I don't want you to worry about anything. Tomorrow morning I'll call Valentine Mitchell, and the two of us will take a trip to Minnesota. I guarantee you will not be a pauper when we get back. Now promise me you won't worry."

"I promise."

"Good. As for your mother's business, I think it's wonderful that both of you will run it. It's too valuable to let it fall by the wayside. Billie is going to be ecstatic when you tell her." He leered across the table at his wife. "Just don't neglect me."

"Me! Neglect you!" Maggie said in mock horror. "Never happen!"

Maggie turned to Susan. "Billie Limited has very little capital. Mam dug into it to pay off the lawsuits from the plane crash. The lawyers are in the process of settling the last three cases. The Colemans are tapped out, as usual, although Sawyer's plane could swing our fortunes around if she can get it off the ground."

"I never understood why Mam felt she had to pay on top of the insurance company. The final resolution was pilot error, not equipment malfunction," Susan said sourly.

"That's the way Billie is," Rand said quietly. "She felt that if money could make up in any way for the families' losses, then she should give the money. It was a Coleman plane. The family agreed. And it wiped you all out.

"When Billie said the family would start over, Sawyer took her literally and ran with the ball. I can't explain it any better than that. I'm behind her. It's a hell of a plane, and I've committed a good chunk of cash to the project. So has Riley, but she still needs a damn fortune. Cole is her only hope. She might pick up some financing, but she doesn't want investors. She wants this to belong to the Colemans. I think she's right. What did Cole say, Maggie? You did call him, didn't you?"

"He said he was going to rework the numbers. He sounded so . . . so unlike himself. I see this blowing into a major storm of some kind. Sawyer sounded different too. This is the first major rift between them. Knowing Sawyer as I do, I know she's taking this personally. And as yet we haven't heard from Riley. Maybe we should call him."

"I'm sure Sawyer already has," Susan said quietly. "We all know she doesn't let any grass grow under those Nikes she wears."

"Does this mean we kick back and wait, or do we get involved as a family?" Maggie asked, worry creasing her fine features.

"I don't recall anyone asking for family help," Rand said. "I also don't recall you calling a family meeting when your mother handed Billie Limited over to you back in January. What makes this different?"

"Billie Limited was never a part of Coleman Enterprises. Coleman Aviation is. Furthermore, Rand," Maggie said with an edge to her voice, "I'm not asking for a loan of a hundred million dollars. As far as I'm concerned, Sawyer's plane and Cole's financial decisions are a family matter, and a very serious one."

"I agree," Susan said. "This family's financial problems are like a roller coaster. One year we're up and the next we're in a deep ditch. Ferris always said it was poor management, which I guess means Riley isn't doing a good job."

Maggie bristled, as did Rand. The disgust in her voice brought tears to Susan's eyes. "Ferris certainly did a good job managing your money, now didn't he? I don't like what you just said, Susan. Riley has done a great job. Our books are open to all the family. Everything tallies right to the penny. You were sent a year-end report. Did you take the time to read it?"

"Ferris read it, or at least he said he did," Susan said miserably.

"For whatever it's worth, I agree with Maggie," Rand said quietly.

Susan stirred the food on her plate, her eyes downcast. "Okay, I'm sorry. It's just that I relied on Ferris for so long. I don't trust my judgment anymore. Don't be upset with me."

"So do we call Riley or not?" Maggie asked. "I vote we do."

"I agree," Susan said.

The bad moments were over.

"I move we head down the beach and walk off this dinner," Rand said, loosening the button on his shorts. "It's a beautiful evening, so let's take advantage of it. We can re-create old memories under the moon and stars like we used to do when we were kids. Remember that, Susan? God, did you ask questions! How high is the moon, how many stars are there, and why is the sky black at night and blue in the daytime."

"Yeah, and you lied to me. You didn't know the answers any more than I did. I thought because you were five years older than me that you knew everything." Susan snorted.

Rand laughed and Maggie giggled.

"I wish I could go back sometime, be a kid again," Susan said quietly. "We're to the halfway mark, and it's scary. At least to me."

They walked, their arms linked, their bare toes digging into the sand. A long time later they headed back to the house. The moon was mellow, the sky starspangled. Susan thought it an omen as she bid her sister and brother-in-law good night.

"I'm going to sit out here for a while. Should I lock up?"

Rand and Maggie laughed. "We never lock our doors. Don't stay up too late. We're going to have a busy day tomorrow. Rand and I get up at the crack of dawn, and I'm driving him to the airport at seven." Maggie kissed her sister lightly on the cheek. "You can relax now, Suse, everything is in capable hands."

Susan ached with loneliness at the sound of Rand and Maggie's easy banter as they walked through the house. She wondered if they were going to make love. She couldn't remember the last time Ferris had made love to her. She couldn't remember the last time they'd had sex, that bodily release that sometimes made things bearable.

Rand's cigarettes, which he smoked infrequently, lay at Susan's side. She reached for one. A terrible, nasty habit—smoking. She'd started after Jessie's death. Ferris chided her, railed at her, ridiculed her to get her to stop, but she hadn't listened. He posted signs all over the house with the Surgeon General's ominous report. She hadn't cared about that either. It was either cigarettes or sucking her thumb. She lit up a cigarette and blew a whirl of smoke toward the potted plants on the lanai. She wondered if she would die. She decided she really didn't care one way or the other.

Susan leaned back on the chaise. The moon shined through the slats overhead, and in its light the trailing vines glowed like dark emeralds. Tomorrow, when she wasn't feeling so shitty, she would walk through the house and savor its beauty. Tears slipped from between her lashes. She hated herself for wallowing. She was weak, but then she'd always known that. All the Colemans had guts but her. Tomorrow Rand and Valentine Mitchell, the family's lawyer, would go to Minnesota to fight her battles for her. Once before, Valentine and Rand had fought for her. That time they had taken on Jerome, her first husband, and they had made it all work out to her advantage. Could they work their magic a second time? Ferris was a powerful man.

Susan wiped angrily at her tears. She'd promised herself she wasn't going to cry, and here she was, slobbering like a child. Well, by God, she was finished with wallowing. Maggie was helping her to get on with her life, and she was going to take advantage of that.

The moon was working its way into hiding when Susan glanced down at her watch. Her mind raced. Cary Assante, Amelia's widower, was an early riser. Right this very minute he was probably wolfing down one of the huge breakfasts that he said made his day possible. She'd lost track of the times she'd called him over the past year. The first time, he'd choked up when she asked him how she was to get through the days after Jessie's death. The second time, they both cried. Whenever she called, in the darkest hours of the night or during the lightest hours of the day, Cary was there for her. They spoke of everything and nothing: of love, hate, betrayal, birds and cats, mush and grits. She thought she had come to know more about Cary Assante than did anyone else in the world. They'd touched on Julie and Cary's guilt, and on Ferris's and her own. She'd told him how beautiful the young nurse named Martina was, and how young. Cary told her she was beautiful too, both inside *and* outside.

On the first anniversary of Jessie's death, she'd traveled back to Texas and walked up the hill alone, to the smallest of all the graves. When a pair of arms encircled her shoulders, she didn't have to see Cary's face to know it was him. At that moment, she'd thought it most wonderful and remarkable that Cary was so attuned to her that he had showed up at exactly the right minute. Later she found out he'd called the house, and Ferris told him she'd run off like a ninny because she was cracking up. "Losing it," Ferris had said.

The portable phone found its way into her hands, and she punched out the numbers. She sucked in her breath while she waited for Cary's voice to hum across the wires.

"Hi," she said softly.

"Hi, yourself. How's it going, Susan?"

"It's not. Will I ruin your day if I unload a bit?" she asked anxiously.

"Not my day," Cary said cheerfully. "Today we're clearing the last piece of land. We'll be ready by July. Then I'm going to take off on a trip around the world. Want to come?"

"If I can afford it, I'd like that very much." She told him about Maggie's offer. "Rand and Valentine Mitchell are leaving for Minnesota in the morning."

"That's good," Cary said cheerfully. "You're too vulnerable right now. You're thinking with your heart, and we can't have that. Let the experts have a go-round. I'm glad you're with Maggie. Family is important at times like this. You're still planning on coming to Texas in July, aren't you?"

"Cary, nothing could keep me away. And Cary, thanks for talking to me. I think I can sleep now."

"My day is just beginning. I'm going out to play with my dynamite charges while you snooze the hours away."

Susan laughed. "I'll call you next week. Be careful with that dynamite."

"I will. Enjoy the sunshine. Give Maggie and Rand my love."

"I will. Wait a minute, Cary. I want to ask you something. This is none of my business, but did you have an offer to sell Miranda?"

"More than one, but I said no. Amelia would never forgive me. Take care, Susan."

Susan stretched out on the chaise lounge. Sleeping outdoors was rather appealing, if sleep was possible. She was wide awake, *wired*, as the young people said. She sat up and lit another cigarette. There was still one call to make.

Her arm shot up so she could see the time on her watch. Ten o'clock. Three o'clock in Vermont.

"She won't be there. She's never there when I need her," Susan said to herself as she punched out her mother's number. Her face turned ugly when Billie's recorded message came over the wire. She angrily broke the connection. She hated that message machine. So what if it was three o'clock in the morning? Mothers, *real* mothers, were supposed to be on twenty-four-hour call. She called again, but this time she waited for the sound of the beep. "Mother, this is Susan. You know, Susan your daughter. I need to talk to you, but as usual, you aren't there for me. I'm in Hawaii with Maggie, your firstborn, your favorite daughter. Do you think there will ever be a time—" The connection pinged in her ear. Disgust was written all over her face as Susan slammed the phone to the table.

It was always this way when she spoke to her mother's machine, worse when her mother called her back. "Well, fuck you, Mother, I don't need you, wherever the hell you are."

Susan was dozing when the portable pinged to life. It had to be her mother. Who else would be calling at this time of night? Her voice was cautious when she said a wary "Hello?"

"Susan?"

How gentle-sounding her mother's voice was, how concerned. Susan stiffened.

"Who else did you expect to answer the phone—Maggie?" Susan's voice sounded so cold, it was hard for her to believe it was her own.

"I didn't expect you to be in Hawaii, but then you don't write, and the only time you call is . . ."

"When something is wrong. Isn't that what you were going to say, Mother? You're known for telling us you're always there for any one of us, day or night, but for some strange reason you're never there for me. Why do you think I'm here in Hawaii instead of Vermont?"

"Susan, what's wrong?"

Instead of answering the question, Susan asked one of her own. "Where the hell are you this time?"

"England. Thad wanted to visit a few of his friends in Parliament. It's a little after ten. I call three times a day to retrieve our messages. Now will you please tell me what's wrong?"

"Do you remember the last time I saw you in the

flesh, Mother? It was at Jessie's funeral. I think that's pretty sad."

"Why do you suppose that is, Susan?"

"Go ahead, Mother, slam it back to me the way you always do. You go to Texas to see Cary, Riley, and Ivy, you go to New York to see Sawyer and Adam, you come here to see Maggie and Rand, and you were in Japan not too long ago to see Cole and Sumi. You've *never* been to Minnesota."

"You never invited me, Susan. I thought you didn't want me there."

"Are you saying you would have come if I asked you to? If I asked you right now to come here to Hawaii, would you come?"

"Darling, I can't right this minute. Thad is . . . we're in England."

"I knew you'd say that, I just knew it," Susan said spitefully. Then her voice broke and she heard herself scream. "You abandoned me, you gave me up, and it doesn't matter if it was to family or not, you gave me up and let Aunt Amelia raise me! I'm not part of this family, I never was. Just go to hell, Mam, just go to fucking hell." Her shaky finger pressed the button to break the connection. In a fit of anger, she released it and then tossed the phone in the general direction of the beach.

A wave of pure hate, unlike anything she'd ever experienced, rushed through her. She had to pay attention to what she was feeling now, experiencing. All those shrinks she'd spoken to had said her problem was deeply rooted in her childhood, and when she was ready to deal with it, to pull it out and look it in the face, she would be on the right road to understanding why she did the things she did, why she kept making the same mistakes over and over. Tonight, she'd finally used the right word, the word she'd always refused to say aloud: abandoned.

"God, how I hate you, Mother. You should die for what you've done to me. And don't think for one minute I'm going to take your first love up on her offer to work in *your* business. Not in *this* lifetime."

Exhausted with her mental and verbal tirade, Susan curled into the fetal position, the knuckle of her thumb in her mouth. She was asleep within seconds.

CHAPTER THREE

Heads turned, male as well as female. The men leered, and the women frowned and sucked in their stomachs. The object of their scrutiny strutted her stuff, her red-gold hair flaming out behind her as she walked impatiently up and down the concourse. At her side she held a Bottega Veneta briefcase. She'd just parked—in a no parking zone—her Lamborghini sports car, which could zip off at 180 miles per hour if one chose to put the pedal to the metal. Valentine Mitchell so chose, and had the traffic tickets to prove it.

She flicked back the cuff of her Armani jacket to check the time on her Presidential Rolex. The jacket, as well as her skirt, had been sculpted for her body by none other than Armani himself.

As the cuff fell back over her wrist, she raised her sleepy green eyes and met those of an aging banker in a three-piece business suit.

"In your dreams, old man," she whispered sotto voce.

The old banker apparently mistook her for a hooker. "I wouldn't give you two dollars," he muttered.

She laughed, and the banker walked out through the door, feeling like a fool.

Valentine was waiting for Rand Nelson. *Lord* Rand Nelson. Now *that* was a hoot. He'd caught up with her in Los Angeles just as she was packing to drive her new

Lamborghini back to Texas. There was no way she could refuse his request, as she was on a retainer from the Coleman family.

Spotting him at the same moment he spied her, Valentine smiled and did a little jig to make sure enough leg showed. Rand whistled approvingly. God, he was handsome, all six feet two inches of him. She approved of his Hawaiian tan, his dark hair shot with silvery strands at the temple. The mustache was new since she'd seen him last, as were the dark glasses he wore to cover his gorgeous dark eyes, which had lashes long enough to kill for. He kissed her lightly on the cheek, inhaling the scent of her perfume.

"Lady," he grinned, "you are a killer."

"And you, Lord Nelson, are as handsome and debonair as usual."

Rand fingered his collar and wondered why his neck felt as warm as it did. He liked her perfume. It suggested faraway places, incense, and veils—veils that came off. For the life of him he couldn't remember what kind of perfume his wife wore. The sudden urge to bolt and run was so strong that he felt he had to dig his feet into the airport carpeting.

"We have time for a drink," he said hoarsely.

"Sounds good. Double scotch on the rocks for me," Valentine said, following him into the airport lounge.

Rand's eyebrows shot upward. "Isn't that a man's drink?" He gave the order to the waitress.

"I work in a man's world, Rand. I've had to join 'em, as the saying goes. Now what are we going to do about Susan and Ferris?"

"I have the key to the house," Rand said, "so we can stay there and map out our strategy. Or we could go to a hotel. Or you could go to a hotel." He held his breath, praying she would say she'd go to a hotel.

Valentine leaned across the table, her perfume wafting about her like a breeze. "The house is fine, Rand. I hate running up a client's bill unnecessarily. By the way, how is the rest of the family? Bring me up to date. It's been four or five years."

"Everyone is fine. You know about my daughter Chesney, of course. Sawyer is designing a new plane, and Cole's wife is due to have her baby any day now. Riley's son is about six months old. Sawyer has twin girls, you know. We haven't seen Billie and Thad for a while but understand they're fine. Cary is about finished with his memorial to Amelia. Maggie and I are doing well, of course, and Susan is the one with the problem. That's about it," Rand said, tossing his hands in the air.

"What's Maggie doing these days?"

The devilish look in Valentine's eyes was upsetting. "Well, yes, there is other news. Maggie and Susan are taking over Billie Limited. I thought you knew. Maggie said she sent you reams of paperwork."

"It's probably on my desk back at the office. I've been in Los Angeles for the past six weeks. These movie people are so hard to deal with."

Rand nodded. He wondered what Maggie was doing.

"Am I bothering you, Rand? You look uneasy, like you want to get away from me."

"Hell, yes, you bother me. I think every man in this bar has a hard-on just looking at you. Can you, you know, tone down or something? Wear a hat or put on a sweater . . . or *something*."

"Wait a minute. Are you saying you're attracted to me? Are you worried that I might try to seduce you? For heaven's sake, Rand, I'd never do that. I adore

Maggie. If you're one of those guys in this bar who has a hard-on, then I suggest you squelch it, because you simply aren't my type."

Well, shit, Rand thought. He had to say something, make some kind of comeback to wipe that victorious smile off her face. "You definitely aren't my type either," he said, rather lamely. "Now that that's out of the way, what do you say we get down to business?"

"Yes, let's," Valentine agreed.

It was a pretty house, Rand thought, surrounded by gracious old elms that were in the process of dressing themselves for spring. Once, when Ferris had been in residence, it must have been manicured to perfection. Now the grass was brown and full of wide-leaf crab-grass, and the flower beds were choked with weeds.

"Gardeners cost money," he said tightly.

Valentine nodded.

"This house kind of looks like the one we had in England," he continued. "Very cottagey, if there is such a word. That's an English garden at the side of the house, and I'd bet five dollars Susan tended it herself. She was happy here. So was little Jessie. I thought they had a good working marriage. I mean, the kind of marriage Billie and Thad have."

"Sometimes people grow apart, things go wrong, one changes, the other doesn't," Valentine said quietly.

"That's well and good, but that didn't give Ferris the right to rob Susan blind. I want you to pull out every big gun you have and shove it in that bastard's face. Make it smoke. Guess the file is here already," Rand said, pointing to the bright Federal Express envelope propped up by the front door.

Valentine looked over the low ranch house with its

added dormers. It appeared neat and tidy, much the way she remembered Susan being. The pink and white brick, and the diamond-shaped windows, reminded her of the foster home she had grown up in. She corrected the thought. She hadn't grown up in a home, she'd grown up in a house, a house full of kids who, like herself, were unwanted. The Delroys hadn't been unkind, but neither had they been particularly kind. She'd been fed and clothed decently with the money the state paid for her keep. There were no extras, no spending money, no parties. No love of any kind was showered on her. Yet she hadn't been truly unhappy, and she still stayed in touch with the Delroys. She always remembered to send a Christmas card as well as a present. But she'd never gone back to visit.

At eighteen she'd struck out on her own, working as many as three jobs at a time to put herself through college and law school. She'd done all right for herself too. She'd graduated from college in the top three percent of her class, and was the salutatorian in law school. Then she'd done a lot of pounding the sidewalks, looking for someone to give her a decent job. In the end she'd had to sleep her way through several senior law partners just to be taken on as an associate at a miserly salary. She never looked back, never chastised herself for what she had done. Her big break, as she always thought of it, had come when she took over a case from a law partner when he went into the hospital for an operation. Not only did she get a whopping three million dollar settlement for the firm's client, but she also managed to get her adversary's business. Afterward, she bought a swanky condo full of chrome, glass, and mirrors. End of story. No, not quite. She still didn't have anyone to share her success with.

Valentine sighed as she watched Rand fit the key into the lock.

"Tell you what," he said, "I'll turn up the heat and make some coffee while you read the file and come up with a plan of action."

"Okay." Valentine kicked off her shoes and looked around, trying to imagine Susan living in this place. "It looks like Mr. Clean lived here," she muttered, grimacing. "Is the kitchen cozy and cute?" she called out to Rand.

"Come see for yourself," he called back.

Rand blinked in surprise when Valentine walked in. Without her three-inch spike heels, she was tiny and didn't seem so . . . so seductive.

Valentine nibbled her fingernail. "All this kind of surprises me," she said thoughtfully. "Susan is a world-renowned pianist. I more or less expected a house filled with exotic souvenirs from all over the globe. This . . ." she said, waving her arms about, "just isn't what I expected."

"Me neither. I suppose it has something to do with being sent off to England at such an early age to live with us. This is like our kitchen there. It broke Billie's heart to send her, but Susan's world was music, and England was where it was going to happen for her. She didn't really have a childhood like most children. All she did was practice the piano. I always had the feeling that Susan must have been starved for love. She still hasn't found it, from the look of things. I just fucking hate it when a man steals money from a woman. I thought more of Ferris."

"Not to worry, Lord Nelson, we'll get him," Valentine said airily.

"I wish you'd stop with the lord bit. I never use the

title, and hearing you say it makes it sound obscene. Sugar or cream?"

"Black. See if you can find the deed to this house, and any other papers you think I should have. Income tax records would do nicely. Are they here?"

"Susan said Ferris took them when he left, but she had enough sense to go to the accountant and ask for copies. The accountant didn't want to give them to her, so she went to the head of the firm and got them. They were afraid of adverse publicity, but since her name was on all the returns, they really had no choice. She told me they're in the piano bench in the music room under her sheet music. I'll get them."

Valentine became so engrossed in the file that she barely noticed when Rand laid a stack of tax returns next to her on the couch. Rand tried not to look at the long expanse of thigh exposed through the slit in the Armani skirt.

"I'm going to call home," he said. "If you want me, I'll be in the kitchen or upstairs taking a shower." The minute the words were out of his mouth, he bit down on his tongue. If Valentine heard him, she gave no sign.

He needed to talk to his wife, he thought as he left the room. He didn't like what he was feeling toward Val. Maggie was his wife, his lover, his friend. Maggie would put it all in perspective for him. "Shit!" he said succinctly.

{{{{{{{{ CHAPTER FOUR }}}}}}}}

Riley Coleman stopped his Bronco, the way he did each and every day, before he drove under the high wooden arch emblazoned with the name SUNBRIDGE. His practiced eye took in the miles of white fence stretching into the distance. Tall oak trees lined the winding drive, and on either side were expanses of bright green lawn watered by pulsing sprinklers.

He lightly pressed his foot down on the gas pedal, the Bronco moving slowly down the driveway, Riley savoring the moment when Sunbridge came into view.

The great house, caressed by the sun, basked upon a gently sloping rise beneath the Texas sky. It was three stories of the palest pink brick, and was flanked by twin wings, which were also three stories high, but set back several feet from the main structure. White columns supported the roof of the veranda, which swept along the entire front. There was a fanlight transom over the two huge oak front doors. The same design was repeated above each window on the top floor. Ornamental topiaries and crepe myrtle hugged the foundation, and a magnificent rose garden surrounded the house, complete with trellises and statuary.

It was a hell of a spread, Riley liked to say, and all of it his and Ivy's. One day it would belong to his son, Moss. A grin stretched across his face. Thousands of acres of prime land where thoroughbreds and cattle grazed contently.

Once, the land had been owned by Riley's great-grandfather, Seth Coleman. It was said that when he first saw it, he felt as though he could reach up and touch the sun. He had come from dark beginnings, and this great house was his major achievement. He hoped that building a house upon the rise would bridge his past with his future. He was not a romantic, but the name Sunbridge was entirely his own conception.

Riley brought the Bronco to a stop outside the front doors. He liked going in past the ethereally graceful rose garden and the feminine sweep of the clematis vine that surrounded the oak doors. He remembered how the house had looked before the tornado swept it all away. There had been shiny, dark wooden floors, massive beams supporting the ceilings, thick, dark Oriental carpets, and man-sized leather furniture. Each time he entered the old house, he imagined the smell of his great-grandfather's cigar smoke, the thudding of high-heeled cowboy boots, and the sound of boisterous men drinking hard whiskey. Now Sunbridge was full of sunlight, earth-tone furniture, white walls and light oak floors. The smells were those of his wife and new son. The sounds were popular rock, Ivy's laughter, and Moss's gurgling. The floor-to-ceiling walls were gone now, replaced with half walls, so that the entire first floor was open and inviting.

He almost had it all, he thought as he opened the massive oaken doors. As always, he stood stock-still and pitched his baseball cap toward the peg on the hat rack, the only thing to survive the tornado that had destroyed the house.

"Hey, anyone home?" he called from the center hallway.

"Only us Colemans," Ivy said, and laughed as she stepped toward her husband and gave him little Moss to hold.

"So, what's for dinner?" Riley wrinkled his nose as he tried to discern the tantalizing smells wafting about. Moss squealed, his chubby arms flailing the air. Riley hoisted him high, then nose-dived him downward. "Ooops, sorry, Ivy, I forgot you don't like me doing that. He loves it, don't you, Moss?" he said, setting the baby down on the floor. "Now it's your mommy's turn."

Riley took Ivy in his arms. She smelled so wonderful, just the way Moss smelled, clean and powdered, with a trace of perfume. Ivy was a constant, a given. He knew when he walked in the door, at the end of either a bad or good day, there would be a smile on her face. Dinner would be ready, Moss would be alert and playful, and they'd each have a bottle of 7UP, their drink for the cocktail hour. He looked forward to his homecoming each day with a passion.

They had their soft drink ritual while Moss crawled about, dragging his stuffed animals with him. After dinner, Ivy warmed the bottle of formula and Riley decked out his son in Billie original sleepwear. Together they read him a story, then Ivy crooned a lullaby while Riley cranked up the Mickey Mouse mobile hooked onto the crib. With the night-light on and the door half open, the contented parents embraced in the hallway.

Riley's favorite room, the den, was where they sat side by side to watch the news. During commercial breaks, they talked about the day's events, their hands clasped together, their shoulders touching.

"Cole called today, so did Sawyer," Ivy said, snuggling against her husband. "Cary called right before you got home and said for you to call him early in the morning. I called Maggie this morning, and your aunt Susan is there visiting. Riley," she said, squirming around to face him, "they're going to take over Billie Limited. Isn't that wonderful! Maggie said paradise was getting to her and it was time to get to work. All of which brings me to something I want to talk to you about. How would you feel about me going back to work, at least part-time?"

Riley's eyes softened. God, how he loved this treasure sitting next to him. "You know, you have the most beautiful eyes, and I heard Grandmam Billie say women would kill for those curly chestnut locks of yours." He hugged her to make his point. "Not yet, Ivy, please. We talked about this, and we both agreed Moss needed you full-time for the first year. Of course, if you feel strongly about it, I won't stand in your way, but remember that Jonquil isn't a young woman anymore, and we shouldn't expect her to take over Moss's care. A nurse or nanny isn't in our budget right now. Have you thought about all this?"

"I thought I'd put out some feelers and work here at home. I don't want to leave Moss. I don't have cabin fever and my brain isn't atrophying. But by the same token I want to do more than garden and cook on Jonquil's day off. I'm a good engineer, Riley."

"The best, kiddo. I've never said otherwise."

"If it gets to be too much, I'll give it up. My family comes first. How'd you like the spaghetti I made today?"

"It was great," Riley said, loosening his belt buckle. "Did Cole say what he wanted? It's the damnedest thing, Ivy. All day I've had this feeling that Cole needs me. We've always been so tuned to one another that I can't ignore the feeling. I was going to call him tonight anyway."

Ivy laughed. Riley and Cole were more like brothers than cousins, and one always seemed to know when the other was in trouble. "Cole said he was probably a few hours ahead of your phone call. He sounded . . . sad. Sumi is fine, expecting any day now. I have this . . . this sense that a phone call isn't going to make whatever is plaguing Cole go away. I'll bet you five bucks he does need you, Riley."

"If he does, how would you feel about me going to Japan?"

"Riley! Family first, no matter what. Call Sawyer, she might know what's going on. Go ahead, I'll do the dishes and take out *your* trash." She kissed him lightly on the cheek.

"I'll do it. I forgot it's my night."

"You can fold the laundry later." Ivy ducked the cushion that sailed through the air.

When the door to the kitchen closed, Riley leaned back against the sofa. The soft murmuring from the television set annoyed him. He pressed the remote. The silence around him screamed. He tried to ease the tension between his shoulder blades by squirming and jiggling in the soft cushions. He punched out Sawyer's number with his thumb. Adam answered.

"Yo, Riley, how's the Texas oil king doing?" Not bothering to wait for a reply, Adam, Sawyer's husband, rushed on, "I want to personally thank you for that lovely—as in very lovely—check that arrived last week. Josie and Katy also thank you, as it's their college fund money. I'm just as happy as shit that you're busting your ass for me and my family." It was a standard joke, an inside family assessment of Riley's capabilities. "Seriously, Riley, I'm glad I sold you the old homestead. If you go dry, that's okay too. No sweat from this end. How's Ivy and the cherub?"

"We're all fine. Ivy's talking about doing some consulting work. Moss is getting bigger every day. He's a happy kid."

"If you want to talk to Sawyer, you'll have to wait a minute. She's trying to get the frizz out of her hair. It's been raining here for two days, and she's meaner than a mercenary when her hair frizzes. You'd think she'd save some of that hostility for the important things in life." The banter was suddenly over. "Does this call have to do with Cole?"

"Yeah, I think so. He's been on my mind all day. I was going to call him when I got home, and then Ivy said both he and Sawyer called, so I assume . . . what's going on? Do you know?"

"Listen, Riley, long ago I made a pact with myself not to take sides. I've stuck to it too. You guys iron it all out. Just try and keep a lid on my wife. She's about ready to blow. Here she comes."

Riley grinned to himself as he listened to the conversation taking place on the other end of the phone.

"What's that thing on your head? Are you going to wear it to bed?"

"It's a snood. Shut up, Adam, just because you don't care if your hair looks like a red cloud of corkscrews doesn't mean I don't care about mine. . . . What do you mean, Riley is on the phone!" Sawyer squawked.

"I called you twice, but you had the old dryer going full blast. As for your hair, I'd love you if you were baldheaded. Talk to your cousin and let me get back to my drawing board."

"Adam, would you really love me if I was bald-headed?" Riley heard her coo.

"Bald, fat, and ugly. Hey, watch it, Sawyer. Riley called collect, so all this messing-around time is on our bill."

"You shithead, why didn't you say something?" Sawyer screeched. "Riley!"

"Yeah, I'm here. I envy your compatibility." He grinned. "I'm returning your call, and no, I did not call collect."

"He's such a wise-ass. We've had a bad day, Riley. Listen, the reason I called," she said, shifting to her business tone, "is I spoke to Cole today about financing the plane. He all but turned me down. The financing he did offer was at loan-shark rates. Is something wrong over there? I spoke to Sumi, but she didn't say anything. Have you spoken to Cole?"

"He called today, but I haven't gotten back to him yet."

"Well, he really copped an attitude, and I didn't care for it," Sawyer said bitterly. "What the hell *is* his problem?"

"Hold on to your . . . snood. I'll call him. In fact, I'm prepared to go to Japan if something serious is wrong. I've wanted to go back for a while, but for some reason the time never seemed right. If Cole is in a bad place right now, then this is the time for me to make the trip."

"Riley, I'm not sure . . . You haven't been back since your grandfather's death. If you aren't ready . . . I can handle this. Cole and I have butted heads before, and we've always been able to work things out. Please, don't make the trip on my account."

Riley felt the urge to confide in Sawyer, to tell her about the dreams he'd been having for the past months, dreams he hadn't even described to Ivy. They took place in Japan, and they had no ending, and they made him cry, made his heart ache. His eyes went to the mantel, to the picture of his Japanese grandfather.

"Look, I'll call Cole. *If* I decided to go over, and *if* I get stuck, *then* you can put in an appearance. Is that okay with you?"

"What you're saying is you think I'm a hothead and you aren't. That you can handle Cole better than I can. I'll buy into it all as long as you remember I'm the brains of this outfit."

Riley hooted with laughter. "I'll tell Cole you said that."

"Be my guest," Sawyer snapped. "Give Ivy our love. When are you coming to New York?"

"Never, now that I'm a family man. Ivy said going to New York City is like going unarmed into a war zone. When are you guys coming here?"

"For the opening of Cary's memorial. How is he? We haven't heard from him in a few weeks."

"He called today too. I think everything is right on schedule. You know that he and Julie . . . Julie went back to New York. I guess it didn't work, and Cary said he couldn't let her think . . . she was the one who made the decision. He said they'll always be friends, that kind of thing."

"She must have loved him very much. How awful for the both of them. If she's here in the city, I'll give her a call or invite her over for dinner. Or do you think I should let her well enough alone?"

Riley had the last word before he hung up. "You did say you were the brains of this outfit, didn't you? If you can't make a decision, fall back and regroup or let Adam make it for you. 'Bye, Sawyer."

"How'd it go?" Ivy asked, placing the laundry basket by her husband's feet.

"She's testy, but then she's always testy. Do you have a snood?"

"What's a snood?" Ivy asked, a puzzled look on her face.

"It's not important. Where are you going?"

"To fill the Jacuzzi. The minute you get off the phone, come upstairs and let's . . . you know, fool around. I'll take off your clothes, you take off mine. I'll oil you, you oil me. I'll scrub you, you scrub me. The whole nine yards. Coconut oil or avocado?"

"Coconut," Riley groaned.

"The black nightie or the peach?"

"Neither."

Ivy pretended to moan as she reached down into the laundry basket for a bottle of chardonnay and two wine flutes. "I'll be waiting," she said as she sashayed from the room.

Riley calculated the time difference between Japan and Texas. Did he fold the baby's laundry and call Cole, or did he . . . ? He bounded from the sofa and took the steps two at a time.

Family first. *Immediate* family, that is.

Riley watched the bright, red numbers on the clock next to his side of the bed. Three-thirty-one and he hadn't closed his eyes. Next to him Ivy slept contentedly, her breathing deep and even. He stretched his long legs, being careful not to disturb his wife. What the hell was wrong? He should get up, go downstairs, make himself some hot chocolate, Ivy's sure-fire cure for sleeplessness, and call Cole. He'd never had the heart to tell Ivy the caffeine in the cocoa gave him a charge of energy instead of putting him to sleep. Ivy took being a wife and mother seriously, and she had cures for everything from sleeplessness to ingrown toenails. Once, she'd forced a cold remedy on him that had curled the hair on his chest. She'd made tea laced with honey, one-hundred-proof whiskey, lemon, and melted Vicks salve. Then she'd stood over him while she watched him down it in two long swallows. She'd pronounced him cured on the spot when his eyes started to water and he nearly choked to death, either from the drink or the Grey Poupon mustard she'd lathered all over his chest. Or maybe it was the string of garlic she hung around his neck. All he knew was that the next morning he was fit to go to work. Not that anyone would come near him. Four days went by before the smell left his system.

Before he could think twice, he swung his legs out of the bed, grabbed his robe, and headed for the hall. He stopped to peek into the baby's room. Moss's chubby fist was clutching the satin binding of his blanket, and his pudgy thumb was secure in his mouth. Riley's heart swelled.

Ivy had spent weeks making the kitchen her domain. The huge fieldstone fireplace that took up one wall was covered with dried herbs, nets of garlic cloves, and shiny copper pots. Tubs of greenery in clay pots graced the hearth along with a basket of logs.

Everything was green and yellow, with touches of red. The floor was red Mexican tile, the cabinets and window moldings honeyed oak. The awning, which Ivy had made herself to shade the huge bow window, was checkered green and white, with a darker green tassel trim. Every appliance was a rich copper color. Bowls of luscious fruit always sat on the counter.

Riley carried the hot cocoa he'd made in a huge mug that said DAD, along with the portable phone, to the old rocker next to the fireplace. The cocoa was cool enough to drink now. Riley sipped, aware that the big old yellow tomcat, Slick, was licking his chops. Slick had wandered up to the back porch one day and had never gone.

Riley leaned back against the cushions. He was diddling, trying to postpone the moment when he had to call his cousin. He ran the time difference over in his head as he punched out the numbers. When he had a clear connection, he spoke in rapid-fire Japanese. He reverted to English when Cole's voice hummed over the wire, though Cole understood Japanese as well as he did.

"How are things back in Texas?" Cole asked quietly.

"Well, it's a quarter to four in the morning, so not much is going on. How's Sumi?"

"Anxious, but then so am I. Look, Riley, the reason I called is . . . What are the chances of you coming over here for a few days? If it wasn't so close to Sumi's delivery date, I'd come to Texas. Can you handle it? I know you said you'd come back when you were ready and not one minute before, but I find myself in need of that cool Japanese head of yours."

"When?"

"As soon as possible. I wish you were here now. Can you clear your decks?"

Riley snorted. "About all any of us are doing is twiddling our thumbs. Yeah, I can get away. Of course, Adam is going to want to know why I'm not tending his wells." The joke fell flat when Cole remained quiet.

"Hang up, Riley, I'll call you back in ten minutes." The connection was broken before Riley had a chance to say anything. He looked at the pinging phone, at the cat who was slinking across the kitchen floor in search of a mouse.

Since he obviously wasn't going back to bed, Riley measured coffee into the percolator and plugged it in just as the phone rang.

"You can get a seven A.M. flight out of Austin, fly to LAX, and from there to Honolulu, where you board a flight for Guam. I'll fly the Dream Machine to Guam, pick you up, and we'll deadhead back. Deal?"

Riley blinked. "Reservations?"

"My girl is taking care of it as we speak. Ivy?"

"No problem," Riley murmured. Guam. His mother had met his father in Guam. They'd been married there and lived in a little farmhouse until his father had been sent to Vietnam to fly night missions over the Mekong Delta, where he was killed.

The coffee was strong, almost as thick as mud. Riley drank it anyway, but not before he poured a generous amount of cream into the cup. It still tasted like mud. Ivy would throw it out when she got up and make her own special blend of Irish cream with a touch of cinnamon. She even ground the beans fresh each morning. Jonquil, their housekeeper, didn't like flavored coffees and kept a can of Folgers for herself in the cupboard, which is what he had used. He decided he didn't like Jonquil's coffee. Neither did Slick when he poured what was left in his cup into the cat's dish.

The first person Riley saw when he stepped off the jumbo jet into Guam's blanket-wet humidity was Cole.

He looks as tired as I feel, Riley thought. He'd never seen shadows under his cousin's eyes before.

When the handshaking, backslapping, and hugs were over, Cole said, "I filed a flight plan. We can either deadhead back or stay over so you can get some sleep. It's your call. I booked a room at one of the hotels we own, just in case."

Riley thought about it for a full minute before he replied. "I slept almost all the way. What I would really like is some ham and eggs and a quick drive around the island. I'd like to see the farmhouse where my parents lived and the church where they got married. What about you, Cole, are you tired? If you are, I can do this some other time. Sumi?"

"Yeah, I am worried. Let's get the ham and eggs. I'll fly you back here when you're ready to return, and you can . . . you can check it all out. You want to be alone when you do that anyway, right?"

"Actually, I'm not even sure I want to do it at all. I feel I should. Let's get the ham and eggs and get back to Sumi. Neither of us will ever hear the end of it if she goes to the hospital and you aren't there. Lead on, cousin. I know you checked this place out already. They're gonna skip the rice, right?"

"Right." Cole grinned.

The two young men who strode down the concourse were almost identical in height and build. The only major difference between them was Cole's blond hair and blue eyes. Riley could have passed for Italian, Greek, Jewish, or Guamanian. Cole's flight suit and the rakish angle of his flight cap immediately identified him as a pilot. Riley's creased blue jeans, low-heeled boots, open-necked shirt, and battered baseball cap proclaimed him a Texan, a fact he constantly wanted to shout to the

world. The slight cast to his eyes that would have re-
vealed his Japanese heritage had been altered surgically
a year before, much to the family's objections, especially Ivy's.

"We must look like giants to these people," Cole said
out of the corner of his mouth. "The tallest man I've
seen so far is around five-eight. I know you're six-four,
and I'm a tad under that. If we lived here, do you suppose it would be an advantage or disadvantage?"

"Well, we'd be able to see far and wide." Riley
laughed as he took his seat in the restaurant. "Like now,
I can see into the kitchen. Looks clean to me." They
spoke of each other's families while eating, then Riley
took a deep breath and plunged in. "Now," he said,
"what the fuck is wrong, Cole? What's with this shit
Sawyer is babbling about? I heard her side. If your side
isn't any better, we're all in trouble."

"I had a bad day. Business is business. You, more
than anyone, should understand that."

"We're talking family here, Cole. Or did you suddenly turn into a loan shark?"

Cole pushed back his flight cap. He didn't like the
edge in Riley's voice. He didn't like the stubborn look
on his face either. "Is that why you're here, to tell me
I fucked up with Sawyer?"

Riley stared across the table at his cousin. "Yeah," he
drawled. He set his coffee cup down carefully. "The
whole purpose of our deal was East and West, remember? United. As one. You agreed. I agreed. Now you're
reneging, like you want to gouge the family. That may
not really be your intention, but that's the way it looks
from where I'm sitting. From where your sister is sitting too. If you have an explanation, I'd sure as hell like
to hear it." This time Riley slammed the empty cup

down on the plastic tabletop. "And, yeah, that's part of the reason I'm here. The other part is I thought you needed me. I'd like to help if you *think* you're in trouble."

"That's big of you, Riley," Cole snapped. "Is this where you remind me that you gave up your Japanese inheritance so I could take over Rising Sun?"

"That's a low blow, Cole, and unworthy of you. I've come halfway around the world to listen to what you have to say."

Cole felt his neck growing warm, a sign that his anger was about to erupt. "That's just another way of saying you're going to interfere."

"Are you afraid of me, Cole?" Riley asked quietly.

Was he? he wondered. "Concerned would be a better word. You control Coleman Enterprises and you still have your hand in Rising Sun. I'm beginning to wonder if I'm not just a goddamn figurehead."

Riley balled up his napkin and then started to shred it. "You control Rising Sun. No strings, remember?"

"*Bullshit!* There's always a string somewhere. I just haven't found it yet, but it will appear like magic if I don't give in and fund Sawyer's plane, right?"

Riley's eyebrows shot upward.

"I'm not aware of any strings, Cole. And you know I've never lied to you. But you and I had a verbal agreement—East and West as one. You're weaseling, and I don't like it."

"I'm not weaseling. I screwed up with Sawyer. I'm sorry about that and the way it looks, so I'm prepared to make a straightforward business deal with her and apologize in the bargain. Does that make you feel better?"

"No. It's not enough."

Cole leaned across the table, his blue eyes burning. "You want me to *give* her the money?"

"My grandfather would have. I would have."

"I'm not your grandfather and I'm not you," Cole snarled.

"Obviously," Riley said quietly.

"Business is business. You don't just give away a hundred million dollars."

"Back in Texas you gave me your share of Sunbridge with no strings. Together we gave Adam back his homestead. That was Coleman money, right? You could be generous with it because you were fed up and didn't give a damn. You thought like I did back then. The bottom line, Cole, is it's the giving that counts. And if you need more proof, just take a look at yourself and what *you* got."

Cole's blue eyes continued to burn. "Let me make sure I understand what you're saying. I give up a hundred million bucks, close the old checkbook and forget about it. Forget interest, forget a share in a plane that will hopefully make history. And at some point in the future maybe five, ten years from now, I'll be paid partial payments on the principal. What kind of fool do you take me for?"

"I never said you were a fool, Cole. You're the last person in the world I'd call a fool. Look, fuck the business end of it. Let's talk about you and me."

"What about you and me?" Cole asked warily.

"We were like brothers, Cole, and now we're not. What is it, we can't afford the phone bills to talk once in a while? I wanted to talk to you so badly while I was waiting in the hospital for Ivy to have the baby. I wanted to tell you how worried I was that something might go wrong, and then when I saw Moss for the first time I wanted to call you and tell you he had all his fingers and toes and that little jigger between his legs was . . . I wanted to *share*."

"Then why didn't you?"

"Goddamnit, I did. I called and left messages and even left the number of the phone booth at the hospital, but you didn't call back. Didn't you ever wonder why we sent a cable announcing Moss's birth?"

Cole's shoulders slumped. "I didn't know. I'm sorry, Riley. I was going through . . . I've been going through . . . I can't sleep, I can't eat right. I drink too much coffee and I'm smoking like a chimney. I'm so wired, I can't think straight these days."

"Is it Sumi?"

"No, of course not. She's upset with me too, and I don't blame her. She'd be entirely justified if she booted my ass right out of the house. I'm not a nice person these days. I have these really awful dreams. I believe—I don't want you laughing at me, Riley—but I believe your grandfather's spirit is in the Zen gardens. Honest to God. I take a bottle of beer out there and set it down. I walk around, and when I come back it's empty. I light cigars, your grandfather's favorite, and then I find ash along the different paths."

"Wait a minute, are you saying that you suddenly believe in . . . ghosts?" Riley exploded in laughter, but when he saw that his cousin was serious, he sobered instantly.

"I went up to the cherry blossom hill, and I swear to God he was there. Your grandfather is disappointed in me. I failed. Do you know something, Riley? Rising Sun is in exactly the same shape it was in when I took over. Almost to the penny. I have not made a difference, and I busted my ass. Jesus, I was working eighteen hours a day, and I still am. I have to be doing something wrong, but I'll be damned if I know what it is. I have this feeling your grandfather is watching over me, and he's shaking his head in disappointment."

"Hey, you aren't in the red, so what's the big deal? It takes a while for ... it's all new to you. The Japanese do things differently than we do back in the States. I think you just need a little more time."

"Riley, I've had three and a half years. If I can't cut it, then I don't belong here. Don't you remember the way you felt when you thought you screwed up and didn't belong in Texas? That's how I feel, but worse. When Sawyer called, I saw it as a way to ... a deal. I thought it was a message from your grandfather. Call it what you like. I saw this whole line of zeros and I went off the deep end. But I know he's there in the garden, Riley, I swear to God. I figured, what I mean is ... I thought if you walked in the garden, you'd feel his presence too. He loved you. You'll feel something. Do you think I'm losing my mind?"

Riley blinked, his heart thudding in his chest. Did he think his cousin was losing it? If Cole backed out of Rising Sun, the whole ball of wax reverted to him, which meant he'd have to give up his life in America and return to Japan.

"Hell no!" Riley blurted. He signaled the waitress to refill his coffee cup. "There's a logical explanation for all this. One of my nieces or nephews must have been playing a trick."

"They were in school," Cole said, impatience written all over his face.

"My aunts, then. They're kind of devilish. Maybe even Sumi."

"At four o'clock in the morning? Give me a break.

Grandmam Billie believes in these things. When Aunt Amelia died she and I both felt Seth Coleman's ... well, whatever it was, we felt it. I remember digging my heels into the ground, and I watched Grandmam Billie do the same thing, though no one else seemed to. We talked about it once. Jesus, I don't know what to think anymore."

"Okay, okay. Then where does this leave us with Sawyer and our immediate problem? Are you going to give her the money or not? And by her I mean the family."

"I'm willing to negotiate, but there's no way I can justify *giving* her the money."

"Okay. That's your decision. Now let me tell you what I want. I want one hundred million dollars transferred to my bank in Texas. I want you to put it in trust for my son. I want it transferred by the close of business tomorrow. Remember, it's my money, Cole. You're just the custodian."

"You'd do that to me?" Cole demanded, his shoulders shaking.

"For my family I'll do whatever I have to do. I think you've lost sight of what's important here. Nothing on this goddamn earth is more important than family," Riley said vehemently. "Nothing."

Cole squared his shoulders and drew a deep breath. "An irrevocable trust, Riley. Anything else is not negotiable."

"No," Riley said quietly.

"Yes. Take it or leave it. You know I would never deny you anything."

"Are you going to make me fight you, Cole?"

"You're double dealing and you know it. If it's not an irrevocable trust, you'll give it to Sawyer. Sawyer is business. Little Moss is your son. If you want the whole ninety billion put in an irrevocable trust for the kid, I'll do it tomorrow. I'll close up shop and go to work for Montgomery Ward selling tires." He looked at his watch. "Time to go. Air traffic at this time of day is a bitch. I don't want to be away from Sumi any longer than I have to." He peeled off a twenty dollar bill and laid it on the table.

Riley grabbed his flight bag and loped after his cousin. He'd do it too; the son of a bitch really would close up shop and go to work for Montgomery Ward. When he caught up to Cole, he clapped him on the back and said, "There's no future in tires. The money's in ride-on lawn mowers. We'll work it out, okay?"

"Okay. I'm glad you're here, Riley."

"Yeah, me too, but I'm not giving in. You need to know that."

"I'm not either. You need to know that too."

"At least we're starting out even."

Cole grinned.

{{{{{{{{{ CHAPTER FIVE }}}}}}}}}

Cary Assante settled his hard hat firmly on his head. Just a few more months and his memorial would be finished. In the beginning he'd had doubts that he was doing the right thing, building this center as a memorial to his wife. A wife he'd betrayed in the last months of their marriage. At first he thought he was doing it out of guilt, but later, when it all started to come together, he cast the guilt aside and knew he was doing it out of love for Amelia.

Whenever he came within a few months of completing a job, he grew happy and antsy at the same time. Everyone was going to be so proud at the dedication. He could see it all now, Billie and Thad, the whole family. It was *his* family now, thanks to Amelia. After her death he worried that they wouldn't want anything to do with him. Instead, they'd drawn closer to one another. A week didn't go by without a call or a letter from some family member. For a year now he'd been sending them all pictures depicting the progress he was making on the center.

He looked toward the heavens and spoke to his wife, as he did every day. He no longer cared if people saw him talking to thin air or if people thought he was eccentric. "We're almost there, babe," he said, then trotted off toward the explosion sight.

He was halfway there when he realized he'd forgotten his safety goggles. Should he go back for them or take a chance that nothing would go wrong? Better safe than sorry is what Amelia would have said, but hell, he was a pro. He'd set thousands of dynamite charges over the years and nothing had ever gone wrong. If he went back for the goggles, he'd be behind schedule all day. He loped over to the dynamite charge and raised the red flag. He had it in his mind to stop by Sunbridge and drop off the set of sponge building blocks he'd bought the other day for little Moss. He was, after all, the kid's godfather. Riley and Ivy didn't know it, but after Moss was christened, he'd changed his will. At his death everything would go to Moss, with Ivy and Riley as trustees. Nothing was too good for his family. He would give the shirt off his back to any one of them. Having a family was what life was all about.

"You ready, Cary?" his foreman, Sam Black, shouted. "On the count of three," the foreman said, holding up his index finger. "One, two, three. Hit it!"

Cary was aware of a burst of flame and scorching heat. He reeled backward and heard Black shout, "Jesus Christ! Call EMS, now! Cary, don't move. Son of a bitch, who checked this detonator cap? Move it, move it! Jesus, do I have to do everything myself? It's gonna be okay, Cary, I'm telling you, don't move, not even a muscle."

When Cary heard the panic in his foreman's voice, he figured he was dying. Thank God he'd made the new will. Get ready, Amelia, I think I'm on my way. Hold open the gates. He blacked out a moment later.

When he awoke, he was in a hospital. He could tell by the smell and the sounds. He'd spent a lot of time here when Amelia was ill. He listened to soothing voices telling him to relax, then felt the prick of a needle.

"What did he say, Doctor?" a young voice asked.

"He said, 'Swing those gates, babe, I think I'm half-way there.' He's delirious. Is his family here?"

"Not to my knowledge, just the foreman who came in with EMS. I'm sure they'll be here as soon as they can."

"Well, we can't wait. We'll have to assume we have their permission to operate." The doctor slipped his hands into latex gloves. "What we have here is . . ."

Thad Kingsley stood behind the French doors observing his wife, Billie. The shrill whistle of the tea kettle jarred him from his unhappy thoughts. He hated tearing his eyes and thoughts away from the woman on the chaise lounge. Every minute, every second, was now more precious than ever. God, what was he going to do? "Measure out the sugar, Kingsley, open the tea bag, Kingsley, pour the water, Kingsley," he muttered. His throat felt tight and he could feel his heartbeat accelerate when he shouldered his way through the kitchen door, with the tray balanced precariously in his hands.

"Three sugars, just the way you like it," Thad said cheerfully, sitting down next to her. "I, on the other hand, take mine like a man—lemon and no sugar."

Billie's hands had been jammed into the pockets of her down jacket, under her lap robe. She reached for the cup, her thin fingers greedily absorbing warmth from the heavy mug. "I can't remember such an early spring here in Vermont, can you, Thad?"

"Now that you mention it, no, I can't remember such an early spring. I hope it means a warm summer without too much rain."

"Me too," Billie said softly. She wanted to scream, to say she loved the seasons here at the farm. She couldn't scream, though, couldn't upset Thad any more than he was upset now. She looked down across the lawn to the rolling farm hills that had been in Thad's family for over a century. It was so beautiful, breathtaking really. Her throat constricted.

"Penny for your thoughts," Thad said quietly.

Billie was tempted to lie, but she'd never been anything but honest with her husband. "I was wondering if you can carry your memories into the hereafter or if it's a whole new ball game. I think that's what bothers me the most—not knowing. Thad, we have to talk about this. At least once. Then we can put it behind us and live our days as normally as we can."

Thad was off his seat in a second, his shoulders twitching unbearably. He knew she was right, but he felt cowardly about it. My God, Billie was dying, and he was a coward. He clutched the railing of the deck banister, his knuckles whiter than any sheet. Maybe he could do it if he didn't have to face her. "Okay," he said hoarsely.

"Sit down, darling, so I can see you," Billie whispered.

Goddamnit, he'd fought a war, flown fighter planes, battled for Billie's love, and then waged war in the Senate day after day for years, and nothing was harder, tougher, than this minute. He knew his smile was sickly when he sat down and reached for Billie's hand. How cold and thin it was.

"Now," Billie said briskly, "let's get on with it. I am not afraid to die, Thad. I'm not anxious to go, but it's been ordained. I truly believe that. So you and I have to accept that my time is limited, that I'm going ... to leave you. I need to know you'll be all right, Thad, and that you'll be there for my family. I know they'll be there for you. I need your promise."

Thad nodded, his eyes full of tears.

"Billie, your family . . . how am I going to explain . . . ? What are we going to tell them?"

"I can't burden them with my illness. They would hover, Thad, and maybe that's the way families do things, but I don't want it. Remember the way we all fretted and fussed over Amelia. She didn't want it either. All she wanted was to have the man she loved at her side. She forbade him to call us, but he couldn't keep his promise. Amelia and I had such long talks about death and dying. She wasn't afraid either. Grieving is such a sad, lonely business, and I don't want my family to go through it one minute longer than they have to. We'll deal with July and Amelia's memorial when it's time. Now, Senator Kingsley, what do you say we go into town so you can buy me lunch? And after lunch, let's go to that flower stall at the end of Main Street and buy an armload of spring flowers. Every color of the rainbow. We'll come home late in the afternoon, make a fire and eat leftovers in the den. Double chocolate fudge ice cream with sprinkles for dessert. Are you tempted?"

"You twisted my arm. But I want rocky road ice cream and chocolate sprinkles."

Billie pretended to sigh. "You got it."

"Billie, I would give up my life for you if I could."

"I know that, Thad. But we've had more joy in our short time together than some people have in a lifetime. Always remember that, and don't be greedy. No one gets it all."

Thad threw his hands in the air. "She's a philosopher too."

"And a hell of a cook." Billie laughed as she made her way to the bedroom at the end of the hall. "I'll just be a minute, Thad."

Thad drove his fist into the back of the recliner. "Son of a bitch!" It wasn't fair. People, good people like Billie, were supposed to live forever. "Please, God, just don't let her suffer. I can bear up to anything but that. She's trying so hard. Just this once and I swear I'll never ask You for another thing. Please, God."

It was four o'clock when Thad and Billie walked into the cedar-shingled farmhouse, their arms full of flowers. Billie headed straight for the vases in the kitchen. Just then, the phone shrilled to life.

They both rushed over and, like errant children, waited for the answering machine to click on. Their M.O., as Thad referred to it, was to listen to the message and return the call a few hours later. In the months since Billie's diagnosis, it had proven a successful strategy for convincing people they were on a world tour and only occasionally checked for calls. It was their way of hiding the effects of chemotherapy from the family.

This time a hysterical voice came over the wire. "Billie, Thad, it's Ivy. It's four o'clock in the afternoon on Thursday. There's been a terrible accident. Cary was hurt in a dynamite explosion and is in the hospital. Riley flew to Japan to see Cole. I called and Sumi said Cole flew to Guam to pick up Riley. They aren't back yet. Sawyer and Adam's machine is on. I called twice, but they haven't returned my call. I did manage to reach Maggie. Rand is in Minnesota with Miss Mitchell.

Something to do with Susan. I called there too, and the operator said Susan's phone was disconnected at noon today. Susan's at Maggie's and she's leaving for Texas on the first flight she can get. Riley said you check your phone messages every other day. I thought you'd want to know. I'm waiting for Jonquil to get back from the market and then I'll go to the hospital. Oh, Billie, I don't know what to do. Cary has no family but us. Will I be doing the right thing if I have to sign? I don't know how badly he's hurt. As soon as I talk to his doctor I'll be back in touch."

Billie picked up the phone. "Ivy, we're here. We just walked in the door. As soon as Thad can make the arrangements, we'll leave. We should be on our way within the hour. You hold the fort, darling, and do whatever you have to do. Cary is . . . Cary is tough, he'll be just fine. I feel that in my heart," Billie said. "I'm going to hang up now, darling, so Thad can use the phone. We'll go straight to the hospital. Ivy, are you all right?"

"Oh, Billie, I prayed you would be home. Thank you for being there. If they let me see Cary, I'll tell him you're on the way. It will . . . give him something to hang on to. Please hurry."

"We'll do our best. Take care, Ivy."

"I'll pack our bags while you make arrangements with the airport. Hurry, Thad," Billie called back to him as she ran down the hall.

Thad dialed and talked to his wife at the same time. "I thought you said you didn't want—"

"We switched to Plan B, darling. Family first. Family always comes first."

It was almost midnight when Thad and Billie walked into the waiting room where Ivy Coleman sat, tears streaming down her cheeks. She ran to Billie and Thad, sobbing.

"Shhh," Billie said soothingly. "We're here now, darling. We're sorry you had to go through this alone. Have you spoken to any of the doctors?"

Ivy nodded. "He's got some second degree burns and a few lacerations. He wasn't wearing safety goggles. He's blind."

Billie could feel herself sway as Thad's arms reached for her. All she could manage to say was, "He's alive, that's what matters."

"Can we see him?" Thad asked.

"Not till morning."

"All right, then, we're all going back to Sunbridge and have some coffee."

"Tomorrow is another day," Billie said softly.

There was nothing bright or hopeful about the new day, Billie thought gloomily as she looked out of the new windows in the breakfast nook. Low, swirling fog danced across the spring grass, which meant that it was going to be a warm day.

Billie shivered. As always these days, she felt cold even though she had on slipper socks and a warm flannel nightgown and velour robe. The coffee cup warmed her hands. She wanted a second cup, but she didn't want to get up. She liked this little nest here on the window seat, surrounded by Ivy's pillows. It was all so beautiful now, this new Sunbridge.

She snuggled deep into her robe and curled her legs beneath her. Thad said she was part cat, the way she curled and snuggled. "You even purr like a cat," he would say. She smiled. She always smiled when she thought of Thad.

The kitchen clock chimed softly, pleasantly, in counterpoint with the Wisconsin wind chime on the patio. That too was a lovely sound, so lovely she'd asked Ivy to send her one for the deck in the farmhouse.

The low fog swirled and evaporated from the garden and lawn. The sun would shine soon and the breakfast room would be warm. Ivy would get up and make breakfast, or perhaps Jonquil would do it. Little Moss was already waiting in his high chair.

"Beat me to it again, huh?" Thad said, padding into the kitchen, his sparse gray hair standing on end. "I thought I'd find you down here curled up with your book. How's Einstein doing?" he demanded, referring to Billie's addiction to Dean Koontz, a writer she'd discovered during her "bad time."

"Thad, listen to this," Billie said. " 'During the rest of June, Nora did some painting, spent a lot of time with Travis and tried to teach Einstein to read.' " Billie rolled her eyes. "Nora is going to teach Einstein to read! Page one hundred eighty-five, Chapter Seven. It's a few pages past the halfway mark. Only one hundred sixty-seven to go. It's soooo good, Thad. Do you want me to wait and read to you later?"

"Absolutely. I want to hear firsthand how Nora teaches a dog to read. Don't you dare read another word! Did the hospital call? How long have you been up?" Thad demanded as he poked around the bread box for something sweet.

"I came down around five. The phone didn't ring. I made coffee, but I'd make fresh if I were you. Isn't this a pretty kitchen, Thad?"

Thad nodded. "You're going to cheat, aren't you?" he asked fretfully. "While I make the toast and coffee, you're going to read. I know your M.O., Billie." He smirked with satisfaction when his wife slammed the book shut.

"Okay, Admiral Senator Kingsley. I closed the book. So there! It's half finished, Thad. I hate it when I get to the halfway mark in a good book. We only have one more of his to read and then we'll have read them all. Do you think I should write him a fan letter?"

"Why not?" Thad grinned. "You wrote one to Sidney Sheldon, Clive Cussler, and Robert Ludlum."

"You forgot Tom Clancy," Billie snapped. "I told him I didn't like parts of *Patriot Games*."

Thad laughed. "I bet he lost a lot of sleep over that letter." It was a game they played. Billie had always loved to read, but since her illness, she read with a vengeance. Most of the time, she read the novels aloud to him. Often she got so caught up in the stories that she forgot about her illness. He made a promise to himself that when he was alone, he would write a letter himself to all the authors Billie adored and tell them how much pleasure they had given her in her last months. He wondered now as he pushed the bread down into the toaster if he would really write the letters or if the thought was just something to make himself feel better.

"Thad, call the hospital," Billie said.

She waited, her heart thumping in her chest while Thad called and identified himself. Her eyebrows rose when she saw her husband's mouth turn grim.

"Of course I'm immediate family. I'm his father. Now, how's my son? Fine, fine, I'll be there by nine."

"Cary's father." Billie smiled. "How is he, Thad?"

"Resting comfortably. The doctor and the ophthalmologist will talk to me at nine o'clock. They won't give out any information over the phone. I suppose that's good."

"Whoa, that's too much butter, Thad," Billie warned. "Remember your cholesterol."

As if he gave a hoot about his cholesterol or his arteries. He scraped off some of the butter because it pleased his wife; he would never give her one moment of anxiety if he could help it. He layered on a thick glob of blueberry jam.

"Remember your triglycerides, Thad," Billie admonished.

He didn't give a damn about his triglycerides either. He scraped off an inch of jam. "Now it's going to taste like shit," he muttered.

"Sit down, Thad, let me do it," Billie said, putting fresh bread into the toaster. "Give me that." She reached for the cold toast and tossed it into the trash.

Thad grinned.

"You did that deliberately so I'd get up and make it for you," Billie grumbled.

"It always tastes better when you make it. Like when you make egg salad and put those little seeds in it. I make it and it doesn't taste the same."

"You're whining, Thad."

"Say good morning, Moss," Ivy said to her son. "My, you're both up early." She looked everywhere but at Riley's grandmother. "The coffee smells wonderful. Jonquil doesn't get here till eight. Usually Riley and I rough it. I'll be glad to make breakfast—eggs, French toast, pancakes. We even have some of your maple syrup left from the last batch you sent."

"Darling, you sit down. I'll make you breakfast. What does Moss eat for breakfast?" Billie asked with a catch in her voice.

"Mashed banana, and then I put some rice cereal in his bottle. I just have juice and toast along with a vitamin. I tend to eat a big lunch. I still haven't lost all my pregnancy weight," Ivy said, fiddling with the suction toy on the baby's high chair.

Billie slipped into her seat across the table from Ivy. "Ivy, please look at me," she said gently, in a voice that would have calmed a terrorist. "It's not the end of the world. Not yet, anyway. Thad and I can handle this. What we can't handle is having this family fall apart. That's the reason we . . . we didn't mention my illness. Since my time is uncertain we . . . we want . . . I don't want hovering, pity, or . . . any of that stuff that goes with it. Can I count on you to help Riley through this?"

"Oh, Billie," Ivy said in a choked voice, "of course I'll help him. It's just that he hasn't come to terms with his grandfather's death and it's over three years. I don't know what this will do to him." There was such sorrow in her voice, Billie found herself reaching for Thad's hand under the table.

"This is life's way of coming full circle. I was thinking about this last night before I fell asleep. You, Ivy, are in the same place I was so many years ago. You're a new bride here in a brand new Sunbridge, a house you and Riley built with the help of your neighbors. It's right that the circle should start again. I feel so . . . so very positive about this." Billie squeezed her husband's hand. He was feeling the same thing she was feeling, she could tell. He recognized the strength in Ivy's young face, saw the love in that same face for her son and husband. So like herself so many years ago. The sadness that welled in her heart was immediately replaced by the knowledge that the family would survive.

"What's our plan for the day?" Ivy asked. "Are we all going to the hospital? I have to pick Susan up at the airport, so why don't I meet you at the hospital. I'll give Moss his bath and Jonquil can take over from there."

"Sounds like a good plan to me," Thad said, draining his coffee.

"Well, if it's good enough for Thad, it's certainly good enough for me," Billie said breezily. "I do like it when a man takes over, don't you, Ivy?" She chucked the baby under the chin, her eyes misting at the cherub whose face was full of mashed banana.

"I'll bring Susan straight to the hospital," Ivy called over her shoulder.

In the privacy of the bathroom, with Moss splashing and gurgling, Ivy let her tears loose. "Why?" she whispered. "We need her, we really do. I didn't understand about Mr. Hasegawa and I don't understand why You need Billie. Riley's grandfather did only good, just the way Billie does. Yes, I'm selfish and I'm sorry about that, but I have to think about Riley and the rest of the family and what it's going to do to them. Should I tell Susan or let her . . . How can I tell her? Help me, tell me what I should do. Is it my place to tell Susan about her mother? Do I tell Riley and Cole or do I mind my own business?" Oh God, oh God, she railed silently.

As she dried and powdered the baby, she thought back to the first time she'd met Riley's grandfather, Shadaharu Hasegawa. He'd been ill just the way Billie was ill. The family chose not to discuss his condition, and the frail old man tried to disguise his illness just the way Billie was trying to disguise hers by wearing fuller, padded clothing. The old Japanese had fought so valiantly, just the way Billie was fighting. Who was she to take matters into her own hands? Ivy asked herself. Yes, it was going to be hard to put what Riley called a happy face on things, but she could do it. So could the others. If it was what Billie wanted, she would play the part, and the others would have to do the same thing. However, it still didn't answer her question: Did she mention Billie's apparent illness or let the family see it for themselves? She buried her face in Moss's sweet-smelling neck, her eyes filled with tears. She hugged the chubby infant even tighter. Billie was right, the family was coming full circle. She wondered why the thought didn't make her feel any better.

When Cary awoke hours later, he was aware of a presence in the room. The voice was familiar, soft and gentle. Of course, it was Billie. And from a distance he thought he recognized Thad's quiet voice as well.

"We only have ten minutes, Cary," Billie said, reaching for his hand. "Thad and I are here. Ivy went to the airport to pick up Susan. They should be here soon. The nurse told us Sawyer is on her way. Don't try to talk, Cary. We just wanted you to know that we're here for you."

Cary struggled through layers of exhaustion to respond. It sounded as if Amelia's family were all coming to see him.

"I feel like shit," he muttered.

"You look like it too." Thad laughed.

"Open the blinds or pull the damn drapes. It's too dark," Cary said.

"Oh, darling, we can't do that," Billie said quietly. "You're in ICU and there are rules. It's dark because of the bandages on your eyes."

It wasn't a shout, it was a scream: "Why?"

Ms. Baldwin, his private duty nurse, was at Cary's

side instantly. "Why what, Mr. Assante?" she asked soothingly.

"Why are my eyes bandaged?" he demanded thickly.

"Because the doctor wants them bandaged. He was concerned that the light in here might bother your eyes. It's a precaution, Mr. Assante."

Fear coursed through Cary as his adrenaline surged. He was almost wide awake now, aware of everything, of the way Nurse Baldwin smelled of antiseptic, and of Billie's sweet-smelling perfume, so like Amelia's. And then he was aware again of the pain in his arm and chest.

He tried to shout Thad's name, but it come out so weakly, he knew it was little more than a whisper. "Thad, what's wrong with me?"

"You were a little too close to a faulty detonator cap. That's what the EMS filed on your report. At first they thought you had second degree burns, but you don't. You were burned, though. That's the pain you're feeling. Your face took some of the heat, but you're going to be okay. Any plastic surgeon worth his salt can give you new earlobes in a heartbeat. You won't even need them if you let your hair grow."

"Jesus," Cary said, trying valiantly to lift his hand to check his earlobes.

"Cary, it was a joke. There's nothing wrong with your earlobes." Thad chuckled. "I was trying for levity here. I guess it wasn't such a good idea."

"What's wrong with my eyes?"

"I don't know, Cary. I haven't seen your doctor. I understand a call went out to the Wills Eye Hospital in Philadelphia and a well-known ophthalmologist is on his way. All you have to do is hang in there and hold up your end. Let the big guys take over, and things will be fine, I'm sure of it."

Cary sighed. If it was anybody but Thad Kingsley telling him this, he wouldn't believe him. Thad never lied.

"Billie?"

"Yes, Cary."

"I thought I saw Amelia. I swear to God. I've dreamed about her so many times, but this time it was different. I saw her. She was blocking my path and wouldn't let me near her. I begged her; I was crying, and she still wouldn't let me near her. Do you ever see her, Billie?" Cary asked fretfully. "You were closer to her than anyone."

Billie drew in her breath. She wanted to tell him she saw Amelia all the time and that she was always beckoning and saying not to be afraid, but Billie couldn't, not in front of Thad. "Only in my dreams, Cary. You've been through a terrible ordeal, and you reached out to the person who was a constant in your life for so long. Darling, the nurse says we have to leave, but we'll be back later." She reached for Cary's hand and brought it to her lips. "Rest, Cary. You'll need some stamina to hear all about little Moss's antics when Ivy gets here with Susan."

Something was wrong, Cary thought. Her fingers were too thin. Her wrist too. Just the way Amelia's fingers and wrists were at the end. His hand held tight, his limp fingers trying desperately to grasp the twig-thin arm. His hand fell back against the white sheet when Billie ran from the room.

"Thad," he cried in a tortured voice.

"Cary, if there was ever a time when I needed a man to talk to, this is the time. You have to get well, and goddamnit, you have to do it soon," Thad said in a strangled voice. "We need you."

"Ah, Thad, not Billie."

"She doesn't have long. One oncologist said six months, another said less. It's uncertain."

"I'd cry if I could. What can I do?"

"Get better and get out of here."

"Yeah, yeah, I'll be out of here in a day or so. Everything is moving, and if the burns aren't too bad, they might let me go. You can sort of steer me around until they take these things off my eyes. How long are you staying?" He sounded exhausted.

"Mr. Kingsley," Nurse Baldwin said sternly.

"I'll be back later, Cary. Rest and take it easy. If you need anything, have the nurse call Sunbridge. We'll be here for a while yet. At least until you're out of the woods."

Cary was asleep before Thad left the room.

Billie sat quietly in the burnt-orange chair in the waiting room. Her hands were folded tightly to stop the tremor that overtook her every so often of late. She had to prepare herself for her daughter's appearance. Sawyer's too. Perhaps this was a mistake. Perhaps she should have gathered the family and . . . And what? Announced her illness? Instead she was putting herself through anguish each time she saw a family member. Cary, sweet, wonderful Cary, had known. Oh, God, give me strength to handle this, she prayed silently. She dozed, her energy depleted.

They were so alike, mother, daughter, and sister, as they came down the hospital corridor. Beautiful, actually, if one paid attention to the interns' and orderlies' overt glances. Maggie was dressed in a multicolored A-line dress, which brought out the rich highlights in her dark hair and a bloom to her cheeks. Susan, in a sea-foam-green suit with moss-green blouse and a strand of Mikimoto pearls, contrasted sharply with Maggie's earthy look. Sawyer, never a fashion plate, was attired in a Liz Claiborne denim skirt with matching blouse. A three-inch brown leather belt rode low on her hips and matched her well-worn boots. Her long blond hair was tied in a knot on top of her head, in messy disarray. Heavy silver earrings dangled from her ears and matched the clanking bracelets on both arms. Her blue eyes were worried.

"Has it occurred to either of you," she stage whispered to her mother and her aunt, "that Ivy acted strangely at the airport and on the drive here? It wasn't just my sudden appearance either. Or yours, Maggie. Ivy's cool, she can handle just about anything. She even said she more or less expected you, Maggie. She was so quiet, and I had to practically pull tidbits about Moss out of her. If there's one thing a mother likes to do, it's talk about her kids. She didn't have to drop us off by the door and park the car. We could have walked together from the lot. Something's wrong."

"Of course something's wrong. Cary is hurt. That's why we're here," Maggie said as a young nurse went by carrying a tray of medication. "I liked it better when they wore those starched caps," she muttered. "I think Ivy is just tired. Riley's gone, the baby takes a lot of care, and here we all are."

"That's just it. Ivy doesn't ruffle. She's ruffled now, though. What do you think, Susan?"

"Maybe she has PMS. In the scheme of things, does it really matter if Ivy is out of sorts? She picked us up and brought us here, so why don't we just drop it at that? When she joins us in the waiting room, we can all ask her what's bothering her. Come on, I'm anxious to see Cary and Mam," Susan said.

"Let's take bets," Maggie whispered. "I say Mam is wearing something in . . . ah, let's see, bright purple. Purple is a spring color. Lace too, maybe on the collar. Five bucks."

"Yellow," Susan said smartly. "Butter-yellow, green accessories."

"Navy-blue-and-white polka dots," Sawyer quipped. Her mother and aunt hooted as the trio moved down the hall.

They were all familiar with the rules of ICU. Maggie led the way to the waiting room, as visiting was limited to ten minutes on the hour. Maggie was almost giddy with the knowledge that she was going to see her mother. Her step slowed as she approached the doorway to the small waiting room.

Three pairs of eyes locked on the sleeping form in the burnt-orange chair. Those same eyes swiveled as one to the hunched-over man with the folded hands. Maggie reached for the wall for support, Susan grappled behind for Sawyer's arm, but Sawyer was slumped against the opposite side of the door. Thad was on his feet in a second, ushering them down the hall.

"Tell me that wasn't Mam," Maggie said in a choked voice.

Susan's world whirled around her. For a moment she thought she was going to faint. Cary . . . Mam . . . just when they were getting to *really* know one another. Oh, God, it wasn't fair. Why did these things always happen to her? Mam. She squeezed her eyes shut to see which person would flash behind her closed lids. Cary first and then Mam. Mam looked like Aunt Amelia before she died. Cary, I need you. How can I handle this? I'm not strong like the others. I need to lean on someone. I need you to tell me this is all going to be all right. She wanted to cry, to throw a tantrum, but if she did that, Maggie or Sawyer would slap her silly. She bit down on her lower lip.

Sawyer cried quietly into a wadded-up hankie. "I can't handle this," she sobbed.

"Well, you all better handle it," Thad said huskily. "Billie, against my advice, chose to . . . to keep her illness from all of you to spare you anguish. When she should have been thinking of herself, she was thinking of you. I didn't want her to come here, but her sense of family is so strong, I knew she'd find a way to get here even if she had to crawl. If you're going to go in there weeping and wailing, I'm taking Billie back to Vermont. I won't have any of you causing her one moment's distress. I mean it," he all but thundered.

"Are you saying you want us to act as if nothing is wrong?" Maggie whispered. "Our world has just crumpled and you want us to act as if nothing is wrong? That's not right."

"I want to hit her," Susan said through clenched teeth. "She can't . . . she can't die. I don't want her to die."

"Will you shut up, Susan, and think about someone besides yourself," Maggie said tightly. "Sawyer, get hold of yourself. We have . . . we have to agree now how we're going to handle this. We came here for Cary. He needs us."

"I want to go home," Susan wailed. She turned and ran down the hall as fast as her legs could carry her.

Ivy, coming down the hall, stiff-armed her, throwing her off balance.

"I can't even go home, damn you. My home is yours now, yours and Riley's. God, I hate you," Susan screamed.

Ivy swayed, her stomach lurching sickeningly. She was aware of shadowy forms in the hallway as she tried to take control of her emotions. She took a deep breath, then literally dragged Susan around the corner and out to the lobby, and from there out the huge double glass doors.

"Get hold of yourself, Susan," Ivy said sharply. "Let's take this outside."

"Damn you, you should have told us. I thought you were part of this family. You're goddamned living in *our house*, so that must make you family. You should have told us, prepared us. But you didn't have the guts, so you parked the car and let us walk ... oh, damn you!"

Ivy gulped in more fresh air. "This is exactly why your mother didn't tell you. Now, I think you'd better get yourself together, Susan, because if you don't, I'm going to slug you right here. This is a time when family needs to come together. As for the house, we'll talk about that later—at length if you want."

"I never took the time ... or had the chance. It's too late for me. I was just talking to Mam. I was so nasty, so unkind. God, I didn't know ... Cary ... we came here for Cary. I didn't mean those things I said, I was trying to punish Mam ... I do love her ... even if ... I'm always too late, after the fact. It's like I burn my bridges too soon. Why is that? What's wrong with me? If Cary was here, he'd know what to say to me. . . .

We're not even thinking of Cary now. That isn't right. God must be punishing me," Susan cried.

"It's never too late to make amends," Maggie said, putting her arms around her sister. "It's when you don't try that it becomes a problem." With her eyes, she thanked Ivy.

"Let's all head for the bathroom," Sawyer said in a shaky voice. "I, personally, have three pounds of makeup in my carry bag, and I think we could all use a little repair work."

"*She* said she would slug me," Susan dithered.

"If she hadn't, I would have," Sawyer said callously. "It's time to grow up and face the world, Susan. Mam and Cary need us."

Ivy would have hung back, but Maggie drew her closer. "Don't you ever, ever for a second, think that you don't belong to this family. You do, and if I ever see you with that look on your face again, I'll slug *you*."

Ivy smiled gratefully, her arm linked in Maggie's.

{{{{{{{{ CHAPTER SIX }}}}}}}}

The house was palatial, and Riley thought it beautiful, but not as beautiful as Sunbridge. The huge wrought-iron gates that shielded it from the busy thoroughfare rolled open with barely a squeak as he and Cole drove up.

What if he got locked in and Cole refused to let him leave? The top of the fence was electrified; how the hell would he get out? God, what if he never saw Ivy and little Moss again. He started to sweat.

Cole watched his cousin, correctly interpreting his thoughts. He reached into the gate house and handed over a key. "All you have to do is open it and you're free."

"You always could read me, Cole," Riley said softly.

"And you me. It doesn't matter if you're East and I'm West. Ah, I see you're West now. That's okay, Riley. You're who you are and I'm who I am. Actually I think both of us are more or less straddling the middle ground here. The real truth is we're just people. Cousins. Can we let it go at that?"

Riley fingered the key for a moment. It felt good in his hand, somehow comforting. He handed the key back to his cousin, who merely shrugged.

"It looks the same," Riley said coolly. "It shouldn't look the same. Change . . ." He let his voice trail off as a gaggle of children, twelve of them, his nieces and nephews, rushed out the front door. As he got out of the car he found himself blinking as they bowed and tittered. He knew all their names; he'd studied the family pictures on the flight over. He called them now by name and smiled. He was Uncle Riley, so he played the part, and he liked his role. When the children straggled off, bickering among themselves, Sumi waddled out the door.

She was tiny and very round. He smiled again when he saw his cousin's face light up.

Cole withdrew a small package from his pocket. "Your present," he said with a flourish.

Sumi giggled. "Mexican jumping beans."

"No, no, no. You drop them in hot water and little spongy animals appear. Look, a present is a present," Cole said loftily.

"I shall treasure it always." Sumi continued to giggle, her dark eyes dancing. "Riley, how wonderful to see you again," she said, doing her best to hug him. "Ivy called. She said you and Cole are to get in touch with her as soon as you can. She called from a pay phone."

"Ivy called from a pay phone?" Riley repeated in dismay.

"Person to person." Sumi smiled. "I didn't take the call. One of my sisters did and wrote down the message. I tried to call back, but Jonquil said Ivy was out, and that she was baby-sitting. That's all I know, Riley."

"We'll call, but first we need some food," Riley said. "In the garden, okay, Sumi? And you are to join us. None of these Japanese traditions that the men eat together while the women giggle behind the door."

"I would love to join you, but I must go to town. I have an appointment with my obstetrician. My sister is driving me. We'll visit later. Go, go," she said, making shooing motions with her hands. "My sisters will make tea and sandwiches."

"You're all screwed up, as usual," Cole said, patting her rump. "Make it Sapporo and liverwurst with raw onion on rye bread. We have an American here who doesn't like Japanese food." He made gnashing sounds with his teeth.

Sumi snorted. "This is what *he* eats every day. Do you have any idea how difficult it is to get rye bread? We have to *make* it for him. Fresh. Every single day. We love doing it." She grimaced.

"Ivy walked the same way. Back home we call it the Sawyer waddle. I overheard Sawyer telling Ivy she had to walk like that so people really would believe she was pregnant. She said a protruding stomach didn't count," Riley volunteered. "Sometimes I think your sister is weird, Cole. The twins are just like her and they drive her nuts. Ivy said she's a wonderful mother, so I guess that's all that counts."

Cole nodded. He didn't want to talk about babies, his sister, or duck waddling.

"Let's walk in the garden. It will take Sumi's sisters at least ten minutes to get our food and beer out here. It will be interesting to see if it disappears."

Riley snorted. "My grandfather didn't like liverwurst and raw onion." He fell into step with his cousin. "You know, this must be the most peaceful place on earth. As a child I thought so. When I brought my grandfather back here for the last time when I made my decision to stay in Texas, I came out here hoping somehow I'd gain . . . insight, wisdom, something that would tell me I was making the right decision. I cried. I thought we were all going to live happily ever after. Crazy, huh?"

Five minutes later, in the garden, Cole said, "Shhh. Listen. Okay, the food is out. Come on, I'm going to prove something to you, Riley. I'm going to lock the door from the outside. We both know there's only one entrance to the garden. No other exit. Do we agree on that?"

"Yeah," Riley said, pushing his cap back on his head. He should be calling Ivy instead of playing games with Cole. He watched Cole throw the shiny new brass bolt on the garden side of the door to lock it.

On the glossy black lacquer tray, which had been set on the white iron table, were four sandwiches, two bottles of Sapporo beer, a plate of rice cakes, a small bottle of sake, a yellow rose with delicate petals in a tiny vase, a pair of linen napkins, and two Havana cigars.

Cole clipped both ends of the Havanas, handed one to Riley, and lit them with his gold Dunhill lighter. The cousins puffed until the ash on both cigars glowed. Cole placed his at one end of a huge onyx ashtray. Riley placed his at the opposite end. He felt silly as hell, though his cousin's face was dead serious.

"What now, Sherlock?" Riley said tightly.

"We take a walk," Cole said.

As they moved away from the table, Riley looked over his shoulder. He didn't sense anything unusual. He wondered if his cousin was having a nervous breakdown.

"Keep your eyes on the path," Cole went on, "and observe that there is not a twig, a leaf, or a pebble on this path. It's clean. You wait, you're going to see cigar ash all over the place. There's no wind, no breeze."

"Cole, I know how you felt about my grandfather, but I do not believe he's here. His spirit, his soul, whatever, is at rest. Ask yourself why he would come back here. Such things don't happen." How desperate I sound, Riley thought.

"Then how do you explain the time Sawyer was in the hospital and we heard the angels sing? Even the doctor said he heard it."

Riley shrugged. He'd never come to terms with the angels singing. As the two men walked slowly through the extensive garden, Riley thought about it. He'd heard what sounded like angels. So had his aunt Maggie, Cole, and the surgeon. Cary said Amelia's spirit was always with him, pointing out right and wrong and making chandeliers tinkle. He'd seen that too. He found himself shivering.

"Cole, we should be going back. I have to call Ivy. There may be something wrong. Otherwise, why in the world would she call from a pay phone?"

"Maybe the phones went out. It used to happen all the time, don't you remember? Then one of us would have to go into town and notify the phone company."

Cole was probably right, Riley thought. The phones had gone out twice in the last two months. Ivy had probably gone to town to call him so that he wouldn't worry if he tried to call home. He should have called her from Guam, he thought guiltily. "How long have we been out here?"

"Twenty-five minutes. Maybe you should call out to him."

Riley would have laughed if his cousin's expression hadn't appeared so miserable. But then the fine hairs on his neck started to prickle, and a chill raced up his arms. His eyes dropped to the footpath.

Cole's fist shot in the air. "I told you," he said, pointing to the little pile of ash to the left of their feet. "That ash wasn't there when we walked this way before."

Cole ran down the path back to the little patio, with Riley at his heels. He triumphantly pointed to the onyx ashtray, where only Riley's cigar now smoldered. Half of one bottle of Sapporo was gone, and the tiny sake bottle was completely empty. One rice cake was missing. The napkins remained undisturbed, and the brass bolt was still in place.

"Now do you believe me?" Cole demanded.

Riley shivered. "Where's the cigar?"

"How the hell do I know? I was with you, remember?"

Riley sprinted down the path, poking and prodding every miniature shrub and bush that came within his line of vision. When he reached the small footbridge from which his grandfather loved to view the garden, he took a deep breath. He knew when he lowered his eyes he was going to see the remains of a mangled cigar. He didn't know how he knew, but he knew. He swallowed hard. Then forced himself to look down, and there it was, two inches of mangled pure Havana. He found himself growing light-headed, and would have fallen but for Cole's strong arm.

"What does he want?" Riley whispered.

"I don't know," Cole whispered back. "You ask. You knew to come to this bridge. Maybe he wants us together."

Riley stepped slowly onto the bridge. When he arrived at his grandfather's favorite spot, he whispered, "Tell us what you want. We don't know what to do. Is it the deal with Sawyer? Grandmam Billie? Cole and me? Wait, wait, let's do it one at a time."

But there was no time to wait. Suddenly a furious wind roared outside the walls of the Zen garden. It ripped up and over the wall, feeling almost as strong as the tornado that had leveled Sunbridge.

"Get down," Riley shouted.

All about them the ageless trees and shrubs were uprooted and tossed like twigs. When it was over, the only things remaining untouched were the footbridge and the discarded Havana cigar at their feet.

"All of the above," Riley said softly.

"Jesus. Why would he destroy this? He loved this garden. He told me once he wanted to die here but it would cause unhappy memories for his family and that's why he chose the cherry blossom hill. He loved this garden. Nah, he didn't do this. That was a freak. That was some—What do you mean, all of the above?" Cole asked in a shaky voice.

"I asked him if it was Sawyer, Grandmam Billie, and you and me. That's when the . . . whatever the hell it was hit. Do you have any idea how much those iron pagodas weigh? Hundreds of pounds, at least. Look where they are, all over the damn place. He must be in a hell of a snit to uproot those banzai trees. They're hundreds of years old. It's totally destroyed. I think we should decide *right now*, just the two of us, if we believe my grandfather did this or if this was some . . . fit of nature."

There was such disgust on Cole's face, Riley found himself wincing. "I guess I know what your vote is. As much as I hate to admit it, it *was* my grandfather. I don't think we should . . . you know, tell anyone. Who the hell would believe us?"

The cousins sat together, arms wrapped around their knees, their shoulders touching.

"What does it all mean, Riley?" Cole asked softly.

"I don't know. The Sawyer thing I can figure out. I

guess you're supposed to hand over the money with no strings. As for Grandmam Billie ... she's the head of the Coleman family, just the way my grandfather was head of this family. Maybe she's going to step down and hand the reins over to Aunt Maggie. She already turned Billie Limited over to your mother. As for you and I, I was prepared to go to the wall with you. I would have, Cole."

"I know. I would have let you win, too," Cole said softly.

"You always were a softie, cousin."

"Look who's talking," Cole said, thumping his cousin on the shoulder.

"Come on, we have to protect the roots of the banzai trees. See that one over there by the pagoda? It's eight hundred years old." Riley ripped at his shirt and light jacket. Cole did the same. When they had the roots bundled, they were shivering in their jockey shorts.

Sumi waddled up the footpath, her eyes dancing devilishly at the sight of her husband and his cousin. "Should I call the gardener?"

"I think that's a real good idea. What did the doctor say?" Cole asked wrapping her in his arms.

"He said I'm about ready. One more week, he thinks. He gave me something new for my heartburn."

"Wait a minute, how did you get out here? The door was bolted from the outside."

Sumi held up a steak knife for her husband's inspection. "I just slid it through the crack in the door and wiggled it till the bolt moved. Someone should tell me what happened," she said, eyeing the destruction all about them.

"A crazy wind," Riley said.

"Like a tornado," Cole said.

"Do you really expect me to believe that?" Sumi giggled. "This garden has been through many storms, as well as a war, and it has never been touched. When the Zen master planned this garden, he said it would last till the end of time. My father did this, didn't he? Somehow, some way, he . . . so you made a believer out of me," she said, tweaking her husband's cheek. "Besides, no one but the owner of the garden can change it, remodel it, or dismantle it. Ask Riley. Old Japanese proverb."

Cole looked at Riley. Riley looked at Sumi. He shrugged.

"See, I'm always right." Sumi smiled.

As Cole and Riley trekked down the hallway to the bedroom side of the house, they heard titters and laughter. Cole knew Sumi was egging her sisters and nieces on. He heard them making comments about nice buns and Chippendale bodies.

"Jesus," Riley said, after ducking into the first bedroom he came to. "When I left here, the aunts and nieces would never even raise their eyes. What the hell did you do to them?"

"Introduced them to our local version of MTV. They're women of the nineties now." Cole laughed uproariously. Riley thought it a good sound.

Thirty minutes later he was on the phone with Ivy. Cole and Sumi sat directly across from him.

After he hung up, Riley's face was the color of old parchment. He repeated Ivy's news, his vision blurred by the mist in his eyes. He rubbed them and saw tears trickling down Sumi's cheeks.

"You must go now, Cole," she said. "I will pack your bags. There is nothing to worry about where I am concerned. I have my sisters and a very fine doctor. Tell your family I will be with them in spirit."

Cole hugged his wife. "Are you sure, Sumi?"

"I am absolutely sure. You will give my love to all and express my regrets."

"Sumi—"

"It is your family, Cole, you must go. Help me up, please."

Cole pretended to grunt. "Two tons at least."

"At least," Sumi sniffed. Riley jerked back when she whistled shrilly between her teeth. The sisters came on the run, their kimonos flapping in a rainbow of color. With her index finger, Sumi pointed to each sister and issued orders in rapid-fire Japanese. Riley tried to get the gist of it, which was, Snap to it, don't drag your feet, and be here with my husband's bag in ten minutes along with a basket of food.

"Do not move, Riley, I have a present for little Moss. I bought it yesterday on the Ginza and was going to mail it tomorrow. Now you can take it to him and tell him it is from his aunt Sumi and uncle Cole." She waddled away.

"She's one in a million," Cole said quietly.

"Try two in two million," Riley whispered.

"That . . . that holocaust out there . . . Grandmam Billie . . . Cary . . . it really is us now."

"Cole," Riley whispered, "I don't have anyone left. My grandfather, Grandmam Billie . . . my mother and father."

"I know what you're trying to say here, Riley, but you're wrong. You have Ivy and Moss. Hell, you're the perfect brother. You have all these ditzy aunts coming out of the woodwork, and you have all the Colemans. You said it before—family is what counts. It's all coming full circle. Grandmam Billie says life does that. Your grandfather and Grandmam Billie—they did their best to make it right for us. It's up to us now. We can handle it, Riley, I know we can. While we're in Texas, we are going to unite our families spiritually and financially. From this moment on we are—"

"One family," Riley said in a hushed whisper.

"One family," Cole agreed.

"In alphabetical order," Riley said airily.

"Now why did I know you were going to say that?"

"Coleman-Hasegawa Enterprises. I like that."

"I do too," Cole said.

CHAPTER SEVEN

The trees with their budding spring foliage rustled softly in the early morning air. Two plump birds sat atop the barbecue grill, tussling over a fat worm. Inside, peering between the chintz kitchen curtains, Rand watched with interest. He noticed that the bird feeders, placed strategically around the small yard, were empty. He wondered whose job it was to fill them—Ferris's or Susan's? Before he left, he would check the garage to see if there was any seed, and if there wasn't, he'd go to the nearest feed store and buy some. Nobody, human or animal, should have to fight for food, he thought.

Rand turned from the window to survey the tidy kitchen. He loved kitchens. His adopted mother Amelia loved kitchens too. All the Colemans loved kitchens. Kitchens were like nesting places, warm and cozy, where families gathered to eat together, to share their day. He liked Susan's little clay pots on the extra wide windowsill. He leaned over and sniffed. Mint, thyme, parsley, and rosemary. The same herbs Maggie had on their windowsill at home. It must be something sisters did.

The sun would be up in a few minutes, and if it was going to be a nice day, the kitchen would flood with light and warmth. His eye swiveled to the huge Mickey Mouse clock on the wall, and he laughed silently to himself. Susan must have hung the clock for Jessie, to try and teach her how to tell time. Or she hung it for the child in herself. Suddenly he wanted to know why the Mickey Mouse clock was in the kitchen. He stored the question in his mind. When the proper time presented itself, he would ask his sister-in-law.

Time to start breakfast. He realized he was ravenous. As he rinsed the coffeepot and added fresh grounds, he thought about the reasons he was here and what he hoped to accomplish. Two days to pay the outstanding bills and have the phone turned back on. Two days to have Susan's car serviced and filled with gas. Two days to buy a few groceries and pack Susan's belongings in the three large traveling cases in the attic. One case alone was full of sheet music, old contracts, brochures, and playbills.

When he heard the first plop of the percolator, Rand added strips of bacon to the frying pan. He'd just finished whipping the fluffy yellow mixture in the bowl when Valentine padded into the kitchen dressed in a thick, sky-blue terry robe with a matching towel on her head. She looked about sixteen, Rand thought.

"What'll it be, scrambled eggs or pancakes?"

"Both. Lots of bacon and three pieces of toast. I like to dip my toast in coffee. Soft butter, and by any chance do you have strawberry jelly?"

"No, but we have apple butter," Rand said, expertly flipping the bacon.

"Sounds good," Val said, lighting a cigarette. "You do that like a pro."

"I always make breakfast on the weekends for Maggie. In the beginning, she'd make me do it over and over till I got it right. One time I used up four dozen eggs till I got them scrambled just the way she likes

them. You should see my pancakes. They're so light
they almost float."

Val laughed as she poured herself a cup of coffee, then sat back down. "In the scheme of things, I'd
say that's pretty important."

Rand laid the crisp bacon on paper towels to drain,
washed the frying pan and added butter just the way
Maggie taught him. She didn't like the little specks of bacon that were in the eggs when you fried them in bacon
grease. He searched for bowls for the pancake mix. With
his head in the cabinet under the sink, he muttered, "You
can use the car. I'm going to be stuck here all day waiting
for the realtor who didn't show up yesterday."

His glance lingered on her for a moment. She looked
cute, he thought, with cold cream all over her face.
Cute, for God's sake. How could a legal barracuda be
cute? Yet he couldn't help but wonder what she had on
under that thick robe. The thought tormented him, and
he replaced it in his mind with a picture of Maggie.

"If everything goes okay," he said, "I think I can
leave tomorrow. I'm going to fly on to Texas. What
about you?"

"I think I'm about ready to make my move today too.
I have a few phone calls to finish up, and then I have
to go over to the bank and wait for some faxed papers
I need from a friend of mine."

"How do you think it looks for Susan?" Rand asked.

"Susan will do fine. Why shouldn't she, as long as
we fight her battles for her? I mean, this is the second
time we've bailed her out and I would be surprised if
it's the last. She's forty-eight, Rand, time enough for
her to have gotten herself together. I can understand
why *I'm* here. I'm the family lawyer. But you? You're
putting the house up for sale; you're closing out bank

accounts with ten dollar balances, serving a car that's ready to fall apart, shopping for groceries, and packing up Susan's belongings. For God's sake, you even called a used furniture dealer to give you an offer on the contents of this house. Susan should be doing all this herself. And don't tell me how she's a creative talent and creative people aren't like the rest of us. That's bullshit, Rand, and you know it."

Rand stiffened. Val was only saying aloud what he had been thinking since his arrival. Still, he felt obligated to defend Susan. "For God's sake, her only daughter died. That has to be the worst thing in the world for a mother. This thing with Ferris made it a double blow. You don't bounce back from something like that overnight."

"Of course you don't. But you don't run away from it either. Running solves nothing. Susan should be here, fighting for herself." She got up to pour herself a refill.

"I offered to come here."

"To make things easy for her. Everyone makes it easy for her. Somewhere deep inside, Susan knows everyone else will make things right for her, and after a suitable period of time, she'll go right back to her old patterns. She's not stable, Rand."

"What do you think we should do? Everyone isn't as tough as you, Val. There are certain things Susan just wouldn't be willing to do to get what she wants." The moment he said the words, he wished he hadn't. Val looked as if she had been slapped. "God, I'm sorry. You know I didn't meant that."

Val blinked. "Yes, you did." She lit a cigarette. "I offend you, don't I? You've made a judgment about me—or at least my morals. You'd prefer me to be more like Susan—irresponsible, weak, someone who needs you to help her out all the time. Well, I'm a survivor, Rand. I survive no matter what it takes, no matter what I have to do, and whatever that makes me, I'm still the one you come to when you have to pull your sister-in-law's chestnuts out of the fire. So don't you ever, *ever* judge me, *Lord* Rand Nelson. Now, where the hell is my breakfast? On second thought, don't bother, I'll eat out." She ran from the kitchen, the terry robe flapping about her ankles.

Now what was that all about? Rand asked himself as he dumped the eggs in the frying pan; he didn't know what else to do with them. He gagged with the smell of burned butter and looked around helplessly before he threw the mess into the sink. A cloud of smoke rushed up from the toaster. The smoke alarm went off at the same time. He rushed to open the window and then the door. "Son of a bitch!"

He reached down for Val's cigarette, which was still in the ashtray. He brought it to his mouth and puffed furiously. The smoke alarm was still shrieking. In a fit of something he couldn't define, he unplugged the toaster, picked it up and pitched it out the back door. It landed with a loud thwack on the concrete patio. A flock of crows took wing, squawking angrily.

"Goddamnit!" With the cigarette between his lips, he climbed onto one of the kitchen chairs and yanked at the smoke alarm. He ripped it from the ceiling. The sudden silence roared in his ears. He climbed off the chair and slammed the kitchen door shut so hard that the glass in the multiframe cracked. "Oh shit!"

Val's voice was soft, just short of apologetic, when she appeared in the doorway. She looked, Rand thought, gorgeous. She also looked like the professional she was. Her suit was the same Pacific-blue as the ocean back home. She wore a trim white blouse, and at her throat an antique brooch. Her makeup was flawless, her hair perfection. The only thing missing, Rand thought, was the sparkle in her eyes.

"I should be back by four," she said, "no later. I'll drop the car off and call a taxi to take me to the airport."

"Val—"

"I'll be sending you the balance of the old family retainer when I wind things up here. I think it's best if we sever our ties when I wrap this up. You can find a lawyer you approve of."

"Val . . . I'm sorry. What happened here? One minute everything was fine, and then, bam, you're resigning from . . . what the hell *is* it you're doing?"

"I don't want to work for you or your damn family anymore, Rand. You obviously don't respect me, but you're perfectly willing to use me for your own ends."

"Use you? It works two ways, you know. You use the family too. It sure didn't hurt your practice to say you were the family lawyer. With the money we paid you, you started up your own firm." He sounded too defensive. Why is that? he wondered.

Val threw her hands in the air. "Truce." She affected a smile. "Have a good day, and try to get the smell of burnt toast out of the house. The realtor won't like it."

A moment later she was gone, with a flash of leg. Rand felt a strong urge to run after her, but dug his heels into the carpet. At that moment he would have done anything in his power to wipe the vulnerable look from Val's face.

The bank was almost empty when Val walked in. She headed straight for the president's office. Her smile when the balding bank officer looked up was of the five hundred watt variety. Her handshake was firm, and her eyes even twinkled when the president held her hand a moment longer than necessary. She kept right on twinkling as she scanned the papers he was handing her one by one. When the stack of faxed papers grew to forty-five, she raised her head and said, "This is all sooo wonderful. I can't thank you enough, Harry, for being so kind to me. This is just what I need. I really appreciate the use of your fax machine."

"My pleasure, dear lady. Here we believe in service, even if you aren't a customer. I'm sorry though to hear that Mrs. Armstrong is relocating. Very talented woman. Her husband is so well thought of here in the community." He let his voice trail off when he realized what the attorney was holding in her hands. "Of course my lips are sealed."

Val waved a playful finger. "I know where to come if word does leak out." She smiled the five hundred watt smile again.

"Mrs. Armstrong is a very nice lady," the bank officer said limply.

"Thank you again, Harry. Perhaps the next time I find myself in your little town, we can have lunch."

"I'd like that, Miss Mitchell. If I can be of further service, don't hesitate to call."

"Oh, I won't."

Every eye in the bank followed Valentine's exit.

Her next stop was a drugstore on Main Street, where she called Dr. Ferris Armstrong's office and requested a consultation appointment. She said her name was Linda Baker and she was referred by the chief of staff at the hospital. She managed to use the word urgent three times in as many minutes. She smiled when the young voice said Dr. Armstrong could fit her in at eleven-fifteen.

Brody's was an old-fashioned drugstore with a counter, stools, and soda fountain. Danish, English muffins, and corn muffins sat on a lace doily under a plastic dome. Old-fashioned sugar bowls with silver spoons dotted the long counter. It smelled wonderful, Val thought. She perched on a stool and looked at her reflection in the mirror behind the service station. She could see containers of egg salad, tuna salad, and plates of greens and tomatoes behind a glass display case. Probably for the luncheon trade. A huge coffee urn with a real spigot brought a smile to her face. The milk pitcher was pink Depression glass. It was pretty. "Coffee and toast, cream cheese on the side," she said to the waitress in the yellow uniform with brown-and-white-checkered apron. Val assumed she was the pharmacist's wife, and gave voice to the thought.

"Yes, I'm Mrs. Brody. I haven't seen you around here before, have I?"

"No, I'm here on business. I was in a drugstore like this once a long time ago," Val said softly. "It has character; I like that."

"Well, we've lived here all our lives. Our customers are comfortable with things the way they are. Change . . . we're too old to change. There's one of those bright, shiny all-night drugstores out on the highway. Prescriptions are higher out there," Mrs. Brody said, pursing her mouth into a round O of disapproval. "We carry everything that's needed, but not a whole bunch of different brands. We sell only what our people want. We give credit too, and I don't mean credit cards. Not many drugstores do that anymore."

"That's important," Val said, biting into her toast. "Do you have cherry phosphates?"

"We certainly do, and lemon squeezes too."

"No!"

"Yes we do."

"I want one of each," Val said happily. "I want some of that penny candy too. One of each. How can you sell it for a penny?" she asked curiously.

"It's for the children. Most of the time we just give it to them. The little ones come in with their pennies, and it's just a joy to see them take a candy stick and lick it. Mr. Brody and myself never had any children. We didn't put the candy crocks there to make money."

"Do you know Dr. and Mrs. Armstrong?" Val asked quietly.

"Very well. It was a shame about little Jessie. She liked the lemon sticks the best. Mrs. Armstrong was always in here, at least once or twice a week. After Jessie passed away, she would still come in and take a lemon stick. She never bought more than toothpaste or shampoo after . . . She had so many prescriptions to fill for the little girl. It was very sad."

Val nodded. "Does Dr. Armstrong come in?"

"Once in a while. He sends all his prescriptions here. He usually buys pipe tobacco and sometimes candy mints. I haven't seen him for a while now, or Mrs. Armstrong either. Are they friends of yours?"

"I know Mrs. Armstrong quite well. I've met Dr. Armstrong on several occasions. What *is* that smell?" Val asked, sniffing the air about her. "Wait, don't tell me." Her eyes fixed on the frosted flowers on the mirror behind the counter. "It's lemon juice, Max Factor powder, pipe tobacco, and fresh ground coffee." She rolled her eyes as she dusted the crumbs from her fingers.

Mrs. Brody smiled.

Val fished in her purse and laid a five dollar bill on the counter. "Keep the change, Mrs. Brody." She swiveled around on the stool to survey the drugstore. She liked the old oak cabinets with the glass doors and wooden shelves. It was all so tidy and neat, with the toothpaste stacked alongside bottles of mouthwash and dental floss. Everything was aligned according to size and color. Remarkable, she thought.

"Do you make black and white sodas in those old-fashioned glasses, and bananas splits in the boat dishes?"

"We do, and the ice cream is homemade by Wilbur Laskin down at the ice house," Mrs. Brody said proudly.

"I might be back for one of each," Val said, sliding off the stool.

"We'll be here till six."

Val nodded.

The tinkle of the bell over the door when Val closed it brought a tear to her eye, though she didn't know why. She'd been traveling in the fast lane for so long, she had forgotten what small-town America was like. She wiped at the lone tear as she settled herself in the car. She lit a cigarette as she studied the papers the bank president had given her.

Forty minutes later Val rolled the papers into a tight cylinder. She snapped the rubber band into place. "Gotcha, Dr. Armstrong!"

The car in gear, Val drove off through the town of Oxmoor. Two blinks of the eye and she was on the outskirts where the hospital sat nestled behind a backdrop of tall, feathery pines. It was pretty, Val thought, just like the town. Small-town living, no matter how gracious and neighborly it was, simply wasn't for her. She liked city lights, fashionable stores, sleek cars, and good-looking men. "To each his own," she muttered as she parked the car at the far side of the hospital.

Ferris Armstrong's office was on the second floor of the seventy-five-bed hospital, the receptionist told Val.

The waiting room of Ferris's office was cute. Cute because Ferris was a pediatrician. Everything, including the chairs, was geared to children. Bright colors, hand-painted pictures, puzzle carpets, and sturdy toys littered the room. A huge bowl of lollipops sat on a low table with a sign that said ONE EACH. Two little boys, dressed in bib overalls, sat on the carpeted floor playing with checkers as big as dinner plates. Cute.

"Linda Baker. I have an appointment," Val said quietly.

"Come with me," the nurse said, motioning Val to follow her. She was young. Was she the *other* woman?

"I like your suit," the young woman said, eyeing Val from the top of her head to the tips of her shoes. "Did you get it at Mason's?"

Val quirked an eyebrow. "Hardly. It's a Scaasi."

"Oh," was all the nurse said. Val noticed that the heel of her right shoe was run-down and there was a run in her stocking.

Valentine stood by the window and stared down into the parking lot. She had counted thirty-two cars in the lot when Ferris Armstrong walked through the door. The moment Val heard the door close, she turned and smiled.

"Val?" Ferris's eyes dropped to the clipboard in his

hand. "Are you the Linda Baker here for a consultation?" he asked stonily.

"No. I'm not Linda Baker. You look well, Ferris. I'll bet it's been at least five years since we've seen each other."

He was handsome. He had a light, even tan—a sun lamp probably—and he was tall and trim, athletic-looking. The gray at his temples made him seem distinguished, especially in combination with the white surgical coat. His sky-blue stethoscope was wrapped halfway around his neck. It matched his eyes perfectly. She almost laughed aloud.

"What can I do for you, Val?" Ferris asked tightly.

She reached into her purse and withdrew the cylinder of papers. When she held them out to Ferris, he backed up a step. Her laughter tinkled around the brightly decorated room. "It's not a subpoena. Take it, Ferris. It's not even a summons. Come on, a big boy like you, a doctor and all, don't tell me you're afraid of me. Actually, in a manner of speaking, these papers belong to you and your wife. I'm more or less delivering your own property to you." Her tone changed to hard-edged steel. "Look at them. In fact, sit down and read them through. I can wait." She was pleased to see Ferris's hand shake as he reached out to take the papers. She was also pleased to see how jerkily he walked. Rather like a puppet on straw legs.

"My income tax records, so what!" Ferris said coldly.

"Not exactly," Val said in a teasing voice. "What you have there are *amended* tax returns, not the originals your accountant gave to Susan. However, the amended returns *do* carry my client's signature." She clucked her tongue. "Or rather, my client's forged signatures. To the IRS. Shame on you, Ferris. All those assets. My oh my.

I had no idea a pediatrician made that kind of money. It almost makes me think I'm in the wrong profession. Now, let's sit down and talk about how much it's going to cost you to make all this go away."

"How much?" Ferris croaked hoarsely.

"Make me an offer," Val drawled, lighting a cigarette. She blew a cloud of smoke in Ferris's direction.

"Five hundred thousand."

Val laughed.

"Seven hundred fifty thousand."

Val giggled.

"Okay, seven hundred fifty thousand and the house in the islands."

Val shook her head. "Think about the word 'forgery.' Then couple that with the initials IRS. Try again."

"Half the bonds. Half the stocks."

"No way."

"One million."

"Sorry."

"How much is it going to take?"

"You figure out what your ass is worth, Doctor. In jail they don't have any little kids to administer to. What's your life here on the outside worth to you? Personally, I don't think much of a man who can't make it on his own and has to steal from a woman. I'll give you one more shot at an acceptable offer. If it isn't agreeable, I'll walk out of here, notify my friends at the IRS, and by six o'clock you'll be on the Oxmoor news. Oh, I also know what you earn in a year. I factored in what you might have invested during the past five years and have a number at my disposal."

Val watched the pediatrician wilt. She'd seen other men fall apart, but Ferris made it an art form. "Okay."

"Okay, let's do it now. Don't think for one minute

I'm going to give you a chance to split. We'll go together to the bank. There's a notary there. For a small fee, one of Harry's secretaries can type up a general release. You know the one, from the beginning of time to the end of time ... I'll want the title to the Porsche. You can have the other car. Rand can drive the Porsche back to Texas."

"You're only leaving me with a heap of a car, a shitbox of a house, and a hundred thousand dollars in savings," Ferris sputtered.

"That's right," Val singsonged. "And you're out of the foundation."

"You're a goddamn bitch!" Ferris seethed.

"I'll take that as a compliment."

Ferris shrugged out of his white surgical coat and slipped into a cashmere jacket. Val commented on the jacket, and Ferris, ignoring her, stormed out of his office. Val sauntered out behind him.

"Dr. Armstrong, what about your patients?" the nurse asked fretfully.

Val leaned over the desk and whispered. "He's just had some very bad news. Have his associate cover for him. I don't think Dr. Armstrong will be back in the office today."

It was three o'clock when Val walked into Susan's house. Rand was watching "General Hospital" when she dropped a manila folder into his lap. "It's done. I gave him this house, so if you put it on the market, you'll have to take it off. He called it a shitbox, so I thought it was worth giving up. I gave him the car out front and told him you'd drive the Porsche back to Texas. The rest is self-explanatory. Your sister-in-law is now a wealthy woman."

Rand was on his feet. He tossed the envelope on the floor. "Val, wait."

"Sorry, Rand, I want to change, pack, and get to the airport on time. Some other time, okay?" she called over her shoulder.

"Don't you want something to eat, a cup of coffee?"

"I had toast, a cherry phosphate, a lemon squeeze, a black and white soda, a banana split, and three peppermint sticks. I'm not hungry," she called from the top steps. "I might be able to gulp down a cup of coffee, though, if you make it snappy."

Rand raced into the kitchen, stopping long enough to pick up the folder. If Val took half as long as Maggie to change, dress, and pack, he figured he had a good fifteen minutes. He measured out the coffee, filled the percolator, slopping water and loose coffee grounds all over the counter. He wiped at them with the sleeve of his shirt.

While the coffee perked, he spread the contents of the envelope out on the kitchen table. He whistled shrilly, his eyebrows nearly meeting his hairline at what he saw. Whatever Val had charged was worth it. Hell, he'd double her fee. No, by God, he wouldn't pay it. Susan would pay it, and he'd tell her to double it, whatever it turned out to be. Val was right, it was time Susan started to stand on her own two feet.

Rand sucked in his breath when he saw Val standing in the kitchen doorway. She had on jeans, sneakers, and a Greenpeace sweatshirt. Her face was bare of makeup and her hair was tied in a knot on top of her head. He cleared his throat and handed her a mug of coffee.

She smelled like a flower garden.

She looked gorgeous, stunning.

She goddamn *sizzled*.

Val reached into her purse for a cigarette. She made a production of lighting it, then blew a perfect smoke ring. As Rand watched it circle overhead, he felt a ring of heat around his own neck. "You shouldn't smoke so much," he said gruffly.

"I shouldn't do a lot of things. But I *do* get the job done, don't I?"

The slow heat Rand felt around his neck crept up to his face. "I'm impressed. I hope you didn't break any laws."

"If you're worried there will be some heat," she said coolly, "don't worry. Speaking of heat, Rand, your face is flushed. Are you coming down with a bug? Or is something else bothering you?"

"Nothing's bothering me. I said I'd drive you to the airport. There's no reason for you to take a taxi. Why are you being so stubborn?"

"Stubborn? It's silly for you to drive me to the airport and then come all the way back here. I told Dr. Armstrong you'd drive Susan's car over there late this afternoon and pick up the Porsche. That's more important than driving me to the airport. I'm a big girl, Rand. My training wheels came off a long time ago. Besides," she said, "I no longer work for the Colemans, so I'd rather you not do me any favors."

"One thing, Val. How do I explain all this to the family? God only knows what they're going to think. You've been with them for a very long time. At least reconsider your position."

"Don't have to. My mind's made up. I never back down, I never compromise, and I never look back. Give my regards to your family."

Rand's tone grew hard. "Who did you have to sleep

with to get amended copies of Ferris's income tax records?"

Val remained cool. She took a final puff from her cigarette, then tamped it out in the sink. "To reiterate, I don't work for you or your family anymore, and furthermore, it's simply none of your business."

"Maybe I don't like the things you do to get the job done." God, did he really say that aloud? The look on her face clearly said he came through loud and clear.

"Why not? I seem to recall *your* having a torrid affair with Sawyer before you dumped her for her mother. And then we all came to find out you slept your way across England—and that's by your admission—and you have a daughter you never even saw until just recently. You know what I think your problem is? I think you still find yourself attracted to me and don't know what to do about it." She laughed then, a sad, vulnerable sound. "You really thought I was going to come on to you, didn't you? You were going to have such noble fun rejecting me so you could go home with a pure heart and clean hands, right?"

"To a certain degree," Rand said tightly.

"What part is right?" She was suddenly curious. She stuffed her hands into her jeans and rocked back on her heels.

"The part about me being attracted to you."

"That's flattering. Every woman likes to hear a compliment. But I've been around the block. I can't believe we're having this conversation. Look, I really have to go. If I ever find myself in Hawaii, perhaps we could have lunch. And Rand, for what it's worth, I'm attracted to you too."

"Val, don't go," Rand said quietly.

"Rand, I don't knowingly mess around with other women's husbands."

"But you do parade around in front of them before breakfast wearing nothing but a bathrobe and cold cream."

The sudden pain in his shins felt like a mule kick. He saw the swinging purse and ducked. He also saw the tears streaming down Val's cheeks. He heard the taxi horn at the same time.

She was in his arms then, blubbering against his shirt front. She smelled sweet and clean, like Ivory soap and lavender. He knew it was lavender because his mother used to line the dresser drawers back in England with real English lavender. He swayed dizzily as he stroked Val's head, crooning words of comfort. Maggie never cried.

"There's a real person in there, isn't there? One who has feelings and passions but is afraid to show them for fear of being rejected and hurt."

Val sniffed and nodded. "How would you know about being vulnerable and feeling hurt?" she asked.

"Men aren't supposed to show that side of themselves, but I'll tell you a secret, Val. Sometimes I just want to go into a corner and howl. I get so damned tired of being someone's extension, someone's reason for living. Sometimes I want to chuck it all and be a beach bum. I suppose it's what the slick magazines refer to as mid-life crisis."

"You're just feeling your mortality," Val said softly. "You want to do things, experience feelings now because you've realized the future isn't forever. I looked that square in the face a while back. We're the same age, Rand."

"I know," he said, wiping the tears from her cheeks. "I think the taxi left; the horn stopped blowing."

Val took a step back, shivering inside the Greenpeace sweatshirt.

Rand ran a finger around the inside of his shirt collar. "Look, let's go pick up the Porsche and come back here and have dinner. We'll build a fire, open a bottle of wine, and curl up on the floor and talk. How does that sound?"

"Premeditated."

Rand laughed. "I like the sound of that."

He felt like a kid again as he scampered from the house, hot on Val's sneaker-clad heels. He wondered if she took aerobic classes. He asked.

Val gurgled with laughter as she settled herself in the front seat of the car. "No time. I have a fully equipped gym at the office and one at home. I'm lucky if I walk on my treadmill once a week. Aerobics take up a great deal of time. Does Maggie take classes?"

They shouldn't be talking about Maggie, he thought. He shouldn't be thinking about Maggie either. "She takes a two-hour class every day. She swims three times a day. She walks two miles a day in wet sand. That's a workout in itself. She stays in shape. She eats very sensibly and gets eight hours' sleep a night."

"Hey, I didn't ask for a dissertation," Val said coolly.

"I guess it did sound like one, didn't it?"

"Maggie is going to be fifty." Now, where the hell did *that* come from? Rand wondered.

"Whoah, Rand. I think I'm missing something here. Is there a rule somewhere that says we have to talk about Maggie and air all that stuff? I don't think it's a good idea. And just as a point of reference, I'm fifty-four years old. That makes me four years older than your wife. And you, being the astute man that I know you are, should know the grass is not always greener on the other side of the fence. It's a tired old cliché, Rand, but very appropriate in this instance."

They drove for a while in silence. "You're being very blasé about all this," Rand finally said as he swerved into the hospital parking lot. He drove slowly up and down the aisles, looking for a Porsche.

"If I'm blasé, it's because dinner and sharing confidences are okay in my book. As far as I'm concerned, we're just friends spending an evening together."

"Now why did I know the Porsche was going to be red, and why did I know Ferris was going to have a vanity license plate that said 'Doc'?"Rand muttered as he ground to a stop alongside the foreign car.

"Because," Val said seriously, "men are little boys, and little boys are predictable." She climbed out of the car and walked around the apple-red Porsche.

"I don't know if Susan can drive a stick shift," Rand said.

"She'll learn."

"You really don't like Susan, do you? Do you like Maggie?"

"The truth?"

Rand nodded.

"Not really. I absolutely adored Amelia, and I'm very fond of Billie. Sawyer is my kind of girl. She's got chutzpah. I don't like what you did to her, and neither did Amelia or Billie."

"Jesus. Would it have been better for me to marry Sawyer when I didn't love her? In any case, goddamnit, it wasn't the way you seem to think. It was over between Sawyer and myself before I fell in love with

Maggie. If you know a way to be kind in a situation like that, I'd like to hear it."

Val shrugged. "So you say."

"Okay," Rand said quietly, "let's scratch this whole scene."

They settled down into the bucket seats, and after pulling out of the lot, Rand set the car careening down a country road. "Are you still up for some wine?" he asked.

"I'd prefer beer. Coors Light. Wine makes me weak in the elbows."

"You know," he ventured, "now that business is settled, you could ride to Texas with me. If you don't have something to rush back to, that is. Or, of course, there's an early morning flight."

"I'll think about it. I still have a few days to call my own. And I should warn you, I hate car trips. Now, what about dinner? All I really had to eat today was a bunch of sugar. I'm getting hungry."

"There's a lot of food in the freezer and there's beer in the garage. I saw it, so I guess we don't have to stop anywhere. Although technically, we're staying in Ferris's house."

"Oh, Rand, didn't you pay any attention to the papers I gave you? I tacked three days on to the house just in case. I didn't know when you would want to leave. I wasn't sure if you packed all of Susan's personal belongings. What about the attic?"

"I didn't think about the attic," Rand said, slapping at his forehead.

"And the little girl's room?"

"I meant to ask you about that. Everything is still there. The dolls, the toys, the clothes in the drawers and closets. I called last night, but the cook said Maggie left for Texas with Susan. I tried calling the house this morning, and there was no answer. Maybe we should pack all the things in boxes, label them, and send them on to . . . where? Texas? Hawaii?"

"What's that *we* stuff, Rand? I'm not packing up Susan's things, which I guess answers your earlier question. I'll be taking the early morning flight since your packing isn't finished. You look relieved," Val added, an edge to her voice.

Relieved wasn't the half of it. For a little while there he'd been temporarily insane with wild imaginings. He felt lightheaded when he climbed from the car, glad that his decision were made for him. As soon as they ate, he'd start packing. Val could watch television and do whatever lawyers did in their free time.

"Who does dinner?" Val asked as she followed Rand into the house.

"I'll flip you. Call it."

"Tails." Val grinned.

Rand flipped a quarter. "You win. Call me when it's ready. I'm going up to the attic."

The phone that had been reconnected at noon took that moment to shrill to life. He reached past Val to pick it up. He knew before he spoke that it would be Maggie. He noticed Val discreetly withdraw from the kitchen. Her absence didn't change his careful tone of voice. He thought about Cary then, and how angry he'd been when Cary had confessed his infidelity.

"What's wrong, Rand?" Maggie asked sharply. He'd never heard her sound this particular way before. "Rand, I need to . . . there's been a terrible accident. Cary's in the hospital. It . . . it's serious. I had Susan call early this morning to have the phone reconnected so I could talk with you. You should be here . . . everyone should be here . . . You aren't saying anything. Why is that, Rand? What's wrong?"

"Wrong? Nothing is wrong. What happened to Cary? What kind of accident? How serious is serious?"

"I only know what Thad told us, which isn't much. Cary's eyes have been severely damaged and he has some bad burns. Mam . . . I need you here, Rand," Maggie said tightly.

"Maggie, listen to me. I'll come home as soon as I can. Look, I don't want to come back here so let me finish up and I'll leave first thing in the morning. If there was something I could do for Cary I'd leave in a heartbeat, you know that." He thought again about Cary's infidelity and didn't know why.

"You sound strange," Maggie said.

"Well, Jesus, Maggie, you just handed me some bad news. How the hell am I supposed to sound? I'm sure if your mother is there things are under control."

"What have you been doing all day? I tried calling earlier."

It wasn't his imagination, Maggie's voice was . . . so down right cold it could chill milk. His eyebrows shot back toward his hairline. "Is there something you aren't telling me?"

"We'll talk when you get here. You still didn't tell me where you were earlier."

"I just picked up the Porsche. Everything is okay on this end with the exception of one thing: What do I do about little Jessie's things? And the stuff in the attic?" He quickly gave her a rundown on Val's day, his voice edgy and cool sounding to his ears.

"I knew Val would come through. I'm glad for Susan's sake. I bet she'll bill us up the kazoo."

"Does that bother you?" Rand asked tightly.

"No. She's worth every penny we pay her. Dudley Abramson says she's the best in the business. I hope you didn't work her to death."

"I don't think so. She's leaving in the morning. She missed her flight this afternoon. She agreed to make dinner, and I'm going to finish the packing. She refused to help."

"At three fifty an hour, I should hope so."

"I thought you liked Val."

"I think she's a fine attorney. I would never hire anyone else. She's just a little too loose and flashy for my taste. Will you be on the same flight as Val?"

"No, I'm going to drive the Porsche back to Texas. Tell me more about Cary."

"He has some burns and he's . . . his eyes were severely injured. That's the bad news. The good news is there's no optic nerve damage. But there's something else, Rand. It's Mam . . . she's ill. All this time we thought she and Thad were traveling, well, they weren't. She was in Vermont undergoing chemotherapy. She has cancer. She didn't want any of us to know. She looks so . . . so different. Susan is behaving like a real witch. Sawyer is here too. Riley and Cole are on their way as we speak. I need you, Rand." Maggie began to sob. "I can't handle this. Rand, say something. Say anything, but talk to me."

"Maggie, I'm sorry about Billie. Truly sorry. I'll be there as soon as I can." He wished he could tell his wife to mix herself a drink, but he couldn't. Maggie hadn't touched alcohol for many years.

Rand looked around the brightly lit kitchen as though seeing it for the first time. Should he leave now and forget about packing Susan's things? Or should he work through the night and leave first thing in the morning?

He could fly back to Texas with Val. He would have to make arrangements for someone else to drive the Porsche, or he could simply park it at the airport lot in long-term parking and hope for the best. Suddenly he hated the Porsche and Susan. He said so to his wife. He listened to the choked silence on the other end of the wire and then hung up.

"Rand, what's wrong? Your face is as white as your knuckles," Val said quietly. He told her.

Val digested the information. She felt a shiver run through her. Billie Coleman Kingsley wasn't *that* old. For some reason, she'd never really thought of Billie as a Coleman, even though she carried the name. Billie was Billie. In her own quiet way, Billie was the backbone of the Colemans. She felt sad, and for once she couldn't control the emotions on her face.

"This must be very hard for you, Rand. Billie is so like your own mother. I wish I had the right words to say to you now, but I don't."

Val stepped away from Rand when she thought he was going to reach out to her. *That* she couldn't handle right now. "Look, I'll make some grilled cheese sandwiches and then I'll help you with the packing. I know I said I wasn't going to do it, but things have changed. We can fly home together. In the scheme of things, that damn car has suddenly lost its importance. So what if someone rips it off? It's insured. All it will take is one phone call in the morning from the airport to the insurance company, and we can fax anything they need when we get home. If we get everything packed up tonight, we can call one of those twenty-four-hour eight hundred numbers in the Yellow Pages and the boxes can be picked up tomorrow sometime."

Rand fretfully combed his hair with his fingers. The

hand that came to rest on his arm was soft and gentle. He looked down through the mist in his eyes.

"I know what you're thinking and what you're feeling," Val said quietly. "It's not the end of the world. I seem to remember that you thought you weren't going to make it when your mother died. We spoke at the funeral. Perhaps you don't remember because of your grief. Life goes on, Rand. Billie . . . she could . . . there's every possibility she could live a long time. They come up with new drugs and procedures every day. The Colemans are a tough bunch. I know you aren't a Coleman, but you *belong*. Someone is going to have to hold them all together, and that someone is you. Cary can't. Thad . . . Thad is going to need you. All of them are going to need you. Riley especially. From what Ivy told me the last time we spoke, he still hasn't come to terms with his grandfather's death. This will be such a blow to him. Cole is very close to Billie. You're the one, Rand. You'll have to hold it all together for them."

"According to Maggie," he said, "Susan is going off the deep end. Sawyer . . . Sawyer will bluster her way through and trample anyone who gets in her way. How do I deal with *that*?"

"Tell Susan to grow up and act like the woman she is. As for Sawyer—you're on your own there. Adam will reel her in and be there for her. He's got a level head. I think you can count on Adam."

Rand placed both hands on Val's shoulders and looked down into her eyes. She had pretty eyes without all the makeup she usually wore. "How'd you get so smart?"

"I don't belong, so I can be objective. It's the lawyer in me."

"You still planning on dumping the family?" His tone was curious.

"Yep."

"Reconsider," Rand said.

"No."

He was too close, she thought, so close she could smell the faint scent of his after-shave. She could also see the late afternoon shadow of his beard. She tensed beneath his fingers. She knew without a doubt that if she took him by the hand and led him to one of the upstairs bedrooms, she could . . . She shook her head. "I'm hungry, and you need to go to the attic and . . . and do whatever you have to do. I'll call you when dinner is ready." She jerked her shoulders free. A moment later, Rand was gone. She could hear his footsteps overhead.

The urge to cry was so strong, Val opened the freezer door and stuck her head inside. The sharp, cold air restored her self-control. It occurred to her that she might be having a hot flash when she yanked her head back out. Maybe she should have cried. Crying was better than the warm flush she was experiencing. Stress, the doctor had told her months ago, could often bring on the hated hot flashes.

She worked automatically, taking food from the refrigerator and freezer, working the microwave and setting the table. Her thoughts refused to be still. For the first time in years she wasn't able to separate her emotions from the business at hand. Her own desire was suddenly clear to her: she wanted to go to bed with Rand. Wanted to see what it was like to make love with someone she really liked, someone she chose. She thought about all the men she'd slept with and the reasons she'd slept with them. She cringed when she remembered the sagging potbellies, the hairless heads, the kinky things she'd done. So many times she'd asked herself, honestly, if she'd be where she was if she hadn't done the things she felt she had to do to get ahead. The answer was always an honest no. No, she wouldn't have gotten ahead; she wouldn't have her own firm, wouldn't have all the wealth she'd accumulated. She'd never been in love, never borne a child, never had even a halfway serious relationship.

By my choice, she thought bitterly. What good was having all this if she didn't have someone to share it with? And when she died who would she leave *all this* to? Who was going to remember her? Who was going to go to the cemetery and cry for her? Who would *care*? She slapped a piece of Kraft cheese between two slices of frozen bread. The frozen sandwich slid down the counter.

As she rummaged in the oven for a baking pan, she thought about her friends—actually, more acquaintances than friends. All were high-priced, fast-track attorneys like herself. All dressed in fashionable clothes; all of them were eagle-eyed and had razor-sharp minds. Occasionally they lunched, attended the same cocktail parties, cozied up to the same judges. But were they the kind of friends you called up at two in the morning and cried to? Not likely. There were no tears when you worked in a man's world. You just kicked and scratched, clawed and fought, and hoped for the best. She was sick of it. Sick of the families she had on retainer, sick of the whole damn legal profession.

A month ago, possibly longer, she'd received in the mail a bumper sticker from some disgruntled person that read: FIRST OF ALL WE KILL ALL THE LAWYERS. Another time she'd overheard two men in the courthouse

say all lawyers were insignificant lumps of snot. At first
she told herself they didn't mean her. She was a damn
good lawyer and won ninety percent of all her cases.
But then, for weeks afterward, she'd taken a good, hard
look at herself and her profession. That was when the
hot flashes started and her period took a leave of absence. Day after day she shrieked at herself in the bathroom mirror: get out, quit while you're ahead! Move.
Make a real life for yourself. Think about adopting a
child, get a dog.

Val flipped the sandwich over. Burned. She turned
down the flame and prepared another one. She shoved
the Tater Tots, whatever the hell they were, into the
oven, and turned off the stove.

She found a can of Budweiser in the refrigerator, behind a Tupperware container of ground coffee. There
were three more, in case Rand wanted one later. Sipping
from the can, she walked out to the garage and brought
in the twelve-pack sitting on the floor near the garage
door. Was Susan a secret drinker or was this a Ferris
leftover? Back in the kitchen, she set the whole package
in the freezer and made a mental note to take it out and
put it in the refrigerator in twenty minutes.

She thought about Oxmoor then and Brody's drugstore. She *liked* the laid-back, sleepy little town with the
Dixon's hardware store on the corner of Main and Elm.
She liked the multipaned storefronts, especially the flo-
rist shop with its array of spring flowers in the window.
There were no franchises here; everything was indepen-
dently owned, even the tea shop. The library was a
small red-brick building trimmed in white, with tubs of
spring flowers on the steps. And next to the free public
library was the *Oxmoor Sentinel*, a weekly newspaper.

Would she be out of place here in this picture-pretty

little town if she decided to take up residence? Would it be possible to open up a law office and take payment in produce and services? Anything was possible, she told herself. All one had to do was make a decision.

"How's it going?" Val asked when she set the plate in front of Rand.

"I'm about done with the attic. There's nothing up there but junk, and if Susan wants it, she's going to have to come here and do it herself. There was a box of baby clothing I brought down and a box of old playbills from some of Susan's tours. I'm halfway through Jessie's room. I packed the photo albums earlier. There isn't much to pack up so I won't require your help. Does that relieve your mind?"

Val nodded.

Rand bit into the sandwich. "It's good," he said.

Val nodded again.

"You look worlds away, Val."

"Just thinking about where I'll live when I retire."

She began to talk about the town. She told him about the drugstore and how wonderful she thought it was. "The smell was . . . comforting. That's the best way I can describe it to you. Do you know the drugstore I go to has displays of condoms in different colors? Some of them glow in the dark. At Brody's they're probably hidden under the counter."

Rand looked thoughtful. "Do they really glow in the dark?"

Val burst out laughing. The uneasiness between them had disappeared.

"Did you make a fire?" she asked.

"No, but I'm going to do that while you do the dishes. I don't do dishes. I don't do windows either."

"Then what good are you?" Val teased.

"I," Rand said imperiously, "Miss Hotshot Lawyer, am a whiz at a variety of things. If you care to draw me out, I might share some of my secrets with you in front of the fire. I like marshmallows in my hot chocolate."

"I do too, so when you make it, add a few extra to mine. God, I almost forgot the beer." Val was off her chair, pulling the box from the freezer.

"Okay, this is the deal," Val said in her courtroom voice. "I'll clean up and call the moving company. You finish up, make the fire, and I'll pop the beer. There's no hot chocolate. Deal?"

"Deal."

It was fifteen minutes past eight when Val settled herself on a pile of petit point cushions. She flipped on the television. A rerun of "L.A. Law" sprang to view. Val snuggled into her nest of pillows and watched an intense courtroom scene. Her eyes were glued to the set as Grace Van Owen, the prosecuting attorney, grilled a witness. She liked the show, but because of her late hours, she rarely got to watch it. Rand sat down next to her on the floor. A frown crossed her face when the scene changed to the local legal watering hold. Grace was begging her lover, Mickey, to understand why she wouldn't be able to sleep with him for at least five days.

"How real is this show?" Rand asked.

A commercial for an air freshener came on. Val tore her eyes from the screen. "About as real as it goes. When you're prosecuting, or defending a client, you eat, sleep, and drink that case. You leave no stone unturned when it comes to your client's welfare. There are nights when I don't get to bed till two or three in the morning, and then I'm up at five, in the office by six-thirty, and in court by eight."

"You must love it," Rand said.

"I did. I think I'm burned out. I find myself turning most cases over to my associates these days. I oversee everything, though, and that's almost as demanding. I need to get out while I'm still on top. Of course, my saying I'm on top is strictly my own opinion."

"What about financially? Can you afford to pack it in?" Rand asked, curious.

"I've made some wise investments. My bank account is quite healthy. And I can sell my practice. My associates are able, capable attorneys, all handpicked. I might consider doing some consulting work just to keep my hand in."

"So then your decision to sever your relationship with the Colemans doesn't really have anything to do with the family and Susan in particular."

"Yes and no. I *am* sick of the Susans of this world. And I'm tired of the dog-eat-dog world of high-priced attorneys and demanding clients. Maybe it's why I'm thinking of retiring to a small town like this."

"I don't know, Val. It sounds lonely to me."

"I'm used to it. I'm not exactly swimming in companionship now."

"Do you miss not being married?" Rand asked.

"You can't miss something you never had. I suppose you mean the family bit: kids, dogs and cats, the whole nine yards."

"Well, yeah."

"I guess I'd have to say no. You got married late. Did you miss it?"

"Not really. But I think as one gets older one wants the security of marriage."

"Comfort. Familiarity. A nurse for your old age. That surprises me, Rand."

"Oh, why is that?"

"You were always a mover and a shaker. It's hard for me to accept that you live on an island paradise and . . . and just exist."

"I don't just exist," Rand said huffily. "I oversee the refinery."

"And?"

"And what?"

"And you lay in the sun, you play, you laze about. You're at least fifteen pounds heavier than you were the last time I saw you. The good life will do that to you, I guess. What *does* Maggie do?"

What *did* Maggie do? He racked his brain. What the hell did she do? She was always available if he wanted to fly to one of the outer islands; she was always ready to walk on the beach, always available to go out to dinner, always ready to make love. She swam a lot and read a lot. He found himself shrugging. "She's going to take over Billie Limited. I thought I told you that." His ear picked up his defensive tone. He gulped at the last of the beer in his can. "Why, do you have trouble with that?"

"No, I don't. What she does with her life is her business. The same goes for Susan. I can't help wondering, though, how either one of them would have survived out in the world without the Coleman cushion. You too, *Lord Nelson*."

"You're too damn bitter, Val. I could make a gallon of wine from your sour grapes."

Val's eyes sparked, but she held her tongue. She knew she could run rings around Rand, his wife, and his sister-in-law anytime, anywhere. She took a swig of her beer.

Rand added another log to the fire. "I miss the cold sometimes," he said. "I try to come back at least once during the winter months, and when I do, I pray all the way over that there will be snow. I also like fireplaces, like this one."

"I have a fireplace, but I've never used it," Val said. "It's one of those insert things and takes those blue flame logs. The decorator put mirror all around it."

"That sounds god-awful."

"Yeah." Val laughed. "That's why I'm enjoying this one so much. Do you know what I saw in town today? A bookstore. I peeked in. There's this fireplace against one wall, with chairs and a table in front. It's like a nook. They serve coffee and tea, and the book buyers kind of sit around and read half the book before they decide if they're going to buy or not. There was a basket of pinecones on the hearth, and there was a tiger cat snoozing next to the basket. They must have a few local authors around here, because their pictures and their books were on the mantel. Neat, huh?"

"Do you like to read?" Rand asked.

"If I had the time, I'd always have my nose in a book. I cut my teeth reading the Bobbsey Twins and Nancy Drew. God, I would have killed to have a life like Nancy Drew. Remember those old Shirley Temple movies when she was little? I used to eat my heart out over those," Val said, yawning. She thought she was slurring her words. But so what if she was? She wasn't going anywhere. She hadn't had a buzz on for years. She was damn well entitled. She stared into the flames. "Do you ever have regrets about things, you know, the important things in your life?"

Rand thought about it. Did he? Everyone had regrets of one kind or another. He wondered if Val had any.

"Well," she said, "do you?"

Rand sucked at the beer can. "A few. I'm sorry I didn't spend more time with my mother. I'm sorry I came down so hard on Cary when I found out about his affair. He confessed, for God's sake. I'm sorry I hurt Sawyer. I'm sorry I didn't hug Sally Dearest more. . . . She was my stuffed cat when I was little. Does that answer your question?" he asked. "What about you?"

"Nope, not a one. Bet you thought I was going to be riddled with them, huh?"

Damnit, he did think that. She'd bested him. "You're a wise-ass," he said.

"That too. You know what? If someone asked me what I'm proudest of, I'd say . . . Do you have anything you're proud of, Rand?"

"Hell, yes, lots of things."

"Name one," Val challenged.

"I send money to Chesney's mother every month," Rand said defensively.

"*That* doesn't count. You can never make up for all those years with money. You weren't there when she needed you. You have to take responsibility for your actions. Money every month won't cut it, Lord Nelson."

"Stop calling me that. And money *does* count for something. I donate a lot of money to charity."

"And well you should. Those less fortunate deserve help. I'm talking about something big, something that made a difference. You're a man, so I guess you didn't."

"Oh, yeah, what about you, *Lady* Lawyer? What the hell have you done that made a difference?" Rand asked sourly.

"I," Val said, enunciating each word carefully, "marched on Selma. And I attended anti-Vietnam marches on Washington. That's what I'm proudest of."

Rand reached out and put his arm around Val. "You're right, that is something to be proud of." He finished off his beer and reached for the pack he'd brought in with him on the last trip. He yanked at the rings on two cans and handed one to Val. "To Selma and Vietnam."

"I never told anyone before. I don't know why I told you." Val squirmed around so that her face was within an inch of Rand's. "Don't tell anyone, okay? It's like a treasure, just mine, that I pull out and think about from time to time. Please."

"Your secret is safe with me," Rand said solemnly. "You have nice eyes, counselor."

"So do you, my lord," Val said breathlessly. "I think we're drunk. That makes both of us vulnerable. Maybe we should go to bed. You in your bed and me in mine," Val said sleepily.

"It's cold up there. I turned down the thermostat earlier. Why don't we just sleep here by the fire. There's a cover on the couch, one of those knitted things."

"What if the fire goes out?" Val muttered.

"It won't. The grate is one of those fancy things with sides for extra logs. That fire will last four more hours. It's hardwood. Hardwood burns slowly. If we get cold, I'll replenish it."

"I hate to shiver," Val said.

"Me too," Rand said.

"Are you warm now?" Rand asked as he shook out a purple and white afghan.

"Toasty perfect," Val said, snuggling into the crook of Rand's arm. "How about you?"

"Val . . ."

"Yes?"

"Val, I . . ."

"Yes?" Val said, snuggling deeper.

"Maybe this isn't such a good idea."

"Don't worry, I trust you. Be quiet and go to sleep. Do you snore?"

"With gusto. What about you?"

"Women don't snore. Can we go to sleep now? We have to be up early."

"It's just that I've been thinking about us," Rand muttered.

"There is no us, Rand. Get that thought out of your head. You're a married man. That means you have a wife, and husbands aren't supposed to cheat on their wives. Wives say . . . damn, what is it they say?" Val mumbled. She thought she was drunk. She giggled.

"Wives say all kinds of things," Rand said. "All the time. Night and day they say things. They have opinions about everything. Sometimes they don't have opinions and they use their husbands' opinions and turn into clones. What do you think of that observation, Miss Attorney? Brilliant summation, eh?"

"Wives say . . . wives say to their husbands you can look but you can't touch. So look, but don't touch," Val said, her voice suddenly full of inebriated hostility.

Rand frowned. "Now you're mad. What are you so mad about?" Maggie never got mad. Maggie never even pouted.

"Who says I'm mad?" Val said, slurring her words.

"You look mad. You sound mad. I think you're mad at the world. This isn't one of your courtrooms. Unwind, loosen up. How about another beer? We have one left. Or we could open up the wine."

"Wine. We should have candlelight. Wine and candlelight go together."

"That's only if there's going to be a seduction. That would mean," Rand said, struggling for the words he wanted, "you are the seductee and I am the seductor."

"You can get that idea right out of your head, Lord Nelson. You are not going to get in my pants!" Val shrieked.

"Lady Lawyer, that statement dates you. Girls used to say that to me when I was seventeen. What does that mean exactly? How do you get in anyone's pants? It would take me an hour to peel those jeans off you." Rand guffawed and then tittered drunkenly as he slurped at the beer can.

Val wanted to cry and didn't know why. She swung her arm wildly, knocking the beer can out of Rand's hand. Suds shot in the air. "That was a lousy, unkind, nasty thing to say to me. I hate people like you. Get away from me, you're married!" She crawled away, closer to the fire, picking up two of the pillows from the floor and hugging them to her chest. Tears rolled down her cheeks. She sniffled, rubbing her nose on her sweatshirt sleeve.

"You look ugly when you cry," Rand observed. He crawled closer.

Val hiccuped. "I'd rather look ugly than have an ugly heart," Val said. "You have an ugly heart. And I hate that oh so veddy British accent of yours. It's so damn . . . affected. Don't come any closer or I'll . . . I'll . . ."

"What?" Rand blustered. "Tell Maggie? She wouldn't believe you. She loves me. She loves me so much she suffocates me. She's made herself an . . . extension of me. That's true love." He inched closer.

Val inched backward. She was afraid she was losing

control. She didn't like what she was starting to feel. A worm of fear crawled around inside her stomach, which had nothing to do with the alcohol she'd consumed.

"We're crossing over the line, Rand, and I don't like it," Val said. "I'm going upstairs to sleep. I'll strip the bed in the morning. I'll get up early."

Rand's arms snaked out to grab her. She threw the pillow at him as she halfheartedly struggled to get up. She slid backward, then toppled to the floor, holding the remaining cushion against her chest like a shield. She felt herself being pulled forward gently. "I think we should think about this," she whispered hoarsely. "Both of us have had too much to drink, and this fire is—"

"Intoxicating," Rand said, tugging at her Levi's. "We're two people caught up in the moment." His voice was full of excitement. "No one will ever know."

"We'll know," Val said throatily as she felt her jeans slide down over her buttocks. Rand's torso flattened her as his hands worked the jeans lower and lower.

Her weak struggles ceased. It had been so long since she'd been with a man. She forgot about Maggie, about the Colemans, and gave in to what she was feeling. Her arms reached up to circle Rand's head, to bring him closer.

"I've wanted to do this since we met at the airport," Rand said huskily.

"You talk too much," Val said, and mashed her lips against his.

They played then like two lovers, teasing one another with their lips and gentle fingers until Rand thought he would go out of his mind. "I feel like a wild animal," he whispered.

"Then act like one," Val whispered in return.

He did, again and again.

"I think," Val said, a long time later, "that was the best sex I ever allowed myself to have."

Rand preened, drawing her into his arms. "I'll second that."

"We're never going to do this again, are we?" Val said sadly.

"It probably wouldn't be wise."

Val thought his gruff voice sounded desperate. "It wouldn't be the same. Nothing is ever the same after the first time."

"I suppose you're right," Rand said, nuzzling her neck.

"I'm always right," Val said sadly.

"I miss you already," Rand whispered.

"Shhh." Val placed her fingers against her lips. "Go to sleep and dream sweet nothings."

"Don't want to go to sleep. I want to make love to you some more," Rand mumbled. "You're a hell of a woman, Valentine Mitchell."

"Yeah, that's what they say," Val said, her voice raspy. Her eyes filled. A lone tear fell on Rand's cheek when she bent over to kiss him lightly on the mouth.

It took ninety minutes for her to shower, wash her clothes, and pack. She walked out of the house and drove to the airport, leaving the car at the curb. She spent the remainder of the night staring into space until her flight was called at seven A.M. She flew into LAX and retrieved the Lamborghini.

Twenty-four hours later Val unlocked the door of her condo in Assante Towers. Only then did she collapse. She cried until there were no more tears left. Then she slept.

{{{{{{{{ CHAPTER EIGHT }}}}}}}}

*With little Moss on her hip, Ivy walked around the din-*ing room table, checking the dinnerware and wine-glasses. "It looks good," she murmured to the baby. "The tulips look just right. Billie loves tulips. I love tu-lips. I think everyone in the world loves tulips. Your daddy is going to be here any minute, what do you think of that?" she crooned to the baby. "And Cole is coming with him. Everything is going to be just fine. Cary will be here too, in a wheelchair, but he'll be here. Everything is going to be just fine. Just fine." She knew she was trying to convince herself that what she was saying was really true.

She brought her lips down to Moss's downy head and kissed him. How good he felt in her arms. Her flesh and blood, hers and Riley's.

"Hey, you're snoozing on me, you little rascal." She tweaked the baby under the chin, but the child was too weary to respond with bubbling laughter the way he usually did. Ivy sighed and headed for the stairs. "Guess your daddy is going to have to wake you up when he gets here." Ivy's touch was almost reverent when she laid Moss in the crib. She smiled when his thumb went into his mouth, his other chubby hand groping for his whuppie. "God, Moss, I don't know if I love you more or as much as I love your daddy." Ivy's heart swelled with love, her eyes filling with tears of happiness.

Billie joined her in the baby's room. "He's so beautiful," Billie whispered. "How blessed you are, my dear."

"I know," Ivy said.

"I used to get all teary when I put the children to bed. It's one of my fondest memories. Sometimes when . . . things aren't going well for me, I turn my memory back and . . . what I do is, I . . . I try to remember things in chronological order. I even write them down, and when I have another restless period, I start from the beginning and add a few more memories. At the moment, I'm up to the time when Riley Senior left to join the service. I was still married to little Moss's grandfather then. It wasn't a good time for me," Billie said sadly.

Suddenly Ivy found herself in Billie's arms. Neither woman knew who was comforting the other.

"It's going to be all right, Ivy. Things are a bit unsettled right now, but like Amelia used to say, life's road has to be a little rocky, otherwise one becomes placid and takes it for granted."

Ivy sniffed and wiped her eyes on the sleeve of her shirt.

"Darling, close the door. I need to talk to you about something."

Ivy perched on a huge red building block while Billie settled herself in the wicker rocking chair. "I need you to do something for me, Ivy. I can't ask the others . . . because . . . I don't think they would be able to. Thad will be the worst. Cary was my first choice, but I changed my mind, not because of his accident, but because . . . I'm babbling, Ivy, because I'm afraid you'll say no. Please, darling, hear me out and think about what I'm going to ask you before you give me your answer. And Ivy, I want this kept between us. For now. I don't want you to tell Riley. I know it isn't right of me to ask you to keep something from him ... dear God, I'm going around the bush, aren't I?"

Ivy smiled wanly, her heart thudding madly in her chest. She watched as Billie withdrew a small square package from the deep folds of her skirt. Without hesitation she reached for it, her eyes full of questions.

"It's my living will, Ivy," Billie said briskly. "I need your assurance that you will do what I want. Thad and my family, they won't be able to. I chose you because you remind me in so many ways of myself at your age, although I do believe you have more guts. Will you do it, Ivy?"

Ivy didn't stop to think, didn't stop to analyze or rationalize. She nodded numbly. Behind her, Moss stirred. Automatically, Ivy reached back to rewind the music box on the colorful mobile hanging over the crib. *Mary had a little lamb.* She cleared her throat. "What ... I mean, what is in this tape? When do you want me to ... to look at it?"

"Why not right now? You have a VCR and television set in your bedroom. Perhaps it will be better if we look at it together." She was still whispering, her eyes clouded with worry.

In her bedroom, Ivy slid the tape into the VCR and turned down the volume. She turned to lock the door before she sat down on the bed next to Billie. She couldn't ever remember being this cold, this numb. Billie squeezed her hand. There was strength in Billie's hard, dry grasp. Ivy didn't want to look at the television screen, but knew she had to. As she watched, she cleared her throat again and again. Five minutes later she pushed the eject button and slid the tape back into the case. She carried it across the room to bury it deep in her knitting bag. She felt like a trapped animal.

"You'll give me your answer tomorrow, Ivy?" Billie asked anxiously.

"I don't need to think about it, Billie," Ivy said, returning to the bed. "I don't need a night to sleep on it. If it's what you want, if you're sure, if you have no doubts at all, I'll do it. Yes, I can handle it. I don't want you worrying about me now." Her arms went around the frail woman. She wanted to hug her hard, squeeze her, to breathe her own precious life into Billie's frail body. She felt as protective of Billie as she did of Moss.

"Will you do one other thing for me, Ivy?"

"If I can."

Billie bit down on her lower lip. "Once in a while, when you aren't too busy, will you go up to the hill and kind of . . . tell me what's going on? Bring me up to date on everything. I'll want to know about Moss, Katy, and Josie. Not right at the beginning, but later on. Amelia and I will be busy catching up. Will you do that for me?" Billie's eyes were misty with tears.

Ivy broke down again, and Billie cried against her shoulder.

"This is my last tear," Billie said firmly, reaching for a wad of tissues on Ivy's night table. "In the beginning all I did was cry, wail, and moan. I wanted to be strong like Amelia was. Amelia was so much more to me than a sister-in-law. She was the best friend I ever had. I loved her as much as Cary did. I've been praying to God, asking Him to give me the same strength He gave Amelia. There are times when I feel He's listening to me, like right now, and then there are times when I feel He's too busy to bother with me. I guess that's wrong.

Either one believes or one doesn't. Amelia told me never to bargain with God, so I don't. Just be kind to our family, Ivy. Time to go downstairs now. The others will be gathering. I'll go ahead. I know you want to check on Moss. Thank you, Ivy," Billie said as she hugged the young woman once more.

Ivy didn't trust herself to speak. She nodded. In the adjacent baby's room, she walked over to the wicker rocking chair. There was barely an indentation in the plush velvet padding. She sat down with a thump and thought about Billie's will.

No life-support measures. Pull the plug. Body organs to an organ bank if possible. Those not ravaged by disease. The word euthanasia sent a shudder through her body. What were the ramifications? She racked her brain to remember what she'd read and seen recently on the news. Had she agreed to do something that wasn't legal? The family ... God, what were they going to say? Would they fight her? She thought of Susan then and imagined her reaction. Her shoulders slumped. Would her husband be on her side?

Ivy was off her chair in a second. The mad desire to fling herself into her son's crib and snuggle with him was overwhelming. What if the family turned on her? What if Riley turned on her? Her hand crept through the bars of the crib. She caressed the downy head. "Then it's just you and me, partner," she whispered to the sleeping baby.

Back in her room, Ivy headed for the bathroom and splashed cold water on her face. She stared at herself in the mirror. How was it possible for her to look the same as when she carried Moss up the steps to put him to bed? She should look ... awful. Terrible. She picked up the powder puff. Billie wanted to be buried on the hill.

What would it do to Thad to see her buried next to her first husband? Dear God, Ivy fretted, what had she gotten herself into? Billie's words ricocheted in her head. "You, Ivy, are the legal custodian of my living will." Ivy closed her eyes as she visualized the battles that lay ahead of her. Tomorrow, or the next day, she was going to go to Valentine Mitchell's office with the tape. Valentine would help her through this. The decision made her feel better immediately.

Now, she had to go downstairs with a smile on her face and play hostess to the family. She crossed her fingers. *Please, God, don't let Susan get to me.*

Ivy used the back staircase to enter the kitchen. Things looked under control. Beef stew, fresh bread, garden salad, and green peas. Jonquil had trouble cooking any meal that required more than one pot. The whole family loved stew made with prime Coleman beef, which was tender as butter. There would be no complaints, and the pot would be empty when dinner ended. There were never leftovers when Jonquil made stew. The peach cobbler looked wonderful, with its little patches of cinnamon sugar crusting the top. It was one of Billie's favorites. Riley's too.

"You best get in there, Miz Ivy," Jonquil said out of the corner of her mouth. "Miz Sawyer is half snookered. Miz Susan is . . . she's been drinking all afternoon."

Ivy took a deep breath and entered the huge family room at the back of the house.

"Well," she said cheerfully, "we're almost all here. Riley and Cole should arrive any minute, and Thad will be here with Cary. Maggie, I'm going to have a ginger ale, want to split it?"

Maggie held her glass aloft. "Beat you to it," she said

quietly. "I told Jonquil to set another place. Rand called from the airport. He's on his way. Guess we'll all be here."

"Well, Miss Hostess of Sunbridge, do you think you can handle *that*?" Susan slurred.

"*Sober,* I can handle anything, Susan."

"Is there a hidden message in what you just said?" Sawyer demanded as she brought the beer bottle in her hand to her mouth.

Ivy forced a laugh that sounded eerie to her ears. "It just means I can handle it. Whatever *it* turns out to be." Her eyes were on Susan when she spoke. "The stew is simmering, and we all know it just gets better the longer it cooks. Why don't we catch up on family matters? I know I would personally love to hear how the twins are. I don't know how you do it, Sawyer. Moss wears me out. Two little girls, it's wonderful. Billie told me about the Easter dresses she designed for them." Her eyes pleaded with Sawyer, who in the past had been her staunchest ally.

"Oh, yes, darling, tell us how the girls are doing," Billie said cheerfully. "And then I'll remind you of the things you did when you were their age."

Maggie's eyes darkened. She hated it when her mother said things like this. She herself had absolutely no memory of what her daughter Sawyer did or didn't do at the age of two.

"You would not believe what they do," Sawyer said proudly. "Adam is better with them than I am. They actually listen to him. Last month they managed to get hold of the phone and called Australia and Greece and a bunch of other places. Adam whacked their bottoms real good. Josie stuck her tongue out at him and Katy kicked him in the shins. Little shits, both of them. However, they're mine and I love them dearly." Her expression became quizzical. "Don't you think it's strange that Katy has straight hair and Josie has curly hair? I mean both Adam and I have curly hair." The question wasn't directed to anyone in particular.

"What's the big deal?" Susan snapped.

Sawyer drained her beer. "I didn't say it was a big deal. I said it was strange. I'm sick of you, Susan. Besides, you're half in the bag, and I don't like talking to a drunk. So why don't you go upstairs and sleep off whatever it is that's crawling in your undies."

"For heaven's sake, girls, what is the problem?" Billie said quietly. "This is a wonderful time. We're all together, and Cary is going to be here any minute. Please, let's not have him come home to a battleground. Now, you're both drunk, and if there is one thing I cannot abide, it is a drunken female. I suggest both of you go to the kitchen and get some coffee."

"Atta girl, Mam," Maggie said tightly. "You tell 'em."

"It was a suggestion, not an order," Billie said, tears forming in her eyes.

"In that case," Susan drawled drunkenly, "I'll pass."

"Well, I won't," Ivy said tightly. "I want both of you to sober up before the rest of the family gets here."

Sawyer set her beer bottle down carefully on the bar. Her eyes were bleak, her hair in wild disarray. "I'm sorry, Ivy. It's just that I felt I needed some bottled courage to face Cole, and before I knew it, I was half lit. I'll get the coffee. Susan, do you want any?"

"Well, I certainly don't want to embarrass *our hostess*, so I guess I will." She tottered after Sawyer, her arms flapping about like a rag doll's.

Billie sighed wearily. Where was Thad? Thad would

have been able to handle this. She looked at Maggie. "What's wrong, Maggie?"

For God's sake, don't you know, can't you see? We're devastated. Right now I want a drink more than I want to take another breath, but if I do that, I won't be any good to anyone. "Susan and Ferris have split up. He pulled a Jerome on her, so Rand and Valentine Mitchell went after him. I'm happy to report, according to Rand, that Suse now has her small fortune intact and will be staying with me in Hawaii. She said she'd help run Billie Limited. It will be good for both of us. Seeing little Moss . . . I guess she thought about her daughter and . . . she's been under a lot of pressure," Maggie said defensively.

"And seeing me like this certainly didn't help matters," Billie said quietly. "Poor Susan, she's been so unlucky in her choice of men." Unbearable sadness engulfed her. She'd never had the opportunity to bond with her daughter, but thanks to Amelia, Susan had the life she'd always wanted, that of a concert pianist. Now, it was too late. She would never be able to help her daughter. Secretly she thought Susan incapable of loving anyone, and for that she blamed herself totally. Susan had never looked at her with love.

The inner trembling that warned of a collapse was starting. She had to get herself in hand or the family would see how weak she was. She brought herself back to the present to hear Maggie speaking.

"That too," Maggie said just as quietly. "You should have told us, Mam. I feel as if we don't count, that we weren't important enough for you to share what you were going through." There was a sob in Maggie's voice that tore at Billie's heart.

"Oh, no, darling, it was nothing like that. I just love

you all too much to make you unhappy for even one second longer than necessary. If it's any consolation to you, Thad badgered me every day. Right or wrong, it was what I wanted. Life goes on, Maggie dear, and when we've resolved the crisis that has drawn us together, Thad and I will return to Vermont."

The steely sound in Billie's voice startled Ivy. She wanted to clap her hands and shout, "Bravo, Billie." Instead, she allowed a small smile to tug at the corners of her mouth as she offered Billie a sly wink.

They all came at once, Thad and Cary, Riley, Cole and Rand. First, there was the sound of three separate car engines, of horns blowing a greeting. Then came the verbal greetings. The men of the family were home.

Ivy ran to Riley, Maggie to Rand, Thad and Cole to Billie.

"Go to your grandmother," Ivy whispered in her husband's ear. She watched as the men crowded around Billie, tears shimmering in her eyes. Billie was so loved, so blessed with her family.

"Hey, what about me?" Cary shouted from the middle of the floor.

"Hey, yourself." Ivy laughed. "What about you? You're here, what more do you want?" she quipped.

"Tell 'em, Thad," Cary ordered.

"We snatched him," Thad grinned. "I couldn't have done it on my own. Rand showed up, and between the two of us, we got him out un-dee-tected."

"Oh, my Lord!" Billie squealed. "Cary, are you well enough?"

"Probably not. It's been four days. I would have signed myself out tomorrow anyway, so a few hours one way or another isn't going to make much difference. Doctors don't know everything. The bottom line is, I wanted to be here. After all, this dinner is for me. I appreciate you all coming like this. I really do. The one thing I have always loved and admired about you all is the way you come together, from all over the world, when one of you has trouble. You stick together like glue, and I'm so grateful to you for your support and love and making me a part of your family. I couldn't have gotten through . . . hell, you know what I mean. End of speech." Cary grinned.

"About time," Susan said. "What would you like to drink, Cary?"

"Suse, is that you?" Cary said, stretching out his hand.

"In the flesh. What would you like?" she repeated.

"Whatever you're having. My nose tells me Sunbridge stew and fresh bread is on the dinner menu. I don't want to spoil my appetite."

Susan's eyes swiveled to Ivy, who smiled. "Soda pop," Susan said. "I had a snootful a while ago and made an ass of myself. As usual. We do have cold beer, though." The tenderness in her voice raised several eyebrows, including Billie's.

"Beer sounds good. Everybody talk so I can get a feel for where you are." Cary laughed when a gaggle of sound erupted around him. "Jesus, not all at once, one at a time. Where's Moss? Ivy, is he here?"

"Afraid not, Cary. He caved in about an hour ago. I tried to keep him up, but he fell asleep in my arms. He might wake up. He does that sometimes when his dad isn't here to put him to bed."

"Here, Cary," Susan said, placing a bottle of Budweiser into his hands. Ivy's eyebrows rose when she noticed how Susan's features softened and the way she touched her hand to Cary's. Her voice was gentle and warm, and she spoke to him in a tone only the two of them could hear. It almost looked as if she was in love with him, Ivy thought.

Cole was the first to break away, his eyes filled with unbearable pain. "So, little mother, how's it going?" he said to Ivy.

"It's going. Some days it's better than other days. The trick is not to get down because it's just too damn hard to get back up. I kind of stick to the middle of the road," Ivy said, hugging him. "How's Sumi? I just know it's going to be a boy. Or a girl." Ivy laughed. Out of the corner of her eye she saw Sawyer approaching from the kitchen. Ivy moved off to stand by her husband. Immediately his arm went around her waist. She laid her head on his shoulder.

Sawyer saw Cole before he noticed her. She stopped. For the first time in her life she was uncertain of what she should do. She told him so.

"When *I* don't know what to do, I just go with my instincts and say fuck it all," Cole said quietly.

"Yeah, yeah, that's pretty much what I do too," Sawyer said hoarsely. "I . . . I guess I got carried away that day on the phone."

"Yeah. I did too. I've been going through a bad time lately. I'm . . ." He wanted to say he was sorry, to take the miserable look from his sister's face, but sorry was just a word. Sawyer wasn't real big on words, not when actions were available. He closed the gap between them and wrapped his arms around her. Her sigh was like music to his ears. Now he could say it. "I'm sorry, Sawyer."

"Me too. Let's pretend it didn't happen and start over. Boy, do I have things to tell you."

"It can't possibly top what I have to tell you," Cole muttered.

"Tonight, when the others go to sleep, we'll talk, okay? Down in Billie's studio. God, I grew up there. I'd kill to have that time in my life back. She's going to die, Cole, and there's nothing I can do for her."

Cole felt like his heart was being wrenched out of his chest. "Smile, Sawyer, or I'll straighten your hair myself. We owe it to Grandmam to be as brave as she is. It's not easy, but you do it because you have to do it. I didn't think I would ever get over Mr. Hasegawa's death. You don't get over it, you just go on. It's part of life. It's that simple, Sawyer. Life goes on."

"But—"

"There are no buts. If we pull together, we'll be able to handle it. God, what *is* that smell?"

"Stew," Maggie said, joining them. "No matter how I try, I can't make it the way it's made here. I guess it's the fresh meat. I plan to make a pig of myself, in case anyone is interested."

"Of course we are," Rand said, slipping his arm about his wife's waist.

Something's wrong, Sawyer thought. Rand was too stiff and his smile didn't show in his eyes. Maggie didn't look right. Sawyer moved away, her eyes full of worry, to where Billie was sitting. She squatted down at her grandmother's feet the way she'd done ever since she was a child. "I've missed you guys. Has anyone heard from Julie?" she asked quietly.

"We've missed you too, but we do love getting the pictures of the girls. We have them lined up on the mantel. They're precious, Sawyer, absolutely precious. And yes, we've heard from Julie."

Thad lowered his voice so it wouldn't travel to Cary

and Susan. "She said she's going to do a bit of traveling and then maybe open her own business in Burlington. She cared deeply for Cary, but like Cary, she was riddled with guilt over their affair. They discussed it all, and both of them agreed parting was the answer. I believe they will always be friends. When we go back, we'll let her know about Cary, but that part of their life is over. Now, what else do you want to know?"

"How do I toilet-train a set of twins?" Sawyer asked ruefully.

"With a great deal of patience, stamina, and fortitude. If that doesn't work, buy stock in one of those diaper companies. You were very difficult to train, darling. You were four years and two months when you finally managed to stay dry," Billie said fondly. "I was about to give up on you."

"But you didn't," Sawyer said softly. "Thank you for that, Grandmam. Did I ever *really* thank you for all the things you did for me?"

"Hundreds of times," Billie said lightly. "You, my darling, were one of the best things that ever happened to me. I wouldn't change one year, one month, one week, one day, one hour of the time we spent together."

"I wouldn't either. My happiest memories were here at Sunbridge. I loved living in the studio. Anyway, thanks again." How husky her voice was. It sounded to her ears like she'd cried too long and too hard. "My God, I'm hungry. When do you suppose we're going to eat?"

"Right now." Ivy laughed.

The family sat down to dinner. Riley said grace.

"Dig in," Thad said happily as he passed one of the three loaves of bread. Riley passed the stew and Ivy passed the salad bowl. Conversation was light, and there were smiles and good-natured bantering back and forth across the table.

When the meal was over, Ivy snapped her fingers. "We ate it all," she chortled. "Every last drop, and we finished the three loaves of bread. Who has room for peach cobbler?" The chorus of groans and opened belt buckles caused a stir when Jonquil carried the plates to the table.

"Real whipped cream!" Sawyer squealed. "Pile it on, Jonquil. Tomorrow I diet!"

"Tuna fish and broccoli tomorrow." Ivy laughed.

The moment dinner was over, the family retired to the huge room at the back of the house, coffee cups in hand.

It was time for family business. An uncomfortable silence settled in the room. Who, Ivy wondered, was going to go first? She nudged her husband.

Riley reacted. "Okay, family, I guess I should mention here at the start of this meeting that Cole and I have more or less come to terms with . . . our families. East and West. We're going to merge these families as one, which was my grandfather's intention all along. I expect things will be bumpy for a while, but I'm confident we can make the transition relatively painless. What all this means is that we will be able to finance Sawyer's plane, and she won't have to seek outside financing. Cole and I agreed to this on the trip back here, so it's not something we thought of on the spur of the moment."

"You're too late," Sawyer said quietly.

Ivy's head jerked upright. Billie squirmed in her chair.

"You're not going to go ahead with it? That's just

like you, Sawyer, get us all riled up, and then you pack it in without telling anyone," Cole said tightly.

Sawyer's tone grew more quiet. "As usual, little brother, you weren't listening. I said you were too late. I didn't say anything about packing it in."

"What are you saying, darling? I'm confused, and I think the others are too," Billie said, matching her granddaughter's tone.

Sawyer was on her feet, her denim skirt swishing about her ankles. One booted foot tapped the oak floor. She moved again to stand behind Cary's wheelchair. "Cary offered me all the financing we'll need. I didn't have to ask. He *offered.* I accepted. What that means, family, is it's a done deed."

"But—" Cole sputtered.

"No buts, Cole. I asked you first and you wanted to gouge the family. This doesn't mean I love you any less, but any profits from this plane won't go into Hasegawa coffers. Coleman Aviation is mine, and don't you ever forget it. Correction," Sawyer said smugly, "I have the controlling interest."

"Why didn't you tell us about Cary's offer?" Riley demanded.

"Listen, I'm not one to let something simmer if I can bring it to a boil. I talked about this to Cary a month ago, and then again the day Cole turned shark. I don't beg anyone in my family to help me. Either you're there for me or you aren't. And let me remind you two," she said, jabbing a finger first at Riley and then at Cole, "it was my husband who pulled your asses out of the fire with his property and his oil. Adam, with my approval—those are the key words, *my approval*—gave this family a chance to rebound. We didn't argue about it, or fight, or make deals. You needed our property, and we sold it to you. I have this absolute, total, blind loyalty where this family is concerned. It was my mistake to think you had it too, Cole."

"That's not fair, Sawyer," Maggie snapped.

"Oh, yeah, what's not fair about it, Maggie? Don't fight your son's battles, he's old enough to do it himself," Sawyer snarled.

"Riley just said . . . you're refusing to take their money, but you'll take money from Cary, an *outsider*?" Maggie railed.

Billie was on her feet and halfway across the room in a second. The slap to Maggie's face was like a gunshot in the quiet, stunned room. "I have never in my life been ashamed of you, but I'm ashamed now," Billie said coldly. "You will apologize this instant," she ordered.

Maggie reeled backward, expecting to find her husband standing behind her, but it was Cole who caught her arm. In all of her life her mother had never laid a hand on her. She was too stunned to do anything but stare at her family. What she saw registered on their faces was shock and disgust. She jerked free of her son's arms and ran from the room. Cole started after her.

"No!" came the iron command.

Cole stopped in his tracks. He'd never heard that tone of voice from his grandmother.

Billie, with Thad's help, walked over to Cary's chair. With great difficulty she dropped to her knees and reached for his hand. "In my heart, Cary, I don't believe Maggie meant what she said. I'm afraid this is all my fault, and I'm perfectly willing to take the blame. This is why I didn't want anyone to know about my illness. It's me Maggie is angry with. She's angry . . .

because . . . because she wants me to live forever, like
I wanted Amelia to live forever. I think I was the only
one who understood what Amelia was trying to do before she passed away. She wanted to spare us, and herself too. But, selfishly, we wouldn't let her. You are not
to think for one second that you do not belong to this
family. You *are* this family. If you want a chorus of
ayes, it can be arranged. Please, I beg you, Cary, don't
judge us by Maggie's outburst. I know my daughter,
and I know she's already regretting what she said.
Words spoken thoughtlessly or carelessly can carry a
lifetime of hurt. I can't change that and I have no right
to ask you to forgive my daughter. I think it's written
somewhere that only a mother will forgive anything her
children do because mothers love unconditionally."

Cary took a deep breath. "There's nothing to forgive,
Billie. I know how Maggie feels." The warm tears
splashing on the back of his hands made his heart
thump. He could deny this wonderful woman nothing.
Next to Amelia, he loved her more than any other person in the world. He felt Thad lift Billie from her kneel-
ing position.

"Now listen . . . family . . . if there's a problem with
my offer to Sawyer . . ."

"There's no problem, Cary," Sawyer said gently.

"Well, if there is, we can work it out. Isn't that what
families do?" Cary asked airily.

Riley's eyes sparked in Cole's direction. "No problem, Cary," he said quietly.

"Carry on, folks," Thad said. "I'm giving Billie a
ride upstairs. She wants to turn in early. I'll be down
later. Cary, do you mind hanging around a bit longer?"

Susan answered for Cary. "No, he doesn't mind. I'm

going to take him for a walk in the garden. It's a beautiful evening and I could use some fresh air."

"That's an offer I certainly won't refuse. Bring some cigarettes, Susan."

"They're in my pocket." Susan giggled. "Hang on now."

"Anyone want a drink?" Rand asked.

"Is it hemlock we're serving tonight?" Sawyer snapped. "Sorry, I didn't mean that."

"I can't believe you accepted Cary's offer," Cole said tightly. "You know that means he has to either mortgage or sell Miranda. You'll be stripping him bare. Is that what you want?"

"Get it through your head, Cole, he offered. He wouldn't have offered if he didn't think he could handle it. It was a drop in the bucket to you, and you . . . look, we're beating a dead horse here, so why don't we just give up, okay?"

"Then what was that business about us meeting down at Grandmam's studio later? I thought things were settled. I screwed up, I apologized, you apologized. Now you tell me . . . ah, forget it."

"Much too little too late. But I *was* going to tell you about Shigata Mitsu. Don't you remember asking me about him? I know who he was . . . is . . . whatever. At first I just recalled the name, and then I asked Thad. He knows all about him. What's wrong with you, Cole? You're white as snow."

Cole forgot about the financing, his mother, and Rand's stony face. "You mean there is such a person?"

"You're a twit, Cole. I just told you so, didn't I? Mr. Hasegawa told me the story once, but it was vague in my mind. Thad repeated it for me. What is it you don't understand?" she asked peevishly, her eyes on Rand.

Before Cole could reply, she said, "Rand, shouldn't you be with Maggie?"

"Why? What she did was unforgivable," he said, pouring himself a second stiff drink.

"I think I'll check on Moss," Ivy said quietly.

"I'll go with you," Riley said, following his wife.

Cole spun around to Rand. "That's a rather unkind remark, coming from you, Rand. I thought you were more understanding. Mother's going through a bad time. Like Grandmam said, she's probably upstairs crying her eyes out and trying to figure out a way to make things right."

"Some things can't be made right. If Maggie thinks of Cary as an outsider, then she must think of me the same way. And what does that make Thad? Ivy? Sumi? Get my point?" Rand said, and drained his glass. "I think I'll go for a walk. Tell Thad I'll go with him when he takes Cary back to the hospital."

"What does *that* mean? That you 'outsiders' are going to band together?" Cole snapped.

"Listen to you, the both of you!" Sawyer said through clenched teeth. "Are you trying to make this family come apart?"

"It's all your fault," Cole snarled. "You started it!"

He never saw the blow, never expected it. He blinked in stunned surprise.

"Goddamnit, Sawyer," he roared, but she was already out of the room.

"Well, that's two down," Rand drawled before he sauntered from the room.

Cole sat for a long time, staring into space. "Sawyer was right," he muttered. "I started this thing, not her. *I'm* making the family fall apart." He was about to get up and search out his sister when Riley and Thad entered the room.

His eyes full of misery, Cole asked, "Is Grandmam all right?"

"She's sleeping. None of this is good for her, Cole. We're going home tomorrow. I'm sure Cary will understand. Ivy and Riley will look after him, and I might be wrong about this, but I think Susan will stay on as well. Billie seems to think they're growing close. It would be wonderful for both of them if they . . . you know, kind of got together."

"Thad, how long does Grandmam have?"

"It's uncertain. At least a few months. Every day I see little things. She tries so damn hard. This . . . trip, this evening wasn't good for her at all. You must have seen it. She was crying when she fell asleep. She kept saying she failed the family, that she should have done more. Of course that's hogwash. No one could be more loving and devoted to a family than Billie. But all this fuss Maggie caused—and Sawyer too, from the way she just looked—has upset her. By the way, how are *you* doing?"

"Right now I feel lower than a snake's belly," Cole said miserably. "I don't know if I can ever make this right. Where do I start. *How* do I start? Sawyer said this family is being torn apart, and she's right."

"I'm afraid I can't help you, Cole. The only thing I'm concerned with is your grandmother. When we leave here tomorrow, I want to see smiles, and I don't want one anxious word to filter up to Vermont. I want Billie to be worry-free, if there is such a thing. I will not tolerate anything less. If one of you crosses the line, I will simply take her away to someplace where there are no phones and no mailboxes. I want you and Riley to relay this to your family."

"Oh, Jesus, not you too," Cole groaned.

"We'll tell them," Riley said.

Cole nodded. "Thad, Sawyer was going to tell me about Shigata Mitsu before she got all strung out. She said you knew the story. Would you tell it to me and Riley? No, wait. Before you do, let me tell you about what's been going on in my head."

Thad listened intently, then said, "Let me be sure I understand all of this. Are you asking me if I believe in spirits, in the supernatural?"

"Guess so," Cole mumbled. Riley looked everywhere but at Thad.

Thad shrugged. "Damned if I know if I do or not. Cary swears he feels Amelia's presence all the time. I remember getting the heebie-jeebies that day when we played 'This Is Your Life' for Riley. Remember how the chandelier tinkled when Cary raised his head and yelled 'Right, babe,' or something like that? We were all spooked. Then there's that business of the angels singing in the hospital when Sawyer was so near death. If this is a yes or no question, then my answer is yes, I hope so, because I'm going to be looking for Billie when ... when ... you know."

"I believe in them," Cole said flatly. "At least I believe in Shadaharu Hasegawa's spirit. I saw with my own eyes whatever it was rip through the Zen garden. So did Riley. Two of us can't be wrong."

"There are all kinds of explanations for something like that. Earthly reasons."

"You'll never convince me."

"Obviously, Shadaharu doesn't frighten you. I guess that means he's a friendly spirit." Thad groaned. "I can't believe we're having this discussion. At least when I tell Billie, she'll have a laugh. She talks about Mr. Hasegawa a lot. I want to cry every time she says she's going to have so many things to tell her old friends when she gets *there*. She's not at all afraid."

Cole hunched into his shoulders. "Tell us the story of Shigata Mitsu."

Thad sighed. "It's not a long story so don't get comfortable. One day Shadaharu and I were in the Zen garden talking about inane things, and I asked him how he came to be the third wealthiest man in the world. He said it was because of Shigata Mitsu. Shadaharu had been a poor tailor at one time with many mouths to feed. He had very little business and worried himself sick about how he was going to pay the rent and buy food for his family. He was walking home along the beach one night with only six yen in his pocket. He thought about drowning himself because he was so ashamed that he couldn't provide for his family. He sat down on the seawall with the six yen in his hand, and was staring at it when a man sat down next to him. The man was neither young nor old, but somehow seemed timeless or ageless. They looked into one another's eyes. Shadaharu said he saw only himself reflected in the man's gaze, but he knew the man was seeing his soul. He couldn't explain how he knew, he just knew. They struck up a conversation, and Shadaharu showed him the six yen in his hand. The man said that Shadaharu was rich, that some people didn't have six yen or even one yen. He told Shadaharu he had to share with those who had less than he had. Shadaharu said he remembered nodding his head in agreement. They talked a little more and then the man got ready to leave. Shadaharu bowed low and the man placed his hand on his shoulder. Shadaharu said it felt wonderfully warm, and his shoulder remained warm for many days. Anyway, on the way home to his family, he met three beggars and he gave each of them a yen. He said he felt good doing it, knowing the poor souls would at least have a warm meal. The very next day when he went to his shop, a man from the newspaper came in and asked him to make three suits. Shadaharu said he worked all day and night and in two days finished the suits. He delivered them personally. The man from the paper called in some people on his staff and they all ordered suits. Many, many suits. Word spread, and soon Shadaharu was the most sought-after tailor in town. *And what he did, Cole, was give half of everything he earned away to those less fortunate than himself from that day on.* He did that until the day he died. The more he gave away, the more he got in return. God has always said give and you shall receive," Thad said quietly.

Cole was on his feet, his hands jammed into his pockets. "Are you telling me the man Mr. Hasegawa spoke with on the seawall was God?"

"I'm not saying that at all. But do you have a better explanation?"

"Was his name Shigata Mitsu?" Cole demanded.

"No. Shadaharu said he never asked the man's name. He gave the man the name Shigata Mitsu himself. He needed a name to go with the story when he told his wife about the encounter, but he told me he thought he was talking to God. Of course, he wondered why God would speak personally with someone as unworthy as himself, so he convinced himself that the man was an *emissary* from God. The Christian God. I think that was another reason Shadaharu was always so open to Western ways, and why he didn't kick up a fuss when his

daughter, Otami, married Riley's father and converted
to Catholicism. He believed it was ordained. He was a
very wise, wonderful, kind, and generous man. You
have no idea, Cole, of the people he helped, of the hos-
pitals he built, the families he supported. He even
funded many churches here in the United States. Did
you ever wonder why he chose this family to befriend?"

"Of course I wondered. We all did. We still do. We
more or less thought it was because of Otami and Riley's father."

"Of course. East and West. He loved this family as
much as he loved his own. He expected Riley to carry
on, but Riley chose to remain here. You were the logical successor, thanks to Riley. That old man adored you,
Cole. He considered you a son."

"And I failed him. Why didn't someone tell me?"

"I think he wanted you to find out yourself. This is
just my opinion, Cole," Thad said hastily.

"How did he explain all those . . . giveaways to the
accountants and lawyers?"

"I don't think he did. They would never dream of
questioning him. He was making so much money, they
were hard pressed to keep track of what he did have.
Shadaharu said the money just flowed in. So now you
sit on ninety billion dollars. Now, as to the tempest in
the Zen garden . . . I'd say, if I were a wagering man,
that Shadaharu was getting impatient for you to get on
the stick. Call it a warning. Call it anything you like.
Maybe Sawyer was your test. Hell, I don't know, Cole,"
Thad said impatiently. References to the hereafter always bothered him.

"Tempest, my ass. Riley and I felt like the wrath of
God was coming down around us."

"Ahhh. On that thought, I will leave you to seek out

my charge and return him from whence he was snatched. Good night, Cole," Thad said, his tone relieved.

The cousins stared at one another. "It would seem," Cole said carefully, "that Thad gave us our answer. Sort of. Now I have to come up with a solution." He babbled then, nonstop, until he came to the part where he said, "Sawyer must have been my test, and I flunked. Cary stepped in, just the way your grandfather did years ago when the family was about to go down the tubes. Now I have to make it right. This is my second chance. I need your help, Riley."

"I'm here. We need a great brainstorming session, and for that, we need a beer bottle in our hands." He twisted the caps off two San Miguels and handed one to Riley.

Settled comfortably with their beers, the cousins stared unblinking at one another.

"What are you going to do about Sawyer, Cole? And when are we going to talk about Grandmam Billie?" He rolled the frosty beer bottle between his hands, enjoying the cool wetness.

"I'm still trying to accept what happened to Cary. My mother . . . I can't believe she . . . Jesus, do you have any idea of what Cary must have felt? I wasn't going after Mother to console her, but to . . . I guess I was going to blast her. I'm glad Grandmam ordered me to stay. I thought Rand would go after her, but he looked like one of those cigar store Indians. He's got a burr scratching him someplace. Cary is what's important now. He was so matter-of-fact at dinner. I couldn't handle being blind, even temporarily, and Cary doesn't know if it's temporary. Did you by any chance notice the little interplay between him and Aunt Susan?"

Riley grimaced. "I missed that, but Ivy saw it. She filled me in when we were checking on Moss. I can see them together. Maybe it will be just your mother running Billie Limited. Maybe Aunt Susan needs someone to nurture, someone who depends on her. She didn't have a problem in the world when her daughter was alive. I guess it has something to do with her going to live in England with Aunt Amelia when she was so young. Rand told me once that she never had a normal childhood and that music was her life. It's sad, if you stop to think about it."

Cole set his beer down with a hard thump. "You want sad? I'll give you sad. This whole family is screwed up. It's the 'outsiders,' to quote my mother, who have their shit in one sock. Thad doesn't have problems. Rand is on top of the heap. Adam is . . . Adam is about as perfect as you can get. Ivy and Sumi, they're in a class by themselves. Cary is one of those rare individuals who is totally giving, warm, and caring. He came through for Sawyer with no questions asked, just the way your grandfather did. It's us Colemans that are screwed up. Go ahead, Riley, tell me I'm wrong."

"I wouldn't touch that with a ten foot pole," Riley said, lining up his empty bottle next to Cole's. He opened two more.

"Does it ever get better? How do we get to that place Adam and Cary are in? God, how I envy the inner peace they seem to have. How, Riley?"

"My grandfather had that same inner peace. Grandmam Billie has it. I think Thad does too. I guess you just have to accept things for what they are. Isn't there some kind of prayer or saying about asking God for the strength to accept what can't be changed . . . or something?"

"I know the one you mean," Cole said, pacing up and down the room. "I don't understand how your grandfather could be so peaceful when he knew he was going to die. And look at Grandmam Billie. She seems as if she's completely accepted her fate."

"Listen, Cole," Riley said, by now sounding slightly drunk, "this is a very heavy discussion, and we're on the way to getting fried, but to answer your question, I can only speak about my grandfather. Until Thad told us that story about Shigata Mitsu, I thought my grandfather was born a loving, kind man. If all Thad said was true, then my grandfather achieved that state of peacefulness by doing good. I bet, Cole, if you go through his personal accounts, you'll be in for the surprise of your life. Knowing him as I did, I bet he gave away more than he kept. Hey, I always feel good when I do something for someone. Remember that high we were both on when we gave Adam back his homestead? Does it compute?"

Cole nodded and lined his beer bottle up with Riley's. He reached into the bar refrigerator for two more.

"This last Christmas, Ivy decided we should not give each other gifts. Instead we made Christmas for six families. We went the whole nine yards: tree, decorations, wreath for the front door, food, toys for the children, gifts for the parents, and a promissory note to all six families to help them throughout the year. It was the best Christmas we ever had. I've never done anything like that before, have you?"

Cole shook his head. "The answer can't be that simple. Give and you get. C'mon, Riley," Cole said.

"Forget the *get* part. It's the giving. It doesn't have to be material things. You gotta forget the gimme part. And I never said it was the answer to all of life's problems, but unless you can come up with something better, I'll stick with my theory." Riley knew he was well on his way to becoming drunk as he watched Cole moving in slow motion.

"Thad said he and Grandmam are leaving tomorrow. That breaks my heart, Riley. There must be something we can do."

Riley shook his head furiously. His stomach heaved with the movement. He sat perfectly still until his insides quieted. "We say, Good-bye, we love you, and if you need us, call. We keep our eyes dry and our voices cheerful. That way Grandmam will think ... think we believe she ... has a chance. It's what she wants," Riley said mournfully. "It's that ... giving thing again. It makes sense, doesn't it?"

"Yeah, it does. Thad said he would take Grandmam away if we didn't do what he wanted. He would too. I don't know about that dry-eye part. My eyes water a lot when it comes to this family. Grandmam's been our rock for so long. She's never failed us. Not once. You want to bawl now so she doesn't see us do it tomorrow?" Cole mumbled.

"Men don't cry," Riley croaked.

"Who the hell said that?" Cole snorted.

"Probably Sawyer. Her tongue should get blisters."

"You're talking about my sister," Cole said sourly.

"Your half sister," Riley said just as sourly. He wiped at his eyes. "She's okay. So what if she has a mouth like a truck driver and wears those ... weird clothes and a ...." Riley struggled for the word he was searching for. "... a snood. She's always there for us too. She has a brilliant mind. She told me that herself."

"She's a pain in the ass." Cole hiccuped. "I didn't come through for her, and she won't give me a second chance, which makes me feel like shit. She won't bend an inch."

"You *should* feel like shit." Riley sniffed. "Furthermore, she lied when she said she would forgive you. Sawyer never forgives. If you don't believe me, ask Adam."

"Naah, he always takes her side. He thinks we're wise-asses."

"He thinks that because Sawyer told him we're wise-asses," Riley said smartly. He peered at the double line of beer bottles. He tried to count them. They were neck and neck. He was searching his foggy brain for something witty to say to his cousin, when he saw Cole's shoulders start to shake. He stumbled his way over to the soft, deep sofa Cole was sprawled on. Clumsily, he put his arm around his cousin.

"Nobody told me it was going to be like this," Cole choked. "I want to be a kid again."

Tears rolled down Riley's cheeks. First my grandfather, then Aunt Amelia, and now Grandmam Billie. He wasn't sure who was trembling, Cole or himself. He clutched at his cousin's arm as sobs ripped from his throat.

They cried then. For the would-haves, the should-haves, the could-haves. Neither of them saw Thad, Rand, and Cary enter and quickly leave the room. Neither of them saw Susan enter and retreat from the room either.

A long time later Cole asked hoarsely, "What time is it?"

Riley squinted at his watch. "Almost ten o'clock. Why?"

"We've been sitting here for a long time. I need to

make some decisions. I feel almost sober. Help me, Riley."

"Sawyer isn't going to bend. That's a given. Were you serious about merging the families?"

"Yes. I wish I knew why I didn't do it sooner. That's going to haunt me forever," Cole said, blowing his nose loudly.

"I don't think it's important anymore. Anything before this moment is ancient history. But if we don't go forward, we're lost. Now that we think we know grandfather's secret to success, we have to follow in his footsteps. Even if for some reason the giving ... wasn't part of his success, I still think we should go ahead. We'll look into foundations. We could do a lot for the homeless. There's churches. I'd personally like to do something for animals. Buy a nature preserve somewhere, fund it so animals don't have to be destroyed. God, we could do so much."

"What about Sawyer?" Cole asked miserably.

"Think about this, Cole. If it wasn't for Sawyer, we wouldn't be uniting East and West. She probably deserves our thanks."

"Get off it, Riley. You're getting carried away. She'll hold it over our heads for the rest of our lives if we admit she was the one who brought us to our senses. You wanna live with that?"

Riley pondered the question. "Yeah, I do," he said quietly.

"Okay," Cole said, "tomorrow we'll kiss her feet and make nice."

He sounds relieved, Riley thought. "What about Cary?" he asked. "With this economy and his present condition, who in the hell is going to lend him money on Miranda? The memorial he's building to Amelia isn't even finished. It was a magnificent gesture on his part to fund the plane, but I don't think he thought it through. They'll kill him with interest payments. He could lose the place. Although we could do it," Riley said slyly.

"Do what?"

"Take the mortgage. We can talk to Valentine Mitchell and see how it's done. Probably a dummy company someplace in New York, or maybe an English one. Cary will never need to know we're behind it. This way he'll never lose Miranda. You control the money, Cole, so once again, it has to be your decision."

"*We* control the money. We shook hands on it on the way over. But what if Cary does find out?" Cole said, a frown building on his face.

"Then we say we're just two wild, crazy kids who got carried away with all that money. The bottom line is we protect Cary. That inner city is his life. You comfortable with this, Cole? The truth."

Was he? "Yes. Jesus, I feel like I've been reborn. And the best part is, we have a secret Sawyer will never know. That gives us the edge." He laughed uproariously. Riley joined in, slapping him on the back.

"Let's make some coffee and work off this drunk," Riley said, teetering his way toward the kitchen.

"You make it, I want to call Sumi," Cole said, lagging behind. "Riley?" Cole whispered.

"Yeah?"

"Thanks."

"You bet."

Sawyer stepped out from behind the wide folding doors of the great room, a gleeful smile on her face. The little shits. She danced a jig and silently clapped her hands. Wait till she told Adam. An hour earlier, when she'd cried her eyes out to her husband, he'd said, "Don't sell those guys short, either one of them. Somehow, some way, they'll come through for you."

When it came down to the wire, when it really counted, you could always depend on family.

Family.

Maggie lay in the darkness. Faint moonlight seeped through the vertical blinds. She had no idea how much time had passed since she'd run up here like a child to throw herself on the bed. She cringed now with shame at what she'd done. How could she have reacted like that? How? She rolled over onto her stomach, burying her face in the pillow. How careful she'd been to stay on her side of the bed. She knew, without having to turn on the light, that there wasn't even one wrinkle on Rand's side.

Rand was the reason she was here cowering like a criminal. Rand was the reason she'd blurted out that hateful word, "outsider." It wasn't just Mam and her illness.

She flopped over onto her back. Ten minutes to twelve. She turned the light off. Earlier she'd heard footsteps in the hall: Sawyer's clumping boots, then Cole and Riley walking past her door. None of them had knocked, none of them had called her name. She was a pariah now. She'd heard Rand talking to Thad and Cary in the courtyard. The three of them had driven off together. She hadn't heard Susan, though. She'd counted on Susan to just open the door and whisper her name, but it hadn't happened.

Her face burned with shame and guilt when she remembered the way she'd pleaded, sobbing at her mother's door, begging her to talk to her, only to have Thad say, "Your mother doesn't want to talk to you right now." Until tonight, no matter what, her mother had never, ever, refused to listen, to offer advice, to help make things right.

That was a separate issue. Tomorrow, today actually, she could attempt to make things right with Cary, to explain why she'd acted the way she had. She could explain to Mam. Mam would understand. Rand. Rand was the problem.

Maggie was off the bed the moment her head started to buzz lightly. She threw open the window, taking great gulping breaths.

Rand was her reason for being. She had no one else. Sawyer was in New York with her family. Cole was in Japan with his. They didn't need her, and that's the way it should be. Mam had Thad. Susan ... would have Cary, even though neither one of them realized it yet. Riley had his family. Rand had his daughter, Chesney.

She'd picked up on the change in Rand during the days he spent in Minnesota with Valentine Mitchell. He'd always admired Valentine, had said so more than once. The two of them had been together in a cozy little house in the Midwest, working side by side, eating together, riding together in the car, having drinks in front of the fire. Rand did love a good fire. She could picture the two of them laughing, talking, sharing secrets of a sort. And then, over drinks, looking into one another's eyes and ...

It had happened. That much she was sure of. As to the date and the exact hour ... well, the poor little wife didn't get to know everything.

How she'd looked forward to Rand returning to Sunbridge. She'd counted on his support. She had needed it to face the fact of her mother's illness. But he hadn't opened his arms to her. She'd run to him, throwing *her* arms around him. He'd had no other choice but to embrace her. He hadn't looked her in the eye, though, hadn't said he missed her, hadn't smiled. She'd known for certain then that he'd slept with Valentine.

Should she confront him? Should she tell him to move out of the house? Cary had done the same thing to Amelia. That's why she'd blurted out that hateful word. Amelia had forgiven Cary, though.

Amelia had confided in her once, late at night. She had admitted she was ill and couldn't give Cary what he needed in the bedroom. She had said she knew about Julie, Thad's niece. She'd gone to extraordinary lengths to cover up her knowledge of the affair and at the same time make it easier for Cary. How noble and unselfish she had been. "Because I love Cary more than life itself, Maggie darling," she'd said. "And I'm so very old, Maggie." Amelia had whimpered then, and Maggie had done her best to comfort her. How could she know then that Cary's betrayal with Julie had happened in her own house in Hawaii?

"Well, I'm not old, and I'm not in poor health. I can't forgive this betrayal," Maggie cried, heartbroken.

Her conscience prodded her. It probably didn't mean anything. These things happened.

Not to me they don't, she told herself. She believed in fidelity, in honoring one's marriage vows. She'd never cheated on him.

Did she have the opportunity? No. She knew she couldn't say what she would or wouldn't do if she were in a similar situation. The right moment, her conscience responded, a drink, your guard is down and . . .

You're wrong, Maggie argued silently. I love Rand. *Loved*. No matter what, she would never be unfaithful.

Rand was going to pretend nothing happened. He thought she didn't know. *I know. Damnit, I know.* He couldn't face her. That's why he wasn't here with her. Under normal circumstances, he would . . . would . . . he would be here with her, consoling her over Mam. She never would have blurted out what she did to Cary if Rand hadn't . . . forget it! Maggie sobbed, running to the bed.

Her conscience pricked a third time. Isn't all this just your jealousy of Valentine? You envy her ability. It's possible she tried to seduce Rand, and he *almost* gave in, and that's why he's feeling guilty. You could be wrong. You must have some doubts.

"None," Maggie said, punching the pillow. "I know, don't you understand?" A woman knows when her husband betrays her. She might not admit it, for whatever her reasons, but she knows. She was relieved when her conscience remained silent.

It was ten minutes past one when the car's headlights arced on the bedroom wall. Maggie slid from the bed and walked over to the open window. Down below she could see Thad and Rand talking in low voices. They must have stopped at a diner for coffee after they dropped Cary off. Would Rand come to the room now? Not likely. Where would he sleep?

Maggie settled herself into a sapphire-blue slipper chair, her eyes glued to the bottom of the door where the hallway light filtered through. Thad had to go past the door. She would hear him or see a break in the light. Through the kitchen, to the back hall, across the family room, out to the center hall and the stairway, and up the steps. She counted, wondering if he knew about the kitchen stairway alongside the refrigerator. Not that it mattered one way or the other. Down the hall now. She waited, holding her breath, for the break in the light at the bottom of the door.

Tears rolled down Maggie's cheeks. She wiped at them with the sleeve of her shirt. As the hours crawled by, she forced herself to think of other things: her mother, her children, Susan and Cary, but she always came back to Rand. Once again her world was upside down.

It was still dark at five-thirty when Maggie washed her face and brushed her hair. An early morning gallop would do her a world of good. A brisk ride in the fresh air might clear the cobwebs out of her head. She was on the landing of the stairs when she sensed a presence nearby. She turned, expecting to see Rand. Sawyer brought her finger to her lips for silence. Maggie nodded and motioned for her daughter to follow her.

"Don't say anything, Sawyer. Please, I'd like you to join me in a ride. I need to talk to someone. What that means is I'd appreciate it if you would listen."

"You didn't sleep at all, did you?" Sawyer said when they were in the stable.

"No, I didn't. Did you?"

"Not really. I'm so used to sleeping with one eye and ear open for the twins, I guess . . . I doubt if anyone in this house slept well last night. But we're talking about you. What's wrong, Maggie?"

Maggie pulled the cinch tighter, then turned to face Sawyer. "Rand cheated on me. He slept with Valentine Mitchell," she said cooly. "Last night, when I said what I did to Cary, it just hit me that he'd done the same thing to Amelia. Nobody knows better than I that it was an unforgivable thing to say. I love Cary. I would never knowingly do or say anything to hurt him. I don't know what to do. I can't . . . forgive Rand. Not now anyway.

The funny thing is, Sawyer, he doesn't even know I know. He didn't come to our room at all last night. That's his guilt. When I was married to Cranston, I became an expert on infidelity. I swore it would never happen to me again. I thought we had such a wonderful marriage. I likened it in my mind to Mam and Thad's marriage."

As they rode off, Maggie took the lead, her heels digging into the horse's flanks. It was still too dark to see well. She's going to kill herself, Sawyer thought. Sawyer's own horse, chomping at the bit to follow the other, reared to show his disapproval. "What the hell?" Sawyer muttered, loosening the reins in her hands. "Follow that horse," she said dramatically.

Forty minutes later Sawyer reined in. They were on Jarvis land. By squinting, she could make out her husband's family home. She wondered if Maggie had lost her bearings in the dark or if this was her destination from the beginning. It was almost full light, that purplish-gray part of the morning that heralds a bright, beautiful day.

"Let's go over to the house and sit on the swing," Maggie called over her shoulder. Sawyer nodded.

This was nice, Sawyer thought. Adam would be pleased that she'd ridden out to check on the house. They really had to think about bringing the girls here for a while in the summer. It would be wonderful to get out of the city in August.

Maggie was already on the swing when Sawyer rode up to the hitching post alongside the house. The mare whickered softly as Sawyer slid from her back. She joined her mother on the swing.

"I always liked this house," Maggie said.

"I always liked it too. Adam had a very happy childhood here."

"I had a miserable childhood," Maggie said.

"I know."

"Thanks to Mam, you had the best."

"I know that too," Sawyer said. "I thank God every day."

"I've always kind of talked to God. I say prayers every night before I go to sleep. I always say . . . said, thanks for giving me such a wonderful marriage. Guess I won't be saying that anymore. In fact, I probably won't be doing much praying from here on in."

"Are you saying you're giving up on God?" Sawyer asked in disbelief.

"I just said I won't be doing much praying. I didn't say I was giving up on God. Only a fool would do that. I'm kind of numb, Sawyer, so don't hit on me right now."

"What are you going to do?"

"Go back to Hawaii this evening. I canceled Rand's flight. I don't want him in the house. I . . . I'll have to tell him, I guess," Maggie mumbled.

"I would think so," Sawyer said.

"Susan is going to stay here. She didn't say so, but I think . . . she will. I'll keep myself busy. There's a lot of work that has to be done to get Mam's old business back in the running. Maybe I'm making a mistake by going back. Maybe I should stay here. I'll be closer to you and Mam. I can get an apartment in town or I can ask Riley and Ivy if I can rent Mam's old studio. What I have to do is make a decision. What do you think?"

"You told me you just wanted me to listen," Sawyer chided gently. She fished around in her jeans pocket and withdrew a key ring. She worked one off and handed it to her mother. "You have to do what is right for you. This is the key to the house. Stay here if you like. Adam will be grateful that someone is here to look after the place."

"What's your opinion of Valentine Mitchell?" Maggie asked carefully.

"I've always thought her a very capable person, and I've always liked her. And yes, she's attractive. That's really what you want to know, isn't it? But then so are you. I've always liked her."

"How could she do this to me?"

"It takes two people, Maggie," Sawyer said gently.

"I'm very well aware of that. It just makes it a little easier if I place some of the blame on Val."

"You said Rand doesn't know you know. How did you find out?"

"No one told me, if that's your question. It's just something I know, something I feel. I'm not wrong, Sawyer."

"You mean you just *think* Rand slept with Val?" Maggie nodded. "What if you're wrong? What if you accuse Rand and you find out it never happened? I just assumed someone told you or you . . . oh, Lord, I don't know what I thought," Sawyer said sourly.

"Come on, time to get back. Don't worry about me, Sawyer, and thanks for the key. If I decide to stay on, I'll let you know. What time is your plane?"

"Eleven o'clock. What time is yours?"

"Five, if I decide to take it. I enjoyed the ride. And the company," Maggie said wanly.

"Me too," Sawyer said softly.

Back at the barn, Sawyer turned the horse over to her mother. "Will you rub him down for me? I have to take another shower and see if I can do something with my hair."

Maggie nodded.

Once the horses were rubbed down and secure in their stalls, Maggie trudged out to the courtyard. She couldn't ever remember being this tired, this discouraged, this betrayed. She wanted to cry, needed to cry, but a release of tears eluded her. How could Rand do this to her? Had he done this before? How was she going to get through this?

She looked at her watch—seven o'clock. She felt like a tired war horse when she struggled up from the milk crate on which she'd been sitting. Time to make the trek up the hill, the only place left for her to go. She brushed at her tears with the back of her hand.

She picked her way carefully, remembering other times she'd gone up to the peaceful cemetery to talk things out. First to her father, then to Riley's father and Amelia. And always she felt better when she walked down the hill.

The path was overgrown, the medallions of stone covered with moss, which was slippery with early morning dew. Obviously Riley and Ivy didn't come to the hill. Why should they? she thought. Thanks to me and Cole, they have everything. She stopped in her tracks and covered her face with her hands. God, what was wrong with her? Why was she thinking like this? She looked at the footpath again, at the overgrown brush and moss. When you were dead, you were forgotten. She sobbed then, in great racking heaves that seemed to echo over the hill.

Maggie hugged herself tighter underneath the shawl as she looked around. The graves were untended. She silently cried out her rage as she dropped to her knees before her father's headstone. This shouldn't be. Riley couldn't be *that* busy. Surely he could afford to have someone clip away the vines and roots choking off the stones. She lashed out at her father's headstone with her clenched fist. Pain shot up her arm, but she didn't care. She stared at her own skin and at the blood trickling over the O in her father, Moss's, name. She reached out with her good hand to wipe it away.

She talked breathlessly then, the words pouring out of her. When she felt purged, she moved on her knees to her brother Riley's grave. She spoke softly there, telling him all about Riley Junior and little Moss. Then she moved to Amelia's stone where she broke down completely.

"He was so changed, Amelia, when he got back. So cool and . . . and almost indifferent. I have this feeling, and it's so hateful, I want to rip out my heart. How did you handle it? I know we talked many times, but you were so . . . accepting, because you genuinely liked Julie. I know you were ill and that made a difference too, but the hurt had to be the same. I'm not wrong, Amelia. I feel it, just the way you did. A woman knows when her husband has been unfaithful. *She knows.* The moment Rand came into the house and looked at me, I knew. My God, I knew. Oh, God, Amelia, you know I didn't mean what I said to Cary. I was lashing out at Rand and . . . and Mam. I hate being helpless. I can't do anything for Mam and Rand, it's a done deal, as the young people say today. It was a double whammy. I almost took a drink, but I didn't. I don't know how to handle any of this. I don't know if I *can* handle it. You know what? There are two words in the English language I hate with a passion. Mortality and infidelity. You know what else I hate, Amelia? That damn saying that you should be careful of what you wish for because you just might get it."

Maggie threw her arms around Amelia's headstone and sobbed.

"I thought I would find you here," Billie gasped, struggling to get her breath.

"Mam! What . . . why?"

"You needed me. Just put your arm around me and ease me down gently. I can sit on this little ledge," Billie said brokenly.

"Oh, Mam," Maggie cried, wrapping her frail mother in her arms.

"Maggie, Maggie," Billie whimpered.

"I don't want you to die, Mam. God, I don't want you to die."

"I'm not exactly overjoyed at the idea myself," Billie said tearfully. "This wasn't supposed to happen. I had it all planned in my mind. It's so hard. I don't have the words to try and make it right for you. Thad and I will be leaving right after breakfast. I need you to understand."

"Mam, come to Hawaii or let me go with you to Vermont. Let me take care of you. I'll stay with you night and day. Please, don't leave us."

"I'm not leaving you, darling. We'll see one another again. Thad . . . Thad needs to be with me. He needs to take care of me, and I need him. It's what I want. Please, Maggie, don't make this any more difficult than it already is."

"Okay, Mam." Maggie gulped. "About Cary . . ."

"I know you'll make it right, darling. Cary is a very understanding person. Be kind, darling. Always be kind. Now, I think we have to figure a way for me to get down this hill in one piece. Thad is going to be so angry with me for coming up here."

"Then let's not tell him," Maggie said lightly.

"Let's not." Billie smiled.

Billie turned to face Amelia's headstone. "I'm on my way. Don't get impatient," she whispered.

Maggie bit down on her lip so hard, blood trickled into her mouth.

When the two women reached the bottom of the hill, Maggie led her mother over to the milk box. "Sit here and catch your breath. If anyone is awake, they'll think we just came out to see the sun come up." After her mother was seated, Maggie said, "Mam, there's something I want to tell you. I think Rand slept with Valentine Mitchell while he was in Minnesota. I don't know what to do about it."

"Darling, when I don't know what to do about something, I do nothing. You said you *think*. That isn't good enough. Please, don't accuse your husband unless you are certain. Right now, our family is in a bit of a turmoil. There is every possibility you're overreacting to the situation. Think before you speak, is all I ask. Can you at least promise me that?"

"Yes, Mam, I can."

"That's good enough for me," Billie said lightly.

"Billieee!" Thad called.

Billie threw her hands in the air. "See what I mean? He gets hysterical if I'm not in his line of vision. I'm over here, Thad," she called gaily.

My God, how does she do it? Maggie wondered.

"Breakfast is ready. What are you ladies doing out here so early?"

"I was watching the sun come up, and Mam joined me. We were having one of those mother-daughter talks, with the daughter doing most of the talking," Maggie said just as gaily.

"Thad, if you'll just help me. My legs are a little wobbly this morning." For an answer, Thad scooped his wife up into his arms.

"You went up the hill, didn't you? I know you, Billie," Thad whispered against her neck.

Maggie smiled when she heard her mother's response. "Thad, did you *see* me go up the hill?"

"No, but—"

"There are no buts, Thad. Either you saw me go up the hill or you didn't."

"All right, already," Thad grumbled.

Maggie trailed behind, her eyes misty with tears. She reeled suddenly, almost losing her balance. Damn, what was that on her shoulder? She brushed at the loosely woven shawl and then a smile spread across her features. "Thanks for checking in, Amelia. I'll give your regards to Cary," she whispered. Overhead the trees rustled and a huge branch dipped and then heaved upward in the early morning breeze.

The feeling she had now, Maggie thought, was the same feeling she'd had in the hospital when she'd heard the angels sing over Sawyer.

As the family gathered at the front door to see Billie and Thad off, the phone rang loudly. No one made a move to veer off to the living room to answer it. Moss, in his mother's arms, chortled happily, his one bottom front tooth showing clearly.

"He loves the sound of the phone," Riley said huskily. "Hold on, everyone, I'll get it." He marched off stiffly, relieved at the break. This parting was going to be just as horrendous as the one with his grandfather. He barked into the phone, listened, and said, "Hold on,

I'll get him. Don't hang up, for God's sake. Yes, yes, I know. Wait now," Riley babbled.

Riley sprinted back to the wide central hall and tapped his cousin on the back. "The call's for you. I'd snap to it if I were you."

"Did . . . is Sumi ready . . . oh, shit . . ."

"Move!" Thad roared.

The moment Cole was out of sight, Riley whispered, "It's a girl. Eight pounds, eighteen inches long, and she has all her toes and fingers."

"Eight pounds!" Maggie and Sawyer chorused in unison.

"How wonderful," Ivy said, hugging her son. "Now you have three girl cousins to play with," she cooed to Moss.

"Cole will make such a wonderful father," Billie whispered. "I think all firstborns should be little girls. Of course, I'm slightly biased."

"I can't wait to buy a baby outfit," Susan said happily.

"I have a daughter," Cole said, coming back into the room. His face was full of awe. "Eight pounds, can you imagine that? Everyone is fine. I'm a father, for God's sake!"

Riley clapped Cole on the back. "Get your gear together, cousin. I'll drive you out to the plane. You sure you're up to flying back alone? You look like you're about to go into orbit."

"I'm fine. I'm really fine. Sumi picked a name. We agreed that if it was a girl, it would be Sumi's choice."

"Don't just stand there like a ninny, can't you see we're all holding our collective breath?" Sawyer grumbled.

Cole walked over to his grandmother. "Sumi said,

and I agreed, to name the baby Billie Otami Amelia Tanner."

"Oh, honey, I'm ... I'm overwhelmed. Riley, darling, your mother would be so happy. Thad," she said, turning to her husband, "I think this might be a good time for us to leave."

Cole hugged his grandmother. "Do you ever get the feeling someone is watching over us?" he whispered. "It couldn't have been timed better."

"I know what you mean," Billie whispered in return. "Promise me something, darling."

"Anything, Grandmam."

"Love your daughter unconditionally. Don't ever deviate from that love for even a second."

"You got it. I think you better get out of here while the going is good. Otherwise—"

" 'Bye, everyone. We'll write and call," Billie said, sashaying through the open doorway.

Cole closed the door. The tear-filled faces staring at him tore at his heart. "Listen up, everyone. I don't care if it is ten o'clock in the morning. I want to toast my new daughter. Break out the champagne. Two bottles, one goes to Cary."

"I'll take it over to the hospital," Susan offered.

The toasts and congratulations over, Maggie walked over to her son. "Will you send pictures of little Billie as soon as you get home? Please don't be angry with me, Cole. I ... ah, I have some things on my mind. I'll be going over to the hospital later to apologize to Cary. I'm going to be leaving late this afternoon. I think Susan will be staying on a bit to look after Cary. I've decided to get started on Billie Limited." She was talking too fast, her eyes pleading with her son for his forgiveness. If she had to grovel, she would. She waited, hardly daring to breathe.

"My Nikon will be clicking every second. I'll FedEx them to you. Hell, I might even develop them myself. Cary is a wonderful guy, Mother, and he's probably the most understanding man I've ever met, next to Adam. Good luck," he said, hugging her tightly. "Listen, now, anytime you want to hop over to see your granddaughter, just do it. We don't stand on ceremony. That goes for everyone!" He laughed happily.

"Wait for me," Sawyer said, her eyes sparkling devilishly. "Adam just called to beg me to come home. It seems the girls woke up at five A.M. and crawled out of their cribs. They squirted whipped cream all over the kitchen, then ate half a jar of sweet pickles and puked all over the kitchen floor. Adam says he thinks they ate a stick of butter too. So I'm going upstairs to pack and head for the airport."

"Oh, we're going to be alone again. I'll miss all of you," Ivy said sincerely. "Susan, you aren't going, are you?"

"No, but I thought I would stay in town. If you need me, I can go back and forth, but I don't have a car."

"Both Riley and I would like you to stay, Susan, but the decision is up to you."

"Town will be better. I'll be open for dinner invitations though."

"You have an open invitation," Riley said. "You can take my car, Susan. The keys are under the mat. I won't be using it for the next couple of days." Susan nodded happily as she made her way up the stairs.

"See? I told you, everything is turning around," Ivy whispered to her husband.

"Wise-ass," Riley said fondly.

"But I'm *your* wise-ass, right?"

"Forever and ever." Riley grinned. "Listen, honey, Cole and I have some business to take care of. Can you make some coffee and bring it into the study?"

"Just as soon as I settle Moss. Where did Maggie and Rand go?"

Riley shrugged.

"Something is wrong," Ivy muttered.

"I know, and whatever it is has nothing to do with Cary. Rand's been acting strange since he got here. He's here, but he isn't here, if you know what I mean."

"Honey," Ivy said, reaching up to kiss her husband, "I think it's a wonderful thing Sumi did by naming their firstborn after Billie and your mother. Billie was so pleased. Did you see how her face lighted? And your own face, darling one, was just as bright. Wait till Cary hears the news. Go, shoo, Cole's waiting for you. Make sure you tell him how wonderful fatherhood is, and don't just tell him the good stuff."

"You want me to tell him about the poopie diapers, and the wakeup calls during the night, and the colic?"

"Yep. If you don't, Sawyer is going to scare the hell out of him. He got a little white when she was expounding away."

"All right. Cole can handle it. Hey, he can call me anytime."

"Don't forget to tell him you always put the diaper on backward." Ivy giggled.

"Enough!" Riley shouted, to Moss's delight.

It was twelve-thirty when Cole leaned back in his chair, his eyes on his cousin. "It's a deal, then. I'll start the legal work the minute I get tired of looking at my new daughter. From this moment on we are ColeShad.

The Cole is from Coleman and Shad is from your grandfather's name. Don't go saying I have a streak of nepotism in me. My last name is Tanner. And we did it in alphabetical order, just the way you wanted." His hand shot out. Riley grasped it in his rock-hard fist.

"You feeling okay about this, Cole?"

"Aside from the headache I'm going to get when restructuring starts, yes, I'm okay with it. I'm sorry it took me so long. You cut me a lot of slack, Riley. I don't know if I would have been as kind if the situation were reversed. I need to know one thing, though. Where's the string?"

Riley thrust his booted feet on top of the desk and hooted with laughter. "There were never any strings. Just the way there were no strings when you deeded Sunbridge to me. We're family, Cole, that's the bottom line."

When the cousins wrapped up business an hour later, it was agreed that Riley would make the appointment with Valentine Mitchell and set the wheels in motion to secure Cary's mortgage on Miranda.

"One last thing, Riley. The moment you . . . as soon as you hear from Thad, get on the horn. I need time to get here."

"I'll do my best, Cole. Grandmam doesn't want any of us hovering and calling all the time. I asked Thad this morning if he would call me every couple of days. He promised. As much as it hurts, we have to do what Grandmam wants."

"Full circle, Riley."

"I think we can handle it now, although it was a little iffy there for a while. Did you ever get the feeling these past years that we—this is going to sound stupid, but— that we were being tested?"

"Every damn day." Cole grinned.

"Me too." Riley guffawed.

"You realize they set us up, your grandfather and Grandmam Billie? Your grandfather with the old switcheroo from you to me, and Grandmam Billie bankrupting the family with the lawsuits. Think about it, Riley, and remember all those trips Grandmam and Thad took to Japan. If it wasn't the lawsuits, it would have been something else."

"It would have been a lot simpler if they had just told us what they wanted," Riley groused.

"Nah, it wouldn't have worked. They wanted us to find out for ourselves. We're it, Riley! From here on in we're on our own. I guarantee there won't be any more ashes in the Zen garden, and no one will snatch my beer and sake. Grandmam Billie will rest easy."

"Jesus," Riley said, his face full of awe.

"Time for me to go, Riley. I'd like to stop and see Cary first, if you don't mind. I want to tell him about my new daughter. He's gonna bust when I tell him her name, and it might take a little of the edge off when my mother goes to see him. I'll meet you by the car. I have to say good-bye to Mother and Rand."

As it turned out, Cole didn't get to say good-bye. Maggie and Rand were nowhere to be found. He scribbled a note saying he would call when he got home. To Jonquil's delight, he kept singing Billie Otami Amelia Tanner over and over as he sailed through the kitchen to meet Riley in the courtyard.

"How did you know where to find me?" Maggie asked from her position on the Jarvis swing, the same swing on which she had sat earlier with Sawyer.

"Process of elimination. That and your favorite horse was also missing."

"Why?" Maggie asked in a disinterested voice. "Since you came back from Minnesota, you have barely said two words to me. You didn't even sleep in our bed last night."

"I was wired up, Maggie. The thing with Cary, it made me realize how fragile our very existence is. Your mother . . . all I could see was my stepmother, Amelia. Your unkind outburst just seemed to bring things to a boil. I felt everything closing in on me. Thad and I stayed with Cary till one in the morning. I didn't want to wake you."

How lame his voice sounds, Maggie thought. She shrugged.

"Don't you think we should be getting back?"

"Why?"

Rand threw his hands in the air. "We have an early evening flight."

"That's not quite true. *I* have an early evening flight. I canceled yours. I don't want you coming back to the house. Ever. I'll pack your things and send them wherever you want. It will be up to you to tell your daughter about your move."

"For God's sake, Maggie, what's gotten into you? I know you're upset about your mother and that . . . whatever that was with Cary, but aren't you carrying this a bit too far? I don't understand. One day things are fine, and the next day you want me to move out of the house! I wish you'd explain things to me. Have you been drinking?"

Maggie shrugged. "No, I haven't been drinking."

"Don't you think I deserve an explanation? Damnit,

Maggie, talk to me." The desperation in her husband's voice brought a smile to Maggie's face.

"I might come back to Texas and work at Billie Limited. Or I can live right here in Adam's house." Maggie held out her hand to reveal a brass key. "Sawyer gave it to me."

"This isn't like you. If it's what you want, fine, but I think I deserve an explanation."

"Why don't we just say I'm crazy and let it go at that? I think this is where you ride off into the sunset. Good-bye, Rand."

Rand reached for his wife and dragged her off the chair. She was like a rag doll in his hands. "Just like that, it's over. With no explanations. Not even a drop dead or go to hell. What the hell did I do?"

"Have you ever been unfaithful to me, Rand?"

The lie rolled off Rand's lips so smoothly, he was stunned. "No!"

"I don't believe you," Maggie said quietly. "I've seen infidelity all my life. My father, my husband, Cary, and now you. I recognize the signs. It's that simple."

"Because you witnessed infidelity in others, you're judging and condemning me!" Rand bellowed, his voice full of guilty rage.

"And found you guilty," Maggie said, anger rising in her. "How dare you! How dare you muck up our marriage like this!" She turned so she wouldn't have to see the awful guilt on her husband's face.

"Maggie—"

"Go away, Rand. Don't make this any harder than it is."

"Maggie, I love you."

"You know what, Rand? I love me too. I don't deserve this. I knew. I knew the minute I heard your voice on the phone. . . . I could hear it in your voice. I felt it. You betrayed me and then you lied to my face. Go, Rand, I can't bear to look at you."

The moment the ground around her was silent, Maggie turned to stare across the prairie. Now she could cry with no one to see or care. *I didn't accuse him, Mam. I asked him and he lied to me. If he'd admitted it . . . no, I can't forgive that. He took something wonderful, something I treasured, and mucked it up. You never forgave Pap for being unfaithful to you. Why should I be any different? I did what you said, though, I asked. I know in my heart what you said to me is . . . is going to be . . . you won't be giving me advice anymore. I followed it, Mam.*

Maggie looked at her watch. She took a deep breath before she got up from the porch swing. She had to make things right with Cary, and she didn't have much time left.

"They all think I'm the strong one, that nothing ruffles me," Maggie muttered as she spurred the horse onward. "Ha. I feel as if my guts have been wrenched out of my stomach."

It was half past twelve when Maggie clicked her way down the sterile hospital corridor in search of Cary's room. Her stomach churned. She swallowed hard as two nurses in starched white crackled by her, medicine trays in their hands. Inside the room she could see Susan sitting on a hard plastic chair, an open book in her hands. Three daily newspapers were piled on the metal table that separated her chair from Cary's. Obviously, Maggie thought, Susan was going to read them all to her charge. How protective she looks. How happy. Maggie's shoulders started to shake the moment Susan noticed her.

"So many flowers," she whispered to Susan. "Would you mind leaving us alone for a minute, Suse?"

"Sure. I'll go get us some coffee." She was gone a second later, the delicate scent of her perfume wafting behind her.

"Cary, it's me, Maggie," Maggie said. She reached for Cary's hand. It felt dry and hot. For some reason, she'd expected it to be sweaty. "I came to apologize. Sorry is just a word, one we all use too often. I want to . . . I need to explain. I'm not sure if . . . what I'm trying to say is I might hurt you even more. . . . Oh, Cary, I . . . Rand . . . Rand slept with Valentine Mitchell. I saw you sitting there and I remembered Amelia and a talk we had and how devastated she was. I reacted badly and I'm sorry. It all sort of slapped me in the face. I had no right to say what I did. I wanted to hurt someone the way I was hurting. Mam . . . Rand . . . your offer to help Sawyer, the look on my son's face. Please, Cary, forgive me."

"There's nothing to forgive, Maggie. I believe I am part of this family. I knew where you were coming from. I felt it. I sensed Rand's . . . guilt. It was so easy to recognize. Don't forget, I've lived with mine for so long, it's part of my skin now."

Maggie nodded and then remembered that Cary couldn't see through his bandages. "I know. I can't be that noble, that selfless. I'm not saying Amelia was wrong, I'm just saying I don't think and feel like Amelia. Betrayal has to be the hardest thing in the world to bear," Maggie whispered.

"I'd say it's right up there with guilt," Cary said quietly. "I live with it every day. Part of me will always love Julie, but I had to send her away. What we had . . . it just . . . I couldn't live with it. What are you going to do, Maggie? What are your options? Wheel me down to the sun room so we can have a cigarette. We can't smoke in the rooms. Don't worry about Susan, she'll find us."

"I am returning to Hawaii tonight. I told Rand to move out. Right now I guess I'll just hang out for a few days and feel sorry for myself. You know, beat my breast and cry a lot. I'm taking over Billie Limited, so that means I have to map out a plan, start up operations, go to Hong Kong and Taiwan."

"It sounds like a good starting place for you. What did . . . Rand say?"

"He denied it. He was never a good liar. I felt it, Cary, just the way Amelia did." Cary squeezed her hand reassuringly. Bolstered, Maggie said, "Cary, I need to ask you a question. Please, for my sake, tell me the truth. If Amelia had asked you, would you have admitted your affair with Julie?"

"Yes. At one point I had, at the very least, one hundred and ten versions of why I did what I did, and not one of them worth the breath it would have taken to utter them. Every single day I waited, expecting Amelia to ask me, but she never did. It's so hard for me to believe, to accept that Amelia knew all along and never said a word. There was nothing about her, no indication. She liked Julie, she approved of her as her successor. Till I die I will never understand *that*. Anyway, I'm glad you came to me."

"Thanks for listening, Cary. Please, I need to hear you tell me you forgive me, that you understand. I think it's a wonderful thing you're doing for Sawyer and the family. Amelia must be smiling from ear to ear. Oh, I forgot to tell you, I walked up the hill this morning, and when I got back I . . . I had this feeling she was touch-

ing my shoulder, telling me she was going to look after
Mam. Don't laugh at me, Cary. It's important for me to
believe this. Anyway, I told her I'd say hello." Maggie
leaned over and kissed Cary lightly on the cheek.

Cary smiled. "She's always there when it counts."

Maggie kissed him again. "I know I'm leaving you in
good hands. Susan, Ivy, and Riley will watch over you.
Susan told you about Cole's new daughter, didn't she?
Billie Otami Amelia Tanner. It has a ring to it. Mam
was so pleased. I'll be in touch, Cary," Maggie said
softly. "Hey, your personal nurse is here, and may I say
I love powder-blue," Maggie said, referring to Susan's
light wool dress. "Susan, take care, I'll call. You'll be at
the condo in Miranda?"

"For a while, Maggie, I—"

"Shhh," Maggie said, hugging her sister. "Take care
of Cary." How bright her eyes are, Maggie thought.
How wonderful Cary's smile is.

She felt cheated when she made her way out of the
hospital to the parking lot.

Four hours later she was airborne. In ten hours she
would be home. Minus a husband.

{{{{{{{{{ CHAPTER NINE }}}}}}}}}

Rand stood alongside Riley and Ivy, who held little Moss, under Sunbridge's portico, his face grim, his shoulders rigid.

"I don't know what to do," he said dejectedly.

"Do you want to come inside and talk about it?" Riley asked. "Neither Ivy nor I know what's going on. Aunt Maggie made peace with Cary. When she got back, she said he was more understanding than she deserved. If Cary forgives her, I don't understand what your problem is, Rand," Riley said with an edge to his voice. He loved Maggie like a mother. She'd stepped in and welcomed him to Sunbridge when he first arrived in the States. More than once she'd taken his side over her own son's when squabbles erupted. In his eyes Maggie could do no wrong.

"You two go along. I think this little fella needs a bath and supper," Ivy said cheerfully. "Jonquil made a buffet, so anytime you guys want to eat, just let me know."

"Sure, honey."

"Do you feel like a walk?" Rand asked.

"How about a trip up the hill?"

"No, not the hill," Rand said. "Let's walk around the garden."

They strolled, each busy with his own thoughts. Riley thought he would burst with the silence.

Rand finally spoke. "I think I'll go back to England."

"Now, you mean? Why?"

"Your aunt Maggie told me not to bother going back to Hawaii. She told me to move out and to take my daughter with me. Earlier she mentioned something about coming back here and either renting Billie's studio from you and Ivy or setting up shop in Adam's house."

"I'm in the dark here, Rand. I don't understand any of this. What I do understand is I've never seen my aunt so miserable, so determined. Are you just going to talk or are you going to explain? If you feel it's none of my business, I can deal with that," Riley said briskly.

"Maggie thinks I slept with Valentine Mitchell," Rand said curtly.

Riley's eyebrows shot upward. He thought about his upcoming meeting with the attorney, and then he remembered the three and a half days Rand and Val spent in Minnesota. A vision of the fast-track lawyer flashed before him. He bit down on his lower lip.

"Aren't you going to ask me if I did or didn't?" Rand asked defensively.

"If I did, would you tell me the truth? Aunt Maggie must believe you did if . . . She usually thinks things through pretty carefully before she makes a decision. She used to hammer that into Cole's and my heads. If that was what she was carrying around inside her last night, it would at least explain her outburst about Cary. Maybe she wanted to go back alone to have a cooling off period, to think about things."

"She's already thought about them. Her leaving alone was her decision."

"You didn't put up much of a fight," Riley said coolly.

"So that makes me guilty, I suppose?"

"Don't put words in my mouth, Rand. However, I do remember another time when you and Sawyer were an item, and you didn't have the guts to tell her it was over. That's when she was so sick and almost died. Then you up and married Aunt Maggie a little while later. Hey, I can add, and I can come up with four like everyone else. To this day, you have no idea how you hurt her. Cole and I know, though. Maybe Aunt Maggie is remembering that too," Riley said tightly, his eyes defensive.

"It wasn't like that. The thing with Sawyer was over before Maggie and I got to know one another," Rand snarled. "That was a low blow, Riley, and you damn well know it."

"It's no such thing, Rand. It's a damn fact. You can't change facts. Like Aunt Maggie, I believe in fidelity." He wanted to ask Rand whether Valentine was worth all that he was going through now, but he didn't. How was he supposed to act around Val when he went to her office tomorrow? he wondered. "So what's your game plan?"

Rand shrugged. "As I said, England, I guess."

"You're welcome here. Stay as long as you like. If you want privacy, you can use Grandmam Billie's studio until you decide what you want to do. I'm not judging you, Rand. If it sounded that way, I'm sorry."

"There's always a but," Rand said. "But you aren't comfortable around me. And you still haven't asked me that all-important question."

He's too defensive, too cocky, Riley thought. "No,

and I won't. I don't want to know. This is between you and Aunt Maggie. Did you talk to Thad about this?"

"No. Thad has enough on his mind. And I didn't say anything to Cary either, if that's your next question. But I think Maggie may have said something to Sawyer."

Riley propped one of his feet on the same milk box his aunt had sat on earlier in the day. "I rarely give advice, Rand, but if I were you, I'd go to Maggie and do whatever you have to do to make things right."

"I'll keep it in mind," Rand said in a neutral voice. "I think I'll skip dinner. Do you mind if I use your truck later?"

"Not at all. I'm in for the night. Is there anything I can do, Rand?"

"No, but thanks for the offer. I'll see you later," Rand said, and strode off in the direction of the house.

The room Rand was supposed to have shared with his wife was decorated in soft, earthy garden colors. The only thing out of place was his suitcase, which was still packed and still in the same position it had been in yesterday, when he carried it here himself. Maggie had spent several days in this room, but there was no sign of her at all. The brown and moss-green spread on the bed was free of wrinkles. There were no telltale flecks of face powder, no stray hairpins, no tissues. In the bathroom the towels were folded neatly, the soap looked untouched, and there were no watermarks on the vanity or sink. The lid on the toilet seat was down. Rand puzzled over the fact that there were no tissues in the waste basket. Maggie required at least half a box when she applied makeup. Then he remembered that she wasn't wearing makeup when she left. Her nose had been shiny and her freckles had shown clearly through her tan.

How many times over the years had she repeated the

words, "Be a good houseguest so you're invited back?" What that meant was to remove the bed linens, empty the trash, hang up the towels, and if there are fresh flowers in the room, change the water. Maggie had taken care of everything. He felt like bawling.

Angrily, he pitched his suitcase at the bed. Now the spread was wrinkled. Good. He undid the straps and peered down at the messy array of clothing. Most of the contents were soiled. He upended the suitcase and tossed it on the floor. At the bottom was a pair of wrinkled but clean khaki trousers and a shirt, also wrinkled. He felt victorious when he noted a clean pair of jockey shorts and one pair of rolled-up socks. Then he felt like bawling again.

In the bathroom mirror, he noticed his two-day-old stubble and winced. He looked like a bum. Jesus. He took off his clothes and pitched them in the general direction of the upended suitcase and pile of clothing on the bed.

Thirty minutes later he was shaved, clean, and wrinkled. "Now what do I do?" he muttered. His gaze settled on the chocolate-colored phone on the nightstand. He noticed the flowers then for the first time. Bright red tulips, which looked limp and tired. So Maggie didn't practice what she preached, he thought irritably. It pleased him no end to carry the vase of flowers into the bathroom to pour out the water and add fresh. He was careful to wipe off the bottom of the vase so it wouldn't leave a watermark on the night table. He felt a little better immediately, as though he'd done something worthwhile, something that really mattered in the scheme of things.

He picked up the phone, punched out his number in Hawaii, and listened to Maggie's voice on the answering machine say, "Rand and I aren't here right now, so leave your name and number at the sound of the beep and we'll return your call as soon as we can." He cleared his throat before the beep and spoke loudly and clearly. "Maggie, we *need* to discuss this. You can't just end things without talking to me. I'm calling from Sunbridge, but I'll be leaving shortly. My plan at the moment is to go to a hotel in town. I don't want to burden the family with our problem. They have enough on their minds as it is. I just wanted you to . . . know I care and that I'm thinking of you."

Rand broke the connection and replaced the receiver.

It was dark now, and the only light shining into the bedroom was from the bathroom. Rand snapped on the overhead light and for the first time noticed the sapphire-blue chair by the window. It looked out of place, more like a woman's chair, or at least a Billie color. He wondered if his wife had sat on it. Was it okay to smoke here in the bedroom? Ivy had never said if it was or wasn't. Riley smoked occasionally, Ivy not at all. He opened the window before he lit his cigarette, spotting a small ceramic ashtray on the wide windowsill.

Where should he go? What should he do? What exactly were his options? What were his legal options? He groaned. Regardless of the mitigating circumstances, Maggie would bend over backward to be fair if it came down to legal defenses. *What goes around comes around.* That's what Sawyer had said to him. He wished now that there had been bitterness in Sawyer's voice instead of sadness. He'd stepped over the line, and Sawyer knew it. She would never forgive him. They'd all forgiven Cary when he fell off the fidelity wagon because Amelia had forgiven him, had given her seal of approval to Julie. They weren't going to forgive him, though. He wondered how long it would take before they *all* knew he'd crossed over the line. The lie he'd told his wife had made things worse. Amelia had raised him to be truthful, to stand up and take his medicine when he screwed up. His shoulders slumped as he realized what he'd done. He'd been unfaithful and he lied to cover up his wrongdoing.

Goddamnit, just because Maggie said he shouldn't go back to the house in Hawaii didn't mean he had to listen to her. He had as much right to be there as she did. Do what she wants, wait it out, an inner voice cautioned. The right time will come for you to sit down and talk. Maggie won't stay in Hawaii alone. She'll come back. She doesn't do well alone. And then another voice accused: Maggie loved you heart and soul, you bastard. Now you've lost her. You're a low-down, stinking, miserable bastard and you deserve whatever Maggie dishes out, *Lord* Rand Nelson.

Rand squeezed his eyes shut. The burning sensation he was feeling made them water. Too much cigarette smoke.

What goes around comes around.

He felt like a thief when he tiptoed down the steps, through the house and out to the courtyard. Since dinner was a buffet, he more or less assumed Riley and Ivy would be eating in the great room. His thought proved right, and he didn't encounter them. He drove around the house and out the three-mile drive to the main road. He never felt more an outsider in his life.

On the highway, driving at a sedate seventy miles an hour, Rand turned on the radio. He almost ran off the road into a ditch when he heard Rod Stewart singing "Maggie May." Shaken, he eased up on the gas pedal and concentrated on the road in front of him. He ended up in the underground parking lot of Assante Towers.

"Your card, sir," the security guard said quietly. Rand whipped out the plastic card Cary had given to all the family members attached to Riley's visor in the pickup. He waited while the card slid through a coding machine. The guard handed back the card and said, "The elevators to the penthouses are to the right of the B section, sixteen through thirty-two are to the left of the A section. The stairs are next to the C section." Rand grunted as he strode off in the direction of the A section.

He stepped out of the elevator on the thirty-sixth floor and walked slowly up the hall until he came to 36A. He pressed the doorbell. He listened to the soft chiming on the other side of the door. He thought it was a tune, but couldn't be sure. He backed up a step when the door opened.

"You were in the neighborhood and thought you would stop by and say hello," Valentine Mitchell drawled. "So say hello and leave. We said we weren't going to see one another again."

Rand stiff-armed the door, which was about to close in his face.

"How did you get in here anyway? We agreed, Rand."

"All I want is to talk to you," Rand said, stepping into the shiny foyer. He didn't think he'd ever seen such an accumulation of mirrors, glass, and chrome in one place. It seemed as if his and Val's reflections were everywhere. House of mirrors, he thought.

Val stepped aside. "Come into my parlor, said the spider to the fly." She made a low, sweeping bow, her face inscrutible. Rand looked at her bare feet. She was wearing jeans and the same Greenpeace sweatshirt she'd worn in Minnesota.

The plush of the white wall-to-wall carpet seemed to cuddle Rand's shoes as he made his way past Valentine into the low sunken living room he'd seen from the foyer. He settled himself in a white leather chair. "This is different," he said as he looked around the huge room. "I like the pictures." On the wall were oversize hangings that were nothing more than gigantic slashes of brilliant color.

"They're my contribution to the decor," Val said tightly. "Since I live in a black-and-white world twenty hours out of every day, I thought I could use a little color. You didn't come here to discuss the furnishings in my apartment, did you?"

"No, I didn't. Maggie knows."

Val fired a cigarette and blew a perfect smoke ring in Rand's direction. "That surprises me. I didn't think you were the type to kiss and tell." She blew another smoke ring, her face impassive.

"I didn't tell her. She said she figured it out herself. She left earlier this evening and doesn't want me to go back to Hawaii. Maggie is not a forgiving person."

Two perfect smoke rings sailed upward. "The first rule in life is you never admit to anything," Val said. "The second rule is, if you fuck up, you deal with it. Usually I charge three hundred fifty dollars an hour for that kind of advice. For you, Lord Nelson, it's free."

"I didn't admit to anything. Maggie asked me point-blank, and I lied. I want you to back me up. It never happened."

"I never look back, Rand, and I never get involved in messes like this."

"Come off it, Val. I'm asking you to help me save

my marriage. All it takes is one phone call. I don't think it's too much to ask."

"I do." She laughed, but it didn't reach her eyes. "That would be an admission on my part that the alleged incident did in fact take place. No thanks, Rand, I'll pass on this one."

Rand's eyebrows crawled backward. "You're refusing to help me?" he asked incredulously.

Val tapped a fresh cigarette on the glass-topped table, looked at the cigarette in her hand with clinical interest before she hung it in the corner of her mouth and then talked around it. "If the alleged incident were reversed, how quickly would you come to my defense? Let's see." She squinted past the smoke spiraling upward. "I'd say your first inclination would be to cover your ass in a variety of ways. You'd have sixteen of the finest, most upstanding citizens you know swear you were in a card game during the time the alleged incident took place. You'd hang me out to dry without blinking. You see, I gave it a lot of thought on the way home from Minnesota. You play, you pay. Now if you don't mind, I have some briefs I need to look over. I have an early day tomorrow."

"Val, please," Rand said huskily.

"Rand, that night, I told you it wasn't a good idea. But we had too much to drink, and we took advantage of each other. As far as I'm concerned, it never happened."

"It happened," Rand snarled.

Val threw her hands in the air. "You see, there are two sides to everything. I told you, I never look back."

Rand was on his feet, his face full of rage.

Val only laughed. "By the way," she said, "yesterday I returned the balance of my retainer from Coleman Enterprises. Certified mail. I also faxed my resignation so there would be no doubt as to the time."

"The family will view that as an admission of guilt," Rand sputtered.

"I don't care how your family views it. It's the way I view it that's important."

"You just dug my grave, Val," Rand snarled. "I'll see that you never get another legal case in this state."

"Really!"

"Yes, really."

Val crushed her cigarette into the ceramic ashtray. She leaned over the cocktail table and took a fistful of M&M candies from a crystal dish. With cool deliberation she popped them, one by one, into her mouth. "This is just my opinion, Lord Nelson, but I'd say Maggie was well rid of you. You aren't the nice person I thought you were. Now, if you don't leave, I'm going to buzz for security. You weren't announced, so that must mean you came up the service elevator and used someone else's card." Her hand was on the phone when Rand slapped it out of her hand.

"Don't ever threaten me, Val."

Rand's arm swept the contents of the cocktail table onto the floor before he stormed out of the apartment. The moment the door closed, Val ran to it and shot the dead bolt home. As Val sat down on the sofa, she realized her anger had turned into something else—a deep melancholy. She needed a friend, but she didn't have one. Not one *true* friend. God, how had she gotten to this point in her life without making at least one?

Well, it wasn't too late. Friends could still be made. She could change her life around if she wanted to.

She'd lied to Rand about having to work on briefs. The pile of papers on the table represented a proposal of sale of her firm, which was now worth a cool eleven million dollars. The six associates were willing to buy her out if they could get adequate financing. Thirty days and it would be over. Right now, this minute, she knew she could walk out of this apartment with her toothbrush and survive the rest of her life in a style that would be more than comfortable.

She thought about Brody's drugstore in Oxmoor, Minnesota. She wouldn't take a toothbrush. A toothbrush, one of those bright yellow ones in the cellophane wrappers next to the mouthwash, would be her first purchase at Brody's.

Fifty-four wasn't too old to start over. Other people had done it. She could buy a little house like Susan's, with a garden. She looked down at her acrylic nails and knew they would be the first thing to go. She could get a couple of dogs and a cat and one of those birds that chirped in the morning. She'd go to Dixon's hardware store and buy a lawn mower, a lawn rake, and a snow-blower. She'd sell the Lamborghini and get a Range Rover. She'd stick the Rolex, the pearls, the diamonds in a safe deposit box and learn to shop at Wal-Mart.

The move, if she went through with it, would be the biggest challenge of her life.

She thought about Maggie Nelson. She'd once heard through the Coleman grapevine that Maggie and Rand had a marriage to equal that of Billie and Thad Kingsley. How sad that it was coming to an end. How sad that Rand screwed it up, and with her help. All the way home on the plane she'd thought about her part in it all.

"But why can't I get Maggie out of my mind?" she asked herself. Maybe she should call her. Not for Rand, but for Maggie. Maggie was sharp; would she believe her? Not likely. She could tell Maggie the truth. Which would be harder for Maggie to deal with? Or was it better to remain quiet? Rand was right about one thing—the family would view her resignation and departure as an admission of guilt. She had to decide now, this very second, if she cared.

Val reached for another handful of the colored candies, popping all of them into her mouth. She munched contentedly. She didn't care.

Thoughts of Maggie stayed with her as she tidied up the papers on the table. At one time Maggie had been tough as rawhide. Now, though, Val thought, she's just as vulnerable as the rest of us. How devastated she must be. Val stopped what she was doing, a terrible expression on her face. What if Maggie started to drink?

Val bolted from the sofa and started to pace, arguing with herself as she waded up and down the long, narrow living room into the dining room, around the table, skirting the four-foot-high pedestal with the bust of Blackstone on it. Up and down she walked, smacking one clenched fist against the other. She stopped once to yank at the Greenpeace sweatshirt riding up around her waist. If only she had a friend to help her, she thought. If only she had someone to listen.

Then, suddenly, faster than she'd ever moved in her life, she ran through the thick carpet to the door, yanking at the chain and the dead bolt. She pulled the door open, stopping for just a moment before she ran down the hall to 36C. She rang the doorbell and stepped back so the occupant on the other side could see her clearly.

Elliot Morrow, publisher of the *Miranda Sentinel* and a client of Val's firm, opened the door. "Val, is something wrong?" he asked, concerned.

"No, of course not. I was wondering if you would do me a tremendous favor."

"If I can," the rotund little man said. "Come in."

Val stepped into an apartment that was almost identical to hers. "I was wondering if you would loan me Isaac for the night. I . . . I have just decided to get a dog, and I . . . I said I would let the man know first thing in the morning. Since I never had an animal, I would . . . ah, like to . . . what I mean is . . ."

"Sure, Isaac knows you."

Elliot whistled. A four-legged whilrwind skittered to a stop at Val's feet. Val dropped to her knees to scratch the taffy-colored spaniel behind his ears. Wet, adoring eyes begged her to continue.

"Val, is anything wrong?"

"Nothing I can't handle," she said quietly.

"Okay. Wait here." Elliot returned a minute later with a shopping bag filled to the brim. "This is Isaac's bed and his blanket. I've included two of his toys, his leash, his snacks, his brush and comb, his toothbrush, and his breakfast. Walk him at eleven-thirty and again at six. Drop him off anytime between seven and eight. His sitter comes in at eight-fifteen. Don't let him on the furniture, and wash his whiskers after he eats. He hates it when his whiskers get stiff. He goes to sleep right after he's walked for the night. His music box is in there too."

"You know, Elliot, you treat this dog better than some people treat their children."

"Isaac and I have been together for a long time. So I spoil him, so what? It makes me happy, and I don't think you could find a happier dog anywhere in this universe. Take care of him," Elliot said, opening the door. To the spaniel he said, "Go with Val and she'll give you a treat." The dog looked backward once, but followed Val obediently, his eyes on the bulging shopping bag.

Val opened the door to her apartment. The moment it closed behind her, Isaac walked straight into the living room and leaped up onto the white couch. He woofed softly and then began to sniff his surroundings. Val watched as he stretched, trying to reach the candy dish on the cocktail table. He woofed again. "Go ahead, help yourself," Val said, emptying out the shopping bag. "A man could go to war with less gear," she muttered.

The moment the dog's belongings were stashed, Val sat down on the couch next to him. She waited, uncertain of what to do next. She wanted to pick Isaac up, to hug him, to feel his warm body and the beat of his little heart. She fondled his silky ears, her eyes misting with tears. She held her breath when the fat little dog slowly inched his way closer until his front paws were on her jeans. He wiggled again, then again, until he was in her lap. A sob worked its way up to Val's throat. Tears rolled down her cheeks. Isaac squirmed and wiggled until he was on his hind legs, his front paws on Val's shaking shoulders. His silky ears flopped this way and that way as he licked first at one side of her face, then the other.

Isaac allowed himself to be petted and stroked, hugged and squeezed. The spaniel's silky head was so wet with her tears, Val had to dry him with a tissue from her pocket. She clung to the animal, baring her soul.

"I was attracted to Rand. I will never deny that. But I would never have acted on that attraction if he hadn't made the first move. I have never lied to myself, and I know in my heart that I wouldn't have. Drunk or sober.

So, Isaac, where does that leave me?" Val sobbed to the dog. "This is pretty much a moral call here, my friend." She rubbed her wet cheeks against the dog's soft body. Isaac whimpered as he snuggled comfortably in the crook of Val's arm.

They slept. Once during the long night, the spaniel crept quietly from Val's arm to circle the apartment, finally choosing the shiny chrome dining room table leg to relieve himself. He was back in the attorney's arms a minute later.

Thirty-six floors below, Rand sat in Riley's pickup truck. He wished now that he hadn't come here. This was his problem, not Val's.

You play, you pay, Val had said. Rand leaned his head back into the cracked leather seat. It made his back itch. His eyes closed and he took roll call of his life. All things considered, it had been a good life. A few ups and downs. More ups than downs. Scene after scene flashed before his closed eyes. He thought about his favorite stuffed animal, a cat, when he was a child. Sally Dearest he'd called it. He wished he had it now, so he could bury his head in the fuzzy, patched-up animal. Back then it had given him so much comfort. The past. Sally Dearest was history. Everything before this moment was history. Exhausted with his soul searching, Rand dozed. When he woke hours later, he looked at the numerals on his watch. Ten minutes past midnight. Time to go home. Home. That was the laugh of the year.

Rand turned the key in the ignition and backed out of his parking space. He proceeded up the ramp and out into the clear starry night. He drove aimlessly because, he told himself, when you didn't have a home, it didn't matter what you did or where you went. He headed east on 290 with no destination in mind. An hour later he pulled the pickup to the side of the road at a phone booth and used his calling card to call Hawaii. He explained to the operator that the machine would come on and he wanted to leave a message.

Rand shivered when he heard Maggie's voice on the answering machine. All about him cars and trucks whizzed by. Where in the hell was all the traffic going at this hour of the morning? He found himself yelling into the phone. "I'm taking the first plane out in the morning. I need to talk to you, Maggie. After I say what I have to say, you can do what you want. But you're going to hear me out. I love you, Maggie. I've never loved anyone but you. I need you to believe me." He choked, his voice breaking. "I *need you*, Maggie."

It wasn't much, but it was a start. Rand half turned in the narrow booth to lean his forehead against the cool glass. All he had to do now was head back to Sunbridge, drop off the pickup, and head for the airport, where he would catch the first flight to Hawaii.

He pushed at the bifold door in time to hear a loud whoosh as a Ryder truck roared down the road. He gasped at the strong wind and smell of the truck's exhaust. God, where *was* this traffic going? He blinked at the blazing oncoming lights. He brought up his hand to shield his eyes, debating if he had time to get to the truck and close the door before the next vehicle barreled past. He opened the door of the cab, his right hip and leg half on the seat, when he heard the sound of an eighteen-wheeler bearing down so close he could see the license plates in the oversize side door mirror. He knew the finely printed words on the side mirror by heart: Objects in mirror are closer than they appear. He was about to slide the rest of the way onto the seat when the behemoth streaked by at eighty miles an hour, slamming him against the door and ripping it off its hinges with a metallic shriek.

He was dead before he was tossed in the air like a rag doll, then down into the deep culvert alongside the road, thirty feet from the telephone booth, his hand still on the door handle.

The driver looked into his rearview mirror, knowing he'd ripped the door off the pickup. "Damn fool deserves to lose his door," he muttered under his breath.

Isaac stirred restlessly in Val's arms. She too stirred with the strange movement. Her eyes popped open to meet those of the spaniel. How warm he was, how soft and cuddly. But she groaned when she realized the dog needed to be walked. "Poor little thing," she crooned as she struggled from her nest in the pillows.

"Okay, Isaac, I know my duty. I'll get my shoes, and we'll head for the nearest fire plug." When she returned wearing her sneakers, she was in time to see Isaac lift his leg on the dining room table leg. "Guess that takes care of that," she whooped, but made no move to clean it up. She squatted down next to the dog, certain he was going to communicate with her in some way. "Don't you have to do something else? Or do you do that at night?" The dog stared at her unblinkingly. Val stared back. "Okay, how about breakfast? Chicken and noodles. Come on, I'll put it on fine china, howzat?"

Val busied herself in the kitchen, dicing chicken thighs and chopped noodles per Elliot's written instructions. When Isaac's food was ready, she slid it into the microwave oven for forty-five seconds, then transferred the mess from the plastic bowl onto the Lenox plate and tested the food with her index finger to see if it was warm enough. Satisfied, she looked around for the dog. She called him and then whistled. "Hey, Isaac, breakfast time!" When the dog still didn't appear, she walked through the dining room and on into the sunken living room. She didn't know if she should laugh or cry. The papers she'd stacked so neatly the night before were haphazardly arranged on the floor where a rather large pile of poop could be seen. Isaac was trying to hide under the glass-topped table, his head between his paws.

Val squatted down again. "I applaud ingenuity in all forms," she said as she tickled the dog behind his ears. She leaned sideways to peer at the mess of papers. The brown stuff was on her resignation letter. She laughed, a strange sound even to her ears. She scooped up the spaniel and carried him to the kitchen. "Good boy," she said, patting the dog's rump as she set him down next to the Lenox dish.

Reassured by Val's tone of voice and gentle hand, Isaac lapped at his food, his long silky ears swishing among the noodles.

While Isaac ate, Val showered and dressed in a soft peach-colored suit and a peach and white polka dot blouse with a demure bow at the neck. She took one last look in the mirror to check her subtle makeup and the French braid she'd become addicted to of late. She padded out to the kitchen, where she proceeded to re-pack Isaac's gear. "C'mere," she said to the spaniel. Brush in hand, she ran it down the dog's back before she threw it into the bag. She looked at the red, white, and blue toothbrush and muttered, "No way." She did, however, moisten a paper towel and wipe the dog's ears and whiskers. At the door she looked down at the spaniel and said, "I think—mind you, this is just my opinion—but I think you got me through the worst night of my life. You are the only one besides myself who has ever set foot in this apartment. Of course, Rand doesn't count, and neither does the cleaning lady. You are the first *invited* guest, and it doesn't matter if you have four legs or two." Isaac tilted his silky head to the side. He appeared to be listening intently to every word. She was stunned a moment later when the dog leaped into her arms, almost knocking her backward. His little pink tongue lapped at her chin. She cuddled him, her eyes as wet as the spaniel's.

"Time to go home," she said.

She carried the dog, inching the shopping bag ahead of her with her leg. The moment her neighbor opened the door, Isaac leaped to the floor. "Thanks, Elliot." To the dog she said, "See you around, Isaac." She was halfway to her apartment when Elliot called to her.

"Are you going to do it?"

Val stopped. "Do what?"

"Get a dog."

"Oh, yes. Yes, I am," she said, and then muttered under her breath, "at some point."

Back in her apartment, Val wrinkled her nose as she walked past the brown lump on the floor. She made no move to clean it up. She slid her feet into beige Ferragamo heels, always the last thing she did before leaving for work. Briefcase in hand, she headed for the door. She was not in the habit of looking back. This apartment was just a place to sleep. It wasn't a home. It could never be a home. Susan had a home. The Colemans had assorted homes. Maggie and Rand had a home.

Maggie.

Val stopped at the door, set the briefcase down, and

retraced her steps to the kitchen, where she picked up the white phone on the wall. She tapped out the area code for Hawaii information, then scribbled the number on a pad on the counter. With a trembling hand she pushed the eleven buttons it took to reach Hawaii. She held her breath, wondering if Maggie would answer or if she'd let her answering machine take the call. Maggie's recorded voice startled Val.

"Maggie, this is Valentine Mitchell," Val said briskly. "I have something to say to you, and I want you to listen to me. Rand came by last evening and told me what you . . . what happened between the two of you. You're wrong, Maggie. Nothing happened. Rand was and always has been a perfect gentleman." The lie was like a lump of peanut butter in her throat. "I thought you knew me well enough to know I would never in any way compromise your family. I also want you to know I am severing my firm's business relationship with the Colemans. In fact, I'm selling the firm and planning to go into semiretirement. Don't for one minute read anything into this statement but what it is. I want a life outside the legal profession, and I just hope it isn't too late for me. Well, that's all I called to say. If I don't see you again, Maggie, enjoy that paradise you live in. And if you doubt what I've said, ask yourself if I've ever done anything but my very best for your family, or if I've ever lied to any of you. 'Bye, Maggie."

The peanut butter was back in her throat. Her thumb shot upward. "That's one for you, Val," she croaked as she made her way to the door.

It was exactly eight o'clock when Val's secretary poked her head in the door and stage whispered, "Riley Coleman is here. What should I tell him?"

Val's mind raced as she looked around her cluttered office. "Send him in," she said in a resigned voice.

How handsome he is, she thought when Riley entered the messy room.

"Riley, we didn't have an appointment, did we?" Val asked cheerfully.

Riley didn't respond. Instead he held out a white envelope with the firm's name engraved at the top. "Would you mind explaining this?" he said, tossing the envelope on her desk.

"There's not much to explain, Riley. I decided I've had enough of the rat race. I want to wind down and have a life of my own. I'm sorry if it comes as a shock to you," she said quietly. "I did return the balance of the retainer."

"Rather sudden, wasn't it?"

Val's lips tightened. "From your point of view I guess it was, but not from mine. I'm selling the firm. If your family wants to stay here, you can negotiate with the new partners. It will probably be to your benefit, and cheaper." Here it comes, Val thought, the biggie.

Riley pushed his baseball cap back on his dark hair. "I can't argue with the part about wanting a life of your own. It's the suddenness that bothers me. Listen, Val, there's no one in the world I have more respect for than you. Both my butt and Cole's would have been in jail if it weren't for you. So I'm not going to beat around the bush here. Rand more or less implied a problem. Aunt Maggie took off. Rand left the house early last night and never came home. I'd like to know what's going on. Not because I'm being nosy, but because you are terminating your contract with us. I also came here today to conduct some business. Or try to."

Suddenly it was important to her that Riley not view

her with suspicion. She was genuinely fond of him, and she absolutely adored Ivy. She got up from her comfortable chair and walked around to him. "Nothing happened between Rand and myself. This thing, whatever this thing is, seems to be coming out of nowhere. I really don't want to get involved with your family's personal problems, Riley. Now," she said briskly, "you said you came here to do some business. What is it?"

Riley explained.

Val laughed. "A piece of cake. I'll tell you what, Riley. I'll do it. We'll call it my going-away present to you. Once I set it up, one of the new partners can take over if that's agreeable with you. Three days, four at the most."

They were shaking hands when the intercom on Val's desk came to life. "Miss Mitchell, there's a call for Mr. Coleman on line two." Val raised her eyebrows and winked. She busied herself at the file cabinet as Riley stretched across the desk for the phone.

She whirled about when she heard Riley say, "What did you say? Yes, that's my license plate number. I loaned my truck to my uncle last evening. It was early when he left my house. No, no, he didn't come home at all last night, and he still wasn't there when I left this morning. No, he didn't call. I'll be there as soon as I can."

When Riley hung up, Val whispered fearfully, "What was all that about?"

"That was the state police. They said . . . they said Rand's dead." Riley's face was drained of all color.

"Dead!" Val said, lowering herself into her chair. "It must be a mistake. How . . . where do they want you to go?"

"The morgue. They said a passing motorist stopped

around six this morning, just as it was getting light, to use the roadside phone booth. My truck was parked on the shoulder of the road with the door ripped off. The motorist called the state police and . . . they found . . . Rand in the culvert. That's all I know."

"I'll go with you," Val said, reaching for her purse. "I'll drive, too. You're whiter than ceiling paint."

"Aunt Maggie?"

"Not yet, Riley."

Val linked her arm through Riley's as she steered him through the maze of offices. To her secretary she said, "I don't know when I'll be back."

They drove in silence. Over and over in her mind Val thanked God for the wisdom he'd bestowed on her earlier. She was glad now that she'd called Maggie, glad she'd lied to her and to Riley. She longed for Isaac's warm, cuddly body. How cold she felt, how very tired.

Ivy was waiting in the corridor outside the morgue, pacing up and down, wringing her hands, her eyes full of tears. She ran to Riley the moment she saw him, her Reeboks making hard slapping sounds on the marble floor.

The three of them stared at one another. Val squared her shoulders. "I'll do it, Riley. I've done it before. Stay with Ivy."

Val was alongside them four minutes later, her face as sheet-white as Riley's. "I signed the paper identifying the body. There was no mistake. It's Rand. We have to go upstairs now." She bit down on her lower lip. God, she needed air. Lots of air. Her stomach lurched sickeningly. Who was going to call Maggie? Who was going to call Billie?

Later, while they waited for Riley to join them in the

corridor, Ivy said, "Riley told me what you said, about you and Rand. You lied. You never did that before, did you?"

Val shook her head. "I didn't want Riley to remember Rand like that. I think . . . I have to get back to the office. You have a car, right?"

"I borrowed Jonquil's. Susan has mine. Val, I need to talk to you in a few days. Friend to friend, if that's okay. Riley told me you weren't going to represent the family anymore."

"I decided to retire. Well, semiretire. I don't know if lawyers ever really retire. And Ivy . . . I'm very sorry about Rand. If there's anything I can do, let me know, and yes, I'll be happy to discuss whatever it is you want to discuss. Friend to friend."

"I always thought Val was tough as wet rawhide," Ivy said to Riley when he joined her minutes later. "She had tears in her eyes. I don't think I ever thought of Val as anything but an attorney who had her head screwed on right. That's terrible, isn't it, Riley? I've never thought of her as a human being. Just an attorney."

"Yeah, Ivy, that's terrible, but it's the way I thought of her too," Riley said hoarsely. "Come on, honey, let's go home. God, how am I going to tell Aunt Maggie?"

"We'll do it together, Riley," Ivy said quietly.

The services for Rand Nelson were held privately. The family left the mortuary in a tightly knit group. Once again their numbers were depleted. This time, though, there would be no burial on the hill. There was to be no grave, no headstone. On Maggie's instructions, Rand's ashes were to be returned to England and placed in his family's crypt. Chesney, Rand's daughter, volunteered to deliver the urn in person, saying she would return to England to live.

Ivy Coleman presided over the gathering. From time to time she wiped at the corners of her eyes, and she was never far from her husband's side.

They were eating now, an exquisite luncheon prepared by Jonquil. The family's voices were little more than hushed murmurs as they stirred and stared at the food on their plates.

We look like an assembly of penguins, Ivy thought, eyeing everyone's black clothing. Only Maggie, in a vivid scarlet dress with matching hip-length jacket, added color to the room. She looked as out of place as a hare in a hound's lair.

"I have to do something," Sawyer whispered to her husband. "I have to say something to wipe that awful look from her face. She's my mother, Adam."

"She's strung too tight, Sawyer. Leave her alone, and by alone I mean keep that mouth of yours shut. You don't see Cole doing anything, do you?"

"Cole's a guy. At a time like this a woman needs a woman," Sawyer said with a catch in her voice. "My God, Adam, do you have any idea how she must feel?"

"Pretty shitty, I'd imagine." Adam gave his wife a nudge. "Talk to her about anything but Rand."

"All right," Sawyer mumbled as she made her way across the room to where her mother was talking to her grandmother and Thad.

"It looks like one of those Texas storms we've heard about is starting to brew," Thad said, motioning with his arm toward the wide expanse of windows.

"I remember one or two of those, don't you, Grandmam?" Sawyer said to Billie.

"More than one or two," Billie said lightly. "Would

you girls mind sitting down with me? My legs are tired," Billie lied. "Thad, fetch us a drink, please."

"Not right now, Mam. I want to talk to Cole." Maggie looked at her watch and frowned. "If there is going to be a storm, I should leave now. I don't want to miss my plane."

"You're leaving?" Billie said blankly.

"You mean you're going back to Hawaii?" Sawyer said, stunned at her mother's words.

"Is there any reason why I should stay?" Maggie asked coolly.

"I don't think it's a good idea for you to be alone right now, darling," Billie said quietly.

"Why is that, Mam?"

"Under the circumstances, I would think you'd want to be with your family," Billie said gently, her face full of sadness.

"The way *you* want to be with us? It was you, Mam, who said we were to peddle our papers and leave you and Thad alone. I'd like to be alone too. I've been alone before. Excuse me," she said, and walked away.

"Did she say good-bye to Chesney?" Sawyer asked.

"Yes. They shook hands," Billie said. "I found that a little hard to accept, but right now Maggie has to do whatever it takes to get through this. If she is going to leave, I hope she goes before Valentine Mitchell gets here. Ivy told me she called and asked to stop by."

"Oh, God," was all Sawyer could say.

"I didn't think Maggie would wear black. But I never expected her to wear red," Billie said fretfully.

"Whatever it takes, Grandmam," Sawyer said, reaching for the glass of wine Thad held out to her.

Across the room, within earshot of Riley and Ivy, Maggie said, "I'd like to leave now, if you don't mind."

"Are you sure, Mother?" Cole asked.

"Yes, I'm sure. I'll go through the kitchen and slip out the back door. I'll meet you by the car."

"Aren't you going to say good-bye?" Cole asked, stunned at his mother's words.

"You know I don't like good-byes, Cole. They're so final. I've had about all the finality I can handle for one day. If it's a problem for you to take me to the airport, I can call a car service."

"It's no problem, Mother. I'll meet you outside. I have to get the keys from Riley."

Riley's eyes were full of unasked questions when he handed over the keys. Cole shrugged. "I'm not going to try and change her mind," Cole said softly. "Once my mother makes up her mind, there's no changing it. We all know that. I won't be long."

Out of the corner of her eye, Ivy saw movements in the courtyard. "It's Val," she said to Riley. "She must have driven in from the back. Don't look at me like that, Riley. She said she wanted to pay her respects to the family. Think what you want, Riley. I like Val. I like her a lot, and since this is my home too, I don't see why there should be any kind of a problem."

"I was thinking more about Val than the family. She's going to feel awkward, I think," Riley muttered. "It's amazing, you know? When you stop to think about it, no one knows anything. Neither Rand nor Val admitted to anything, and yet ... oh, skip it. Civility has always been this family's long suit." He gave his wife a gentle squeeze before he walked to where Cary and Susan were sitting.

Ivy made her way to the kitchen as unobtrusively as she could. Damn, Val's timing couldn't have been worse, she thought fretfully. She wondered for the thou-

sandth time if the attorney and Rand had really, as Riley
put it, *done it*. She remembered their fight, and how
she'd defended Val, her voice shaking with emotion.
She'd flounced out of the room yelling over her shoulder, "Valentine Mitchell would never do anything to
hurt this family." It had been hers and Riley's first serious disagreement, and one Riley had apologized for two
hours later.

Outside, the sky was darkening rapidly. The wind
whipped through the tunnel-like courtyard. Maggie had
the car door open when Val parked next to her. Maggie
turned, the skirt of her red dress fussing about her knees
in the whipping wind.

"Val," she said quietly.

"I came to pay my respects to your family, Maggie."

"I have no objection. I'm leaving myself," Maggie
said tightly. "Cole's driving me to the airport. I think
it's commendable of you to show up like this. If I had
even the slightest doubt in my mind that Rand or you
told the truth, just the teeniest little doubt, I'd throw my
arms around you and weep with sorrow, but, you see, I
know. In my heart I know Rand was unfaithful. Under
the circumstances, if I were in your place, I might have
done the same thing. Then again, maybe I wouldn't
have. Emotions are the one thing in the world you can't
count on. I've learned that the hard way." Unexpectedly,
Maggie's hand shot out. Val reached for it. "Maybe
we'll talk about this someday," Maggie said, getting
into the car.

"Just call," Val said in a whispery voice.

Only Ivy saw Val knuckle her eyes. Only Ivy saw her
slide back into her car, where she leaned her head over
the steering wheel, crying. She watched the attorney
back the car out of the driveway and head out to the

road that ran perpendicular to the house. An immense surge of relief flooded through her. Relief for Val. She ran then up the back stairs of the kitchen, taking the steps two at a time. Gasping with the exertion, she ran down the hall to the baby's room. Only here was it normal. Only here in this bright, colorful room were things the way they should be.

Ivy's eyes fell on the cartoon-figured hamper that held Billie's VCR tape. She'd removed it from her knitting bag and secured it in an airtight Ziploc bag before placing it in the bottom of Moss's hamper, because Riley liked to rummage. She felt like a criminal when she lifted the lid on the wicker chest, and heaved a sigh of relief when she saw the tape untouched in its plastic bag.

"There you are," Susan hissed from the doorway. Ivy dropped the lid, her face full of guilt.

"Susan, you startled me," she chided.

"Sorry." She didn't sound sorry at all, Ivy thought.

"I was just checking on Moss. Maggie left." Ivy whispered until she was out in the hall, the door safely closed behind her.

"I know. Maybe it's best for her." Susan made it sound like no matter what happened or where it happened, it would be for the best. "I just came up to tell you I'm taking Cary back. This whole thing has upset him terribly. This is not a good place to be right now. Things always happen here. Sunbridge was never a happy place."

"That's a terrible thing to say, Susan. A place isn't unhappy. It's the people in the place that are unhappy."

"Maggie was never happy here. Cole wasn't either, since he deeded his half of the place to Riley. Mam wasn't happy here, she said so. Grandfather Seth banished Aunt Amelia, and she hated Sunbridge. Mam said Grandmother Jessica wasn't happy here, so who does that leave? Riley? You? That mean-spirited tyrant who was my grandfather was the only other person who actually lived here, and no one knows to this day what made *him* tick. No, you and Riley are the only ones who *say* they're happy here. Anyway, I only came up here to tell you we're leaving. It was a nice luncheon, Ivy."

As Susan made her way down the steps, Ivy stood at the railing, looking down into the great room.

Riley's family. Hers now. Ivy's shoulders slumped. They straightened almost immediately when Riley looked up and smiled. She smiled back.

It was four o'clock when Sawyer and Adam, the last of the family to leave, said their good-byes. "We seem to be doing this a lot lately, saying good-bye," Sawyer said sadly.

"Good-byes are never easy," Ivy said quietly.

"Aunt Maggie can't bring herself to say those words," Riley remarked. "She'll say so long, see you around, or something to that effect, but she'll never say good-bye. I wonder why that is?"

"I don't think it's important right now, Riley," Sawyer said gently. "Maggie will cope. She's tough. She put up with all of us for a long time, didn't she?"

"Yeah, she did. Cole said he'll take Sumi and the baby to see her as soon as the doctor gives the okay for the baby to fly. Aunt Maggie will like that."

"Yes, she'll like that," Sawyer said happily. "Chesney didn't stay around very long. She didn't say two words to me. I thought that was a little strange."

"What's even stranger," Ivy said coolly, "was how fast she made an appointment with Val to go over

Rand's will. I didn't see any tears in her eyes at the church service, and I looked."

"No kidding. I missed that," Sawyer muttered.

"She was probably in shock, like the rest of us," Riley said.

"Grow up, Riley," Sawyer said nastily. "Months ago, Maggie told me Chesney was never at the house and that the relationship Rand wanted with her never really materialized. Chesney, Maggie said, was ever so polite, but ever so indifferent. For a while Maggie had convinced herself that she had a second daughter, but it turned out to be wishful thinking. Chesney is a very wealthy young woman today. She gets half of everything, and *everything* is considerable."

Riley smiled. He loved it when Sawyer was off and running. "Except the house in Hawaii," he said. "Val told me herself that last year Rand had deeded it over to Maggie because she loved it so. I assume Aunt Maggie knows this, but knowing Rand, he may never have told her."

"That's something, at least." Sawyer turned to Ivy. "Ivy, thanks for putting up with us," she said, hugging her. "Riley, take care of things, and don't let Susan get to either one of you. Production on the plane starts two weeks from Monday. Cary assured me the money would be in the coffers in less than a week. He must know some pretty influential people."

"That's great, Sawyer," Riley said. "Cary is one in a million. I'm glad he's the one who's getting the project off the ground. Cole feels the same way. You really stepped in it, old girl."

"Didn't I, though?" Sawyer said smugly.

Another round of hugs followed. Both Riley and Ivy watched until the rental car was out of sight.

The moment Riley closed the door, Ivy said, "This was such an awful day. All I want to do is curl up in a corner and pretend it never happened. I felt so bad for Maggie. I wanted to slap Susan till she bounced off the walls. That doesn't say much for me, does it, honey?"

"It says you care. Let's put a slicker on Moss and go out for a chili dog with lots of onions . . . real greasy french fries and onion rings, and one of those giant-size slushes. Blueberry. Later I'll drink a quart of Mylanta."

"Just the three of us?" Ivy said, her eyes shining.

"Yep."

"You're on. I'll get Moss."

"Ivy?"

"Yeah?"

"I love you."

"Not as much as I love you."

"I'm never gonna win this one, right?"

"Nope."

{{{{{{{{ CHAPTER TEN }}}}}}}}

Maggie's eyes were glued to the sun creeping over the horizon. Sunrises and sunsets should be shared. A soft whimper escaped her lips. She squirmed, the chill of the vinyl lounge cushion sending chills through her body. She struggled with the oversize beach towel she'd used for a cover, yanking and pulling at it to no avail. She had to get up, brave the new day somehow. She had to make coffee and eat something, possibly take a vitamin pill. There were so many things she had to do; the list was growing longer each day. In the ten days she'd been back, she'd done nothing but sleep, drink coffee, and swim. She gave up her struggle with the beach towel and entered the kitchen.

The kitchen was warmer than the lanai. In another hour it would be warm and sunny and filled with the scent of the plumeria outside the open windows. She loved plumeria and all the island flowers.

Maggie carefully measured out coffee, added just the right amount of water to the Mr. Coffee, and pressed the red button. The refrigerator surrendered bread, butter, and mango jelly. There was no milk and no juice or eggs. A jar of pickles with cloudy brine was the only thing left. She was going to have to go to town to the market. "Tomorrow," she muttered. Everything was scheduled for tomorrow.

She listened for the last little gush of bubbles as the water in the machine dribbled down to the pot. Ten cups. She'd drink it all by mid-morning. Her toast popped up. It looked as dark as the coffee. She knew the butter wasn't spreadable, but she tried anyway, finally settling for little pats, which she covered with three spoonfuls of jelly. She chewed slowly and methodically.

When she finished, she donned a clean bathing suit. She poured fresh coffee into a giant-size mug that said MAGGIE on it and carried it down to the beach, where she would sip at it and stare out across the water until her eyes started to burn, at which point she would head back to the house for more coffee, which she would drink on the lanai.

With the exception of her caffeine nerves, she felt better today, more rested and not as restless. She could think clearly now and was probably capable of making a decision.

She shuddered in the warm, fragrant air, her eyes sweeping her private stretch of beach, the beautiful palm trees and the squat palmettos and the gorgeous white sand. It was all so perfect, this place she'd called her personal paradise. If she didn't watch herself, it was a place where she would lose touch with reality.

She brought her mind into the present. She'd given herself ten days to deal with Rand's death. During that time, she'd allowed herself to settle into a dark, emotional place that was full of nightmares and boogeymen. Ten days. Not much, but all she allowed herself to mourn, to hate herself, to wallow in self-pity. Now it was time to rejoin the world.

Maggie ran the list of things "to do" over in her mind. At the top was changing the message on the answering machine, listening to ten days' worth of messages, since she hadn't been answering the phone, going through her mail, then packing up Rand's mail and sending it to Chesney.

Chesney. Rand's daughter. Her stepdaughter.

Nobody was what they seemed, she thought sadly. Not Rand, not Chesney, not even her own mother. She wondered if what you saw was ever what you got.

Chesney was gone, bag and baggage, and Maggie felt only a sense of relief. Chesney had been an intruder. She'd had her own life, had asked for nothing, and had openly said she didn't love her father, though she did admit to liking him. She reminded Rand over and over that she would one day return to England. Brian, her fiancé, she said, was perfectly willing to make his home in England and perhaps fly for the same airline she did.

It occurred to Maggie at that moment that Chesney was as unforgiving as she was. The only difference was that Chesney had said from the beginning—from the moment she found out Rand was her father—that she wanted nothing except to see him, to see the man who'd let her grow up in an orphanage believing she wasn't loved or wanted.

Inheriting half of Rand's sizable estate was poor compensation for spending one's young life in an orphanage. The girl deserved whatever Rand left her. Maggie wondered how long it would take Chesney to stake a claim to this slice of paradise. Not that it mattered one way or the other. Chesney deserved more than whatever Rand had left to her in his will.

"Miss Maggie!" Addie, Maggie's three-day-a-week domestic, called from the lanai.

Maggie stood up and brushed the sand from her bare legs, then drained the last of her coffee before heading toward the lanai. "I'm sorry, Addie, I forgot you were coming today." Addie, Maggie thought, was the neatest, tidiest, nicest person she'd ever met. She was tiny, no more than four feet eight inches tall, but she said her coronet of braids added an entire inch to her height, making her four feet nine inches tall. She took the extra inch very seriously. She had dark licorice eyes with a double fringe of dark eyelashes. Her age was a mystery which she refused to discuss. She also refused to tell Maggie where she bought her muumuus, one-of-a-kind, gorgeous creations, which Maggie adored. Today she was attired in a straight-lined, boat-necked muumuu of a pinkish lavender. On her feet were sturdy L.A. Gear sneakers.

"What would you like me to do today, Miss Maggie?"

Maggie inhaled deeply, letting her breath explode in a loud shoosh. "Today, Addie, I want you to . . . pack up all of Mr. Nelson's things and take them back to town with you. I mean everything. Give them to the Rescue Mission, or if you know someone who needs them . . . I don't care. I would appreciate it if you'd call one of your brothers or cousins to come for the bedroom furniture in my room and . . . and Chesney's. I don't care what you do with it either. I know you might not get to all this today, but if you're free, come back tomorrow and pack up Mr. Nelson's office. There are a lot of boxes in the garage. Ask Mattie when he comes to do the lawn if he'll carry them up to the crawl space over the garage."

Addie's licorice eyes were full of concern. "If we take the furniture, where will you sleep, Miss Maggie?"

Maggie grimaced. "Out here on the lanai, where I've been sleeping for the past ten days. And, Addie, throw away the red dress and jacket. The shoes too," she added as an afterthought.

The black eyes snapped. "There is no food in the refrigerator," Addie said, wagging a finger at Maggie. "I will tell my brothers to stop at the market before they drive up here. Will there be anything else?"

"Would you mind bringing me the leather case in my room? The big one leaning up against the wall. And I'd appreciate it if you'd make some more coffee."

The black eyes snapped again. "You still haven't been out of the kitchen, have you?"

Maggie dug her heels into the sand at the edge of the lanai. "No, I haven't. I've been using the bathroom off the kitchen. I can't ... I'm not ready ... Later, when you're finished I'll ... maybe then I can ... Right now, it's not important, Addie."

"You've lost weight, Miss Maggie. Tonight before I leave I will cook you some food. You must promise to eat."

Maggie nodded absently, then headed back down to the beach and into the water. She swam till she was exhausted. She rolled onto her back and let the waves rush her to the shore. Exhausted with her effort, she struggled toward the house, where she snuggled into the lounge chair, the beach towel snug around her to prevent an attack of the shakes. The MAGGIE cup was full to the brim, steam spiraling upward. She inched one of her hands free of the towel to the cigarettes next to the cup. Where had Addie found them? Over the past days she'd wanted them desperately, but she wasn't desperate enough to drive to town or to walk through the rooms of the house to search for one. She lit one now, inhaling deeply. Terrible, terrible habit, smoking. Her eyes fell on the Surgeon General's words. As if she cared. She puffed and sipped. Sipped and puffed. Rand loved to smoke, got great enjoyment out of cigarettes. Maggie smoked and sipped until the cup was empty.

"Life goes on," she muttered as she bent to pick up her leather case, which once belonged to her mother. It was full of sketches, color samples, Billie's formulae for dyes, every color of the rainbow and some that weren't in any color formula anywhere in the world. She stuck the cigarettes and lighter into the bra of her swimsuit before she trudged with the heavy case out to the monkeypod tree, where she laid it down and unzipped it.

The sun crawled high in the heavens and then started its downward descent as Maggie studied the contents of the case, scribbling notes, matching colors, writing questions to herself. Once, she looked up and fantasized she was meeting with one of her mother's clients. "Gentlemen, the offices of Billie Limited are under a monkeypod tree." Her adrenaline was flowing, she could feel it coursing up through her body. A good sign. She went back to work, stopping again at four o'clock to stare at the descending sun. "If I can get the color and blend it with . . . what? What I want is a color that's the same shade as the sun over Sunbridge." She would have to do some experimenting with the pots of paint in her bedroom closet. It occurred to her then that she was going to need some work space. "Sorry, gentlemen, I've closed up shop under the monkeypod tree. From now on, Billie Limited will be conducting business out of the garage."

It was a decision. She'd actually made a decision. Out loud. "When you say it out loud, it makes it real, definite. All I'll need is a chair and two folding tables," she mumbled.

"Miss Maggie," Addie called from the lanai, "I have your dinner ready."

Maggie looked around, an expression of shock on her face. The sun was starting to set.

"It's not much this evening, Miss Maggie. Just a chicken pie, but I made the crust myself. There's enough for your lunch tomorrow. The vegetables are from my own garden. My brother's wife sent the dessert. I know you like banana cream."

"Thank you, Addie," Maggie said, sitting down at the table. "It looks delicious. Tell me, where did you find those cigarettes?"

Addie opened one of the kitchen drawers and pointed. She clucked her tongue in disapproval and then pointed to the large glass of milk next to Maggie's plate. Dutifully, Maggie picked it up and drank. Addie gleamed with pleasure.

"Tomorrow I will come back and do the laundry. The office will be finished by noon. What will you do for a bed?"

"I guess I'll have to go to town and get a new one. I have to get some folding tables too. I know you must be tired, Addie. I can clean up here. Go home to your family. And, Addie, thank you."

Maggie stopped eating long enough to thank the cousins and brothers trooping through the kitchen in Addie's wake. She started to eat again, realizing she was ravenous. She dug into the remainder of the chicken pie and finished it off. She finished the milk and poured more. Then she ate two slices of banana pie. Before the night was over, she'd probably finish that too. She could walk off the calories on the treadmill in the garage, if she felt like it.

It would take her ten minutes to wash her dishes and

tidy the kitchen. The night loomed ahead of her. She hated this time of day, that fragile time when day crept into darkness and the blackness was sprinkled with artificial lights.

Was she wrong? she wondered. Would the question haunt her forever? *Don't think about Rand. Rand no longer exists.* The realization brought such an ache to her chest, she doubled over, fighting for her breath. Her eyes started to water. She wiped at them angrily with the back of her hands. She *wasn't* crying. How could she cry when she was dead inside? If I'm dead inside, then why do I feel like this? she asked herself as she slammed her dishes into the sink. Scalding hot water poured from the faucet, steam rushing upward. She added detergent. She watched curiously as the frothy bubbles rose up and poured down the front of the sink. She turned off the water. *You could be wrong. Valentine said you were wrong. You judged and condemned a man you loved based solely on your feelings, on instinct, and now he's dead. You could be wrong. Val said you're wrong. Rand denied . . . Rand said . . . I don't care what he said, he lied. Val lied because . . . Val lied.* "Period," Maggie said coldly. She looked at the pie crust crumbs on the table. She swept them to the floor with her arm. The ants had to eat too.

Now what was she supposed to do? What did she normally do after dinner? Walk on the beach with Rand, hold hands, make love in the sand, play Scrabble, watch television, read. All of the above.

Maggie turned and yanked at the kitchen drawer. She pulled out a pack of cigarettes, ripping at it. She looked around for the MAGGIE cup, but the water in the sink was too hot for her hands. She opened the cabinet door for a clean cup and saw the RAND cup, the mate to hers.

Her eyes burning fiercely, she reached for it, hefted it in her hand, then threw it across the kitchen. The shattering sound was deafening. She ran from the kitchen, through the lanai and down to the beach.

You aren't perfect, Maggie. Admit that just maybe you're wrong. Look it square in the face and admit the possibility. "I saw the guilt in his face," she said aloud, "heard the lie in his voice. I'm not wrong." *What if you are? What if, what if?*

Maggie stomped her way down the beach fighting the tears burning her eyes. "I know! I know!" she shouted, to be heard over the lapping waves.

She walked for a long time, stumbling and righting herself in the wet sand. When she was exhausted, she turned to see how far she'd come. At least two miles, she estimated. She could barely see the lanterns strung on the lanai.

She ran back, tripping and falling, stumbling and cursing, until she reached the lanai, where she collapsed, her breathing ragged and uneven. "I know I wasn't wrong. I know it!" she cried brokenly. "Oh, God, I need you, Mam."

The moment her breathing was back to normal, she reached for the portable phone with shaking hands. She was stunned at how normal her voice sounded when Thad's voice came over the wire. She almost hung up when she realized it was the middle of the night in Vermont. She apologized. "I'm sorry, Thad, I forgot the time difference. I don't suppose Mam is awake."

"No, Maggie, she's sleeping. I'll tell her you called when she wakes in the morning. Are you all right?" The question sounded to Maggie as though he didn't care if she was or not. It was something to say, something polite. Thad was always polite.

"Fine. Look, don't even tell her I called. I know she doesn't want to be bothered . . . right now. Take care of her, Thad," Maggie whispered.

"I will, Maggie. Stay well."

Maggie's next call was to her daughter, Sawyer. Adam, his voice groggy answered the phone. "Maggie, is anything wrong?"

"No. I just wanted to talk to Sawyer. I know it's late."

"She's dead to the world. The twins have chicken pox, and we haven't had any sleep for three days. Can she call you first thing in the morning?"

"No, that's okay. I'll call later in the week. Make an oatmeal paste for the girls. It will stop the itching. Good night, Adam."

Susan. Maggie punched out a new set of numbers. She let the phone in the Coleman condo ring eighteen times before she hung up. Where was she? At Cary's? At Sunbridge? She tried Cary's apartment and wasn't surprised when there was no response. Susan once admitted that she never answered the phone after eleven o'clock at night, fearing a disaster of some kind. She had said she could only handle disastrous news in broad daylight. It was all a crock, Maggie thought. Susan couldn't handle anything. It was a wonder she could brush her teeth on her own.

Ivy. Ivy would understand what she was going through. She dialed Sunbridge's private, unlisted number, which only the family knew. She listened to Ivy's message: "Riley and I have gone to Florida for my mother's birthday. We'll be back home on Tuesday. For any of you who are interested, Moss now has his second tooth."

Maggie lit a cigarette from the stub of the old one.

She counted the filters in the ashtray. Six. She snorted in disgust. Did she dare call Cole? He would be at the office now. She closed her eyes, trying to visualize his office number. The moment it came to her, she called. His secretary said that Cole had gone to Kyoto and wouldn't be back in the office until tomorrow.

How unavailable her family was. Each of them had someone running interference for them. As her mother had always been there for her, Maggie had made a point of always being available to the family, no matter what was going on in her personal life. Always. Now who was there for her? Maggie buried her face in her hands. Everyone had someone.

Because she didn't know what else to do, she entered the house, snapping on lights as she went along. She walked into the empty bedroom to where the phone and answering machine rested on the floor in the middle of a nest of tangled wires. She dropped to her knees and pressed the message button, then rocked back on her heels as she listened to the calls for Rand from the refinery. Those had been made before . . . before anyone outside the family knew . . . One call from Sawyer, one from Ivy telling her about the trip to Florida. There were no calls from Susan or her mother, but there were six, one after the other, from Valentine Mitchell, and one from Cary, who wanted information, if she had it, on the refinery. The last call was from Cole, saying baby Billie was now a pound heavier.

Maggie rewound the tape. They had stayed in touch after all. But she didn't feel any better.

On her way back to the lanai, she passed the foyer, where mail was stacked neatly. Most of it, she knew, would be for Rand, probably refinery business, household bills, charge accounts, insurance bills, tons of magazines, and sale flyers. Nothing really personal or directed to her. Someday she'd look at it.

Someday.

Back on the lanai, Maggie toyed with the idea of calling Valentine Mitchell and waking her from a sound sleep.

She was wired now, there was no doubt about it. Wired and angry. That was good, the anger part, she thought. "Up till now I've been in a stupor," she muttered.

Should I call Valentine Mitchell or shouldn't I? To what end? she asked herself. Call her, ask her again, beg her to tell you the truth. "No!" The word exploded from Maggie's mouth.

Maggie got up and paced. Should she make coffee? Should she light another cigarette? Already her mouth tasted like a pair of old sneakers. Should she brush her teeth? She moaned. God, she couldn't even make a simple decision.

She had to do something physical. Work of some kind. She slid her feet into a pair of zoris and marched around to the garage at the side of the house. The sensor lights came on as soon as she stepped on the walkway, bathing her in six hundred watts of light. She opened the door and put on the inside light. Like all garages, this one was a mess, so messy that she couldn't park a car inside. She looked around. Which one of us was the messy one? she wondered. She remembered her intention to walk on the treadmill. It was in here somewhere, along with a stationary bicycle and a stair machine. Rand said they needed the machines, along with his Nautilus equipment. To her knowledge, he'd never used any of them. Swimming had been their major exercise, that and walking miles up and down the beach.

Maggie worked through the night, clearing away a section of the oversize garage she planned to use as a work space. Once the canvas beach chairs, picnic coolers, bags, boxes of shells, and junk they'd collected over the years was stored on the far side of the room, she realized she might not have to buy folding tables at all. The workbench, once it was scrubbed, would serve nicely as a work surface. The shelves above it, which now held jars and cans of rusty screws, nails, nuts, and bolts, would be perfect for her jars of paint. If she left the garage door open, cleaned the windows, and painted the concrete floor white, she'd have more than enough light to work by. She could bang nails into the walls to hang up her sketches, and stretch a line to hang the wet, painted fabrics that would later be dyed. Who needed five thousand bucks a month overhead? Clients wouldn't be coming here. She'd go to them, the way her mother had.

She did need more paints, though. She ran back to the lanai for her mother's case. Inside was a catalog from which Billie ordered paints. Federal Express could have them to her in twenty-four hours. The swatches too. She looked around to see if there was a phone in the garage. She found the jack but no phone. A simple matter to rectify. A business phone she would answer, the house phone—no.

It was almost full light when Maggie set the scrub bucket on the driveway. *Her* half of the garage literally sparkled. Not only had she scrubbed the workbench, she'd painted it too, along with the shelves. She'd wet-vacuumed the garage floor and slapped a thick coat of paint on it. By evening it would be dry.

"You do good work, Maggie *Coleman*," she muttered.

By eight o'clock she'd showered, washed her hair, braided it, and donned a pair of clean chinos and a polo shirt. She washed the dishes, made coffee and breakfast, washed dishes again, smoked four cigarettes, and was ready for her trip to the Ala Moana shopping center.

Before she left the house, she wrote a note to Addie and left her check on the kitchen table. She blew her horn when she passed Addie in her open Jeep on Kam Highway.

She'd never come to the center this early in the morning. Usually, she had to fight for a parking space. This morning she sailed into one with no cars on either side of her.

Maggie used up an hour buying the first two bedroom sets she set her eyes on. Both were white bamboo, the headboards intricately carved. From there she meandered down the outdoor concourse to a linen shop where she ordered sheets and new towels, telling the clerk she'd pick them up at the delivery door later. At a stationery store, she stopped long enough to fill a shopping bag full of pencils, pens, markers, notepads, colored chalks, and construction paper. She was about to pay for her purchases when she saw a decorator phone with numbers so huge, she blinked. "I'll take that too," she said.

Her next stop was a coffee shop, where she ordered a mahi-mahi sandwich, a glass of root beer, and a slice of coconut custard pie. She then walked over to Liberty House, where she bought herself a bottle of Ysatis perfume and talcum powder. From there she went to Liz Claiborne and bought one of everything in the designer's spring collection. She asked to have it sent to Sawyer.

Out on the concourse again, she stopped at a phone center and made arrangements for the telephone company to install a new number for her in the garage the following day. From there she retrieved her car, picked up her linens, and drove to the market, where she bought everything in sight, completely loading down the trunk of the car.

She was back home at three o'clock. The kitchen smelled wonderful. She was sniffing in appreciation when the phone rang. She stared at it and muttered, "Where were you when I needed you?" She sniffed again when she opened the oven to reveal a plump oven roaster that would provide many lunches, decorated with baby carrots and small red-skinned potatoes. A salad waiting for dressing was covered with Saran Wrap in the refrigerator. The note on the table from Addie said the chicken would be done at five o'clock. The P.S. said all the office boxes were stored in the attic over the garage.

Maggie stocked her cupboard shelves and refrigerator before she carried the shopping bags with the sheets and towels into the empty bedroom.

In the bathroom off the kitchen, she stripped down and donned a tangerine one-piece bathing suit. She carried the shopping bag with her supplies out to the garage. The floor was dry, but she didn't walk on it. Back on the lanai, she opened the catalog to the pages she wanted, dialed the eight hundred number and placed her order. She was promised delivery by ten o'clock the following morning.

She walked the same distance she'd walked the night before, swam for an hour, and returned to the house at exactly five o'clock. She turned off the oven before she curled up on the lounge chair on the lanai. She slept until midnight, when she got up, ate, did the dishes, and slept again until morning.

Her life, Maggie told herself, was under control. For now.

{{{{{{{{ CHAPTER ELEVEN }}}}}}}}

Maggie stirred, then stretched, flexing her legs beneath the new blue-and-white-striped sheets. Should she go back to sleep or get up? The realization that she was now a working woman with a real job made her swing her legs over the side of the bed.

Her morning ritual was different these days. She took a five-minute shower instead of one that lasted until the hot water heater ran cold, tied a rubber band around a ponytail instead of wrestling with a braid, and dressed in shorts and T-shirt instead of donning a bathing suit.

Bedmaking, at best, took a minute, unless her pillow was wet, which it usually was from crying in her sleep. In that case, she stripped the pillowcase and put on a new one. Today it was wet. After she had stuffed the pillowcase in the wicker hamper in the bathroom, her watch told her she'd used up eight and one half minutes.

Time for breakfast. Three cups of coffee, a corn muffin with mango jelly, and a glass of orange juice. Two superduper vitamins for women who were fifty or over were next to her orange juice. She swallowed them knowing they made her ravenously hungry during the day. In the last five weeks, since the day she'd cleaned and painted the garage floor, she'd put on seven of the ten pounds she'd lost.

She wasn't swimming as much, and most of her tan was gone. In the scheme of things, she didn't think it mattered. The only thing that made sense to her was her daily schedule. She went around to the garage and sat down to work from seven o'clock to twelve, then ate a huge lunch, and returned to work until three, when she took a break and a fifteen-minute swim. Refreshed, she worked until six, ate a dinner that Addie had prepared in advance, and was back at her workbench by seven-fifteen. With a new Mr. Coffee machine and the MAGGIE cup at her elbow, she worked until she felt her eyes cross with weariness. A mile walk on the beach with an apple in one hand and a banana in the other, followed by a quick shower, allowed her to sleep soundly, if not dreamlessly.

Maggie looked around the garage. It had become a nest. A smile tugged at the corners of her mouth. It seemed as if an artist had gone berserk. Colored swatches, sheets of plain white paper with colored streaks and splashes, were clipped with colorful clothes-pins to a length of dental floss tied to nails on the wall. There were more swatches, more sheets of paper, on a pegboard that was at eye level with her workbench. The workbench she'd painted white was now a rainbow of color, spills, streaks, and dots of mind-boggling hues.

Maggie felt anxious, nervous, when she took her place at the table. Today was a test of sorts. The Baby Ben clock she wound each morning stared at her. Next to the clock was an Amalfi shoe box with three jars of paint, a sheaf of fabric, and a stack of white papers. At exactly ten o'clock she had to run to the beach and stare out across the water to try and match the colors she was working on.

There was nothing on paper, no formulae, no idea of

how, if she succeeded, she was going to present her lines to the people in Hong Kong who would eventually make up the material she needed. In her head she was calling one set of colors Pacific Jewels, the second Egyptian Lights.

Her goal, the same as her mother's, was to set the fashion world on fire with her 1993 line of colors. She'd talked with many of her mother's suppliers, who promised to wait until June for it. Not the end of June, the first of June. She had less than five weeks now till the deadline.

Today she was striving for the electric-blue of the Pacific, the color that appeared where the sky merged with the ocean, a color so vibrant, so alive, she'd so far been unable to capture it on fabric or paper. She'd captured the green of the ocean by staring out at the ocean for endless hours, waiting for that one moment when the water changed color right in front of her eyes. Nile Green was the result.

Egyptian Lights now had two perfect colors: Nile Green and Egyptian White. Cleopatra Gold was giving her as much trouble as Pacific Blue, and she knew she was going to have to go back to Sunbridge, to the hill, to study the sun, then somehow combine that color with the hues of the sun here in Hawaii.

Maggie squeezed her eyes shut. It wasn't the manufacturers' and suppliers' timetables that were really bothering her, it was her mother's timetable, and of course her own timetable for success. Subconsciously, she knew she was putting unbearable pressure on herself, but she was unable to ease the mounting tension that was increasing steadily each day.

Today was momentous in more ways than one, Maggie thought as she stared at the Baby Ben. Late this afternoon she was expecting an overnight delivery from Hong Kong of raw silk, chiffon, and pure silk swatches. And she'd promised herself to go through the three Liberty House shopping bags full of first-class mail. Time permitting, she'd also promised to call the family members and Valentine Mitchell. Half of the mail in the Liberty House bags was from Valentine. What she *really* wanted to do was carry the bags down to the beach and set fire to them.

The Baby Ben ticked on, the hands moving so slowly Maggie wanted to scream. She lit a cigarette and fingered the swatch she called Firecracker Red. She wasn't sure what she should do with it, as it didn't fit either end of her color spectrum. Could it stand alone? She doubted it, but the color was so stunningly beautiful, she knew she had to do something with it.

The Baby Ben continued to tick. She smoked, drank coffee, rinsed the pot with the garden hose, made more. She drank more, smoked the last cigarette in the pack, ripped open a new carton.

Both hands on the Baby Ben settled on the ten.

Maggie grabbed the Amalfi shoe box and sprinted down to the beach, where she settled herself with the open jars of paint. She flexed her fingers before she laid out the swatches and papers and said a silent thank you for a windless morning. Her fingers were feverishly poised over the pots of paint, her eyes glued to the marriage of sky and water taking place in front of her eyes. She worked frantically, smearing, blending, dotting, streaking the colors on both paper and material. She had only five minutes until the colors changed.

Maggie's breath exploded in a loud exhalation. Until this moment she hadn't realized she'd been holding her breath. She blinked as a cotton-ball cloud drifted downward toward the marriage taking place. She dabbed again, smeared, blended, stroked. Blueberry. Dresden Blue. Hyacinth. Cerulean. Cornflower and, God Almighty, Pacific Blue!

She had it! But would it look the same when it was dry? By mid-afternoon, when the swatches had dried, she'd know for certain. Wet paint and dry paint were totally different, but she knew, felt, that she'd captured a true marriage of color. When made into dye it would be perfect. The same way you knew, felt, that your husband was unfaithful? an inner voice niggled.

"Yes, damnit," Maggie said hoarsely. "I wasn't wrong then, and I'm not wrong now."

Maggie withdrew a folding aluminum cylinder from the shoe box and stuck it in the sand. With paint-stained fingers she Scotch-taped each swatch, each sheet of paper, to the pole. The shoe box under one arm, the pole in the other, Maggie made her way back to the garage, where she carefully removed each swatch and paper and hung them on the dental-floss line with bright red plastic clothespins. She crossed her fingers and danced a jig before she poured coffee and lit a cigarette. Tomorrow she'd start to work on the actual dye.

Her mind whirled, her eyes ricocheting from one end of the dental-floss line to the other. More than anything in the world, she wished she could call her mother and give her a progress report. Did she dare? Maybe it would perk up her spirits. The worst thing that could happen was there would be no answer or Thad would say her mother was resting. She could explain to Thad that she wasn't calling to whine and fret or . . . chastize her mother for . . . for dying, for God's sake. She'd been whacked in the face so many times lately, one more time wouldn't matter if Thad got defensive. Or offensive.

Maggie looked at the swatches again. Oh God, oh God, they looked ... they looked just right. She reached for the phone. She was stunned when her mother's voice came over the wire, all quivery and shaky, but still her mother's voice. Maggie started to talk, the words rushing from her mouth. Then she was babbling, trying to get everything out at once before her mother said she had to go or Thad came on the line and said "time's up."

"Maggie darling, that sounds wonderful. I love the names you've given to the lines. Tell me again, what does Cleopatra Gold look like?" Billie asked in a thin, reedy voice.

Maggie told her. "Mam, what do you think of a gossamer scarf with either gold or metallic threads? Oversize, of course, or would it be better to bleed the colors? Both? I think I'm going to go back to Texas this week. I've got the Pacific Jewels collection, I'm so sure of it. I wish you could see them."

"No metallic threads. You have to be careful with metallic thread. You've always had a good eye for color, Maggie. I'll tease myself by imagining them, and when you have them completed, we'll see how close I come. I'm so glad you called, darling. How *are* you?"

"I'm okay, Mam," Maggie lied. "Vermont must be beautiful now. I can hardly believe it's the end of April. I love April. Actually, I love all of the months, December is my favorite, though." She was babbling again. "How's Thad?"

"Thad went to town for a haircut, and he said he was going to stop and pick up some cheese. He wants to make a cheese and mushroom omelet for dinner. He's turned into a rather good cook. Of course, I supervise. I think I hear him now. Call again, Maggie."

Maggie stared at the pinging phone in her hand. She felt worse now than before she called. Tears burned her eyes. She rubbed at them, not caring what the cosmetic manufacturers said about thin eye tissue.

What was she doing? What was she trying to prove and to whom was she trying to prove it? Finding no ready answer to her questions, Maggie flip-flopped her way to the kitchen, where she made herself a baloney, cheese, liverwurst, and raw onion sandwich. She munched as she dragged the Liberty House shopping bags out to the lanai.

She separated the mail into four categories. Bills, family, refinery business, and Valentine Mitchell. "Obviously," she muttered, "I am going to have to pay these bills or I won't have water or electricity." Her charge accounts were demanding payment in full. Insurance premiums were past the grace period, and she was being given ten days to come up with the premium or risk losing her valuable coverage. She snorted. God, she was hungry. She marched into the kitchen, trampling over the bills she tossed on the floor, for a box of Fig Newtons. She devoured one entire package as she moved on to the family mail. Pictures of baby Billie made her cry. Pictures of Sawyer's precocious twins made her mouth twitch. She really had to give some thought to whether she should put all the pictures in an album or frame them. It would be something to do on a rainy day.

Someday.

Everyone, according to the notes, was well. The Snoopy card from Susan said Cary was doing as well as could be expected, though he was depressed. Cary's doctor had placed him on a list for a donor transplant.

Maggie cringed at the scrawled P.S. at the bottom of the card. "I haven't heard from Vermont, nor has anyone else to my knowledge. Personally, I don't give a hoot if I don't hear anything until after it's a fact."

Maggie balled her hands into fists. "Susan, you are a first-class, unadulterated snot," she said aloud. "Someone should tie your tits in knots."

Maggie tossed Susan's card and envelope onto the pile of trash.

Eighteen letters addressed to her from the refinery glared up at her. She had nothing to do with the refinery. Chesney would have inherited Rand's half, and Cary owned the other half. She pushed them aside. One of these days she would send them on to Chesney in England.

One of these days.

Maggie puzzled over the thick stack of legal envelopes from Valentine Mitchell. For someone who no longer represented the family, she had sent much too much mail. Tying up loose ends, she supposed. Well, Val's loose ends, whatever they were, didn't have anything to do with her. Maggie ripped at one of the envelopes. She hated the crisp, crackling sound and wondered why all lawyers felt they had to use such stiff paper.

Rand's will. She threw it on top of Susan's card.

The deed to the house. She puzzled over that for a moment before she tossed it onto the pile of trash. She looked at the rest of the legal letters and decided she didn't want to know what messages they contained. Unopened, she pitched them in the general direction of Rand's will and the deed to the house.

Maggie trotted into the house for a trash bag. She smacked her hands together in satisfaction when she dumped it at the end of the driveway. *"Fini,"* she muttered.

The sun was gone, she noticed as she made her way back to the kitchen. Rain would be good, she decided while making a second sandwich, this time with two slices of Bermuda onion. She carried it with her to the dining room, where she wrote out the household checks. When she came to the insurance bills, she stared at them a moment before she ripped them up. "So bury me in a pine box."

Munching on the sandwich, her eyes watering from the onion, she walked out to the mailbox. She moved the red flag to indicate mail was to be picked up.

Her lights and water were secure.

The rest was history.

{{{{{{{{ CHAPTER TWELVE }}}}}}}}

Valentine Mitchell propped her bulging briefcase on top of the newsstand while she rummaged in her purse for money to pay for copies of *The Wall Street Journal* and *Business Week*. She counted her change, then tossed in a pack of Life Savers and a package of peanut butter and cheese crackers. Now she could nibble on her way to Los Angeles. She hated making the trip, but it was something she had to do. Make nice, do a little hand-holding, make promises on behalf of the new owners of her firm, give reassurances that if things didn't work out with the new partners, she would step in.

The last month had been so hectic, she had felt like pulling out her hair on more than one occasion. She'd gone to more parties hosted in her honor than she'd gone to in all the years she'd practiced law. Champagne breakfasts, catered luncheons, cheese and wine parties, cocktail parties, and elaborate dinners, all to honor her contribution to the legal profession.

It was all winding down now. Another day and she would be as free as the proverbial breeze. It hadn't been as easy as she anticipated, because no one was willing to put up the eleven million for the associates to buy her out. Even when she opened her books, the answer had been the same—no. She'd hated to do it, but she cut a deal with Riley and Cole. "You finance the associates' buyout, and I do the deal for Cary's inner city with ColeShad," was the way she'd presented it on a three-way conference call. They'd haggled, but she'd pulled it off and everyone got what they wanted.

Time to check in. She still had twenty minutes before boarding. She headed for the door marked LADIES. While she was washing her hands, she saw her. Maggie eyed her Scaasi suit. She eyed Maggie's Carolyn Roehm raspberry confection. Both women's eyes turned wary.

"Val," Maggie said quietly, by way of greeting, as she reached for a paper towel.

"Maggie," Val said, pushing the button of the hot air blower. She carried her greeting a step further. "I heard you were in town. Why haven't you answered any of my letters?" She asked a second question on top of the first. "Are you going to Los Angeles?"

Maggie adjusted the waistband of her skirt. She played with the collar of the silk blouse beneath the jacket. "Yes, I'm going to L.A. and on to Hawaii. You?"

"L.A. You didn't answer my first question," Val said, blotting her lipstick.

"I know." Maggie turned to walk away.

"We'll talk on the plane. I'm assuming you're taking the same flight I am."

"I have work to do," Maggie called over her shoulder.

"So do I. They serve subpoenas in Hawaii, you know. You can be forced back here. On the other hand, it will be relatively painless if we conduct business on the plane. Forty-five minutes and we're done."

"You can't force me to come back," Maggie said irritably. "Not for something so stupid as a will."

"Maybe I can't, but the IRS can. Inheritance tax and all that good stuff is a come-on for the IRS. Think about it. I have a bulkhead seat, so I can spread out. I just have to check in. Midsection," Val said, walking off.

Rand had been paranoid about the IRS. So was she. Never mess with them, Rand always told her. "Okay," Maggie said. People turned to look at her, but Val didn't turn around.

Maggie walked toward the gate where boarding was in progress.

When the pilot announced they were cruising at thirty thousand feet, Maggie unbuckled her seat belt and walked forward to the bulkhead seat where Val was sitting, her briefcase open in her lap. Maggie took the seat next to her.

"Plane's almost empty," Val said.

"I guess people don't like early morning flights. I prefer them myself," Maggie said.

"I do too. I hate to waste time. I'm taking the red-eye back tonight."

"That's a long day," Maggie said indifferently.

"If you'd read the mail I sent you, you'd know I'm trying to wind down all your family's business before I leave. I sold the firm to my associates. It's definite now. All I have to do is sign on the dotted line. Retirement sounds ominous now. It didn't when I made the decision."

"Why are you doing it, then?" Maggie asked coolly.

"I'm fifty-four. I've never had a life outside law. It's time. I'll find a house somewhere in a small town, grow some flowers, get a cat, go to pot-luck suppers, join the Grange, and learn to knit and cook. Not necessarily in that order."

"It sounds deadly." Maggie grimaced.

"Doesn't it, though? I might do some *pro bono* work. I'll decide that as I go along."

"You're a good lawyer, Val. It will be a shame to let all that go. *Pro bono* is good, but I rather thought you liked to sink your teeth into *really* big cases and walk off a winner."

"Are we communicating here?" Val smiled.

"We could really communicate if you'd tell me the truth," Maggie said coldly.

"I did tell you the truth." Their eyes met. Val was stunned to see the *nothingness* in Maggie's gaze. She was more certain than ever that she'd done the right thing by lying to the woman sitting next to her.

"Why don't I just sign a power of attorney for you in regard to Rand's estate? That will make it easy, won't it?"

"Easier than it's been. Thad and Billie were executors. They both signed over a power of attorney. Judge Freize okayed it. I did all the preliminary work, but I'll turn it all over to the firm. They'll be in touch with you. Can you deal with that, Maggie?"

Maggie nodded. She pulled up the arm tray and straightened it out, then signed her name on the form Val handed her without bothering to read what it said. After she had handed over the paper, she got up. "Good-bye, Val. I hope you enjoy your retirement."

"Maggie, wait. What are you going to do?"

She sounds, Maggie thought, as if she cares. "Take it one day at a time. I'm working on Billie Limited. I manage to use up my time. And I still don't believe you," she said with a catch in her voice.

"I know you don't. I'm sorry about that," Val said earnestly.

Maggie walked back to her seat. The seats next to hers were empty. She tucked the gored raspberry skirt tightly around her legs. She was asleep in minutes.

In the bulkhead section, Val replaced the tray table Maggie had been writing on. She moved the armrest and slid across to stare out the window at the carpet of marshmallow clouds below the plane. They look like *warm fuzzies*, she thought, something you could hug to yourself to garner comfort. All their lives the Colemans had warm fuzzies to comfort them. All *she'd* had was textbooks, a law library, briefs, trials, appeals, and lots of money in the bank. Not a warm fuzzy in the bunch. But it was by my own choice, Val thought.

What was going to happen to Maggie? What would happen to the Colemans when Billie was gone? Riley, Cole, and Sawyer would be all right. They had families, children, spouses. And they had all that *money*. Susan was as wired as a tomcat on diet pills. A wild card. There was no telling what Susan would do. Cary, according to their last conversation, was going to take it one day at a time, the way Maggie said she was doing. She'd felt sad when Cary said the memorial to Amelia was in a holding pattern. There would be no completion date and no ceremony in July the way he'd planned. Thad would crawl into a shell, and if she was any judge of love and devotion, he'd be gone inside of a year. Childishly, Val crossed her fingers and wished the best for Thad.

Val rummaged in her briefcase for the peanut butter and cheese crackers. She noticed her hands trembling when she ripped at the cellophane wrapper. Ivy. Steady on her feet Ivy. Rock solid Ivy. She understood perfectly why Billie had entrusted her living will to the young woman. She cringed, remembering how sick Billie looked on the video and how hard she'd tried to cover up her emaciated appearance. Hot tears pricked at Val's eyelids.

Now all the Colemans would have to stare at their own mortality. When Billie was gone, there would be no more buffer shielding them from the inevitable.

Below, the carpet of marshmallows parted, then moved together to form a giant cotton ball. Her eyelids pricked again.

Not for all the money in the world would she want to walk in Ivy Coleman's shoes. She wished now she hadn't given Ivy the advice she had, which was in direct opposition to Billie's wishes. She was clearheaded, impartial, and could see down the road to what was going to happen, which was why she'd told Ivy to tell Riley *now*. She'd also insisted Ivy turn the tape over to her for safekeeping. To her knowledge, Ivy hadn't followed her advice, for if she had, Riley would have demanded to see the tape.

Val finished the crackers, wished for more. She looked up to see the stewardess handing out salted peanuts. "Two," Val said. "And a glass of tomato juice, if you don't mind."

Val ripped at the vacuum-sealed bag. They certainly didn't give you many peanuts. It was a good thing she'd asked for two bags. If there was one thing she hated, it was to get her taste buds going and then be cut off just as she was starting to enjoy something. She wondered if there was such a thing as cholesterol-free, fat-free peanuts.

Why did she care what happened to the Colemans? They were clients. You represented your clients, you got paid, and that was supposed to be the end of it. Not so with the Colemans. Somewhere along the way she'd become attached to them, allowed the family to sneak into her heart, where they carved their own little niche, and now she was . . . not stuck with them, that was unkind. No, it was more like she felt responsible for them. Even though she'd severed her relationship and returned the balance of their retainer, she hadn't been able to turn them away.

How was she supposed to walk away, go to Oxmoor and start her new life, with that family standing in the shadows?

There was really no *pending* business with the Colemans. Ivy's *problem* had been presented on a friend-to-friend basis. Was Ivy going to need an ally, someone in her corner? She supposed she could give Ivy her new address and swear her to secrecy. "This whole thing is just *shitful*," Val muttered. She'd broken the first rule of any good lawyer—she'd allowed herself to get involved. She ripped at the roll of tropical fruit Life Savers, separating the ones she didn't like from the ones she did. Coconut and lemon were wadded into a napkin. The tangerine and melon went into her mouth.

What was Maggie doing? What was she thinking? *What was she feeling?*

Life goes on. Val bit down on the candies in her mouth. She ground them between her teeth. Now what would she eat? "Miss," she called to the stewardess, her voice fierce, "do you have any more peanuts?"

Val followed the hordes of people heading for the baggage area, her eyes searching for the Carolyn Roehm suit. She half turned before she stepped onto the moving stair, but she didn't see what she was looking for. She shrugged. She and Maggie Nelson would never be friends, so why was she persisting in worrying about her? Because, she answered herself, Maggie looked so fragile, so vulnerable. What she *should* be doing, Val told herself, was thinking about her upcoming meeting and the whopping bill she was going to present for services rendered.

Time permitting, she might take a stroll down Rodeo Drive to pick up gifts for the office staff. She'd meant to do it earlier, but she hadn't gotten around to it.

Val stepped off the moving stair. There was still no sign of Maggie. She could check out the United gates for Hawaii, if she cared to, but she decided she didn't care to. She kept on walking, her eyes alert for a limo driver holding up a placard bearing her name. The moment she saw it, Val switched into her legal mode and forgot everything but the business at hand.

LAX had to be one of the busiest airports in the world, Val thought as she looked around at the weary travelers, some lugging oversize suitcases, others carrying crying infants and children. Everyone looked tired. She was tired too, but in a different kind of way. She looked at the plates of deep fried onion rings, deep fried cheese sticks, deep fried beer-batter shrimp. The odds of her not dripping grease on the Scaasi suit had to be one in a million, she thought irritably. She looked at the greenery on the plates, wondering if it was scallion tips or green weeds. She pushed the plates away and concentrated on her second glass of white wine.

The table next to hers was suddenly filled by a young woman and three youngsters, the oldest no more than six. She blinked when she saw a baby peeking over the canvas sack attached to the young mother's shoulders. The young woman looked so tired, Val's heart ached for her.

The woman was pretty, with a wealth of red-gold hair trailing down her shoulders. The infant in the shoulder harness yanked at the hair, snapping the woman's head backward. Her voice was gentle, patient when she admonished the child. At the table the three children whispered among themselves. "Hamburgers, french fries, ice cream, Cokes."

"I told you," the woman whispered, "you can split some french fries. We only came in here to heat the baby's milk. If I don't have the money, I can't pay for it. Do you understand?"

Val watched from the corner of her eye as the children nodded solemnly.

Val waved down the waitress and asked for her check. She followed her to the cash register and said, "See that family over there? I want to pay for their order." She handed a fifty dollar bill to the waitress. "The change goes to the woman, okay?"

"Sure," the tired waitress said.

Val walked over to the newsstand, where she browsed through a copy of *Time*. She watched as the young mother shook her head, her eyes swiveling around the restaurant. Finally, she nodded. Val grinned from ear to ear when the children clapped their hands in glee. Val paid for a Tom Clancy novel, two packages of peanut butter and cheese crackers, two mint patties, three peanut butter cups, and two packages of tropical fruit Life Savers. She headed for the gate to wait for the boarding call, thinking about the check in her purse and how happy her accountant was going to be when she told him to put it into her retirement account.

Her future was secure and looking better with each passing day. Tomorrow would be her first day of unem-

ployment in so many years ... she grew light-headed
just thinking about it.

At noon the following day, Val snapped her briefcase
shut, took a last look around the office that was no
longer hers, and headed for the door. She knew the minute she opened it the staff was going to yell "Surprise!"
At which point she would yell, "Surprise yourself!" and
hand out the gifts that had arrived by Federal Express
two hours earlier.

"Fog lights!" she squealed moments later. "Mono-
grammed floor mats! A down sleeping bag! Mud flaps!
Don't tell me this is a tent!" Val shrieked with laughter.

The oldest member of the firm spoke. "You said you
were going to get into a Range Rover and just drive until you came to a place that suits you. As we speak, the
maintenance people are installing a brush guard on your
vehicle. In case you run into a cow or something at a
crossing."

Tears rolled down Val's cheeks. "I don't know what
to say."

"My mother always told me if you don't know what
to say, don't say anything. Just smile. Like *you're* smiling," Val's secretary said, hugging her. "Thanks for the
Gucci watch," she whispered. "And the bonus."

"I'm really going to miss all of you," Val said in a
choked voice.

"Hey, we have an eight hundred number, call us anytime," someone shouted.

"Don't think I won't either," Val shot back.

"We have one last present for you, Val," the se-
niormost man in the office said. "We talked about this
and we all agreed we would worry ourselves sick with
you driving wherever it is you're going alone, so we ...

ah, we decided to . . . hell, open the door," he said to one of the secretaries standing next to the kitchen.

Val's jaw dropped. More tears rolled down her cheeks.

"This is Samantha. She answers to Sam. Note the Gucci collar and the Gucci lead."

"Ohhhh," Val said, dropping to her knees to cradle the golden retriever's head. More tears rolled down her cheeks. "I don't know what to say."

"Whoof."

"Sounds good to me." Val grinned. "Is she house-broken?" She was remembering Isaac's contribution to her decor months before.

"Completely," the senior man said. "She was on a list to go to the Seeing Eye Farm, though at the bottom of the list, I admit. The owner seemed to think she was too playful, and he didn't want to take a chance. She's yours, Val."

"Okay. Listen, I'll be in touch. I'll call in. I'll be back from time to time. When I finally light in one place, I'll let you know. Thanks for everything."

In the parking lot, out of sight of her office staff, Val unhooked the leash from the dog's collar. All of a sudden she felt like the kid she never had a chance to be. She kicked one spike-heeled shoe in the air and then the other. She ran, feinting to the right and then to the left. Sam chased her, her tail wagging furiously. In and out among the cars they ran, spooking one another. Exhausted with her efforts, Val backed up against her new brush guard, her chest heaving. Sam stood on her hind legs, her front paws on Val's shoulders. She growled softly, her eyes wet and adoring.

"God, I just love you," Val said, rubbing her face against the dog's silky head. "Come on, let's get this show on the road. You can either have the front passenger seat or all of the back." She opened the door to let the dog leap in. Sam settled herself comfortably on the passenger seat. Val wiggled her butt on the seat before she swung her legs inside. Designer, skintight skirts were not conducive to four-wheel drives, she decided. She'd remedy that as soon as she drove to her condo to pick up her bags. Her jeans, endangered species sweatshirt, and L.A. Gear sneakers were all laid out, just waiting for her to arrive home.

Val backed the Range Rover from her parking space. She looked at her name on the metal marker and saluted smartly before she swung the four-by-four about. She drove carefully, mindful of the dog on the seat.

"We," Val said, "have one stop to make before we head for the open road. Not to worry, it's in my building. We can do our visiting while my bags are being loaded into the car. There's somebody I want you to meet." The dog looked at her expectantly. "Okay, two stops. Food for you. God, I hope you aren't going to need all that stuff Isaac needs. He's a sissy. He even has a toothbrush. I draw the line at that." She grinned and almost swerved off the road when one silky, shaggy paw stretched out to touch her arm. "I guess that means you like me," she chortled happily as she tooled down the road. She felt like singing, but she didn't know the words to any songs. Instead she switched on the radio, fumbling with the buttons. Lionel Ritchie's voice exploded into the confines of the truck. Val switched stations until she heard Carly Simon's voice. She turned down the volume and hummed along.

When they arrived at Assante Towers, Sam leaped out of the truck, as if she knew they were home. Home for another thirty minutes.

In the apartment, Val called down to the security station to ask for help in getting her bags to the car. She watched as Sam checked out her new surroundings, stopping twice at the dining room table leg Isaac had christened. Val looked at her watch. In thirty minutes, noon actually, the electricity and phone would be turned off. One week from today the new owner was moving in, a dentist who had his offices on the fifteenth floor. She hoped he would be happier here than she had been.

"I'm happy now," Val chortled as she punched out a new set of numbers. She was glad when Cary Assante answered the phone. "I'm coming up to say good-bye, and I'm bringing a friend, is that okay?"

"Sure," Cary said.

"Okay, see you in a bit."

Sam was at the door before the doorbell rang. She backed up, her tail between her legs, as she waited for Val to open the door. She gave one sharp warning bark before she growled softly. Val pointed to her four oversize French bags and the three boxes of personal papers and the few files she was taking with her. She handed the porter a ten dollar bill before she closed the door.

"We'll get some cheeseburgers when we hit the road," she said to the dog. She bent over to tie the laces in her sneakers. "I hate shoes," she said to the dog. "Come on, I want you to meet a friend of mine. Well, he's sort of a friend. Closest thing to a friend. I think so anyway," she muttered.

"Come in," Cary called. "Door's open. I'm on the terrace."

Val looked around. Nothing had been changed since Amelia's death. She just knew all of Amelia's clothes were still in the closets, her things still on the dresser,

her robe still on the hook on the bathroom door. Cary
was not a man to change.

Val bent over to kiss Cary's cheek. "This is Sam. My
office staff gave her to me at my going-away party.
She's a golden retriever." Val smiled when Sam plopped
one of her paws on Cary's leg.

"He feels silky. Is his coat shiny?"

"She. Yep, you can almost see your reflection in her
back. I never had a dog. I love her. How's it going,
Cary?"

"It isn't. I pretty much hang out here on the terrace.
I listen to the television; Susan reads to me. I have
stacks of books on cassettes, though I never was much
of a reader. I go to the doctor's twice a week. I'm on a
donor list. Friends call. I've put the memorial on hold.
My heart isn't into much of anything these days."

"It hasn't been all that long," Val said softly.

"Depends on who's doing the counting. This is July.
The memorial was supposed to be finished by now."

"It's just a temporary setback, Cary. Is there anything
I can do before I leave?"

"Like what?"

"Like I don't know. That's why I'm asking."

"I am a little worried about the payments on the
mortgage," Cary said quietly.

"Well, don't be. I structured it with your condition in
mind. Some people owed me some favors, and I called
them in. You don't have a thing to worry about. By the
time the first payment comes due, the plane will be
ready for testing. Sawyer tells me it's going full-speed,
and, to quote her, 'is lookin' good.' Don't frown, Cary.
The year's interest is tacked on to the last balloon payment at the end. There really is no problem here. Trust
me."

"If it was anyone but you, Val, I'd be chewing my toenails worrying if I bit off more than was wise. Tell me, what's your game plan?"

Val sighed. "I'm just going to drive. West. When I see something that pleases me, I'll stop, stay awhile and see if it's what I want. I'll let you know where I end up. I have all the files and records in the car. I plan to keep my eyes and ears on things."

"Have you heard anything about Billie or Maggie?"

"Not really. I saw Maggie on a flight out to L.A. yesterday, but I haven't heard a thing about Billie. I would think Susan would know. Doesn't she?"

"No," Cary said curtly. "She's refusing to deal with it. She's blaming her mother for dying. I don't know how to deal with *that*. She's starting to smother me, Val, and I don't know what to do about that either. I like Susan, I really do. Part of me wants her to leave and part of me—the part of me that's afraid to be alone—wants her to stay. Can you understand that?"

"Of course. Why don't you have a talk with her?"

"She's in a very shaky emotional state, but then so am I. I don't want her to get ... I'm afraid she's becoming too attached to me. How do you tell someone something like that?"

"Very carefully, I would think. Do you want me to talk to her before I leave? By the way, where is she?"

"She went to get her hair and nails done. What time is it?"

"Almost noon."

"She should be back by now. She may have stopped by the market. She likes to cook. She says I need to eat more. I probably would eat more if someone wasn't watching me slop my food all over myself. Jesus, Val, I don't know what to do."

"You didn't answer my question. Do you want me to talk to her? Believe it or not, I can be subtle. It will be up to you to follow through, though. Can you handle that?"

"No. Look, don't worry about me. I've pretty much come to terms with it all. I've been through the denial, the grief, the anger. I'm trying real hard to get to the acceptance part. I'm not ready to sell pencils yet. I'm not ready for anything."

"Life goes on, Cary. I've heard that term so many times lately, I feel it was created just for me. I don't think Amelia would approve of what you're doing. She'd tell you to get the lead out and put some grease on your sneakers. This is just my personal opinion, and I probably have no right even to voice it, but we've been friends for a long time. Stop wallowing. Boot Susan out of here and take responsibility for yourself. That's the end of my lecture. I don't *have* to leave today. I can stick around and set some things in motion for you."

"What kind of things?"

Val smiled at the curiosity in Cary's voice. Until now it had been resigned and pitiful.

"Things like Sam here. Man's best friend. I was told she was supposed to go into a Seeing Eye program, but the people that train the dogs said they felt Sam was too playful, and they didn't think she would outgrow her playfulness. With a Seeing Eye dog, you could get out and about on your own. There's a foundation in Austin that has trained people who will come here and mark off your stove, teach you to cook, and show you how to arrange your cabinets. And then, of course, there's Braille."

"That pretty much makes this a . . . hopeless condition. If I do that . . . it means I've given up." He started to shake, his body trembling uncontrollably. Sam whined deep in her throat as she pawed Cary's legs, trying to get to his face so she could lick at it.

"It doesn't mean any such thing, Cary," Val said gently. "It's *something* for you to do now. Something to get you through until things are more in your favor. You can't just vegetate. It's been five months."

He was calmer now. Sam nuzzled his hand to get her ears scratched. Cary obliged. "I'll think about it. I'll have to . . . psych myself up. I'm scared, Val. Piss-ass scared. I feel so helpless, and I'm so goddamn angry. Christ, I'm still trying to come to terms with Rand's death and . . . Billie. It's all closing in on me. If I don't stick my neck out and just sit here, nothing else can happen. I'll . . . I promise to think about everything you said. And, no, I don't want you to hang around. Get on with your life. Check in with me, let me know how you're doing."

Val bent over to hug him. "Thank you, Cary, for not asking."

"I've known you for a long time, Val, and it didn't compute. I've never been judgmental. I think you know that."

"Yes, yes, I know that. I think this might be a good time for me to take my friend here and leave before I start sobbing all over your carpet. Take care of yourself, Cary, and I'll be in touch. Say good-bye, Sam." The retriever woofed happily.

"Be happy, Val," Cary said huskily.

"You too."

Sam suddenly barreled to the front door, her huge paws slapping at the painted wood.

"Susan must be home," Cary said sourly.

Val's eyebrows shot upward. She called the dog, who immediately came to sit at her feet.

"I've always heard dogs are better judges of people than people themselves. Let's see what Sam thinks of Susan," Cary said sotto voce.

"I'm home," Susan trilled, closing the door behind her with her rump. She stopped in mid-stride when she saw Val and Sam. She set the grocery bag she'd been carrying on the end table. "What have we here?" She motioned to the dog, who was growling deep in her throat.

"Susan, this is Samantha, Sam for short. My new roommate. I came up to say good-bye. As a matter of fact I was just leaving. You look well, Susan," Val said with a bite in her voice.

"That's because I am well. I don't think I've ever been *more well* in my life." Her eyes slid from Cary to Val and back to Cary.

"For heaven's sake, I almost didn't recognize you in that *getup*." Susan looked down at her own pricey outfit, clearly a Billie original. "Are those *sneakers* I see on your feet?" She made the word sound obscene.

Val smirked. "I own stock in L.A. Gear. I'm wearing Jockey underwear. The jeans are Levi's, the shirt is Greenpeace. As you can see, Sam's collar and leash are Gucci. It's a question of priorities."

Cary chuckled and then guffawed. Sam ran to him, barking happily at the strange sound of his laughter. He tussled with the big dog, laughing as he did so. Val thought it a wonderful sound. Not so Susan.

"I don't like dogs. They breed germs, they shed, and they make messes, plus you have to walk them and feed them. They slobber all over the place."

"That's too bad, Susan, because I'm getting one,"

Cary said. "Val said she'd take care of it for me. I expect they'll deliver. . . . Do they deliver dogs, Val?"

"You bet. I'll take care of those other things we discussed too if you want."

"I do," Cary said.

"What other things?" Susan asked suspiciously. *"What other things?"*

"A live-in housekeeper, a male companion to help Cary over the rough spots until the foundation can set things up for him. And, of course, the dog."

"Cary doesn't need any of those things. I'm here. I cook for him, I take care of him. Everything is working out just fine. Cary, tell her you don't want or need other people. That's why I'm here, why I stayed on. Caryyyyy, tell her," Susan whined.

"Val's right, Susan. I have to start getting on with things," Cary said firmly. "I'm going to . . . to learn Braille. I'm going to get out on my own. I'm going to learn to take care of myself."

"They're not going to care about you the way I do. They'll take advantage of you. You're *handicapped*, for heaven's sake," Susan said shakily.

"I don't like that word, Susan," Cary shouted.

Sam barked sharply, her ears flattening against her silky head. She continued to bark.

"Guess that answers our question," Cary said. "It was nice of you to stop by, Val. Stay in touch. I'm going to take a shower and go for a walk. See you around, lady," he said smoothly, ruffling Sam's sleek back.

"Wait a minute, I'll get you a towel and soap," Susan said. "We aren't scheduled for a walk until after dinner. Cary, you can't upset our routine like this."

"I know where the goddamn towels and soap are. I can open and close the shower door myself, and I want to go for a walk now," Cary said, feeling his way into the room.

"I'll lay out your clothes," Susan bleated.

"I can do that myself," Cary snorted.

"But they won't match," Susan whined.

"Who cares? When those people from the foundation come, they'll show me how to arrange my clothes so I do match. I read about that once. So long, Val. I keep saying that, don't I?"

Sam ran over to Cary, a whirlwind of motion, and nuzzled his leg. *"I love Paris in the spring,"* Cary bellowed. "That was Amelia's favorite song," he called over his shoulder.

"What are you trying to do?" Susan snarled at Val. "What *did* you do? You've spoiled everything. You ruined Maggie's life and now you want to ruin mine. You're jealous. You've always been jealous. I know all about Rand and Maggie. If it wasn't for you, Rand would still be alive."

"All you do, Susan, is breathe air other people need to live. It's not what I did, it's what you did. You took Cary's life and made it yours. You can't function on your own. You need to be an extension of someone else. You've been feeding off Cary. You need to grow up, Susan. I won't even bother to dignify your last statement."

"Bitch!" Susan seethed.

Sam tensed and growled, her teeth showing. Val never felt more protected in her life. From deep within the apartment she could hear the sounds of the shower. Val jerked her hand in the direction of the hallway. "Guess Cary was right. He can take a shower by himself. Bet he even found the soap and towel."

"Eat shit, Val," Susan spat.

Val laughed as she made her way out to the elevator. "I can't believe she said that. Miss Holier-Than-Thou. It just goes to prove, Sam, first instincts are usually right. I had Susan pegged from the first. It looks like we have more work to do," she said, fondling the dog's ears. "If the phone company is on schedule and the phone's been turned off, we'll have to fall back and regroup."

Back in her apartment, Val headed for the phone, praying for a dial tone. Dead. "Nuts," she muttered. "Okay, we'll go to the garage and call Ivy. Come on, girl, we're splitting this place."

She didn't look back and felt no regrets when she locked the door behind her. This part of her life was history now.

In the garage, Val settled Sam in the car and rolled down the window. "Stay," she said, her voice ringing with authority. Sam stayed. "Cheeseburgers within the hour," she promised.

Ivy answered the phone on the second ring. Val explained her visit to Cary's apartment and her encounter with Susan.

"You didn't!" Ivy squealed.

"I did. My phone's off, so will you make good on the promises I made to Cary? I'd really appreciate it."

"What are friends for? I'll get right on it. And Val, take care of yourself and call me once in a while, okay?"

"Of course. Right now I have to pick up some cheeseburgers. 'Bye, Ivy."

" 'Bye, Val."

"We're free as the breeze," Val said, climbing into the Range Rover. She studied the map and the route she'd marked with a felt-tipped pen. When she had it firmly in her mind, she started the engine, slid a Carly

Simon tape into the tape deck, ruffled the dog's ears, and drove down the ramp of the garage to the outside world.

"Six cheeseburgers coming up, complete with pickles, ketchup, and mustard. Helloooo world!"

Susan sat with her head in her hands, tears streaming down her cheeks. Damn Valentine Mitchell, damn her to hell, she thought. Always sticking her nose into my business. Cary was hers. She'd devoted so much time to him, done everything for him, anticipated his every need, put him ahead of herself. A sob escaped from her throat.

She saw him out of the corner of her eye, a brilliant cherry-red towel wrapped around his middle. She tried to square her shoulders, tried to gather her dignity, but it seemed a hopeless task. Then she remembered Cary couldn't see her. She stood, her knees wobbly.

"Guess I screwed up again," she said pitifully. "I just wanted to help."

"I know. I'm not blameless here," Cary said from the doorway. "It was easy for me to let you do everything. The plain truth is that I acted and you reacted, or vice versa. I appreciated everything you did, but Val is right and we both know it. I need to do for myself. Can we leave it that if I need you, I'll call you?"

Susan gulped. "Story of my life, Cary. Sure. Well, guess I'll be going. The groceries are on the table. Do you think you can put them away, or do you want me to do it?"

"Hey, I'll just dump them on the counter and work from there. If you brought cold cuts, I'll be fine. I've been making baloney sandwiches for years now. I can wash a piece of celery as good as the next guy. Apples are good. Cheese is okay. Finger foods. Don't worry about me, Susan. And I don't want to have to worry about you."

"Can I still call you?" Susan whimpered.

"Hell yes. Are you giving up Billie Limited? Maggie could probably use some sisterly intervention about now."

"Is that another way of saying hit the road?"

"It means whatever you want it to mean," Cary said quietly. "You need direction, Susan, and I'm not the right person for that. I have so many problems and hang-ups of my own, I can't give sound advice. Think about a therapist or a . . . someone who can be impartial."

His voice was so kind, Susan started to cry all over again. "What you're saying without saying it is that you think I need a shrink, that I'm not stable."

Cary, holding on to the walls, made his way into the kitchen, where he fumbled around in the utility closet till he found the broom. Using it as a cane, he swept his way back to the living room and advanced to where Susan was sitting. "What I'm saying, Susan, is you need to talk to someone other than me. I've been a sounding board, nothing more."

"I was falling in love with you, Cary."

Cary shook his head. "No, you were feeling sorry for me, just the way you feel sorry for yourself. You saw in me an extension of yourself. We'd exist, flounder around, and be miserable. Amelia was and still is the only woman I'll ever love."

"You betrayed her, you had an affair with Thad's niece Julie. Don't stand there and tell me she's the only woman in the world for you!" Susan snarled.

"That was a low blow, Susan, but I guess I deserve

it. But knowing Amelia forgave me makes it a tad easier to live with.

"I've been wallowing, and Amelia *wouldn't* like that. She would approve of every single one of Val's suggestions. Amelia liked Val, just as I do. Val's real. She doesn't make excuses. And there isn't a mean bone in her body. You owe her a lot, Susan."

"She was paid," Susan said bitterly.

"There are some things money can't buy. Just look what she did for me in the space of fifteen minutes. Jesus, I feel alive, all charged up. I can't wait to get dressed and mess around in the kitchen. So what if I look like a nightmare, so what if I live in squalor until I get it down to a science? So what, Susan?"

When Susan let herself out the door, she could hear Cary singing "Pretty Woman" at the top of his lungs. She slammed the door so hard that one of the brass plaques fell to the floor. "So hang the damn thing up yourself. See if you can find the nail and the hammer. See if I care."

In the Coleman condo, Susan looked around. No one lived here. It was for visiting guests or for family to stay over when they didn't want to make the trek home. Spartan, hotel-suite decor. Susan flopped down on a long sofa that was covered in a scratchy nubby material the color of sand. The whole apartment was done in bland earth tones. It was depressing. She got up, jerked at the draperies to blot out the sun. She turned on the television, then turned it off. Tea. She looked at the box. Celestial Seasonings. It sounded, she thought, like something that would give you an orgasm. She pitched it in the general direction of the sink and was rewarded with fine bits of herbal tea showering all over the kitchen.

She was homeless. Literally homeless. Unless she wanted to go back to Minnesota and live in the house she'd once shared with Ferris. She could take it off the market. Or go to England. She hated England and its dreary weather. Homeless. At forty-eight.

In a fit of rage she grappled for the phone on the table next to the nubby couch. She dropped it twice before she managed to punch out her mother's telephone number. When Thad's voice came over the wire, Susan said, "I want to talk to my mother and I want to talk to her now. If you don't put her on the phone, I'm taking the next plane to Vermont. If you take her away, I swear to God I'll track you down. Now, get her!"

Thad's stinging voice hummed over the wire. "I will not allow you to upset your mother. Tell me what the problem is, and I'll decide if Billie is up to taking your call."

"You'll decide!" Susan screeched. "God is going to strike you dead for what you're doing. I told you I need to talk to her. This is all her fault. Everytime I need her, she's never around or she's too damn busy. She's so damn busy dying, she can't talk to me, is that it?" Susan heard the click. She stared at the phone in her hand. "You son of a bitch!" she dialed again and got a busy signal. "You bastard, you took the phone off the hook!"

Her rage was uncontrollable. She stomped about the apartment looking for a weapon of sorts, and found a cast-iron meat mallet in the kitchen drawer. She smashed everything in sight, all the mirrored walls, the sliding glass drawers, the porcelain sink in the bathroom, the tile on the wall. In the kitchen, she banged and pounded at the appliances until they were dented to her satisfaction. From the same drawer where she got the mallet, she picked up a huge carving knife. She ripped and gouged, sending fiberfill in all directions. Exhausted with the destruction she had caused, she slumped to the floor, but not before she threw a china vase at the television screen.

Almost at once she felt appalled at what she'd done. God, who was going to pay for this? She must be going crazy. At forty-eight, she was homeless *and* crazy. Ferris had said, among other things, that when you think you're crazy, you aren't. It was when you denied having problems that you did indeed have a problem. She wouldn't believe anything Ferris said if his tongue were notarized.

The sound of the phone ringing was louder than an explosion. Susan stared at it with glazed eyes. It was probably a wrong number, but at least it would be a human voice. She picked up the phone, her voice scratchy and gruff. "Hello."

She had to strain to hear the whispery words on the other end of the line. "Mam? Mam, is that you? Mam, I'm sorry for yelling at Thad. Mam, I need you. God, I'm homeless and I think I'm crazy. Do you think I'm crazy?" She rattled on, her voice shrill at times, dropping to a whisper and then turning shrill again. "I tried to help him, to be there for him. He said I need a goddamn shrink, so that's two people who think I'm crazy. Him and me." She finally wound down, her voice a whimper.

"Darling, you aren't crazy, but I do think you could do with some professional counseling. You need friends, Susan."

"I haven't had time to make friends, Mam."

"You have the time now, darling. There are so many

wonderful support groups out there. You need to get involved in things, to start a new life, and you can't do that
through someone else. I think, and I may be wrong, but
I think you tried to take Amelia's place with Cary. No
one, and we both know this, can ever do that. Things are
mixed up in your mind with regard to Amelia and myself, and that's why I think you need to go for counseling. I did not abandon you, Susan. I tried to do what was
best for you. If I was wrong, I'm sorry. Parents don't
always . . . We make mistakes too."

"I've disappointed you, haven't I? I'm sorry, Mam.
Tell me what to do, where to go. I can't seem to make
a decision."

On the other end of the phone she could hear Thad
saying, "One more minute, Billie, and then I'm cutting
off the phone." And then her mother's weak, gentle
voice. "Shush, Thad, my daughter needs to talk to me.
I'll rest when I hang up."

"Mam, it's okay. Thad's right. I'm just being selfish.
I'm sorry I bothered you."

"Darling, you aren't bothering me. I want to help, but
you have to be open and want to help yourself. What
can I do for you, Susan?"

"Just tell me what to do."

"If I do that, will you take my advice?"

"God yes. Do you think I like being like this?"

"Good, that's the first step. Do you have paper and
pen?"

"Yes, yes, right here by the phone. Mam, I destroyed
this apartment. I wrecked it with the meat mallet and
carving knife."

"Then you're going to have to pay to repair everything. If you did it, it's your responsibility. Now, write
this down."

Susan scribbled as her mother's weak, wan voice trailed off. "But that's what you said earlier," Susan complained.

"Yes, Susan, but now you have it in black and white. You can see it. Think of it as a road map to your . . . recovery. Will you promise me to act on it?"

"I'll do my best." As an afterthought she said, "How are you, Mam?"

"I'm not going to run the mile when we've hung up, but Thad is taking wonderful care of me. I'm comfortable."

"All right. Good-bye, Mam. Oh, Mam, will you tell me you love me?"

"My dearest Susan, of course I love you. I loved you the minute I saw you. I will love you into eternity."

Billie was crying. Susan realized she had made her mother cry. She wanted to say I love you too, but the words wouldn't slide past her tongue. She replaced the phone in the cradle. "Yeah, sure you love me. I had to ask you to say the words." She cried bitter, scalding tears.

Forty-eight. Homeless. Crazy. Unloved.

{{{{{{ CHAPTER THIRTEEN }}}}}}

The lazy July sun cast its last shimmering light across the Pacific waters. The lanai was cloaked in its mystical glow. The air was redolent with the scent of plumeria. Scattered about were wet beach towels, chattering children, sand pails, shovels, vibrant, vinyl beach toys, and a set of parents ready to pull out their hair.

"You're sure you want to do this?" Sawyer demanded of her mother.

"Of course I'm sure. I think I'm capable of handling the twins. All you need is discipline. I can manage. You and Adam can go off to Japan without worrying. I know how to be a grandmother. I've been reading up on the matter. Like Adam says, all-day suckers and cookies mixed with discipline will do it. I'll teach them how to swim, and we'll build sand castles and all that good stuff."

"What about Billie Limited?" Sawyer asked anxiously.

"Hey, I'm Billie Limited, and I can take time off. Things are running smoothly since I decided on going American. I saw the labels two days ago. They gave me goose bumps. Made in the U.S.A. Next year's colors are in the running. Later, when the children are in bed, I'll show you the scarf. God, it's gorgeous. My first article, my first color. I can't wait to send it to Mam. Have you heard anything, Sawyer?"

"I called this morning before we left, but the machine was on. I left a message. At least you got to speak to her a few months back. Lord, I cannot believe it's the middle of July. Where is the time going?" Sawyer moaned.

"Don't think of time in the past, think of it as now, as in whose turn it is to give these children a bath," Adam grumbled.

"It's yours and you know it," Sawyer said sourly. "I gave them one this morning at home and this afternoon after they fell asleep on the beach. I washed their hair too. They're half asleep, so they won't fight you and drown. Please, Adam, I'm too tired to move."

When father and daughters were gone, Sawyer bustled about the lanai, popping cans of iced tea and setting out crackers and cheese. "So, tell me what's going on."

Maggie laughed with genuine mirth. "Absolutely nothing. You know I went back to Texas for a while. We spoke about that. Ivy called a few weeks ago to bring me up to date on Cary. She said he has a magnificent dog, which he absolutely adores. He's getting out and about on his own. He's got this nice older gentleman who works on a voluntary basis for the foundation. A part-time companion of sorts. He's doing just great. He told Ivy he owes it all to Val."

"What about Susan?"

"I haven't heard from her. Ivy said she's staying in the family condo, and when Cary can fit her into his schedule, she visits. Ivy said she thinks Suse will go back to England. It wouldn't surprise me. She's never called me, not once."

"And you, Maggie, how are you?" Sawyer asked softly.

"I'm here. It hasn't been easy. I have bad days and I have good days. Today is a good day. I'm so glad you decided to stop here and leave the girls with me. I hardly know them. It shouldn't be like this. I really would like the chance to be a grandmother. I can't wait to see Cole's daughter. He promised to bring Sumi and the baby here at the end of the month. He sounds so happy, Sawyer," Maggie said happily.

"That's because he is happy. I keep getting this vision of him and Riley *playing* with all that money. I'm going to tell you a secret, and you have to promise not to tell anyone."

Maggie nodded, her eyes dancing with interest.

"Cole and Riley think I don't know, but I overheard them talking back in the spring when we were all at Sunbridge. You'd just done *your number* and the family was in a turmoil. Anyway, those guys decided to finance Miranda through Valentine Mitchell. She set it all up. Cary thinks he got the financing from some English firm. It was Cole's way of securing Miranda in case anything goes awry with the plane. They're twits," Sawyer said fondly, "but as Adam says, they always come through when it counts. I just wanted to bust when I heard it. The only person I could tell was Adam, and he just said, 'I told you so.' You have reason to be proud of Cole."

"Val set it up?"

"Yes, she did. She was very good to this family, Maggie. I'm sorry she won't be representing us anymore. You could always count on Val. I don't think anyone has heard from her."

"In the beginning I was so certain she lied to me. Now I'm not sure. I don't know why that is, Sawyer."

"I don't know why either, Maggie. Does it really matter now?"

"I thought it did ... does ... maybe, I don't know. I try to block it all out, to keep busy. I got rid of all the furniture. At first I just got rid of the bedroom stuff, and Chesney's too. Then the office stuff and then the rest of everything. I would walk around here thinking I smelled Rand's after-shave, *him*. He never even told me he deeded this house to me. I had a real crying jag on the day Val sent the deed. It reminded me of the day I got the deed to Sunbridge. God, I was drunk as a skunk, but that sobered me up real quick. I never took another drink after that. I don't want to talk about this, Sawyer."

"That's fine with me. What do you want to talk about?"

"Mam, I guess. Your plane. Whatever."

"I'd rather not talk about Grandmam. I don't want to cry anymore. I'm so glad Adam agreed to this move. Sumi is looking for a little house for us to rent. I think it will be good for the girls. All those little cousins over there will be wonderful for them. I bet they learn Japanese with ease. The cousins will learn English. Sumi promised to get me a girl to watch the twins, and a housekeeper. Adam is going to be really busy. He's had an offer to do a book of his favorite cartoons for Random House. But don't think we're going to neglect the girls," Sawyer said hastily. "We'll have more quality time with them. They are a handful, Maggie."

"I don't doubt that for a minute. If things get wild, I'll call on Addie and have her get me some schoolgirls to help out. Take as long as you need. You said production is under way?"

"Yes, I made two fast trips over there. Things are under control. A year and it will fly. The switch over from Coleman Aviation to ColeShad Aeronautics throws me every so often. Cole thinks we should go public with CSA. I can't make up my mind. What do you think?"

Maggie shrugged. "I don't know much about it, but I don't think Cole would steer you wrong. Val can probably . . . well, someone can . . . talk to a lawyer." Maggie averted her eyes.

"Were . . . *are* you jealous of Val?"

"That's as good a word as any. In many ways I admired her. She did everything on her own. It really doesn't matter how she did it, she did it. Ivy talks to me about her a lot. Ivy considers her a friend-friend, if you know what I mean. She said every club, organization, and legal firm in Miranda and Austin threw going-away parties for her. She said her picture was in the paper every day with glowing testimonials from judges, lawyers, and clients. She did it all on her own. I'm envious of that. Look at you, Sawyer, you did it. What have I done? Nothing. All I did was take. I was no mental match for Rand.

"I've had a lot of time to look back on things. The last year or so, Rand spent so much time away. He *said* he was going to Maui. He *said* he was going to Hilo. He *said* he was going to England. He *said* he was going to Hong Kong to see Chesney. He said a lot of things. I think I did to Rand what Ivy said Susan did to Cary. I made myself an extension of him. What was my contribution? I walked on the beach. I swam. I prepared food. I went to exercise class two or three times a week. I shopped. I read. My God, what kind of life is that? The worst part is, I didn't see . . . didn't think I should do anything differently. Rand must have been bored out of his mind. When Chesney returned from one of her trips, he came *alive*."

"Don't do this to yourself . . . Mother," Sawyer said, taking Maggie in her arms. "Let it go. That's what you used to tell me. Take each new day as it comes."

"Easy for you to say," Adam said, flopping down on a beach chair. "The terrors are clean and asleep. They rise and shine around the time the sun comes up. Sometimes before the sun comes up."

"That's interesting to know. I'm an early riser myself," Maggie said.

"They're very demanding," Adam said.

"They are little shits," Sawyer said. "What one doesn't think of, the other one does. Then they both act on it. If you had told me twins run in your family, I never would have married you."

They argued back and forth good-naturedly, then heatedly, almost coming to blows. Maggie watched and listened. They were so passionate about everything. She couldn't ever remember having had such a discussion, such a fight, with Rand.

"I could punch your lights out with one hand behind my back," Sawyer blustered. "You were the one who forgot to buy the Fig Newtons. Don't lie, Adam!"

"While you're *trying* to do that, I'd be snatching you baldheaded," Adam stormed. "Jesus, I'm tired. Let's go to bed, honey."

The tempest was over, if that's what it was. Maybe this was the way young people *communicated*.

Sawyer leaned over to kiss her husband's cheek. "I'm kissing you now because when we get to bed I won't have the energy. You don't mind if we turn in, do you, Maggie?"

"Good heavens no. You both look exhausted. What time is your plane tomorrow?"

"Ten-thirty. We'll have to leave here at nine. 'Night, Maggie," Sawyer mumbled. Adam waved wearily.

"Sleep tight," Maggie said.

Maggie walked down to the ocean, the damp sand tickling her feet. She sat down, cross-legged, and stared out across the moonlit water. How beautiful. How peaceful. The waves' soft lapping was music to her ears. She hummed a few bars of a popular ditty until tears gathered in her eyes.

She was alone.

She thought about her family. Their lives seemed to be in order. No one needed her. Baby-sitting the twins for a week or so didn't really qualify as having someone. If Cary was on track, that left only her and Susan at odds with life. Maybe she should call Susan when she went back to the house. And say what? Ask her to come here? Not a good idea, Maggie. Make the offer anyway. You know she'll refuse.

Mam. Don't think about Mam. If you think about Mam, you'll set yourself back months. Maggie hugged her knees, her toes digging into the sand.

Sand castles.

Maggie leaped to her feet and ran back to the house and into the kitchen, where she rummaged in the cabinet for a bowl, a plastic glass, and a bucket from under the sink.

Grandmothers built sand castles.

Maggie worked diligently, lugging buckets of water to a spot high on the beach so it would stay intact until morning when the twins awoke. She molded and sculpted with the Tupperware bowl and Burger King plastic glass. When she finished at four o'clock, she rocked back on her heels to stare at the wonder she'd created. It had turrets, windows, a moat, and a drawbridge. The girls would love it. It was almost perfect. But every castle needed a flag. She raced to the garage, where she searched for a swatch of suitable material. She decided on one from the Pacific Jewels collection. She grimaced. What good was a flag without a flagpole? She bounded out of the garage and into the house. In the bathroom she found the perfect flagpole—a cuticle orange stick. She was back in the garage a moment later, dabbing Krazy Glue on the stick. When she had pressed the small flag around the cylinder, she reached for the pinking shears and snipped at the edges.

Perfecto.

Maggie ran back to the beach and positioned her flag to the right of her drawbridge—the shiny cardboard tray chicken cutlets came wrapped in. She felt pleased with herself, almost as pleased as the day her color swatches were made final.

In the shower, she remembered her intention to call Susan. She felt like singing and wasn't sure why.

Back on the lanai, dressed in a one-piece playsuit the color of the Hawaiian sky, Maggie reached for the portable phone. "Suse, it's Maggie."

"You're up early, aren't you?" Susan's voice accused. She sounds depressed, Maggie thought.

"Actually," Maggie said, and laughed. "I didn't go to bed last night. I stayed up and built this gorgeous sand castle for the girls. They're here, you know. I am going to baby-sit. Can you believe that? I don't know for how long. Adam and Sawyer are going to find a house in Japan. They're moving there temporarily, but then you know that, right?"

"No, I didn't know that," Susan snapped. "No one tells me anything."

"Sawyer said she spoke to you," Maggie said gently. "Is something wrong?" Of course there was something wrong. There was always something wrong in her sister's life. This conversation was already a downer. Think positive, she cautioned herself.

"She did call weeks ago, and she did say she was *thinking* about it. I'm out of sorts. What have you been doing since . . . are you all right?" Susan asked in an uninterested tone.

"I finished the dyes a few weeks ago. Look for Pacific Jewels and Egyptian Lights next spring. If you like, I can send you a scarf. I've been working on them. I want Mam to see them. Have you heard anything, Susan?"

"Hardly. Have you?"

"Not recently. How's Cary?"

"Cary's just fine. He's so fine, he's never home. He's so fine, he doesn't return calls. He's so damn fine, he told me to *do* something. I hate men, Maggie. I gave up my life for months for him, and I did everything humanly possible to make his life pleasant. I was there for him every hour of the day and night. Now he has this dog, and he has people over to his apartment all the time who are teaching him how to . . . how to cope. I *wanted* to do all that for him. He was so grateful until that bitch showed up and turned him against me. She did to me what she did to you, Maggie. She snatched Rand from you and . . . She just stirs up all this trouble in our family and then she takes off! She's a slut, a tramp, and a no-good bimbo!"

I will not let her ruin my day. I simply will not,

Maggie told herself. "I assume the bitch in question is Valentine Mitchell," Maggie said quietly.

"Of course. Who else do we know who does the things she does? She's always been jealous of us. Though we were good enough to pay her hundreds of thousands of dollars over the years."

"Maybe you should stop and think about what you just said, Susan. A few months ago you showed up on my doorstep with . . . what was it you said? Eighty dollars in your checking account? That's bread-line, pauper level. You're sitting on a velvet cushion now, thanks to Val. Give credit where credit is due. And don't forget that she was the one who bailed you out the first time around, when your first husband did the same thing to you your second husband did. Maybe you should take a long, hard look at yourself, Susan. You know, I called you to see how you were. We're sisters, and I care about you, but you are so bitter, Susan, so angry at everyone and at the world. You should be thrilled and delighted that Cary can do things for himself, that he isn't so traumatized that he sits and sucks his thumb. Instead, you're angry. Mentally, Cary is in a healthier place than you are right now. You think about *that* for a while, and if you want to call me back later with a smile in your voice, *maybe* I'll talk to you. Good-bye, Suse," Maggie said, slamming the phone down.

"*That* was a mistake," Maggie muttered as she filled the Mr. Coffee.

"Froot Loops," a tiny voice by her knees said. Maggie whirled about.

"Shoclit bears," a second tiny voice said.

"No. Scrambled eggs. Toast. Juice."

The tots shook their heads wildly.

"Oh, yes," Maggie said. "Sit!"

"No," the girls chorused in unison.

"Aha, well, then I'll eat by myself. You go pick some flowers for your mother." The twins watched, uncertain at the sternness in her voice. They continued to watch, thumbs in their mouths, as Maggie set one place at the table. "This is my plate," she said. "Shooo, go get the flowers. Pretty ones."

"Froot Loops," Katy said.

"Shoclit bears," Josie said.

"Eggs," Maggie said.

They cried, at the same time, both their lower lips trembling.

Maggie scooped some of the scrambled eggs onto her plate and sat down. She started to eat. The twins sobbed. Maggie ignored them. "Want some?"

"Popsicle," Josie said.

"Cookie," Katy wailed.

"Eggs," Maggie said.

"Sugar bread," Josie, the ringleader, pleaded.

"Gummi Bears," Katy hiccuped.

"Eggs," Maggie said.

The twins looked at one another. They stopped crying at the same moment their thumbs came out of their mouths. As one they scrambled onto their respective chairs. They wiggled until they were on their knees. "Eggs," they said.

"I thought you'd see it my way." Maggie smiled. The girls wolfed down their eggs and toast and finished their milk.

"Cookies?"

"Apples," Maggie said, wiping their faces with a wet paper towel. "Let's pick some flowers and make a lei for your mommy. That's a necklace of flowers. We'll have to work quickly before Mommy wakes up."

Darning needle and nylon thread in hand, Maggie led the twins out to the garden at the side of the house. "You pick them and I'll string them."

Chubby fingers piled the fragile blossoms at Maggie's feet. She worked quickly, stringing the sweet-smelling flowers on the thread. "For mommy."

"Daddy," they chorused.

"Okay, Daddy too." Maggie's needle worked furiously. "How about one for Josie and Katy?" Maggie kissed each of the girls as she placed the small leis around their necks. "Now take these to Mommy and Daddy and tell them to get up. Hurry." She smiled.

"Prize."

"When you get back I'll show you the surprise." She watched as they scampered off. What had she gotten herself into? Who cared? She was going to love every minute of it, if she survived.

"They smell wonderful," Sawyer said happily. "What a wonderful way to wake up. The girls said you made eggs for us. I'm starved."

"No. I made eggs for the twins. How do you like yours?"

"Over easy. *They ate them?*" Maggie pointed to the plates on the table. "Look, Adam, they ate eggs."

"I'm no authority on children, but did you two ever stop to think about how much sugar those children eat? That's probably one of the reasons they're so wired-up all the time."

"Pepsi," Josie said.

"Pepsi," Katy echoed.

"Juice," Maggie said.

Sawyer watched, her eyes round, as the girls drank their juice without a fuss.

"Prize?"

"Just as soon as I make breakfast for Mommy and Daddy. Pick some more flowers for me." Sawyer watched her children as they trotted off to do her mother's bidding without a fuss.

"Here you go," Maggie said, sliding the eggs onto Sawyer's plate. "I have to go now. Adam, you can push your own toast down, can't you?"

"Yeah, sure. What's your hurry?"

"I stayed up all night and built a sand castle for the girls. That's the *prize*. There's a lot of traffic Monday mornings, for some reason," she called over her shoulder. "Maybe you better leave fifteen minutes earlier."

"And you were worried?" Adam scoffed, dipping his toast into his wife's egg yolk. "When we come back for the terrors, they probably won't want to go with us. In which case we could board them out here and visit on holidays."

Sawyer threw her napkin at him.

"This is probably the best thing we could have done for your mother. Let's take a shower together," he said, leering at her, "wearing our leis."

"My dear, that is the best offer I've had since ... God, since when?" Sawyer said, dashing off to the bedroom, her husband right behind.

The moment Sawyer and Adam drove off, Maggie took the girls by the hand and led them around the side of the house and down to the beach. Josie, the more verbal of the twins, had laid claim to the sand castle. Now it was time to build one for Katy.

It was almost noon when Maggie called a halt to the building. She had heard her name being called from the garage area. She never had visitors, and Addie was off today. She felt a flurry of panic and didn't know why.

It was probably the meter reader. She called out, "I'm down here."

He's huge, Maggie thought. He was six-two, at least, with a crown of thick dark hair mixed with silvery strands at the temples. He was dressed in creased navy chinos, with a crisp white shirt open at the throat and sleeves rolled to the middle of his arms. His tan, if it was a tan, was a glorious bronze color. Dock-Siders adorned his feet, along with white tennis socks. Obviously, Maggie thought, whoever he was, he wasn't trying to make a fashion statement. He looked comfortable in his clothes and with himself. From where she was standing, she thought him ugly, but as he approached with a smile on his face, she revised her opinion. She looked into warm, dark eyes the color of melted chocolate chips.

Maggie brushed the sand off her hands, her eyes wary.

"Mrs. Nelson?"

"Yes."

"I'm Henry Tanaka. Your stepdaughter's attorneys approached me in regard to selling her ten percent interest in the sugar refinery. I was wondering if you had any intention of selling your interest as well. I spoke personally to Mr. Assante yesterday, and he suggested I come up here to talk to you. He told me about his condition and expressed an interest in selling out, either to you or to me. I understand you'll want to verify all of this, but I would like to make an offer."

"I hadn't thought about it, Mr. Tanaka. As you can see, I more or less have my hands full right now. When would you want my answer?"

"I'm not in a hurry, but your stepdaughter seems to be. Take as long as you like. I haven't built one of those in years," he said, pointing to the sand castle. "My wife and I used to build them all the time for our grandchild. Then my son decided he wanted to work on the mainland and they moved. My wife died two years ago. For a while we would build them ourselves. . . ."

How sad he looks, Maggie thought. "We could use some help, if you have nothing to do. You see, I stayed up all night to build one, and I forgot how proprietary twins are, so we now have to build another. By the way, this is Josie and this is Katy. I'm baby-sitting. For a couple of weeks. I think."

"I'd like that. Would you mind if I change? I keep a swimsuit in the trunk of my car."

"Not at all. The bathroom is off the kitchen. You're sure you're an expert at this?" She twinkled.

"The best. We could have a contest. You take one of the girls to help you, and I'll take the other one."

"Before or after lunch?"

"If that's an offer, I accept. I'll just be a minute." He beamed.

The moment Henry Tanaka was out of her sight, Maggie started to worry. God, what if he was some kind of pervert? An ax murderer?

"Hims nice," Josie said.

"Yeah, hims nice," Katy agreed.

"I think you're right," Maggie said, "but I'm still going to call Cary."

"He's got a good reputation," Cary said. "Rich as sin, I hear. He more or less implied he'd pay cash if we want to sell. It's your call, Maggie. I won't be able to do much overseeing in my condition. Rand was the one who knew the refinery, not me. I'll go along with whatever you decide. Are you out on the lanai? A sand-castle building contest, huh?" he said wistfully. "Do you still have all those beautiful purple and pink flowers?"

Maggie looked around.

"Yeah. I'll call you back and let you know who wins, okay?"

"Promise?"

"I promise."

"Checking up on me?" Henry asked.

"Yes. Cary said you are who you say you are. He left the decision up to me. Grilled cheese and tomato soup for lunch," Maggie said, leading the way into the kitchen. "The bathroom is off the kitchen."

"Popcorn," Josie said.

"Jelly bread," Katy said.

"Grilled cheese and soup," Maggie said. She could hear Tanaka laughing in the bathroom.

"Hims nice," Josie said.

"Hims nice." Katy grinned.

"Let's wash up first," Maggie said. "While I fix lunch, you can pick some flowers for Mr. Tanaka. Maybe he'll help you."

Lord, he's big, Maggie marveled. She wondered if he was Hawaiian. She asked.

"My mother was a *hale*, so was my grandfather. It explains my height. I've lived here all my life. About two miles up the road. We've been neighbors for a long time. I knew your husband. Not well, of course. I'm sorry about his passing."

"Thank you."

"You must be very lonely here. I know I am. When my wife died, I went around the world. I thought I would never come back, but I did. Now I'll never leave. As a matter of fact, I couldn't wait to get back. One has to learn how to deal with memories. It isn't easy."

Josie tugged at his hand. "Flowers." Katy tugged at his other hand.

"They said, and this is a direct quote from both of them, 'Hims nice.' "

"I'm impressed."

"And well you should be." Maggie laughed.

The moment they were out of sight, Maggie ran to the bathroom to run a brush through her hair. She couldn't put on makeup now; it would be too obvious. She couldn't splash on perfume either. Thank God the playsuit was attractive. When she walked back to the kitchen she felt giddy. Hmmmmn. But her good mood soured almost immediately. Henry Tanaka wanted to buy the refinery, so naturally he would be nice and ingratiate himself with her. So what? she said to herself. For now, it's pleasant, and he's someone to talk to. She flipped the sandwiches onto a plate. She cut them up in little squares for the twins and poured their soup into small cups with thick handles.

"I think," Henry said thirty minutes later, "your charges are falling asleep in their soup."

He sounded so disappointed, Maggie said, "Let's carry them out to the lanai, and you and I can get a start on the castles. When they wake up, we'll finish them. Are you sure you can spare the time?"

"That's about all I have these days. Time."

"But you said you want to buy the refinery. Don't you work?" *That's about as blunt as you can get, Maggie.*

"I don't work. My daughter-in-law uses that term all the time. I acquire things."

"I see," Maggie said.

Tanaka laughed. "My wife used to say that all the time. Usually it meant she didn't fully approve. Ooops,

I think we better get these youngsters to someplace soft before they fall off their chairs."

"I don't understand. Sawyer said they never take naps. She said they don't sleep through the night and they don't eat anything," Maggie dithered. "God, you don't think there was anything wrong with the food, do you?"

"I think they're just tired. The sun and sand will do that to you. They do jabber a lot. You should have heard them when we were picking the flowers. This one," he said, indicating Josie, "is solid as a rock."

"So is this one." Maggie laughed. "Do you think I should cover them?"

"It's eighty degrees. Is this your first time with the girls?"

"I guess it shows, huh? I'm enjoying it, though. I promised I would teach them to swim. Now I don't think it's such a good idea. Josie is afraid of the waves."

"Come up to my place and use my pool. We have two ponies and three horses. Do you ride, Mrs. Nelson?"

"Call me Maggie." She told him about Sunbridge and the horses there. "I couldn't impose on you. Thank you for the offer, though."

"Tomorrow morning. I'll come down and get you and drive you up to my place. We have some new kittens in the barn."

"If you're sure we won't be taking you away from anything, then yes, okay, we'll accept."

"Have you given any thought to how you'll teach *two* children to swim at the same time? You need eyes in the back of your head when they're this age."

"Yes, I see what you mean. You'll teach one, and I'll teach one."

"Listen, I really don't care about the refinery. If you want to sell, that's fine. If you don't, that's fine too. I don't want you to think I'm buttering you up for the kill."

She believed him. "The thought did cross my mind."

"I like an honest woman. I like you, Maggie Nelson."

"Thank you," Maggie said, flustered. God, who could she call and tell?

They talked then, forgetting about the sand castles.

"You're Billie Limited," Henry said in amazement.

"You know about Billie Limited," Maggie said in surprise.

"My wife did. She wouldn't wear anything else. Now, there's a company I wouldn't mind acquiring."

"Too late. I'm running it now. Would you like to see my new line? I work out of the garage." She told him about that too.

They were as old friends, comfortable with one another, calling each other by their first names, when hours later Henry proclaimed himself the winner of the sand castle contest. "The winner gets to take the ladies out to dinner. Ice cream, soda pop, and hamburgers."

"Vegetables, chicken, fruit, and milk."

Henry looked at the girls. "She's the boss. I'll pick you up in an hour."

The twins clapped their hands in glee. Maggie did too. Now she could wear makeup and perfume. And a dress. Thank you, God.

"All right," Maggie said. "We'll be ready."

Maggie spent so much time pressing the girls' polka dot sunsuits and polishing their sandals, she had barely enough time to shower and change. She chose a gauze two-piece outfit with a straw belt riding low on her hips. She slipped her feet into matching sandals and was about to start on her makeup when she looked at the clock. No time for makeup, but time enough for a quick spritz of perfume.

She looked at the two cherubs sitting side by side on the bed. "We have a date." She laughed. "And," she said, dropping to her knees and lowering her voice, "I bet if we play our cards right, we can have even more. Dates, that is." The girls nodded solemnly.

They were off the bed in a flash when Henry blew the horn.

It was a date. Of sorts. A beginning.

CHAPTER FOURTEEN

The trees rustled softly overhead in the weak, struggling breeze. Blue jays settled on the leafy branches, their eyes searching the water fountain and bird feeder in the middle of the yard. As they watched, their provider scooped out thick, fat worms from a Chinese-style container and placed them in the feeder along with sunflower seeds and crumbs from a strawberry Danish.

The oversize birdbath had been fashioned by Billie and himself in a pottery class they'd taken years ago. "Big enough for hundreds of birds, Thad," Billie said. "One that will take gallons of water." And that's what they had. Thad turned on the hose and tested the lukewarm water with his finger. When the bath was filled, he felt like jumping in himself, or at the very least, turning the hose to drench his perspiring body. It was a silly thought, and lately he hadn't had many silly thoughts. He sprayed his feet.

Today, according to the weatherman, was the hottest day of the year. The thermometer on the deck registered ninety-six degrees.

Thad dragged the hose over to a two-hundred-year-old maple tree, where he filled two buckets of water for any squirrel or chipmunk who cared to visit. He also filled the square wooden box at the base of the tree with acorns and the assorted animal food he purchased at the local feed store. His last chore was to fill the narrow metal tray with rabbit pellets, carrots, and lettuce for the family of rabbits that lived under the toolshed.

It was a job. Something to do. Something to take his mind off Billie. He knew that the minute he joined her on the deck, she was going to pick up the discussion they'd had before he'd come down to the yard to tend to the birds and animals. He dawdled to delay the moment of his return as long as possible. He knew he was going to do what his wife wanted, because he could deny her absolutely nothing. If she asked for a slice of the moon, he'd try to find a ladder big enough to climb to get it for her.

Thad coiled the hose and carried it back to hang it on the rack attached to the house. He noticed the lid to the barrel that held the acorns wasn't closing properly. Should he attempt to fix it and delay his return to the deck, or should he wait for another day?

He knew exactly what Billie was going to say. "Thad, why are you being so stubborn?" He felt like cursing. Suddenly he wanted to shout all the obscene four-letter words he'd ever heard during his stint in the Navy. Damn, he should be praying instead of cursing, but then he'd already tried both, and neither worked. What was going to be was going to be, and nothing he did or said was going to change a thing. He cursed then, every dirty, filthy word he knew, and when he ran out of words, he made up new ones. When he was finished he said, "I'm sorry, God, I had to do that."

Thad did his best to control his anger and to put a smile—even if it was a sickly smile—on his face when he flopped down in the lounge chair next to Billie. Here it comes, he thought. *Thad, why are you being so stubborn?*

"Why are you being so stubborn, Thad?" Billie asked quietly.

"Because you are in no physical condition to make a trip, any trip. What you want to do is make a pilgrimage. No."

Billie smiled wanly. "You've never refused me anything. I want to do this. I *need* to do it. I already spoke to Dr. Blake, and he said if I was up to it, to go ahead and do it. You're just being obstinate. I understand your concern and I truly appreciate it, but if you don't go with me, I'll hire someone to take me. Now, make your decision," Billie said. "I won't take no for an answer."

"Then I guess you have my answer," Thad grumbled. "When do you want to go?"

"What's wrong with right now? Our bags have been packed for the last ten days. That's how long you've been arguing with me, Thad. I gave in on the Hong Kong part because even I know the trip would be too much. But going to Philadelphia, Pennsylvania, is almost around the corner. We can stop every hour if need be."

Thad gaped at his wife. "You mean just get in the car and leave . . . now?"

Billie smiled. "Uh-huh. All we have to do is lock the door. Oh, Thad, let's do it!" Billie cajoled.

"You're whining, Billie." Thad smiled.

"No, this is my coaxing voice, my wheedling voice. Please, Thad."

"Oh, okay. Go to the bathroom. I'll get the car out. I can't believe I'm doing this," Thad pretended to grumble. "I suppose the *packed* bags are inside the closet."

"Thad, you are so astute, you amaze me," Billie said

as she got up to go to the bathroom. Thad watched her out of the corner of his eye. She was rail-thin now and wobbly on her legs. She reached for the pronged cane, waving him away. "I can do it," she said tightly.

"I just didn't want you to trip over my feet," Thad said, working his facial muscles into a smile.

"You're hovering, and you promised not to. Get a move on, Thad, time waits for no one."

Inside the bathroom, Billie leaned up against the door. Why was she doing this? Why was she insisting Thad take her to Philadelphia? Was the trip down memory lane for herself or for Thad? "For Thad," she muttered. He needed something to do, something to think about other than her. "I don't have much time left," she murmured.

She had to go to the bathroom, but did she have the strength to . . . Such a simple thing as going to the bathroom had become a major obstacle in her life. Give me the strength, she prayed.

"Hey, lady, what's taking you so long?" Thad called from the other side of the door.

"If you think I'm going to tell you, you have another thought coming," Billie shot back. She swayed dizzily. Her hands, she thought, looked like claws. She opened the door. "I think I need some help, Thad."

"That's what I'm here for." Thad scooped his wife into his arms. She couldn't weigh more than eighty pounds. More like seventy-five. "I'll come back for the cane. Do you think you'll be warm enough?" he dithered.

"Thad, it's over ninety degrees. I have my shawl on and a long-sleeved dress. It's August, remember?"

"I just want to be sure," Thad groused as he settled

Billie in the front seat of the car. "Put your seat belt on."

"It's on, Thad," Billie said, snapping the buckle into place.

"Okay, I'll get the bags. Want an apple?"

"Sure, bring all the fruit, and some crackers too. I know how you like to munch when you drive. Soda pop too, you get thirsty."

"That's going to take at least ten minutes."

"So I'll snooze while you do it."

"You had better be awake when I get back."

Billie nodded.

Satisfied that his wife would be all right, Thad went back to the house. He carried the two small bags to the front door. The trip to the kitchen for the fruit, soda, and crackers took all of a minute. He dropped the bags by the front door with the suitcases, then walked back to the kitchen and picked up the phone.

He thought this day would never come, that he would never have to make this call. He'd hoped, he'd prayed, he'd done everything humanly possible to ward off this moment. He squeezed his eyes shut and tapped out the numbers he wanted. He was in total control when he spoke to Ivy. It wasn't until he hung up that he thought he would completely fall apart.

Billie was wide awake when he settled the suitcases in the trunk. He handed her the bag of fruit and soda he knew he wasn't going to eat or drink.

"See what you think of this," Thad said, backing out of the driveway. He thought his heart would shatter when Billie looked back, her eyes drinking in the sight of the house and lawns. Almost as though she knew she wouldn't be coming back. My God, she does know that, Thad realized. She's doing this so she won't . . . so she won't die in the house and leave me that terrible memory. Oh God, oh God, oh God.

"Yes . . . ?" Billie drawled.

"Well, we'll drive through Connecticut, and if you aren't too tired, we can go through to New Jersey. Or we can stop in Connecticut at a five-star hotel and the following day head for New Jersey and Philly. Philly is only three hours from the Connecticut state line. I'm personally for the five stars, what about you?"

Billie giggled. "Okay, let's drive to Connecticut. Unless, of course, you get too tired." She was needling him, telling him in her own inimitable way that time was of the essence. He felt his heart skip a beat.

"I suppose you'll want to dine on greasy hamburgers and greasier french fries," he said.

"Absolutely. And one of those apple pie things that taste like cardboard."

"You got it. When was the last time we had one of those greasy killer meals?"

"Four days ago," Billie smiled. "It's un-American to take a trip and eat health food."

She was asleep a minute after she finished the sentence. From time to time Thad wiped at his eyes as he drove along. She would sleep for forty-five minutes and then awaken, unaware that she'd dozed off.

Thad glanced at the dashboard clock when Billie said, "Speaking of American, Maggie is going American. She said she isn't going to do business in Taiwan or Hong Kong. She asked my permission, and I gave it, to label our fabrics 'Made in the U.S.A.' I'm so pleased at the way she's taken over . . . under the circumstances. I can't wait to see the Cleopatra Gold scarf she said she's working on right now. She said those ten days she spent at Sunbridge staring at the sun were worth the blisters she got on her eyeballs. Those two lines are going to be all you see next year, mark my word, Thad. I'm so proud of her."

"I know you are, honey. I am too. I think turning over Billie Limited to her was the best thing that could have happened to Maggie."

"I'm just delighted. What was it you said you wanted to tell me? Or are my days mixed up again?" Billie said fretfully. "Can I have a pill, Thad?"

It was two hours ahead of schedule, but he didn't give a damn. "Sure, honey, wait till there's a break in traffic, and I'll pull over. Is the pain bad?" What a damn silly question that was.

"It's bearable. I thought with the trip and your driving, you just forgot. Take your time, darling, we don't want to have an accident."

"Here we go," Thad said, moving from the middle lane to the right and then off to the shoulder of the road. From his pocket he withdrew a bottle of capsules and shook one into the palm of his hand. "You'll have to take it with soda, is that okay with you?"

"That's fine. Now what was it you were going to tell me?"

Thad shifted his mental gears. "Sawyer sent me an article in the mail. I was going to read it to you this afternoon when we had our reading orgy, but I'll tell you instead. She also sent a note. She says she thinks Cole is into 'high-tech love hotels.' Rooms by the hour. The high-tech part is for discretion. They use state-of-the-art automation to choose a room, check in, eat and drink, pay the bill, and check out, and no one is the wiser. A guest checking in is greeted by tape-recorded check-in instructions and a floor plan showing room locations and availability. They even have frequent-customer cards, which go into a slot for payment. They have this oh-so-discreet-sounding bell that reminds guests when it's time to leave. Rooms go for thirty to ninety bucks for two hours. Two hours, can you believe that? It's twenty percent higher for an all-nighter. Repeat guests get a discount. Sawyer said she called Cole to ask him if he was involved, and he just laughed." Thad chuckled; Billie giggled.

"Would Cole really do that?"

"Wouldn't surprise me. Guess there's big money in sex."

"Good Lord, Thad, don't tell that to the family."

"I won't, but Sawyer loves to babble. I'm sure she's apprised everyone and sent them the same clipping. She does love to involve the family in all things that generate income. And she loves to one-up Cole, as you well know. How are you feeling, honey?"

"Almost normal," Billie said tiredly. "What was on our reading schedule today, Thad?"

"*Tokaido Road* by Lucia St. Clair Robson. It's that novel about feudal Japan you said we should read. That was your choice. My choice was *Under Siege* by Stephen Coonts. We can read them this evening when we stop." She was asleep again. Tears rolled down Thad's cheeks. God in heaven, what was he going to do without her at his side? How could he go on? Why go on? He blinked, dislodging the tears from his eyes. He continued to drive because it was what Billie wanted.

Fifteen minutes later Billie stirred, mumbled in her sleep, and said, "Is there really money in high-tech sex hotels?" Thad threw his head back and laughed uproariously. Billie slept, a smile on her face.

* * *

While Thad's Lincoln Town Car chewed up the miles and Billie slept, Ivy Coleman paced, her eyes those of a trapped animal. She shoved the VCR tape behind the cushion on the sofa. A second later she retrieved it and slid it under the couch, only to pull it out and hide it behind a book. She continued to pace, around the low-backed sofa with its oversize cushions, around the table with its yellow bowl of daisies, around the recliner and foot stool. Angrily, she walked back to the bookcase, where she yanked at the books. She snatched the tape and laid it on the coffee table. She shoved aside two copies of *Architectural Digest* and the August issue of *Better Homes and Gardens*. She slid the crystal ashtray to the far end of the table. The tape glared at her like a giant, square black eye. She started to shake. Her eyes turned to the clock on the bookshelf. Her mother would be walking through the door in less than twenty minutes to take Moss back to Florida with her. Riley would be home in a little over an hour.

Oh, God! She wished she'd followed Val's advice and told Riley about the tape. But she hadn't! She'd told Sumi, though. Sumi understood. Oh, God! She had agreed with Val's advice, and followed through by having an extra tape run off and left in Val's possession. Just in case, Val had said.

Five o'clock. By eight the family would be here. All of them. Riley didn't know that either. Would he forgive her for taking things into her own hands?

The calls had been so hard to make, but she'd done it. To spare Riley.

The moment Ivy heard her mother's voice, she calmed. She hugged her, her eyes brimming with tears. Her mother wiped at them with a tissue.

"You have to be strong," Tess said. "You're doing

what Billie wants, and if the family doesn't understand, then it's their problem. That goes for your husband too."

"What if they don't, Mama? What if they fight and carry on? What do I do then?"

"You just keep saying over and over it's what Billie wants. It's right there on that tape. Did that lady lawyer call you back?"

"Not yet, Mama."

"Honey, I don't have time to talk. I have to get right back or I'll miss the plane. Is Moss ready?"

Ivy pointed to the playpen and the pile of luggage by the door.

"Lord, Ivy, I'm not taking any of that. Coots is out buying everything we'll need." She held up her hand as Ivy was about to protest. "He feels important doing it. I just told him to get one of everything and to assemble it by the time I got back. He dropped me off at the airport, just *itching* to head for Burdine's. All I need for now is a diaper bag, Moss's bottles, and one change of clothes. That's all, honey."

"Okay, okay. Here, I wrote out—"

"Ivy, we'll manage. Where's his whuppie?"

"Right here," she said, handing it over.

"Ivy, if . . . if you need your daddy, you just call."

"I will, Mama. Give Daddy a kiss for me. Well, here he is, my bundle of joy," she said, giving Moss one last hug.

"We're going to spoil him, Ivy."

"I know that, Mama. Take care of him."

Tess nodded. "You stand up for yourself. Billie trusts you. Don't let her down. Not now. You tell the family I'm real sorry. I always liked Billie. I was jealous of her for a while, but I came to realize you can't be jealous of *good people*. You can only like good people. 'Bye, honey."

"Call me when you get home, okay?"

"Of course."

Ivy cried then, great, hard gulping sobs as she watched the airport limo until it was out of sight.

When Riley walked through the doorway at six-fifteen, Ivy was listening to Dan Rather on the news, her eyes on the VCR tape.

"Hey," Riley shouted, to be heard over the news, "are we going somewhere?"

Ivy took a deep breath as she lowered the volume on the television set. She was amazed at how steady her voice was when she said, "No, my mother came to pick up Moss. She took him back to Florida. I had his stuff all piled up, but she said Daddy wanted to go out and buy . . . what she said was, Daddy needs to feel important."

"Don't you think you should have told me?" Riley said quietly.

"Yes, I should have, but the circumstances . . . I just thought it would be better if Moss was away from here for a while. He'll be well taken care of."

"I don't doubt that for a minute, but what do you mean 'would be better,' and why didn't you tell me?"

"Because . . . because I gave my promise that I wouldn't. What that means is . . . sit down, Riley, I have something to show you. It will explain about . . . about Moss."

Riley watched his wife change the television channel to three and then turn on the VCR. He grew uneasy when he watched her walk over to the television set and insert the tape that had been lying on the table.

Ivy's eyes never left her husband as he watched the

tape. When it ended, she asked, "Do you want me to play it again?"

"Jesus Christ, no!" Riley exploded. "How long have you had this?"

"Since March."

"And you're just showing it to me now!" Riley sputtered.

"I promised your grandmother, Riley. She asked me not to tell you. She didn't want me to tell anyone. I told Val, who advised me to tell you. I wanted to, Riley, but your grandmother . . . how could I refuse to do what she asked? If it was wrong, I'm sorry. I have to tell you, though, I'd do it again."

"I'm sorry, honey. It's just that I thought this would never happen. It was . . . in my mind, I think, but . . . I wanted to think it wouldn't happen for . . . for a year, maybe longer," Riley said, his voice full of sorrow.

Ivy reached for his hand.

"The family?"

"I called them all. Cole is bringing Adam and Sawyer. Sumi, of course. Sumi's sisters are going to watch the children. They'll stop in Hawaii and pick up Maggie, who, by the way, is bringing a friend. Someone named Henry Tanaka. I said that was okay. Maggie needs a friend right now more than she needs family. I said I had no objection."

"What about Cary and Susan?"

"They'll be here around eight. Separately. I don't quite know what that means. Cary said his companion would drive him over, but he said he would have to spend the night, because the man has to pick up another . . . person early in the morning, to take . . . I don't know. I just said yes. Susan said she would leave for England in the morning. I'm sure she'll change her mind. She said, and this is a direct quote, 'These family get-togethers are getting to be a pain in the ass, and I can do without them.' End of quote."

"*She's* the pain in the ass," Riley said through clenched teeth.

Ivy pressed the rewind button on the VCR.

"Ivy, let's walk up the hill."

"Are you sure you want to?"

Riley nodded.

"Then I think we should take the shears and those clippers, along with a couple of trash bags. Your Aunt Maggie was very upset when she was here the last time. She said there was no excuse for the way you let the hill go."

"She's right. There is no excuse. Let's go, the stuff is in the barn."

It was something to do. Something that needed to be done. Something to pass the time until the family arrived.

While they worked, they talked: about Sawyer's revolutionary plane design; the prototype; Cole's progress in restructuring ColeShad; Maggie's new friend, Henry Tanaka; Cary's Seeing Eye dog; and about how similar the cherry blossom hill was to the spot on this hill. From time to time they both cried.

It was dark when they walked down the hill. Riley dragged three huge gun-metal-gray bags behind him; Ivy carried the basket of garden tools.

While they were washing their hands at the kitchen sink, Ivy whispered, "Riley, we didn't do that because . . . because . . ."

"We did it because it needed to be done. I want you to keep on top of me in regard to the hill. It's important that it be kept up. I'm ashamed I let it go so long. Do we have time for a quick shower?"

Ivy looked at the clock. "Sure."

Together they walked into the great room at ten minutes past eight. Cary arrived at almost the same moment, Susan soon afterward. The others arrived at twenty-five minutes to nine. Ivy had a moment to take Henry Tanaka aside and talk to him.

"I feel like I know all of you," Tanaka said, afterward, shaking hands all around. His eyes, Ivy noticed, turned wary when he reached for Susan's hand.

"Are you Hawaiian?" Susan asked.

"More or less."

"Does that mean you're like a half-breed?"

Tanaka laughed. "That about sums it up. Does it make a difference?"

"Not to me it doesn't," Susan snapped. "We could take a vote."

"Shut up, Susan," Sawyer ordered.

Riley watched tight-lipped. Susan was the instigator here, and she was going to cause more than one problem.

"Don't tell me what to do," Susan snarled.

"Somebody should tell you," Adam said quietly. "If you can't keep a civil tongue, then you should leave. I, for one, won't miss that smart mouth of yours."

"I've had a hell of a long day, crossing datelines and all," Cole said through clenched teeth. "None of us have had any sleep, and I'm not in the mood for a family harangue. I thought we left that behind us the last time we gathered here in this room."

They were in pairs, Ivy thought. Everyone had someone but Cary and Susan. God, here it comes, she thought as she visualized a nightmare scenario: Susan going berserk and killing all of them with a gun hidden in her purse.

"Well?" Riley said.

"Well what?" Susan demanded. "You called this get-together, so get on with it. I have things to do."

"I hope dropping dead is at the top of the list," Sawyer said.

"Enough!" Riley roared. "You all know Thad called yesterday. He called again this afternoon and spoke to Ivy. He said he's taking Grandmam to Philadelphia because she wants . . . to see it again, the place where she grew up. He told Ivy he thinks . . . she won't . . . she won't make it back home. He also said it's his opinion Grandmam didn't want to die at the farm. She didn't want that for him, for any of us."

" 'Ivy says,' " Susan put in. "Why did Thad call Ivy? Why not Maggie or me? We're Mam's daughters. Ivy is just a granddaughter-in-law."

"Well, I can tell you why Thad didn't call *you*, Susan," Sawyer shouted. "You're about as stable as a yo-yo. What that translates into in English is, you're nuts. Why does it matter who Thad called? We're all here. We all know. The question is, what are we to do? What does Thad want us to do?"

"Thad wants us all to be together so when it's . . . time," Riley said, "we'll be . . . we'll be a family. Grandmam entrusted Ivy with her living will. We're going to show it to all of you now. Thad hasn't seen this. According to Grandmam, he doesn't even know she made it. I don't think there will be any doubt in any of your minds when you . . . when you see with your own eyes what Grandmam wants."

Ivy pressed the play button on the VCR, then took her place next to Riley, who reached for her hand.

The family stared at the blank screen. The soft whirring of the machine was the only sound in the room. Billie's face flashed on the screen. She smiled a wan, weary smile before she clasped her thin hands in her lap. She was stick-thin, her eyes deep-set behind her tinted glasses. Ivy knew the preparations for this video must have taken a lot of time and effort on Billie's part. She was dressed in a meadow-green, flowing caftan with matching turban. Billie had designed the caftan, Ivy was certain, to hide her thinness.

The tinted glasses were new, a prop, Ivy felt, to hide the sunken hollows of her eyes and to draw less attention to her thin cheeks and sharp cheekbones.

A tear slid down Ivy's cheek. Riley leaned over and kissed it away. She snuggled deeper into the hollow beneath his arm.

Billie smiled and addressed each of them by name, then thanked them for leaving their lives to come to Sunbridge. Her smile was tired, but in place.

"As Thad always says, listen up, family. I had hoped to keep my condition a secret, but Cary's accident made that impossible. A secret to spare you. Perhaps I was wrong. If so, I apologize. You see, I love you all so much, so very much. When I first found out I was terminally ill, I wanted to run to each of you, to have you hug me, to hear you tell me things like 'It will go away, it's just one opinion, they're making medical advances every day.' I realized I just wanted to fool myself.

"I know you're all weeping now. It's very hard for me to sit here in front of this camera . . . and not cry myself. But I promised myself that I'd be strong, that I couldn't go with any less dignity than my old friends who've gone before me. I ask myself over and over, how did Amelia leave us with such dignity, and yet with a sense of humor I still marvel at? I finally decided it was because she had all of us, was certain of our love. She told me . . . she told me once near the end, that what bothered her most was what would happen to all of us. I assured her we were family and would always be there for one another. She . . . please wait just a minute while I . . . wipe my eyes. She said she knew I would keep us all together, and then she thanked me for being . . . her friend . . . all those years.

"Shadaharu, who was a wonderful friend, simply said to me before his passing, 'Life must go on.' And that's what I'm telling all of you now. I do not want any of you to grieve for me. What I want is for all of you to go on with your lives, remember me with love, and to visit me on the hill once in a while. I know there's a perch someplace in heaven, and . . . and Amelia, Shad, and I will be sitting on it watching over all of you. If that sounds silly or unbelievable, allow me this last small indulgence. I am crying. I'm sorry, so very sorry. I think it's the medication, the steroids I'm taking.

"Bear with my . . . roll call. I can't leave without one last word for all of you. Maggie darling, I remember you the day you were born. You were so pink and pretty and so very perfect. I was a mother for the first time. Some of our years weren't too easy, but then life is not always easy. You turned your life around against all odds. I am so very proud of you. I know I leave Billie Limited in good hands.

"Susan, darling, I also remember the day you were born. You were pink and blond and perfect too. I know you believe your father and I abandoned you. . . . We didn't. We did what we thought was best for you. And now, with all your efforts, you are one of the world's most renowned pianists. I don't know who was more proud of you, Amelia or me. I love you, Susan, with all my heart.

"Sawyer, sweetheart, Maggie and I shared our love for you. Like Susan, you had two mothers. I will always be grateful for the love you showered on me. Without you in my life during those bad years, I fear I wouldn't have made it. Love Adam and the twins with all your heart.

"Cole, Riley—I'm doing this in alphabetical order—you are the young blood who will keep this family together. You are both like bright, shining lights, taking the family out of the darkness and into the sun. East and West . . . West and East . . . No one could love you more than me except your wives.

"Ivy and Sumi—again in alphabetical order—I entrust to you these two fine young men who are my grandsons.

"Cary, my friend, I leave you my family, for they love you as much as I love you. Amelia asked me to look after you when she passed on, and I did my best. Now I ask that you look after my family. Thad . . . Thad won't be able to. . . . He's going to need you, Cary. Please, be there for him, all of you, help Thad through . . . the bad times.

"I want you all to pay close attention to what I'm going to say now. I do not want to be hooked up to any life-saving equipment. If there are any of . . . my body parts that are not eaten away by disease, I want them turned over to a donor bank. There will be no open casket. Thad won't be able to handle that. I want a one-day service, and I want to be buried on the hill. A private funeral. I don't want the state of Texas or Vermont to attend.

"I've anguished over who I should entrust with this

tape. As I sit here before you, I don't know who that person will be. You need only know the person who plays this tape has the final say in regard to my last wishes.

"I say good-bye now to all of you and ask only one thing. Please take care of Thad. Good-bye, dear ones. You were mine for such a little while, and now I must give you up. I love each and every one of you. I will carry my memories and my love for you into eternity, and share that love with Amelia and Shad. I truly believe they're chomping at the bit for me to get there. I'll give them both your regards."

When the tape ended, Riley turned the machine off. The silence in the room was so loud he shook his head to clear it.

Ivy stood to take her place beside her husband. "There is one last thing. Please, all of you, remember Billie chose me to be custodian of her living will. She believes you would all be too emotional to carry out her instructions. I gave her my promise to do what she wanted. At seven o'clock this evening, I discussed this with Riley for the first time. He's in agreement with me. But you need to know I spoke to Billie last week and she said . . . she trusted me to make sure her eyes went to a donor bank. The recipient of her eyes is to be Cary. There is no room for discussion. There is a plane waiting at the airport to take Cary to the hospital. I've spoken to Mr. Tanaka, and he has kindly agreed to go along to handle matters. It's what Billie wants, and as custodian of Billie's will, it's what I want too. Billie will . . . Billie will live on for all of us through Cary."

Cole and Riley jumped to their feet as one. Both of them offered to fly the plane.

"I'll fly the plane," Henry Tanaka said quietly.

"You're both too emotional, and I want Cary to arrive in one piece. It will be my pleasure to do this for your family."

"Wait," Cary said. "I don't know what to say. I want to say something wonderful and meaningful, but I don't know the words. I can't believe Billie would think of me during this time."

"Billie predicted you would say exactly that," Ivy said. "She said, and this is a direct quote, 'Tell him not to sweat the small stuff. I need to take a message to Amelia so I can see her smile. Knowing Cary is going to view the world the way Amelia and I viewed it is all the thanks I need.' End of quote. I'd get going if I were you, Cary."

Cary choked up, "She said that?"

Ivy smiled. "Word for word."

"Then I guess we'd better get going."

There were hugs and kisses, slaps on the back, handshakes, and more kisses. Susan stood to the side, her eyes full of bitter hatred, refusing to join the family.

"What a family" were Cary's last words as he was led from the room by Henry Tanaka.

CHAPTER FIFTEEN

Thad's chest hurt. His head ached, and he had muscle cramps in both his legs. The lump in his throat was so large, he could barely swallow past it. Any minute now he was going to bawl, he could feel it building up in him. He risked a glance at Billie, who was peering out the window with such intensity he almost ran onto the curb.

"It's so pretty, just the way I remember it. The trees are bigger, of course, more leafy. They're elms, you know," she said in a voice he could barely hear.

How in the name of God was she doing it? She was hanging on by a thread, and they both knew it, but she wouldn't give in. Not yet. She belonged in a hospital. They both knew that too.

"There it is, Thad, Four seventy-nine Elm. Oh, they painted it. It used to be white. The shutters were black."

"It looks like baby-poop yellow," Thad said gruffly. "I guess the brown shutters go with it. I think I like black and white better. If I close my eyes, I can visualize it the way it was back in 1941."

"That was fifty years ago, Thad. Where did the time go? It seems like yesterday that I lived here. The day I met Moss was the day my mother rented out my room because we needed the money. I don't think I ever forgave her for that. Where are we staying tonight, Thad?"

"The Radisson." He wanted to say the hospital, but he didn't. Billie still had things to do.

"I'm ready now to go to the Navy Yard. It's not far. Not quite two miles. I walked that day with Tim Kelly and my friends. He was killed in the war. I can still see him clear as crystal."

"There's Loews Theatre," Billie said minutes later. "Moss took me to a movie there. I was supposed to go to a matinee with my friends the day I met him."

He didn't want to ask, but he did. "Do you ever regret . . . any of your life, Billie?"

"I wouldn't change a thing, Thad. I never came back. Why do you suppose that is? Fifty years is a very long time. I should have come back. I meant to. I wanted to, but I didn't. Now, now when it's too late, I . . . I guess this is where it began and where it has to end."

"I guess so," Thad mumbled heartbrokenly. "There's the USO building. Do you want to stop?"

"No. Seeing it is enough. I danced with you that first night. I remember that. I loved your New England twang. Moss kept calling you his Yankee friend. Moss loved you, Thad. You said I looked like an angel on top of a Christmas tree. I thought that was such a wonderful thing to say to someone you just met."

"And you said I reminded you of an Uncle Sam poster. I remember everything about you, Billie. I loved you the moment I met you, but you belonged to my best buddy."

"Well, here it is, the Navy Yard."

Thad bit down on his lower lip. He hated this kind of memory. Why was she doing this? So she could tell Moss when she saw him that she'd made this pilgrimage? The thought was so upsetting, Thad fought to get his breath. "You don't want to get out, do you?"

"No, darling. That first day there were so many ships here. Battleships, destroyers, camouflaged green and brown. Huge superstructures that seemed to reach for the sky. The chain-link fence was so awesome. Moss came up behind me and asked me how I liked it. He pointed out the aircraft carrier and told me about the *Enterprise*. Moss had summer-blue eyes. He absolutely mesmerized me that day. He took me home. Somehow he managed to borrow a 1938 Nash from someone. I felt so grown-up."

Thad choked up. "Anything else, Mrs. Kingsley?"

"No. I think I've seen enough. Thank you for bringing me, Thad. I'm sorry if this stroll down memory lane has upset you. I felt it was something I had to do."

"Hey, I'm the one who ended up with the girl."

"Thad, I love you so much. I think I loved you that night when I met you at the USO, and was too stupid to know it. Moss was so . . . he was bigger than life. He simply overwhelmed me. I did love him, though, for a very long time. How far is the hotel, Thad?"

"Not that far. Out by the airport. We can check into a hotel in town if you prefer. You're exhausted, aren't you? You're shivering."

"I am a little chilly," Billie whispered.

Sweat trickled down Thad's face. His shirt was soaked and clinging to his back. He rolled up the windows, praying he wouldn't pass out from the heat.

"How many puppies did Duchess have, Thad?"

"Eight, honey."

"Where's my green dress, the one I wore for you in Hong Kong?"

"At home in the closet. It's in a plastic bag," Thad lied.

"How could I forget something so important?" Billie murmured.

He knew exactly what she meant. He'd also seen it in the bottom of her bag, wrapped in tissue paper. She'd thought of everything. He wiped at the sweat and tears on his face.

"It's time to go, Thad. How far are we from New York City? I should know that, shouldn't I?"

"An hour and a half, two at the most." He knew exactly what that meant too. Sloan Kettering was in New York. He turned the car around, checked to get his bearings, and headed back the way they'd come.

It was dusk when Thad pulled up to the back of Sloan Kettering. He looked at the huge red letters that said EMERGENCY. He thought the color was the same as Maggie's Firecracker Red.

"We'll take over from here," an attendant said quietly. He looked at Billie, blinked, and said, "Park the car, sir." His voice was so kind, Thad cried.

"I won't be long, honey," Thad said, leaning over to kiss his wife. His tears mingled with hers. She tried to smile. The effort it cost her broke Thad's heart. A moment later she was gone from his sight.

He had to move the goddamn fucking car. He had to put it in reverse and back out and then put it in gear and park it. Climbing the Himalayas would have been easier.

The moment Thad had parked the car, at a crazy angle, he lost whatever sanity he had. Bellowing obscenities at the top of his lungs, he beat the wheel with his clenched fists until his hands were swollen and red.

An eternity later he found himself in a waiting room. All the necessary papers had been signed. He was waiting now for word from Billie's doctor in Vermont. He was also waiting for the oncologist who had treated Billie from the beginning to make an appearance. He stared down at his swollen hands and the Styrofoam cup of muddy-looking coffee he was holding.

He felt a thousand years old when he made his way to the phone booth. He didn't have the energy to rummage in his pockets for the change he needed to make the call. Somewhere in his wallet he had a phone card, but he didn't have the energy to look for it either. He pressed the button for the operator and placed a collect call to Texas.

"Riley," was all he could say. He could see them all, gathered in the great room, their eyes filled with tears, dreading the moment the phone would ring. He wondered if the sound was different for this particular call. How long would it take them to get here? Three hours at most. He was a pilot, for God's sake, he should know to the very minute how long it would take Cole to clear a flight plan, get off the ground, get airborne and . . . he should know, but he didn't. He couldn't think. He stared at the muddy coffee. Billie made such wonderful coffee. Ivy did too. The family was probably drinking it by the gallon. "Riley."

"I'm here, Thad. We're all here. Well, Susan isn't here, but the rest of us are. She left for England this morning. Where are you?"

"New York. Sloan Kettering. I've been here a couple of hours."

"We're on our way," Riley said quietly.

"Good. That's good, Riley. I'll wait for you. I'll be right here. I mean I'll wait right here. Jesus, will you hurry, Riley?"

"Hang up, Thad," Riley said in a strangled voice.

"You want me to hang up? Why is that, Riley? We need to talk. I . . . Billie packed the green dress. I didn't know it was in her bag until last night. She knew. That's why she packed the dress. I should have looked earlier. Do you think I should have looked earlier, Riley?"

"No, no, you did the right thing. Green is Grandmam's favorite color. I'm going to hang up now, Thad. You . . . you wait for us."

"I'll wait, Riley. Right here. I won't go away."

He waited.

Twice they let him see his wife for a total of ten minutes. He wanted to die when he saw the tubes and machines that monitored her progress. They said she was in a coma.

He questioned God and received no answer. He drank the muddy coffee.

The oversize clock in the waiting room read twelve-ten when the family walked into the waiting room.

"I can't bear to see her like this," Maggie said against Sawyer's shoulder.

"Mother of God," Sawyer whispered tearfully.

Sumi reached for Cole, who was leaning against Riley, his eyes filled with tears.

"Billie is hooked up to life support systems," Ivy whispered to Maggie. The break in her voice tore at Maggie's heart.

"Now, we have to do it now," Ivy said to Riley. "Billie said not one minute longer than necessary." Her voice was strong, firm, when she spoke.

"Can you do it, Ivy?"

"I can do it, Riley. I gave my word. Thad's down in the office."

"It's up to you, Cole, to see that things go forward for Cary. He's got to be ready. I'll do my job, you do yours."

The family was in the waiting room, each with a cup of the same cold, muddy coffee Thad had had earlier.

Riley spoke quietly to Thad, explaining about the tape.

"Don't do this, please, don't do this," Thad cried. "Don't take her from me. Riley, please, I'm begging you." He turned to Ivy, his eyes imploring her, pleading with her to change her mind. She shook her head, her eyes full of sorrow.

"If it's what Billie wants," Thad whispered, relenting. "It doesn't matter what we want. Not anymore."

"When?" Sawyer said.

"Now," Ivy said in a voice no one recognized, as she walked away. "I'll tell them."

"One at a time," the doctor said quietly.

The family looked at one another. Maggie stepped forward, her eyes swimming in tears. She walked over to the hospital bed. How gaunt, how emaciated she was. This wasn't her mother. Her mother was vibrant, always smiling, always warm and caring. Always loving. Her tears overflowed. She should have a pretty gown on, one of the Billie colors she loved so much. Maggie plucked at the cotton stocking cap on her mother's head, seeing the fine, thin baby hair that had grown back in wispy tufts. From her purse Maggie withdrew the Cleopatra Gold scarf wrapped in tissue paper. She looked down at the embroidered logo and the label she'd sewn herself: Made in the U.S.A. Her hands were steady when she raised her mother's head to wrap the scarf around it. She bunched the folds with care under her mother's chin. "You can't go to meet Aunt Amelia and Shad in that tacky stocking cap. You gotta go in style, Mam." She leaned over, the tears splashing on the scarf, to kiss her mother one last time. " 'Bye, Mam."

She ran from the room, straight into Ivy's arms. "I forgot to tell her about Susan. I wanted to explain. . . . When it's your turn, Ivy, will you tell her?"

"Yes, yes, I'll tell her."

"Do you think she'll come back for the funeral?" Maggie whimpered.

"No. Susan will never come back. I like your fella, Maggie."

"He's not my fella, Ivy. He's a wonderful friend, though. He insisted on coming with me. I'm glad he did. Everyone seems to like him. I know Mam would . . . would have liked him. This has been awful for you, hasn't it, Ivy?"

"Billie said she chose me because none of you would have been able to do it. I think she was wrong. Not that it matters."

"No, Ivy, she wasn't wrong. I know myself. I would have kept her hooked up to those damn machines forever. Sawyer too. Cole and Riley could have done it, maybe, but I doubt it. Thad never could have done it. How are we going to handle looking at Cary, knowing Mam's . . . oh, God, Ivy, how?"

"I don't know, Maggie. I have to go now, it's my turn."

The family sat together on the two ugly brown sofas that faced each other. All their eyes turned to follow Thad when he entered the room.

They waited.

Thad sat down on the chair next to Billie's bed. The tubes running into her nose and arms had been removed. He reached for her thin hand. He talked, his voice barely a whisper, telling her things she already knew, and then whispered things only the two of them knew. Once, he thought her eyelids fluttered. He talked faster, his voice more urgent. His voice cracked and then steadied. He thought he felt her thin hand squeeze his. "Nobody ever loved you the way I love you, my darling. Let go, Billie. They're all waiting for you: Amelia; Moss; your son, Riley; your mother; Shadaharu. They'll . . . they'll take care of you until I get there. Let go, Billie," Thad said gently.

He knew the minute Billie slipped away. He took her in his arms and cradled her to his breast. "Rest, Billie," he whispered against her cheek. He laid her down gently and pulled the stark white sheet up to meet the folds of the scarf. How peaceful she looked.

"Shadaharu, Amelia, take care of her, you hear me?" Thad whispered. He watched as the flat line blipped to the top of the screen, did a crazy jig, then flat-lined again. "Thanks." He smiled wanly.

Outside, he nodded curtly to the doctors and nurses before he walked over to the family. "I left her in good hands." He told them about the blip and the jig. He was rewarded with smiles as tired as his own.

Billie Ames Coleman Kingsley's death was recorded at 5:55 A.M. At 6:45 A.M., Cary Assante was undergoing anesthesia while the family waited in the waiting room.

At noon Henry Tanaka ushered them all into a limousine waiting to take them to Kennedy Airport. There they boarded the ColeShad corporate jet that would transport them all back to Sunbridge. Billie's body was in the cargo hold.

Billie Kingsley was laid to rest next to Amelia Assante the following day.

On the walk down the hill, Cole inched close to Riley. "I smelled the cigar smoke, did you?" He sucked in his breath, waiting for his cousin's answer.

"Yeah, I did. I heard Aunt Maggie say she smelled Aunt Amelia's perfume. Guess they came to pay their respects," Riley said shakily.

"Wouldn't surprise me," Thad said airily. "Right now, I bet they're all lined up in a row watching us. If we believe that, I think we'll be okay." The others nodded.

"Stew for lunch?" Adam said to Ivy.

"Yep. Homemade bread too."

"I gotta get back home," Thad said. "I have a whole menagerie to take care of, and at least fifty letters I promised myself I'd write to different authors telling them how much pleasure they gave Billie."

"What a wonderful idea," Maggie said, squeezing Henry's arm.

"I miss the twins," Sawyer grumbled.

"My mother and father are bringing Moss home this evening." Ivy beamed. Riley grinned from ear to ear.

"Little Billie is getting a tooth." Cole laughed. "I can't wait to see it."

Sumi giggled. "Me too."

They were in the courtyard when the sun dimmed. When it crept from its cloud cover, it was brighter than ever.

"That's Mam telling us things are under control." Maggie smiled. "Either you believe or you don't."

The family, as one, chose to believe.

{{{{{{{{ EPILOGUE }}}}}}}}

In delicate, oversize script, the brass plate read: The Amelia Assante, Billie Kingsley Memorial.

Thad hefted the bottle of champagne in his hand. Cary did the same.

The gathering was small, family only.

Cary grinned as he stepped up to bat. "This one's for you, babe," he said, swinging wildly. The family clapped in approval.

Thad's swing was just as wild, connecting with the same cornerstone as Cary's.

"I have to sit down," Sawyer complained.

"Twins again," Adam said, his eyeballs bulging from their sockets.

Sumi sat down next to Sawyer. They compared their stomach sizes. Sumi was the winner. "Cole said it's going to be a boy this time. If it isn't a girl."

Ivy squeezed onto the bench. She patted her protruding stomach. "Riley says this one is going to be a girl. If it isn't a boy."

"I think it's wonderful!" Maggie chortled. "Oh, Henry, isn't it wonderful? Eight grandchildren!"

"I guess I have to get six more ponies and enlarge the swimming pool. But not till after I marry Maggie!"

Cole grinned. " 'Bout time."

"I get to be maid of honor!" Sawyer said sourly.

"Sumi and I are bridesmaids!" Ivy giggled. "Josie, Katy, and little Billie are the flower girls. Moss, the ring bearer."

"It's a deal," Henry said, his smile embracing the family.

"Well, I'm at loose ends now, how about you, Thad?" Cary grinned.

"Hey, my time is yours."

"Three months from today!" Henry said, getting into the spirit of things.

"To Maggie and Henry," Cary said, holding up an unopened bottle of champagne.

"To the best family a guy ever had," Thad and Cary said in unison.

"Hear! Hear!" the family chorused together.

Available in bookstores everywhere

SEASONS OF
HER LIFE

by Fern Michaels

Published by The Random House Publishing Group.

Read on for the opening chapter of
SEASONS OF HER LIFE . . . .

{{{{{{{{{ CHAPTER ONE }}}}}}}}}

1950

Almost free. Almost.

Ruby Connors looked around her room for the last time.
She was really leaving this house, this room, and if she had
anything to say about it, she'd never come back. Her eyes fell
on the white curtains hanging stiffly at the window, starched
in sugar water and stretched on curtain stretchers. No more of
that, Ruby thought gleefully. No more pinpricks. And no
more white iron bed with its crazy quilt made by her mother
with patches from her older sister's dresses. She hated the
quilt, just as she hated Amber.

Someday she was going to have a pretty bedroom like the
pictures in the Sears, Roebuck catalogue. She'd have a dressing table with a white organdy ruffle with curtains to match—
and not the kind that had to be stretched, either. She'd have
a meadow-green carpet and a real bedspread. Every table and
corner would have plants and flowers, mostly daisies. On her
dressing table would be silver frames with pictures, maybe of
her dog or cat. Everything would be alive. Maybe she'd even
put her picture of Johnny Ray in it, the one she'd sneaked out
of a *Photoplay* magazine.

Ruby sat down on the edge of the bed, and the springs

squeaked under her ninety pounds. The room was sweltering hot, even though it was only June. In the summer she baked alive, and in the winter she froze with cold drafts from the attic.

Almost free. Almost. "I'm leaving and I'm never coming back, neverneverneverneverneverneverneverne," Ruby singsonged quietly.

Her suitcases were packed; she was wearing her sodality medal and the scapular that her mother always insisted on. Her dress wasn't new, but it wasn't as faded as her others and a ruffle had been added to cover the let-down hem. Her hairstyle, if it could be called a style, was a dutch boy with bangs. As soon as she could, she was going to get a permanent and some colored barrettes, maybe a ribbon or two if that's what the girls wore in Washington, D. C.

Ruby scuffed at the braided rug with her polished saddle shoe. The shoes were almost new, and so were her socks, but they smelled like No Worry. So did her underwear. If only she weren't so skinny and plain-looking. She was starting to worry now and have doubts. She *was* doing the right thing. There was no way she wanted to stay home and work in the shirt factory. She'd seen girls that graduated a year or two ahead of her getting off the bus at the railroad tracks with threads all over their clothes. They always looked so tired and listless. Her mother called the shirt factory a sweat box. Living with her older sister, Amber, was not going to be divinely wonderful, either. Amber was prissy and meticulous, and she was a liar. But it would be better than living here and working in the factory.

Ruby carried her suitcases out to the hall. Two hours to go. She put the rag rug back in place at the side of the bed. Two quick swipes and the quilt was wrinkle-free. She backed out of the room. Her hand stretched toward the door. If she closed it, she would no longer exist, she thought. Her parents would walk right past it and never think of her. If she left it open, they just might think, this is Ruby's room. *Maybe . . . could be . . . dumb thought, Ruby.* She pushed the door shut, a defiant look on her face.

The house was so quiet, Ruby thought as her saddle shoes snicked at the rubber treads on the stairs. Her mother, Irma, was probably on the back porch, shelling peas for dinner. Her father had gone uptown for the mail and to shop at the A&P because he said Irma didn't know how to shop and look for bargains. Opal was at catechism class. She was going to miss Opal. Out of necessity she and Opal had banded together against their parents and Amber. She'd promised to write to

Opal, but to send the letters to her grandmother's house. Opal had promised never to show the letters to their parents. Opal was going to have a tough time with her gone.

In the wide center hallway, Ruby listened for any sound that might mean her father had returned. The screen door squeaked when she opened it and squeaked again when she closed it. She waited a moment on the front porch to see if she would be called back into the house. A bee buzzed about her knees. Ruby swatted it and killed it with her bare hand. Amber would have squeaked and gone white in the face the same way she'd always gotten white in the face when it was her turn to scrub the porch floor. Because of Amber's regular weekend illnesses, Ruby scrubbed this porch every Saturday for as long as she could remember. She would never again have to do it. Now it was Opal's turn.

Ruby ran, careful not to scuff her shoes, down the street, past the lumber mill, over the railroad tracks, past Riley's Monument Works, where her father worked. She raced past her uncle's garage, over the bridge and up the hill. The smell of stale beer from Bender's beer joint made her hold her breath as she careened around the corner that led to her grandmother's house.

A smile tugged at the corner of Ruby's mouth. She'd said good-bye to Bubba every day for the past two weeks, but when you weren't ever planning on coming back, you couldn't say good-bye often enough. Besides, she *needed* this last visit, this last good-bye.

Almost free. Almost.

Ruby took a moment to drink in the sight of her grandmother's house, to commit it to memory. It was a squat little house made from fieldstone with a matching wall. She'd never sit on that wall again, never lie under the old chestnut tree in the front yard. She loved the old chestnut and the way its branches hung down and covered her like a grand umbrella. She would forget the house she grew up in, but she would never forget this house. Never.

Inside, the kitchen was big and square with cabbage-rose wallpaper that sometimes made her dizzy, but her grandmother loved bright things. The windowsills and shelves held glossy green plants in colorful clay pots, and the room always smelled of cinnamon and orange. The curtains, as cheerful as the wallpaper, were made from linen and trimmed with inch-wide red rickrack, handsewn by her grandmother. They were changed twice a year, when the mullioned windows were washed. The crazy quilt linoleum on the floor was blinding.

What she loved most, though, were the old-fashioned coal stove and the pots that constantly simmered with orange peels. It was a kitchen of pure love. This house was similar to her parents', having been built by the same lumber company, but love had made it into something very different. Love was something she was never going to be without again.

"Ruby, is that you?" her grandmother called from the back porch.

"It's me, Bubba," Ruby trilled as she made her way past the snowball bush, which was in full bloom. Once she'd picked a bouquet from it for her room, and her mother had thrown it out, saying she didn't want any bugs in the house. Later Ruby had pulled the wasted bouquet from the trash.

Ruby planted a noisy kiss on top of her grandmother's head. "Apple pie tonight, huh?" Her uncle John loved apple pie. Uncle Hank liked rhubarb. Ruby knew there would be two kinds of pie tonight. "I came to say good-bye again." Ruby laughed.

"I knew you'd come this morning." The old lady smiled in return. "You look pretty, Ruby. Did you have breakfast?" Ruby nodded. "Are you nervous about going on the train all the way to Washington?"

"No. Well, maybe a little. About Amber mostly. She's supposed to meet me, and she won't like that. But I bought a present for her last week at the company store, so she'll have to be nice to me. I'm going to do my best to get along with her." She could tell by the anxiety in her grandmother's eyes that she wasn't convincing her.

"You know, Bubba," Ruby went on, "I feel different . . . inside . . . I'm changing or else I already changed . . . it's not just me going away, either. It's something else, something I can't explain. Maybe it's because I'm turning eighteen next month. But whatever it is, I think it means you don't have to worry about Amber and me. It's going to work out, really it is."

"I hope so," Mary Cozinsky mumbled under her breath. "You stand your ground with your sister, Ruby, and don't let her push you around."

"You're not going to worry about me, are you, Bubba?"

"Every single day until I know there's nothing to worry about. But I'm happy for you, too. Do you remember when we talked about the seasons in a woman's life? You're in the spring of your life, Ruby, the best time of all. Everything is still before you. It's your time to grow, to spread your wings, to turn into the wonderful woman I know you will become.

By the time you reach the summer of your life, you'll be married with children of your own. I think by then you'll understand how the cycle works. Right now your head is so full of anticipation and excitement, it's hard for you to think about things like seasons."

Ruby wanted to tell her she understood perfectly, but then she would have to admit that she knew her beloved grandmother was at the end of the winter of her life. The thought, the words, were unbearable. Better to pretend she was excited. Better just to change the subject.

"I'm going to write to Opal and send the letters to your box number," she said. "Opal will read them to you. She's going to scrub your kitchen floor on Fridays, and on Wednesday she'll go to the farm for your pot cheese. She'll pick the blueberries and help you make jelly whenever you're ready. She can iron real good, Bubba. She can do the Sunday shirts if you want her to. You can depend on Opal, Bubba, and I think you should keep her money the way you did for me. Pop will make her put it in the collection if you give it to her." Ruby's eyes snapped angrily. "Pop gave me my bill this morning. It's so much money. I have to pay rent, buy food, buy tokens for the bus, and a bunch of other stuff. I'll be an old woman before I pay it off. Your parents are supposed to give you a present when you graduate from high school. I didn't get a present. I got a bill for my keep and for all the money I put in the collection basket on Sunday. Eighteen years worth! I figured it out, Bubba, it's ten cents for every Sunday Mass." Ruby cried heartbrokenly.

"How much does it all come to?" Mary asked quietly as she stroked Ruby's dark hair.

"Church is $93.60. The bill for my keep is six thousand." Ruby felt the tremor in her grandmother's body.

"I have a present for you, Ruby," the old lady crooned. "You have to stop crying now, or your eyes will be red and swollen when you get on the train. Smile for me, Ruby," she said in a quivering voice. Ruby wiped her eyes on the hem of the sweet-smelling apron her grandmother wore.

"A present?" Ruby's moist eyes glistened. "How big is it?"

"Very small, sweetie. I'm glad you have a pocket in your dress. This . . . present has to be a secret. You must promise me that you'll never tell Amber, even if she makes you so angry, you want to shout about it. And you must not tell your father. Not now anyway. Someday, perhaps, when you're secure and happy. Will you promise me, Ruby?"

"Oh, Bubba, you know I will. I never broke a promise. Not

a peep. Amber is the last person I'd spill my guts to, you know that."

Mary fumbled in the pocket of her apron and withdrew a rumpled-up ball of linen. Ruby knew what it was the moment she saw it. She gasped and the old lady's eyes twinkled. Ruby held her breath. It was years since her grandmother had shown her the prize that was wrapped so carefully in cotton and then once again in the white handkerchief.

"The czarina's ring! Oh, oh, oh, it's more beautiful than the last time I saw it. Truly, you're giving it to me? I know you promised, but I thought you . . . you just wanted to make me feel good. What if someone steals it?" Ruby said, holding out her hand.

"It's your responsibility now, Ruby. It's up to you to make sure it's kept safe."

It was so heavy, but it felt good in the palm of her hand. The band was wide, reaching almost to her knuckle, where it crested into a cone shaped pyramid of diamonds and rubies. Ruby sucked in her breath as she struggled to count the stones in the ring. "How many stones are there, Bubba?"

"Lord, child, I don't know."

"Do you think it's worth two hundred dollars?" Ruby asked naively. The old lady smiled secretly and nodded.

"I'll keep it safe, I swear I will. I won't ever wear it, I promise."

"You'd look kind of silly if you did." The old lady chuckled. "This ring is fit only for royalty. The president's wife doesn't have anything half as grand. Only you, Ruby."

When Ruby's grandfather had been alive, he would regale her with stories of the ring every Sunday after Mass. The more beer he drank, the wilder the stories became. To this day, neither Ruby nor her grandmother knew for certain if the czarina had bestowed the ring on her grandfather for a deed well done or if he stole it, like he said, as he was falling into his beer stupor that was permitted only on Sunday.

"I think she gave it to Grandpop because he was so young and dashing, a true cossack. Don't you, Bubba?"

Mary did not answer, but instead gave a mysterious little smile, then handed over a small square of white paper. "There's a man's name here who lives in Washington, D. C. He will buy the ring if you ever want to sell it. Your grandfather was going to sell it before he died to make sure I was taken care of, but I wouldn't let him. He was so proud of that ring. Your uncle John and uncle Hank take care of me. Besides," she chuckled, "my fingers are all crooked. What do I need with a ring? It's yours, child. Although there's going to be a war around here when I die and your father finds out the ring is missing."

Ruby's eyes filled. She bundled up the ring and stuffed it into her pocket. "I can't wait till I'm eighteen." she said.

Mary smiled. "Hand me that apple bowl and don't go wishing your life away."

"Do you think anyone will ever love me besides you?" Ruby blurted out.

Mary pretended to think. "What I think is you're going to have beaux standing in line, waiting to take you to the picture shows."

Ruby giggled. "I'm so plain and ordinary. Maybe if I get a permanent. I'm going to get a tube of lipstick, too, and maybe some pearl earrings. I have thirty-four dollars I put away. Pop doesn't know I have it. I think it's enough for maybe two new dresses, shoes for work, and a brassiere," she said impishly. "I'll grow breasts, too, you wait and see. My hormones are just slow right now." The old lady laughed in delight at her granddaughter's gamin face.

"You better start home, Ruby, before George comes looking for you. Be a good girl now. I mean a proper young lady."

"I won't shame you, Bubba. Don't worry about me. Opal is going to take care of you, but I'm not coming back here, ever, even when . . . you know . . . I'm not!" Ruby said adamantly.

"Ruby, I know that. I don't want you coming back. I want you to remember me like this, not the way I'll look in those purple dresses the undertakers put on you. That's why I gave you the ring now. There's nothing for you here, Ruby, so you stay away. Send me pictures. Amber sent me a postcard and said she had a camera."

"Boy, was Pop mad about that!" Ruby giggled. "She paid off her bill, so he could only holler at Mom. She sent pictures and Pop threw them in the stove. Said they were the devil's handiwork. It was a nice picture of Amber, too. She was sitting under the cherry blossom tree and had her legs crossed. Her skirt was up to here," she said, pointing to the middle of her thighs.

Ruby dropped to her knees. She looked earnestly into her grandmother's face. "I don't think I'll ever love anyone as much as I love you. You've never said a cross word to me even if I deserved it. I'll think of you every day. I'll keep all my promises, and you'll never have to be ashamed of me. I'll remember you sitting here like this. When I'm old I'm going to peel apples just the way you do, all in one curl."

Ruby leaned closer and hugged her grandmother. "Are you sure," she said huskily, "that you don't mind if I don't come to your funeral?"

"I'll mind if you do come. If you do, you'll have to see your father. Make up your mind, Ruby."

"I'm not coming," Ruby said in a jittery-sounding voice.

"That's good. Now, get along," Mary said firmly.

Ruby kissed her grandmother one last time and raced off the porch and down the walkway to the street. She didn't want to think about the tears on her grandmother's cheeks.

Almost free. Almost.

Mary Cozinsky slumped back on the old wicker rocker. The dearest piece of her life was gone now. So many pieces were gone. She set the apple bowl on the floor and withdrew her rosary from her apron pocket. She raised her eyes upward and prayed, simple words from the heart. "Protect my little Ruby," she pleaded. "And, God, if you decide to send her father, my son George, to hell, I won't question your decision."

She'd known this day was coming; still, she wasn't prepared for the empty feeling, the devastating sense of loss. She'd given birth to seven children, and she loved them dearly, with the exception of George, but none of her own children touched her heart the way Ruby did. When Ruby was seven and permitted to cross the road and the railroad tracks, the child had begun visiting daily, sometimes twice. By the time Ruby was eight, she was tightly ensconced in the hearts of both her grandparents. When George objected, her husband had straightened him out in the blink of an eye. The handsome cossack had stepped on George the way he would have stepped on a piss-ant, telling him that Ruby was to visit whenever she wanted. George recognized the threat: either he allowed Ruby to visit or he would foreit his share of any inheritance.

Still, Ruby paid for her visits in other ways: gross punishments, hand-me-downs, and the loss of her freedom. While the other children played and had fun, Ruby was reading scripture with a Nancy Drew book inside the Bible. The wiry little girl had cooked and cleaned, run errands, and lived in fear in that damnable cell she called a bedroom. Only at her grandparent's house could she be herself, and she blossomed under the umbrella of their love, willingly doing any of the chores asked of her. In the beginning, it was hard for Ruby to accept the rewards—a quarter here, a half-dollar there, wonderful desserts, the love of Sam, the old bloodhound who had died right after Ruby's twelfth birthday. It was an awful birthday for her that year. Just days before, George had told her she hadn't been named Ruby for a precious gem at all, but because she was all red and ugly when she was born. Old Sam spent hours licking her tears. Her grandfather had to physically restrain her the day they buried the old hound, for she would have crawled into the special burying place along with him.

She had so much love, that little girl. Often, late at night, when Mikel had been so sick near the end, they would talk about Ruby and what would happen to her. Wanting to leave no stone unturned, Mikel summoned Ruby's mother, Irma, and spoke with her at length. Irma, in her squeaky voice, mumbled that she would never go against George, and Ruby would do as they said. After graduation she would go to Washington to live with Amber, and work. Although it hadn't been said aloud, it was understood that Ruby would begin paying her debt just the way Amber had paid hers. They'd offered, on the spot, to pay on Ruby's behalf, but Irma had squirmed in her chair, frantically shaking her head. From somewhere she summoned the gumption to ask what made Ruby so special to her in-laws. Mikel had looked at her with pity and told her to go home. The moment the screen door banged, Mikel asked for the czarina's ring and said, "This is to go to Ruby when you think it's time."

Two hours after Mikel's funeral, when the beer had flowed and the food was all eaten, George had asked Mary when she was going to sell the ring. She remembered her words as though she'd just uttered them. "You might think I'm a dumb Polack and your father was a dumb Russian, George, but you're wrong. Your father made a will and the ring is mine. I can do whatever I want with it." And then she blurted out without meaning to: "Ruby told us to make a will; she learned all about wills in school." The others, George's brothers and sisters, were all behind her chair in the kitchen, supporting her words, when George dragged a screaming, crying Ruby from the house. With Mikel gone, there wasn't a thing any of them could do. Ruby's punishment was compounded daily and ran for months at a time, but Ruby wrote notes that friends delivered and read to her grandmother after school.

Mary wiped her eyes with her apron. She smiled through her tears. She'd done the best she could for the child; the rest was up to Ruby. As long as she had the ring and her picture of Johnny Ray, Ruby would be fine. Her watery eyes took on a special sparkle when she thought of Ruby's eighteenth birthday and what she could give to her. Money, of course. Hank and John would contribute, and she'd take all her change in the lard can to the bank. Maybe, just maybe, she could scrape up a hundred dollars. She smiled then, picturing the look on Ruby's face. She could buy all the things she wanted. A real pocketbook, some nylons, maybe some nail polish and new underwear. All the things a young girl would need when she lived and worked in the city.

As for George, Mary made a mental note to deduct $6,093.60 from his share of her estate.

There were so many things she'd never forgive her son for, though she knew there were reasons for the way he'd turned out, reasons almost too horrible to think about. In a town as small as Barstow, with only seven businesses on a small main street, a tiny high school, telephone party lines, conversations over clotheslines, wintertime quilting bees, and summertime garden clubs, there could be no secrets.

The gossip had filled in the details—an older boy had done terrible things to him, sexual things, all while a local tomboy named Bitsy Lucas stood by laughing and taunting and urging the older boy on. But Mary had seen the violation in his eyes the minute he had walked into the house and he had never forgiven her for the insight. He'd been only eleven years old at the time, and she'd had to take him to the doctor's, so Mikel inevitably found out. From that day forward, father had looked at son with disgust in his eyes.

And from that day forward, whether because of Bitsy Lucas or herself Mary didn't know, George hated all women. He hated her the way he now hated Irma and even his own daughters.

The familiar pain was creeping around her chest again. That old fool of a doctor had told her she shouldn't upset herself. She snorted. With George in the background, how could she be anything but upset? Obviously, a second rosary was called for. The comforting prayers calmed the pain in her chest almost immediately.

Ruby slowed her steps and shifted her mental gears the moment she crossed the railroad tracks. Her right hand was in the pocket of her dress, her fingers caressing the tightly wrapped ring. She hoped it didn't bulge too much. Her hand worked to flatten the linen handkerchief as much as she could. They'd just think she had a hanky wadded into a ball.

She crossed the fingers of her left hand. Sometimes she thought her father had X-ray vision.

Skirting the gravel lot at the lumber mill, Ruby headed up the street to her house, knowing her parents would be on the porch, waiting for her. She wasn't late. In fact, she still had almost ten minutes before it would be time to leave for the train station. She sucked in her breath as she cut across the Zacharys' lawn next door. She stepped behind an ancient white pine and observed her parents for a minute. They were both tall, but there any similarity ended. Irma was incredibly thin with large, bony feet, red hands and short fingernails. Her hair was a soft brown, the color of the spring wrens. Ruby was never sure what color her mother's eyes were because she rarely looked directly at her. Probably a greenish-brown. Hazel maybe. She had a warm smile though, particularly when Amber did something that pleased her. Overall, her mother was a tired, weary woman. She worked tirelessly, never sitting down for a cup of coffee or tea. She couldn't, Ruby thought, because George made her perform. The bathroom had to be scrubbed every day from top to bottom. The kitchen floor had to be scrubbed, too. Monday was wash day; Tuesday was ironing day; Wednesday was baking day; Thursday was for changing beds and window washing; Friday was clean-the-whole-house day, and Saturday was for scrubbing the porches, dusting the jars in the fruit cellar, and going to confession. If there were any free moments, they were spent at the sewing machine or mending by hand. Idle hands were the devil's work, her father said. If that was true—and Ruby didn't believe it was—then Irma Connors was damn near a saint. Right now her mother looked nervous, Ruby thought. She was always nervous when she was in her husband's company, always fearful she would say the wrong thing. Irma survived the only way she knew how, by obeying her husband and keeping quiet. Ruby's eyes darkened. Her father wasn't around *all* the time. There was time enough for an occasional hug or pat on the head or kind word, time her mother chose not to give her.

George was pacing on the porch, his face surly and mean. As far back as she could remember, he'd always looked just the way he looked now. Muscular and hard, long-legged in creased work pants, his shirt ironed to perfection. Her girlfriends thought him handsome; she thought him ugly, inside and out. He was strong and arrogant. Every day of her life she'd felt that strength and arrogance. Cold, piercing eyes were scanning the sidewalk, watching for her. Even from this distance Ruby could see how his lips thinned out. He was angry—at her, at life. Twice she'd seen those cold blue eyes become warm, and both times he'd been staring at Grace Zachary, their neighbor. He often said Grace was the devil's own disciple, in her scanty shorts and halter top. Her mother said she was trash. But nothing could make Ruby deny her affection for Grace, who called her honey and sweetie. She'd liked her even more the day she saw her stick out her tongue and make a face behind her father's back.

The Angelus rang. Noon. Ruby ran around the pine through the yard and along the side of the porch. She wouldn't be late until the last peal of the bell.

"You're late, girl!" George said harshly. Ruby lowered her gaze, staring at the cracks on the porch floor. Early on she'd learned never to look her father in the eye. "Where you been, girl?"

"I went over to Bubba's to say good-bye . . . sir."

George's eyes narrowed. "Your grandmother give you a going-away present?"

"No, sir." Ruby lied with a straight face. She crossed her fingers inside the pockets of her dress. Bubba hadn't given Amber anything when she went away, so there was no reason for her father to think this time would be any different. Because it was so important that he believe her, she raised her eyes and said, "She did give me a hanky because I started to cry."

She withdrew the square of white linen with the shirt-tail hem. Her heart took on an extra beat, but she didn't lower her gaze.

"Did you clean your room, girl?"

"Yes, sir. This morning."

"Did you pack your Bible?"

"Yes, sir. Last night." Before she got off the train at Union Station she was going to ditch the Bible. If Amber was dumb enough to ask her where it was, she'd lie and say someone on the train stole it. Girl. He'd never called her anything but girl. Was Ruby so hard to say? Or dear or honey? She risked a quick glance at her mother, who immediately looked away.

"Get your bags, and don't be slow about it. Close the door, and don't slam it. I'll bring the car up."

Ruby climbed the steps to the truck room, a lump in her throat. Close the door, and don't slam it. She'd like to slam the damn door so hard it fell off its hinges. They'd never think of her again until her payments started rolling in. Angrily, she pushed her suitcases down the hall to the top of the stairs. She closed the door quietly, and in a last fit of rebellion, she kicked both suitcases down the steps. They landed with a loud thud. Ruby clapped her hands and grinned, then went downstairs again. Her suitcases upended on the front porch, Ruby stared at her mother, willing her to say something, something kind, something personal. Even a look would do, Ruby thought desperately. She wanted to throw her arms around her mother and cry, but she didn't. You must love me a little bit, she thought, I'm your daughter. She cried silently, never taking her eyes from her mother's face. Hurry, Mom, he'll be here in a second, just a word, a look. Please, Mom. Oh, God, please say it. Now, now, before it's too late. Ruby didn't need to see her father's car come to a halt at the side of the house; she saw the relief in her mother's face.

"I think it's going to rain before long," Irma said loudly enough for George to hear.

"There won't be any rain today, woman," George said coldly.

Irma blinked and looked overhead at the dark gray clouds that would erupt shortly. "I'm sure you're right, George," she said.

Ruby carried her bags to the car. God, wasn't her mother even going to say good-bye?

"Say good-bye to your mother, girl," George ordered.

Without turning, Ruby mimicked her father, "Say good-bye to your mother, girl."

At the same moment the words tumbled from Ruby's mouth, Opal skidded around the corner of the house screaming at the top of her lungs, "RubyRubyRuby! I thought I would miss you. I asked Sister Clementine to let me out a few minutes early. She said to say good-bye for her."

Ruby saw George's hand move, and Opal took the blow high on her cheekbone. His slap caught her full in the mouth, cutting off anything else she might say. Opal's eyes filled with tears. Ruby caught her sister close and whispered, "Don't you cry, don't you dare! That's what they want, especially *him*. Don't ever let them see you cry. Soon as we leave, go over to Bubba's. You can roll out the dough for the pies. She's waiting for you. I'm leaving that damn Bible on the train. Think about that tonight when you fall asleep. Go on now, get up on the porch and I'll wave to you."

Ruby rolled the window down, fixing her gaze on her mother. Irma looked away. Ruby waved at Opal, who was struggling not to cry.

Almost free. Almost.

Three hours into the trip, shortly before the train groaned to a stop in Harrisburg, Ruby finally felt confident enough to get up and go to the bathroom, knowing all eyes would be on her lurching walk to the end of the car. It wasn't so bad walking down the car because she was looking at the back of people's heads. Coming back they'd be staring at her. She knew she was dressed all wrong. Her hair was wrong, too. Even the saddle shoes were wrong. So was the sandwich and apple her mother had packed for her. She'd be damned if she'd eat the egg salad sandwich. That would be left behind with the Bible.

It took Ruby a full five minutes before she figured out how to flush the toilet, and when she did, she smiled from ear to ear. She had a lot to learn, so much was new to her: the train ride, the strange countryside, the washrooms, the colored people. How could she be so ignorant about these things and yet so smart in school? She *was* smart, too; she could take dictation faster than anyone else, faster than her teacher, Miss Pipas, and her typing was almost sixty words a minute with no mistakes. Miss Pipas said she was the best, the most accurate student she'd ever had.

Head high, aware of the stares she was receiving, Ruby marched back to her seat and sat down. Miss Pipas had tried, in her own way, to prepare Ruby for what she'd called the outside, but she hadn't paid that much attention. Now she wished she had listened more carefully.

Ruby looked at the backs of the passengers' heads, all curly hair set with Wave-Set. Even the men had some kind of stuff on their hair. There were young people her age on the train near the front of the car. They were having a grand old time, laughing and teasing one another. Ruby ached to join them, to be part of them for a little while. She settled deeper into her seat and watched the countryside through the window. The wheels clicked on the tracks seeming to say Amber, Amber, Amber.

Regardless of what she'd said to her grandmother, Ruby knew things would not go well with Amber. Amber didn't want her; Ruby had read the letter and heard her parents talking. The gist of that conversation was George telling Irma that if she, Ruby, didn't obey Amber, she would be sent home to work in the factory. "She'll listen or else," George growled. "You tell *your* daughter in your next letter that if she can't keep a tight rein on Ruby, I'll go down there and fetch them both back here." And he would do just that.

Not me! Ruby screamed silently. You'll never get me back

here! What it all meant, Ruby decided, was she had to toe the line and do *exactly* what Amber said.

But God, how she hated Amber. All the reasons for her hatred rivered through her, leaving her weak and trembling. She thought about how, when she was five and her sister was eight, Amber had pushed her under the water in the field pond. The memory made her gasp, just as she had then. If it hadn't been for one of the older boys, who fished her out, she would have drowned. Amber didn't want to be saddled that day with a younger sister. She hadn't wanted to be saddled with her the day she left her with her foot caught in the railroad tracks to go on with her friends to play stickball. She'd been lucky that day, too, when an old miner worked diligently to free her foot, though she'd gotten a whipping for her torn shoe.

Ruby never understood Amber's hatred of her until her grandmother explained that Amber had always wanted to be an only child, as if that would make her loved and wanted.

That in part explained why Amber had always said she had been born an angel, complete with wings and halo. She said she was supposed to go back to heaven, but her wings had been injured on the trip down to earth. Arms had sprouted from the injured wings and their mother had found her in the nick of time. Ruby believed all this, but when she found the nerve to repeat the story to her beloved Bubba, the old lady had scoffed and told her it was a big lie. She smarted for over an hour at her own gullibility. For years she'd actually believed the terrible lie that her sister was somehow special, more deserving of love than she, Ruby. She'd gone home and stalked her older sister like an animal, catching up with her at the crick and beating her almost senseless. Amber had crawled home bawling and calling her a devil. For that Ruby had been whipped with a belt, banished to her room for five days, and told to read the Bible from cover to cover. At the end of the five days she'd read only twenty-three pages and was whipped again when she couldn't answer any of the questions her father asked her. The real punishment this time was far worse: she wasn't to go to her Bubba's for a month.

Ruby braced herself as the train came to a grinding, crunching halt in Harrisburg. Ahead, some girls were counting out money and buying pop and snacks. They wore earrings and charm bracelets and seersucker playsuits with matching sandals. She knew they were her age, possibly younger, but how sophisticated and confident they were. She'd bet the thirty-seven dollars in her suitcase that their parents, both of them, had kissed them good-bye at the train station. If she ever had children, she would smother them with love and affection.

Ruby morosely fished a dime out of her pocket for a bottle of Orange Nehi.

She set the bottle on the floor and reached overhead for her suitcase. This was the perfect time to fish out the Bible and slide it under the seat. She made a mental note to rip out the first page with her name on it. She didn't ever want to see the Bible again.

People were looking at her, but Ruby didn't care. None of them, she noticed, offered to help her with the smaller of the two cases. Lickety-split she had the Bible out, facedown on the seat. Stretching to her full height, she jammed the case into the overhead rack. She inched the book across the seat before she sat down.

She thought about the egg salad sandwich then as she watched the girls laughing and eating potato chips. She'd die before she did something to embarrass herself, and eating a homemade sandwich on the train was embarrassing. Besides, egg salad always smelled like her father's smelly underwear on wash day.

Ruby relaxed. The empty pop bottle was now safely under the seat along with the Bible and the egg salad sandwich. She leaned back and stared out the window. Gradually, the clickety-clack of the train wheels hypnotized her to sleep.

The girls in the front of the car squealed in glee when the train pulled into Union Station. Ruby found herself jolted forward and caught herself before she slid from the seat. To her horror the Bible and the egg salad sandwich slid out from under the seat. She bent over to look for the pop bottle and saw it three seats ahead. With the toe of her shoe she shoved the Bible and sandwich as far back as she could. She hoped the couple in the seat behind her hadn't seen the garbage she was leaving, but when the man offered to get her bags overhead, she realized they couldn't care less what she left behind.

With her suitcases banging against her shins, Ruby found her way to the end of the car and struggled down the three steps to the ground. It was dark and gloomy. As Ruby trudged along with the other travelers, she could hear over the hissing steam from the trains the young girls shrieking with laughter. She wondered what was so funny about lugging suitcases all this way.

The moment Ruby set foot on the concourse, she spotted Amber leaning nonchalantly against a wall. She set her suitcases down as she fought for a deep breath. She watched her sister for a full three minutes before she walked toward her. She looked almost elegant, Ruby thought, with her upswept hair and summer sundress. She thought her yellow sandals the most beautiful shoes she'd ever seen. Ruby felt ugly and angry at the same time.

If she smiles, things will be okay. If she doesn't smile . . .

"Amber, I'm here," Ruby said, setting down her suitcases. She stretched out her arms to hug her sister. Amber stepped back, her eyes snapping furiously.

"I've been waiting for almost an hour!" There was no smile. Ruby's arms fell to her sides.

"They had to add water or something in Harrisburg. I heard someone complain that we'd be late. It isn't my fault, Amber," Ruby said quietly.

"I suppose it's mine. I had things I wanted to do today, and you've managed to foul things up as usual. Don't just stand there, pick up your bags and let's go."

"If you'd help carry one of the bags, we could move faster," Ruby grumbled.

Amber stopped in mid-stride. Ruby, struggling to keep up with her long-legged sister, literally bowled her over. She found herself apologizing as she reached out to help Amber to her feet. "Get away from me. Now look what you did. The strap on my sandal broke. You're here five minutes and already everything is wrong. No one helped me when I had to come here. I had to find my own way."

Ruby sat down on one of her suitcases. Her eyes shot daggers at her sister. "I didn't ask you to pick me up. I'm not so stupid I can't find my own way. So leave. I don't need you."

"You're just what I need, Ruby. If I leave you, you'll call for a cop and God only knows what you'd say, not to mention calling home and telling them I deserted you."

"No, Amber, that's what you would do, not me," Ruby said softly.

"This is not going to work," Amber said.

"You're telling me," Ruby muttered. "Just see if I give you your present. When crows turn pink and grow a third leg, you'll get it."

"What did you say?" Amber demanded.

"I said"—Ruby enunciated each word slowly and distinctly—"I hate your guts."

Amber laughed, a fiendish sound in the hubbub following them out of the station. She continued to laugh as they boarded the bus that would take them to the YWCA.

Follow the saga of the Coleman
clan from the beginning!

The TEXAS
Series:

TEXAS RICH
TEXAS HEAT
TEXAS FURY
TEXAS SUNRISE

by

Fern Michaels

Published by Ballantine Books.
Available in your local bookstore.